KISSING IN COVENTRY

Jandy began to laugh as dogs and people scattered in all directions, turning over crates and kennels and toppling pedestals. She looked again at Sam, who held tightly to Sue's leash while he watched and laughed at the chaos. Their eyes met, and before she knew what she was doing, Jandy began walking toward him through the bedlam.

Sam and Sue met her halfway. She wasn't sure which of them made the first move, but Sam's free arm went around her and she held Grayson's camera behind her as she tilted her head to avoid his cowboy hat. It could have been a friendly kiss or a happy kiss, but it was a different kind of kiss, the kind that sent a shock wave down her spine, then radiated out to every nerve of her body.

Between one moment and the next, she forgot it was broad daylight and that most of the population of Coventry and all of its tourists could get an eyeful if they were so inclined. She forgot caution and her fiancé in California and lost herself in the kiss that she hadn't allowed herself to want or dream about for four weeks. . . .

Books by Becky Cochrane

A COVENTRY CHRISTMAS

A COVENTRY WEDDING

Published by Kensington Publishing Corporation

A Coventry Wedding

Becky Cochrane

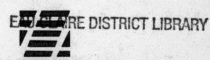

ZEBRA BOOKS
Kensington Publishing Corp.
www.kensingtonbooks.com

In loving memory of my mother,
Dorothy Cochrane,
who gave me my love of words, and
John Riley Morris,
who always gave
my imagination
a soundtrack.

Acknowledgments

Sometimes books and maps and the Internet aren't enough, and the following people shared their time and knowledge, earning my deepest gratitude: Jim Carter, Simmons Buntin, Mark G. Harris, Jak Klinikowski, and Gary Beagle and his students at Volunteer State Community College.

Thank you to my editor, John Scognamiglio (a patient man), my copy editor, Debra Roth Kane, and my agent, Alison J. Picard; my husband Tom; and Timothy J. Lambert, Timothy Forry, Lynne Demarest, and especially Jandy, who loaned me her name without conditions.

The list of people who give me support and encouragement gets longer and longer. Thank you to my friends and family in Houston and elsewhere, the booksellers who are just amazing, my fellow writers whose good opinions and good will help keep the words coming, and my blogging and AOL, LiveJournal, and Yahoo friends. If I named you all, I'd have to cut a chapter from the book, so take the chapter of your choice and consider it your gift.

Thank you, Todd, for the family names, Jess and Laura for letting me borrow Sue, Lisa B. for the Florence story, and all those readers who sent e-mail about *A Coventry Christmas*. I hope you enjoy your summer visit to our town.

I'm grateful to John, Paul, George, and Ringo for giving me dreams and ideas about love, peace, and romance.

Finally, for lightening my load and brightening my world every day, thanks Guinness, Margot, Rexford G. Lambert, the visiting EZ, and the late Lazlo.

Chapter 1

"Call me Jandy."

She cringed a little inside every time she remembered saying those words aloud. Technically, she hadn't lied. When she was a little girl, her grandpa had called her Jandy. But she hadn't thought of that in years, and even the way she'd presented it—"Call me Jandy" instead of "My name is Jandy"—sounded dishonest. Lying about her name was ominous, much like the sign a few feet away with its warning: POISONOUS SNAKES AND INSECTS INHABIT THE AREA.

She dismissed her feeling of doom. She'd never been superstitious; she believed in cold, hard facts. She also believed in things she could see, and so far, those things hadn't included snakes or spiders. She was more concerned with a pest that walked upright on two legs, called itself Sam, and belonged to a gender that tended to boast that it ran the world. Considering the state of the world, she wasn't sure that Sam had much reason to brag. Nor did she think his current suggestion of a coin toss to settle their argument over custody rights indicated any great intellect.

Maybe it was the effect of the desert heat on her brain that made her agree to his proposition. Or maybe it was her memory of *Burger v. Burger* (Los Angeles County Superior Court). Perhaps if Theodore Burger and his former wife Mary Therese had settled *their* custody dispute with a coin toss, they'd have spared themselves millions of dollars in damages and attorney fees.

Maybe a coin toss was a quick solution to an unexpected and unwelcome roadblock on her road to liberty.

With a pang of guilt, she nodded at Sam. He took a quarter from his pocket and flipped it in the air while saying, "Heads I win; tails you lose."

She pressed her knuckles against her lips to stop herself from protesting. No matter how infuriating it was to be considered stupid—did he really think she didn't understand that "heads I win; tails you lose" meant that she lost either way?—the last twenty-four hours were proof that her judgment skills had faded almost as fast as her cell phone battery. She needed sleep. She needed food. She needed help with her stolen truck, which only a half hour earlier had suffered a much noisier death than her cell phone. What she didn't need was a custody battle under the broiling Arizona sun.

She could tell by the sweat running down her face and the way her hair was plastered to her skull under the yellow bandanna—and yellow was *so* not her color—that she wasn't looking any better than she felt. She was hideous, hot, and hopeless. She was five hundred miles from home without a soul to call to rescue her. Not that she believed in being rescued. And not that she could call anyone anyway, with a dead cell phone.

The single advantage of losing phone service was that she no longer had to dread a possible phone call from her mother. Unfortunately, having Dear Prudence along for the ride was nearly as bad—even if Dear Prudence was nothing more than the name she'd lifted long ago from a Beatles song and given to the nagging voice inside her head. Dear Prudence didn't smile, didn't play, couldn't see or hear the beauty in the world, and cast a pall over everyone else's good time.

When she'd been a child, Dear Prudence kept her from making mud pies with the fresh dirt the landscapers put in the flower beds. Dear Prudence kept her from running through the jets of water that kept the grass a brilliant green on the golf course behind their house. When she became a teenager, Dear Prudence kept her out of messy entanglements with boys and away from dirty tricks the mean girls played at school. Dear Prudence ensured that she never drove without a license, shoplifted an article of clothing, cheated on a test, smoked a joint behind the gym—in fact, had any fun at all.

As an adult, she still heard the voice, though she'd shortened its name to Pru, and it often seemed more grimly real than her mother. Some people had imaginary *friends*. But *she* had to come up with an imaginary mother, as if the one who'd given birth to her wasn't hard enough on her nervous system.

This is not *the way you were supposed to be spending this week,* Pru chimed in on cue.

She couldn't argue. Buried somewhere in the bottom of her purse, probably wrapped around the twelve thousand in cash that she was supposed to have put in the bank, was a piece of white card stock embossed with cascading roses. Its words were burned into her brain by remorse hotter than the sun that shone on the Grand Canyon State.

*The honor of your presence
is requested at the marriage of
Miss January Day Halli
to
Mr. Henry Hudson Blake
Saturday the third of June
Two thousand and six
at half after seven o'clock*

Blah blah blah. Instead of looking like he'd been cast in the role of the perfect bridegroom, Hud was in Minnesota, and she had changed her name from January—or even the name she was usually called, Jane—to Jandy and embroiled herself in a custody fight with an annoying man named Sam who thought she was stupid.

Heads I win, tails you lose.

Seeming to hover in the air, the coin looked like a flame, an illusion caused by the reflection of the unrelenting sun. Memories of Theodore and Mary Therese Burger again pulsed through her heat-addled brain. Three million dollars in fines and fees and damages. The swimming pool of their Hollywood Hills mansion filled with headless chicken and duck carcasses purchased at Hong Kong Market. A Land Rover dredged out of Lake Arrowhead. Careers ruined. Families divided. All because two adults who desperately wanted to be free of each other couldn't agree about which of them had the greater claim to an award-winning, eleven pound bichon frisé named Wallace.

No. She didn't need that kind of drama. Let this Sam person win his coin toss and with it, custody.

She glanced down at the stocky dog who was scratching its ear with a hind paw, indifferent that its fate was being decided by a bogus coin toss. Except for being white, *this* dog was nothing like the pictures she'd seen of the Burgers' little Wallace. In a world of canine celebrity, this dog would be the barrel full of muscle and fat that acted as bodyguard to the petite powerhouse that was Wallace. This dog would be invisible, in fact, unless some overly ambitious fan or photographer got too aggressive toward Wallace. And then . . .

She glanced again at the dog's benign expression and thought, *Not even then. This dog is just a big, dumb flea carrier. Although thanks to this dog, at least the fleas are getting somewhere, unlike me.*

As much as it rankled her to admit it, Sam was probably right. If the dog had a choice, would it want to end up with a woman who thought of it as a big, dumb flea carrier? A woman who knew nothing about taking care of a dog? A woman who was sweat-soaked, exhausted, and couldn't manage to steal a functioning truck?

The dog yawned, as if bored by the outcome of the coin toss.

Fine. Let Sam think she was that stupid. The sooner she stopped arguing with him, the sooner he'd take the dog and get out of her way. She was waiting for someone and didn't need to be distracted by man or beast.

"Heads," Sam said and let her see the coin in his palm. "I win."

"I guess you got yourself a dog." She looked down to see the dog staring up at her, its tongue hanging out from between pink and black gums. "What'll you name it?"

Sam had removed his belt from his cargo pants and was making a loop to put around the dog's neck. He glanced at her, squinting against the sun—her initial assessment that he was no genius was backed up by his failure to realize that his sunglasses were hanging from the front of his shirt—and said, "I don't know. Maybe I'll *call it* Sue."

She scowled at the way he emphasized his words, and Pru jeered, *Maybe he's smarter than you think. Sounds like he knows Jandy's not really your name.*

Whatever, she answered. *It's not like I'll ever see him again.*

"A boy named Sue?" she asked.

Sam looked puzzled and said, "I would never have figured you for a Johnny Cash fan."

"What?"

"What?"

They stared at each other, and finally she said, "Why would you name a boy dog Sue?"

"I wouldn't. I chose Sue because that eye with one black ring made me think of *Rudbeckia.*"

Too much heat and too little sleep were apparently affecting her comprehension skills, so again she said only, "What?"

"The flower," Sam said. "You might know it as black-eyed susan, but its real name is *Rudbeckia.* Perfect for her, because she looks like she has a black eye."

"Oh!" she said, looking again at the dog. "It's a *girl* dog."

The expression on Sam's face, and maybe the dog's face, too, made it clear he was sure that the right person had won the coin toss and with it, possession of the dog. After all, if she couldn't figure out a dog's gender, what ignorance might she show regarding more serious matters like when to feed it, what shots it needed, and whether it had worms?

Ugh. Worms. Maybe it really was best that the dog was now wearing Sam's belt.

"I hope you two will be very happy together," she said.

Sam raised an eyebrow, probably because of her dismissive tone, but simply said to the dog, "C'mon, girl. Sue. Let's go for a walk so you can take care of business before we hit the road."

She felt a twinge of regret as the two of them walked away without a backward glance. She again thought of Wallace Burger, the bichon frisé. The big, dumb flea carrier wouldn't have been Wallace's bodyguard after all. She was a graceless, lumbering female who would probably never have been allowed near the little champion. And if she had been, onlookers would have wondered, *What's he doing with* her? *She's way out of her league with him.*

She shook her head. She was so tired that she was attributing unattractive human qualities to dogs. It was possible that she was just bothered by the dog's indifference as it walked away from her. Who wanted to be judged unworthy of friendship by a dog? Dogs were supposed to like everybody, weren't they?

She certainly didn't care what Sam thought of her. So what if he'd been kind enough to help a dog? So what if he had nice eyes, interesting eyebrows, good skin, and a semi-attractive smile? He thought she was stupid, and she had no patience for that. One thing Hud never did was treat her like she didn't have a brain. In fact, Hud almost always deferred to her decisions, including the one she'd made to postpone their wedding less than a week before it was scheduled to take place.

She glanced at the two-carat, emerald-cut diamond on her left hand and remembered to twist it around so the stone wouldn't show. Then she climbed back inside the hot cab of the crippled pickup and stared at the flatbed tow truck she'd noticed when she pulled off the freeway. At least she was out of the sun. She didn't dare go inside the rest stop and miss the tow truck driver. As soon as he showed up, she could get the pickup taken somewhere for repairs and then turn back the way she'd come. She'd been in the grip of some kind of road hypnosis, but now she was clearheaded.

Mostly.

Her eyes felt gritty, and she longed to close them. To keep herself awake—and maybe to silence Pru—she mentally replayed the last twenty-four hours. If she could make sense of her impulsive behavior, she might be able to face her mother and anyone else who had reason to question her.

She'd awakened the day before with the feeling of a certain harsh reality settling in as she stared blearily from the balcony of Hud's Los Feliz apartment. In only a few days, she would wake up there every morning, watching him rush out the door to make it to the studio by seven. There would be some days he'd be gone for twelve to fourteen hours, finally coming home to eat and memorize his lines for the next day before falling into bed.

The three days a week he wasn't taping, he'd be busy playing softball, golfing, or surfing with the Foundlings, his group of friends who'd given themselves that name when they hadn't made it into the Groundlings, L.A.'s famous improvisational group. She suspected that rather than being self-deprecating with their name, they secretly thought they were too good for the Groundlings. She had to admit that none of Hud's friends had turned into the slash clichés: waiter/actor, stylist/singer, personal trainer/comic. The Foundlings were moderately successful, but almost nothing they did reflected the glamorous lifestyle people outside the industry associated with show business. They were just normal people who happened to be actors, writers, comedians, and musicians.

The Foundlings' ordinary lives didn't bother her; she wasn't interested in glamour. But she did wonder why they always had to be around and part of everything she and Hud did, and she had a feeling marriage wouldn't change that. She wasn't sure she was ready to drastically alter her life when Hud's would basically stay the same.

While she'd stared from his balcony at the hazy L.A. sky, she suspected it was a bad sign that the week of her wedding, she was already missing her tiny studio apartment on the edge of Silver Lake. Her rent was paid through August, so she didn't have to rush moving her possessions into Hud's place after their wedding. But shouldn't she be looking forward to starting their life together as a married couple, instead of yearning for her creaky old hardwood floors and the shaded sidewalks of her neighborhood? Even the burglar bars on her apartment windows and her aloof neighbors seemed charming compared to Hud's apartment full of gray granite, smoked glass, black leather, and stainless steel.

She'd stopped her random, brooding thoughts when her fiancé joined her on the balcony wearing nothing but a pair of Calvin Klein boxer briefs and holding out a steaming cup of coffee for her. She might be losing an apartment, but she was getting the hunk of *Sweet Seasons*. Thousands of women would be thrilled to spend a single night with their favorite soap actor, and he was going to be with her every night for the rest of their lives.

She'd opened her mouth to thank him for the coffee and instead heard herself saying, "I want to postpone the wedding."

She still couldn't understand what had motivated her. It was as if someone else had taken over her brain and spoken for her. Certainly not practical, dutiful Pru, who'd been filling her head with recriminations ever since. Maybe she had yet another personality inside her. Maybe someone would end up writing a book about her. They could turn her disorder into a network movie: *Three Voices of a Reluctant Bride*. Or better yet, a dozen episodes on

HBO or Showtime. They'd get some actress with long red hair to play her. Not Nicole Kidman; she was too old. So was Julianne Moore. Lindsay Lohan was too young. Maybe Alicia Witt. Hud could play himself.

Hud, Pru reminded her. *You were remembering Hud's reaction.*

Hud had been amazingly understanding. Once he realized that she was serious, he assured her that she was having a bad reaction to the way the wedding had gotten beyond their control. Instead of trying to talk her into getting married anyway, he agreed to the postponement. He called the network and had someone arrange his flight to Minneapolis so he could join several of his cast mates at *Suds and Studs,* a meet-and-greet for fans of daytime TV. He wasn't even upset that she didn't want to go to Minnesota with him. He suggested that she treat herself to a few days at a resort of her choice, where she could relax and stop thinking about the wedding. Chandra, the agent/publicist/raving lunatic who took care of Hud, could notify the minister, the church, the string quartet, the caterer, the band, and the five hundred wedding guests. He would even ask Chandra to cancel their honeymoon plans.

All *she* had to do was tell her mother. Hud refused to burden Chandra with that job.

She squirmed uncomfortably and looked at her silent cell phone. She *had* attempted to call her mother. Several times. It was impossible to catch Carol Halli in her office, so she'd finally tried to leave the message with her secretary.

"Oh, no you don't," the secretary barked. "You deliver your own bad news. I've got one word for you: liposuction."

"Huh?"

"Here's a test. If you can tell me my name, maybe I'll give your mother the message."

"Uh . . ."

"Can't do it, can you? Do you know why you can't remember my name? Because over the past five years, your mother's had more assistants than Baskin-Robbins has ice-cream flavors. I've kept my job a record seven months. I only have two paychecks to go before I've saved enough money to get this cottage cheese suctioned from my ass and thighs."

"What does your surgery have to do with my wedding?"

"This wedding is your mother's ultimate networking opportunity. If I tell her it's off, she'll fire me on the spot."

"That's crazy," she said, even though she had to admit that her mother was incapable of hanging on to an assistant. "Anyway, the wedding's not off. It's just delayed."

"I'm sending you to voice mail," the secretary sang in a warning tone.

"It's Frida. No, Francie."

"So close," the secretary said before adding, "It's *Nelda*."

The next thing she heard was her mother's *I'm-not-in-leave-your-number* message. After a hostile moment of wishing she could tell Nelda that she should keep her ice cream and cottage cheese strictly metaphorical, she tried to break her news in a tone that sounded as forceful and confident as possible. Then she hung up and raced to keep her appointment in Palm Springs with the man who'd made an offer on her car. Even though she was no longer days away from becoming Mrs. Hudson Blake with legal rights to the second set of keys to his Audi, she'd been counting the minutes until her wretched SUV paid back some of the money she'd spent to keep it running. Nothing would have stopped her from unloading it.

She checked to make sure the twelve thousand dollars was still in its tight bundle at the bottom of her purse. When the tow truck driver showed up, she couldn't let him know she was carrying that much cash, just as she didn't want him to see the diamond that seemed too heavy for her slender fingers. Being desperate, stranded, and apparently affluent would make her an easy mark for him or whatever mechanic he took her to.

She squinted at the name on the driver's door of the tow truck: REVERE AUTO REPAIR. The letters beneath it were too faded to make out at this distance. It looked like CONVENT-something, but that made no sense. Although if she thought about it, nuns probably didn't take a vow renouncing auto repair. Judging by how much car repairs had cost her, a garage seemed a more practical way for a convent to raise money than selling honey, sewing choir robes, or doing whatever nuns did. She wasn't Catholic, so she had no idea. The closest she'd ever come to a nun was Sister Francesca on *Sweet Seasons*. Sister Francesca would never be mistaken for an auto mechanic, although Delaney Stewart, the actress who played her—

Fatigue was taking her on mental journeys that would only end in sleep. She stretched her neck and tried to focus. After giving her the twelve thousand for her SUV, the buyer made arrangements to get her back to L.A., but at the last minute, she'd asked to be taken instead to her grandpa's house in Redlands. A visit with Grandpa Bagby and Aunt Ruby would settle her frayed nerves and give her courage to deal with her mother. At least when her mother deigned to speak to her again.

She didn't want to think about her mother. Instead, she let her mind drift again, this time to summers at Grandpa's when she was a little girl. Most of the local orange groves were gone by then, but he'd held on to

some of his land and his trees. Enticed by the fragrance
wafting through her bedroom window, she'd wake up
early in the mornings, throw on shorts and a T-shirt, and
run to the grove, plucking juicy oranges right off the
trees to eat them for breakfast.

Everything had been so much simpler then. She
closed her eyes as she savored the memories, then jolted
herself back to alertness and stared again at the tow
truck. Where was the stupid driver? How long did it take
to go to the bathroom or do whatever he was doing?
She'd been to weddings that had taken less time—

Yes, about weddings, Pru said. *You went running from your
groom to your grandfather hoping that he'd deal with your
mother.*

Maybe that was true. But Grandpa was the only
person who could keep her mother in line. Unfortunately, Grandpa hadn't been home. It was only after she
took the key from its hiding place and let herself inside
Grandpa's house that she remembered it was the week he
and Aunt Ruby were gambling in Laughlin. They hadn't
planned to come back until just before her wedding so
they could be at the rehearsal dinner on Friday night.

There she'd been, stuck in Redlands without a car,
too nervous to sleep, and trying not to regret her decision or to worry about whether Hud was sorry he'd been
so nice about it. Just before dawn, she took the key to one
of Grandpa's trucks from a hook inside the pantry and
drove to the 10 freeway, intending to find a place to eat
breakfast.

Which was when that irrational force kicked in again.
Instead of stopping for food, she kept driving. The freeway was hypnotic, stretching in front of her like an enticing gray ribbon. She wasn't sure what thoughts made her
lose track of time before she finally realized she was near

Phoenix. She stopped to fill the pickup with gas and told herself that she couldn't keep driving east. She hadn't left a note for Grandpa to let him know she'd taken the truck. What if he came home unexpectedly and reported it stolen? It was one of several old pickups that he refused to sell, but he would surely notice it was missing. And even if Grandpa had taken the most tender care of it, it had to be at least thirty years old. She was crazy to be driving alone so far from home in a truck that was five years older than she was.

They just don't make 'em to last like they used to, Grandpa always said whenever he was nagged to get rid of any of his battered old pickups. For no apparent reason and with no real plan, she'd trusted his faith in Ford Motor Company enough to keep driving east after Phoenix, still unwilling to go back and face the consequences of her actions. Or more accurately, to face her mother. It was never a good idea to thwart Carol Halli.

When she saw the sign for Tucson, she promised herself she'd take the exit and turn back. If it hadn't been for the annoying van in the right lane that wouldn't speed up or slow down enough for her to move over, she would have.

Of course, that didn't explain all the other exits she hadn't taken. She'd been ignoring the voice of Pru, fighting her sleepiness, and steeling herself to make a U-turn when the real trouble started, because the boring view was interrupted by a startling change of scenery.

She'd never seen anything like the enormous boulders that were lying in piles on either side of the freeway. Even though she'd been forbidden to read fairy tales when she was a little girl—*That's not the way things turn out in real life,* her mother always said in the no-nonsense voice that eventually morphed into Pru—the boulders evoked images of a lost tribe of giants throwing them in some kind of game. There were rest stops on both sides of the freeway, and travelers had parked so they could walk through the canyons of rocks. Some people were even climbing them. She slowed down, lured by a sense of magic that went against everything her mother had ever drilled into her head.

Just as she pulled off the freeway, something under the hood of Grandpa's truck began making an alarming clanking noise. She turned into a parking space and grimaced as the truck shook, wheezed, and died. That was when she discovered that her phone battery was also dead. She got out, intending to approach the first sane-looking person who came along so she could ask for the use of a cell phone. Then she spotted the flatbed tow truck and relaxed. As soon as the driver came back, she could put her problem in more capable hands. Mechanic's hands.

While she'd been waiting, anxiously eyeing the snake and insect sign, a white Jeep sped past her and came to a squealing stop. A lanky man wearing a baseball cap pulled low over his eyes climbed out and spit. He snapped his fingers, and a big white dog with a few black spots tumbled out on clumsy paws.

She smiled. A man taking his dog for a walk was good scenery. But then the man jumped back inside his Jeep, slammed the door, and burned rubber driving off.

After a moment's shock, she yelled, "Hey!" and jumped out of Grandpa's pickup to run toward the abandoned dog. She heard her cry echoed by a masculine voice and glanced up in time to see a man sliding down from where he'd been sitting atop one of the more accessible boulders.

They met at the dog, each of them bending to give it a reassuring pat. They'd barely managed to avoid bumping heads, and their fingers touched briefly before both of them drew back and stood up straight.

"I'm Sam," the man said.

After a pause, she'd said, "Call me Jandy."

Why, *why* had she given him that name? Was it because she'd been reminiscing about being a little girl running through Grandpa's orange grove?

Sam gave no indication at first that he noticed her choice of words. He stared in the direction the white Jeep had taken and muttered, "Loser."

"I can't believe he just dropped the dog and took off," she agreed.

He shook his head, patted the dog again, and said, "Apparently it's my destiny to get a dog today."

Just like on Hud's balcony the morning before, a strange compulsion overtook her and made her say, "How do you know it isn't *my* destiny? Maybe *I'm* supposed to get a dog." Since she didn't believe in destiny, nor had she ever been allowed to have a pet after an unfortunate incident with a turtle named Martha, she had no idea what provoked her to claim the dog for herself.

After a few minutes of bickering over rightful custody of the dog, Sam suggested the coin toss. *Heads I win; tails you lose.* He'd "won" the dog, and she was stuck waiting for a tow truck driver who was apparently reading a Russian novel in the rest stop's bathroom.

"Poor dog," she said aloud. She looked for Sue—

Sue! What an unimaginative name. She was sure she could have come up with something more original.

Like Jandy, Pru said.

"Oh, shut up," she muttered, continuing to scan the area. Sue and Sam had either left while she wasn't paying attention, or they were concealed among the rock canyons.

She wanted to leave, too. Instead, she would probably drop dead of heatstroke. Or a rattlesnake or scorpion would get her. Maybe a tarantula. She shuddered. Were there tarantulas in Arizona?

She looked around again, intending to go back to her original plan. But no one was nearby, with or without a cell phone.

Anyway, who would she call? Her mother wasn't speaking to her. Grandpa and Aunt Ruby were out of town. Hud was in Minnesota. Her most recent temp job, working for the attorney who'd handled the appalling *Burger v. Burger* divorce and dog custody case, had ended a few weeks before. Even if she still had coworkers, none of them had cared enough about her to drive over five hundred miles to help her. She didn't even have a best friend who'd do that.

In fact, most of her friends were actually Hud's friends. They were nice to her because she was engaged to him. But once Hud's publicist contacted the Foundlings to tell them about the postponed wedding, they would probably forsake her one by one. It gave her a hollow feeling. Sue the abandoned dog was better off than she was. There was no one to fight over who got to keep January Day Halli.

Are you really that pathetic? Pru piped up again.

The relief that flooded through her when she suddenly spotted Sue, who didn't give a damn about her, returning with Sam, who thought she was dumb, was a clear answer that yes, she was. Pathetic, friendless, stranded, and—

"Hey!" she yelled again as Sam reached for the door handle of the tow truck. For the second time, she jumped out of Grandpa's pickup. "Wait!"

Sam turned and gave her a quizzical look as she ran

toward him, then he said, "You need to let it go. I won Sue fair and square."

"You won her," she said, "although fair and square had nothing to do with it. That's not important right now. You're the man I've been waiting for."

His eyebrow shot up again, then he grinned and said, "And I thought it was only the *dog* you were after."

Chapter 2

As much as she wanted to cut Sam's ego down to size, she reminded herself that she needed his help. Before she could explain, he held up a hand to silence her. "First things first," he said. "Dehydration is always a possibility in this kind of heat."

She'd been sweating buckets, and her throat was parched, but he was crazy if he thought she was going to accept some kind of drink from him. She didn't need the voice of Prudence to remind her that was a sure way to end up as the victim on a segment of *America's Most Wanted*.

She watched while Sam reached inside a cooler in the back of his spotlessly clean extended cab. It was hard to believe this was a mechanic's vehicle. She'd expected stained rags, empty cigarette packs, and crushed beer cans. Maybe that was just *her* mechanic, whose nickname was Hog. She'd gotten to know Hog only too well because of her unreliable SUV. She should have sent *him* a wedding invitation and gotten a little of her hard-earned cash back in the form of a toaster. Actually, if there was any justice in the world, Hog should buy her a commercial-grade range. She wondered if the mechanic would miss her and her frequent checks. She'd probably paid for some little Hog's braces. Or more likely, Mrs. Hog's breast augmentation.

The bottle of Ozarka water Sam held looked so cool and clear that she could almost feel the liquid sliding down her throat. There was no reason not to accept it since the seal around the nozzle hadn't been broken. She'd never wanted water so much in her life as she watched him uncap the bottle and fill a red plastic cup. Then he set it down in front of Sue, who took a couple of indifferent laps before clambering into the truck, looking back as if to say, *We all understand whose needs come first here, right?*

Sam drank the water that remained in the bottle, tossed the water from Sue's cup toward a patch of sand, put the bottle and the cup in a plastic bag, and tied the bag. Then he brushed off a miniscule smudge left by Sue on the truck's seat before he turned back and said, "Sam Revere. What can I do for you?"

The easy and honest response was to say *January Halli* and let him assume Jandy was her nickname. Instead, she heard herself saying, "Jandy Taylor."

What was wrong with her? Even though Taylor had been the name on her birth certificate, it hadn't been her name since she was four and her stepfather adopted her.

She shook off her self-recrimination, gestured toward Grandpa's pickup, and said, "Something's wrong with my truck."

Victim! Pru warned. *Don't let him think there's no one else you can call to help you. Don't give him the impression you're an easy mark. And don't let him think you've got enough money to pay a big repair bill.*

There had been a few times in her life when she'd lied to her mother just to avoid a confrontation, but she was usually honest. She hoped the lies she began fabricating along with her fake name were provoked by weariness and thirst. She hated to think that in addition to having a schizophrenic tendency to hear and be controlled by voices inside her head, she was turning into a pathological liar.

"My husband's been out of work for five months, but he finally got a job in"—she paused momentarily to search her brain for a city, any city—"Dallas. I stayed behind to sell our trailer, and now I'm on my way to join him. I've got enough to pay for a tow somewhere. After that, my husband can take care of everything."

Sam seemed a little amused as he looked across the parking lot at the pickup. "You'll probably be stuck waiting for parts. Maybe several days. That truck was new when Ford was in the White House. *Saturday Night Live* still had its original cast. Fleetwood Mac was still an obscure British—"

"I get it," she interrupted. "That'll be my problem. I just need you to tow it in."

"I could look at it," he offered. "Stay," he ordered Sue, who was sniffing the inside of the tow truck and paying no attention to either of them. As he walked toward Grandpa's truck, he paused to toss the plastic bag in a garbage can, noticed that the dog wasn't the only one who'd stayed, and called, "It's worth checking out, right? Maybe it's not as serious as you think."

She glared at his back. Once again, he assumed she was stupid. She looked at Sue and said, "I hope he continues treating you better than he does other females."

In answer, Sue shook her ears. A trail of saliva left from her drink of water ran down the seat, leaving a satisfying blemish on Sam's clean truck.

By the time she got to Grandpa's pickup, Sam had the hood up. She got in and turned the key. Of course, there was no horrible noise. The stupid truck hummed. Typical. Cars never made the same noises for mechanics—

A sudden clanking broke the silence, and Sam stuck his head around the hood and motioned for her to kill the engine. When she did, he stepped over to the window.

"Yep," he said, "that's definitely a problem."

"What do you think it is?" she asked.

He stared toward the engine with a thoughtful expression and finally said, "Sounds like it could be your rotary beater."

"My . . . my *what?*" she asked.

"I could be wrong, but you definitely shouldn't be driving—"

"Isn't a rotary beater a kitchen utensil?"

"Same principle," Sam said. "Where do you think they got the name?"

She noticed he had a little bit of a drawl. She narrowed her eyes. She'd been willing to go along with his fake coin toss because she could admit—at least to herself—that inexperience would make her an inadequate dog owner. But now he'd gone too far. She'd been in this situation before, with men like Hog who gouged her for hundreds of dollars in car repairs with a *don't-you-worry-your-pretty-little-head-about-what's-wrong* attitude. That was why she'd unloaded the SUV on the man in Palm Springs in the first place. She was sick of being taken advantage of because she was a woman with a bum car. She was sure that no truck part had the same name as something she'd seen Aunt Ruby use to beat eggs. In fact, she'd used a rotary beater herself, although it had been a while. Did this Sam Revere person think she was stupid about cars *and* kitchens?

"Then again, it could be your defibrillator," Sam added.

After a stunned moment—*defibrillator*!?—he must also think she'd never seen an episode of *E.R.* or *Grey's Anatomy*—she looked down at his hands. Just as she'd suspected, the nails were nicely cut and no more stained by grease than his hands or clothes were. He clearly wasn't a mechanic. But if he only drove the tow truck for Revere Auto, why didn't he just say so? Why make up fake engine parts? Had her inner pathological liar sought and found its soul mate?

She knew all too much about tow truck drivers from *Greer v. Wilkes d/b/a We-Haul-It* (Los Angeles County Small Claims Court). Sam was about to discover that he wasn't dealing with a neophyte in the ways of rip-off artists.

"Actually, if you're going to Dallas, this is your lucky day," Sam was saying. He slammed down the hood. "Revere Auto is in Coventry, Texas. That's where I'm headed. It's an hour or so west of Dallas. I can practically deliver you into your husband's arms."

You had to pick Dallas, Pru chided. *And you must need glasses. It's Coventry, you imbecile, not* convent *printed on the side of the truck.*

The name Coventry seemed familiar to her, but she couldn't imagine why. She knew next to nothing about Texas.

"I'm not sure my husband would want me riding so far with a man I don't know," she said. The lies were almost automatic now, but there really was no reason in the world for her to go all the way to Dallas to be ripped off. Especially not with Grandpa's truck.

Sam shrugged and said, "You can call him. Give him my business name and tag number. Or I can tow you back to Tucson. Or you can call somebody else to tow you somewhere. Makes no difference to me. I'll be glad to stay with you until someone else comes to tow you."

"That's awfully nice of you," she said sweetly, "since you cheated me out of a dog and couldn't be bothered to offer me a drink of water."

"Haven't you ever watched a movie on Lifetime Television for Women? Never take a drink from a stranger."

Since his words merely repeated her own thoughts, she decided to ignore him and focus on her truck dilemma. Tucson seemed like the best choice. At least she'd be heading in the right direction. If a city offering no job, a sterile new apartment, no wedding, five hundred disappointed wedding guests, and a hostile mother could be considered a place she wanted to go.

She sighed. She'd feel better after a night's sleep. Once Sam located a garage for the pickup, she could manage to find a motel, a phone, a bathtub, and a bed without his help.

Before she could suggest as much, Sam said, "If it'd make you feel safer, there's a gun in my glove box that you can use if I try to take advantage of you."

She couldn't decide if he was teasing her or not. She'd always heard Texans were gun-crazy.

"Is it loaded?" she asked, attempting to sound nonchalant, as if she handled firearms every day of her life.

"I have no idea," he said. "It doesn't belong to me. Since I don't hunt—hunting is stupid when there's Kroger—I don't do that manly gun thing."

A window in her brain opened and she saw the light—or else she was overdosing on sunshine. He was the kind of man who got all sappy about an abandoned dog. It was possible that his fingernails had been manicured. The cab of his truck was spotless. He didn't seem to be interested in females unless they were canine. He watched Lifetime. Plus the more she looked at him, the more his appearance improved.

Sam wasn't a looker like Hud. He was just a regular guy. But his brown hair was shaped in a cute, short cut. He had a little stubble that gave him a scruffy appeal. And if she wasn't sure he was laughing at her, she would have liked the way his eyes danced with humor. He might think she was dumb, but he really wasn't at all threatening, even if he was pretending to be a mechanic. Her brilliant deduction: Sam Revere was gay.

Then again, the hair peeking over the collar of his shirt gave her pause. Hud was ordered by the suits at *Sweet Seasons* to keep his chest shaved. His character was forever removing his shirt, and apparently the show's viewership of teen girls and gay men liked their soap studs with hairless chests. Did the presence of chest hair mean Sam was straight? Things would be so much clearer if he was wearing one of those ball caps with an equality symbol on it, or a necklace with rainbow rings. Or if he was sporting a big sticker on the back of his tow truck with some slogan like "I Don't Even Drive Straight."

Since the lack of a wedding ring meant nothing, she decided to test her theory and asked, "What about your wife? Would she want you driving"—she had no idea how far it was to Dallas, but at the very least, they had to get through New Mexico—"hundreds of miles with a strange woman?"

"You don't seem that strange," he said. "And I'm not married."

Gay. She was sure of it.

She relaxed and thought things over. Why not go to Coventry, Texas? She had no reason to rush back to L.A. She had money. She could get Grandpa's truck fixed—by someone who knew more about engines than Sam—then drive back to California at her leisure. Instead of feeling like she was in the middle of a disaster of her own making, she could consider this the getaway that Hud had urged her to take. An adventure. For a few days, instead of being Stan and Carol Halli's disappointing daughter, January, or Hud Blake's friendless fiancée, Jane, she could be Jandy. The name made her sound like someone fun, almost jaunty. Being Jandy for a few days could make her a more interesting person.

The decision was made. From that moment on, she would maintain her carefree Jandy persona. She would introduce herself as Jandy, even think of herself as Jandy. When the truck was fixed, she could go back to L.A. and her identity as Jane Halli feeling rested, rejuvenated, and ready to set a new wedding date.

And with enough time and opportunity, she might even talk Sam out of the dog. Or she'd become resigned to the idea that a dog was the last thing she needed.

"How much will a tow to Coventry cost me?" she asked.

"I was on my way there anyway. Maybe you could buy a tank of gas to make up for the extra weight."

She frowned and said, "That dog probably weighs almost as much as I do."

He laughed. "I wasn't talking about *your* weight. I was talking about the weight of your vehicle."

"Oh. Right. Fine. I'll go inside the rest stop and call my husband while you load the pickup on your tow truck."

"Technically, it's not a tow truck. It's a rollback," he said.

Suddenly he knew the right name for everything. She just smiled, grabbed her purse and her useless phone, and headed inside to use the bathroom and get something to drink. It was none of his business if she didn't really have a husband—or anyone else—to call.

* * *

By the time they were on the freeway, Jandy felt quite a bit better. Just being in motion helped. She tried to remember the last time she'd taken a road trip anywhere. When Hud had vacations, they usually flew to his sport resort of choice: Utah and Colorado for skiing and snowboarding, Grand Cayman or Cabo for snorkeling or surfing, and places where he could play or watch golf while she shopped or sat next to a pool and slathered the highest possible SPF sunscreen onto her fair skin. Though she occasionally drove to Redlands to see Grandpa, most of her road time was just going to and from work. At least when she had a job.

She sighed, waiting for Pru to list all the careers she could have if she just applied herself. The voice would sound tremulous, like Sally Struthers on one of those late-night commercials: *flight attendant, paralegal, welding, gun repair* . . .

Pru's nagging voice must have been lulled into silence by the cool air, however. Grandpa's air conditioner hadn't worked, which had made the drive through Arizona unbearable once the sun was high in the sky. When she'd finally used the bathroom at the rest stop, she'd used wet paper towels to give herself what Aunt Ruby called a whore's bath, so she no longer felt quite as repulsive. It would be nice to have some toiletries and a change of clothes, but she could worry about that later.

She'd half-expected Sam to let Sue ride shotgun and make her sit behind him, but Sue was stretched out on the bench seat in the back and occasionally emitted a loud snore. After a few miles in the quiet, cool cab, Jandy realized she was struggling to keep her head up. Sam reached behind his seat to get a pillow.

"If you put this against the window and lean on it, you'll stop giving yourself whiplash trying to stay awake."

"Wasn't Sue just drooling on this?"

"It's either her drool or yours," he said and waved the pillow in a final offer. She grabbed it and tucked it between her head and the door. She hated to admit it, but it felt wonderful. And it smelled good, too, clean like shampoo. It was a struggle not to close her eyes and just breathe, especially since there was nothing compelling about the scenery. Certainly nothing as interesting as the giant boulders at the rest stop.

"Where do you think those came from?" she asked sleepily.

If Sam said anything, she didn't hear him. The next time she opened her eyes, the sun was dipping toward the horizon behind them. She was confused, hot, and fearful that she really had drooled on his pillow. She hoped she hadn't also snored, but there was music playing, so maybe he wouldn't have heard it anyway. She smiled as Paul McCartney crooned about the long and winding road.

"Why?" Sam asked, and she realized he'd already said it once.

"Why what?"

"You said that the Beatles always make you think of Barbie dolls."

"I must have been dreaming." She sat up and hugged the pillow to her chest. She stared out the window. "How long have I been asleep? Where are we?"

"A little over three hours. Near Las Cruces. We'll stop in El Paso in about an hour."

"To eat?" she asked, wondering if he could hear her stomach growling.

"That and a night's sleep."

"But El Paso—that's in Texas. Can't we just drive on to Dallas? Or Coventry? Wherever."

He glanced at her and said, "Did you look at a map before you started this trip?"

"Sort of," she said, wishing he wouldn't ask so many questions. He was practically forcing her to lie to him.

"We've got an eight-hour drive ahead of us tomorrow. There's no way I'm going straight through. Not to mention you look like you could use more than just a nap."

"You always say the nicest things. I don't know why you're still single."

"Just because I'm not married doesn't mean I'm single," he said.

She ignored him while the Beatles continued going back to that same old winding road. When the song changed, she cut her eyes at him and said, "Texas isn't exactly the most enlightened state, is it? How did your parents handle the news that they had a gay kid?"

He stared straight ahead, looking a little surprised, then he grinned and said, "Unlike Texas, my parents are *very* enlightened. They handled it just fine."

She couldn't help but smirk. Her assumption that he was gay had turned out to be a lot more accurate than his assumption that she was stupid. She turned around and looked at Sue, who was on her back with her legs all spread out. The dog clearly had no sense of modesty or propriety—

"Wait," she said anxiously. "What? We're spending the night together?"

"You're not my type, remember?" he asked, keeping his eyes on the road and flashing that crooked grin again.

"I meant," she said, her tone icy, "do you expect me to sleep all night in this truck on the side of the road?"

"No. We'll get a couple of motel rooms. If you don't have enough money—"

"I can pay for both rooms," she interrupted. "In exchange for the tow. I just thought it might be hard to find a place that'll take your dog."

"Oh, so if someone has to sleep in the tow truck with her, you're suddenly willing to admit that she's *my* dog."

"Technically, it's not a tow truck," she reminded him. She saw the shiny trails of dried dog saliva on the backseat and smiled. "As for the dog, I think you and Sue are perfect for each other." When he didn't say anything, she added, "I'd never have called—er, named her Sue."

"What would you er-name her?"

"Something with more panache. Something dramatic and uniquely hers."

"She's a dog," Sam said. "Not America's Next Top Model."

"You have no imagination."

"I've got plenty of imagination," he disagreed. She noticed that his eyebrow slipped up again in that way it had.

"Puckish," she said, wondering if that was the right word to describe his expression.

"That's the dumbest name for a dog I ever heard."

"I wasn't—never mind."

"Puckish," he muttered. "And dramatic? I suppose you'd call her Juliet?"

Jandy glanced back at Sue with a dubious expression and said, "I don't think so. She's not quite delicate enough. I was looking for something more substantial. Isis. Or Natasha. Natasha's a strong name."

"Then she'd have to contend with moose and squirrel," Sam said in a funny accent.

"Huh?"

It was his turn to cut his eyes at her and say, "Moose. Squirrel." When she didn't say anything, he added, "Bullwinkle? Rocky?"

"Oh," she said. "The cartoon. I never saw it."

"You never saw *Rocky and Bullwinkle*?" he asked in an incredulous tone.

"I've never watched cartoons."

After a minute of stunned silence, he said, "Daffy? Bugs? Roadrunner?"

"Nothing animated."

"Speed Racer? Homer Simpson? Ninja Turtles?" He sounded dazed.

"Nope. And before you get worked up over Disney, no Mickey, Dalmatians, or dwarves."

"How is that possible?"

"My mother didn't believe in watching cartoons. Or animated films. She thought it was ridiculous for a child to grow up thinking that mice could talk or dogs could drive cars."

She didn't add that a long-ago summer job had made her all too aware that Anaheim wasn't really the "Happiest Place on Earth," just a place where tourists spent a lot of money to mingle with people in animal costumes. Even the news that the freshly painted yellow submarines were scheduled to return to find Nemo couldn't lure her back to Disneyland.

"Snoopy," Sam said. "You must have seen the *Peanuts* specials on holidays."

"Nope." She thought about it and added, "I knew Snoopy from reading the comics when I visited my grandpa. And *Foxtrot, Luann, Cathy,* and *Doonesbury.*"

"That's something, I guess," Sam said, still sounding a little dazed.

"Too bad Sue's not a boy. She could be Zonker. Or Hobbes. I loved reading *Calvin and Hobbes.*"

"No Great Pumpkin," Sam mused as if talking to himself. "No Wile E. Coyote. No Betty Rubble. No Scooby . . ."

She let him ramble on without comment. She had more practical things to worry about, like whether gifts had to be returned if a wedding was only postponed and not really canceled. It had been daunting to write thank-you notes for a zillion presents. She couldn't imagine having to box them up and return them.

What would the forever single Cathy *do,* she wondered.

That, Pru scolded, *is exactly why your mother knew cartoons were bad for you. Get real.*

Chapter 3

The sky was awash with dozens of variations of orange, blue, and yellow by the time they got to El Paso. Jandy wanted to enjoy the beauty, but she was uncomfortably aware that she needed a restroom and suggested that Sam might want to pick an exit with a promising motel sooner rather than later.

Sam said it would be better to eat first and then find a motel, explaining, "I'd rather leave Sue alone in the truck with the windows cracked than in a motel room."

Jandy nodded, remembering *HoliTyme Hotel, Inc. v. Randolph, et al.* (San Diego County Superior Court), and said, "Yeah. She might chew through a wall. Or use the bed as her bathroom. Who knows what bad habits she has? Something made that guy ditch her."

"Meanness made that guy ditch her," Sam said, pulling into a Denny's parking lot. "She's probably his wife's dog, and they had a fight. Jerk."

Jandy covertly checked out the area and had to admit that Sam couldn't have chosen a better place to eat. Not only were there motels within walking distance of Denny's, but she spotted a Target at the nearby mall. All she had to do was get away from him, buy a suitcase, and fill it with a few necessities and a change of clothes. She didn't want Sam to know that she had no luggage. Not that it was any of his business. But if he found out she'd lied to him, she'd lose her moral high ground against a person who cheated at a coin toss and pretended to be a mechanic.

She went inside the restaurant, used the restroom, and washed her face and hands, then got them a table while Sam walked Sue and gave her more water. By the time he joined Jandy, she had a plan.

"Why don't we check into that La Quinta after we eat?" she asked. "Then, if you wouldn't mind dropping me at the mall, I need to pick up a few things. Female things," she added, knowing any man, straight or gay, shunned shopping for such items. "I don't want to be rushed through the store, though. You and Sue can get settled into your room, and I'll just walk back to the motel when I'm finished."

"Fine with me," he said, studying the menu.

She wasn't sure whether she was relieved or exasperated not to get more of an argument about walking alone in a strange place. He didn't seem at all concerned about her safety, yet with that strange compulsion of a man to let a woman precede him through doors or to light a woman's cigarettes, he insisted that Jandy be the first to order food. Then, while he talked over his options with the server, she looked at her hands. Even though she'd washed them, they still felt grimy. She began digging inside her purse, pulling things out and dropping them on the table as she searched for her hand sanitizer.

"You can figure out a lot about a woman by the contents of her purse," Sam commented.

She would never let him see the bundle of money or the now inaccurate wedding invitation, but she took inventory of everything else as she emptied her purse. She wondered what he thought he was learning from her Estée Lauder lipstick; Clinique compact; Prescriptives eyeliner pencils in various colors; Maybelline Great Lash Mascara—Blackest Black, because she ignored makeup advice for redheads; hairbrush; two tampons inside a little case—she hoped he didn't guess what that was, or he might wonder about her proposed shopping trip to Target; multiple key chains with keys to various apartments and cars; several computer disks; a copy of Jennifer Weiner's novel *Good in Bed*—she'd been carrying that around for months and even though she liked it, she was still only on the third chapter; a half-finished résumé in a tattered envelope; three hairclips; four pens—she was sure at least three of them didn't work; several crumpled receipts and ATM slips she'd never put in her check register; cell phone; cell phone charger—that would come in handy at the motel; book of stamps; a Dooney and Bourke wristlet case that held three condoms and her birth control pills; two pairs of sunglasses from a dollar store that were in Oakley cases discarded by a long-ago roommate; Burt's Bees lip balm; a tin of Altoids Peppermint Smalls; a Coach wallet that contained other people's business cards, a MasterCard, a Bank of America debit card, a faded photo of Hud, her driver's license, and a five-dollar bill; and at last, a tiny bottle of Purell Hand Sanitizer.

She had no idea what her Fendi knockoff and its contents said about her. Which prompted an assessment from Pru: *You're a fraud with fake sunglasses and a fake purse. You have cosmetic promiscuity. You have more keys than a cat burglar. You don't finish things. But at least you'll have germ-free hands, fresh breath, and no sexually transmitted diseases or unplanned pregnancies.*

She used the hand sanitizer and said, "What do you think my purse says about me? That I'm a big, disorganized mess?"

"You don't have kids. You have a sore shoulder from lugging all that crap around. And you haven't been living a low-income life in a trailer."

"It's a Fendi knockoff," she said.

"With real Dooney and Bourke and Coach accessories inside it."

Oh, yeah, he was gay. She would never let him see the fake Oakleys.

The server came back with their coffee. Jandy noticed that Sam took his black, while she loaded hers with cream and Sweet'n Low.

"I would have figured you for the blue package," Sam said.

"No. I'm all about the pink. You really don't know anything about me, Sherlock."

"Tell me about the Beatles and the Barbies."

She stared at him. Maybe he was more perceptive than she thought, because he'd bypassed stupid judgments based on her purse contents and gone right to one of her deep, dark secrets. After a few seconds, she decided there was no reason why she shouldn't tell him. Sometimes it was easier to confide in total strangers. After all, as soon as the pickup was fixed, she'd be on her way back to California and would never see Sam again.

"The Beatles broke up way before I was born," she said. "I probably wouldn't have known who they were except that every time a Beatles song came on the radio, or there was something about them on TV, or even if they were mentioned in random conversation, my mother always got this sour look on her face. She'd change the station or the channel. She threw away magazines if they had articles on any of the Beatles. I thought it was weird, so I started doing things to test her."

She paused when the server came back to top off their coffee. Sam pushed the cream toward her. He didn't say anything, but his face had an expectant look, so she went on.

"I listened to a classic rock station to hear their songs. I named my pet turtle Martha after Paul McCartney's dog. Sometimes my Aunt Ruby would keep chickens, and I'd call them names from Beatles songs: Lucy, Rita, Julia, Loretta. I didn't dare name the rooster Ringo—that would have been too obvious—so I settled for Dr. Robert."

Sam laughed and said, "Wasn't Dr. Robert somebody's drug dealer?"

"Allegedly, but hey, how would I have known that? I was just a little kid at the time. After school, I usually stayed at the library until somebody picked me up on the way home from work. I'd check out books on bands, including the Beatles. Not racy memoirs or unauthorized biographies or anything like that. Books that it would be okay for kids to have, mostly with pictures. My mother always made the same unpleasant face if she saw Beatles books in my backpack. And one time, I paid a boy at school thirty dollars—that was a lot for a kid to scrape together—for a T-shirt with a picture of John and Yoko on it. My mom went ballistic about that."

Once again she had to pause while their plates were set down. Sam barely waited until the server was out of earshot before he said, "Did you ever find out why?"

"That *is* when I found out why."

"Don't tell me. You're supposed to be John Lennon's illegitimate child."

She laughed and said, "Close, but no."

"Yoko's?"

"Do I look Japanese?"

"Good point."

"Since my mother wouldn't break her no-Beatles rule and tell me herself, I got the story from Aunt Ruby. When she was in college, my mother fell in love with a man—well, supposedly she married him, but I don't think that part could be true, because my grandpa and Aunt Ruby never even met him. His name was Thomas Taylor, and he was a huge John Lennon fan. He apparently had every Beatles-related object he could get his hands on. Albums, posters, books, photos. Just like John, he drew and wrote songs and played guitar and piano. When John Lennon got killed, Thomas was crushed."

"I'm sure."

"Apparently, he got it into his head that if he went to Japan, he'd make peace with the loss of his idol. Find consolation."

"Or find his own Yoko."

"That's exactly what I think!" Jandy agreed. "He told my mother he felt like he had to go on a pilgrimage to honor John's memory. He was going to Japan, then Liverpool and London, then New York, and finally back home. Maybe he did find his Yoko, because he never came back, at least that I know of. Aunt Ruby said he didn't know—even my mother didn't know—that when he left for Japan, she was pregnant with me."

"So you never met him?"

Jandy shook her head and said, "Now that I'm older, I think it's more likely my mother was involved with someone who didn't want to marry her. The rest of it sounds like some story she or Aunt Ruby made up."

"But that wouldn't explain your mother's dislike for all things Beatle," Sam said.

"I guess. Anyway, after Aunt Ruby told me that story, I

never talked about it to my mother. Of course, then I *really* wanted to know everything about the Beatles, especially John Lennon. By that time, my mother had been married to my stepfather for a few years, and he'd adopted me. Stan's an okay guy, but you know how kids are. If I was mad at my parents or got in trouble, I'd always think my *real* dad would come back and take me away. The two of us would bond over the Beatles. He'd think I was the perfect daughter."

Do you have any idea how lame you sound? Pru asked.

"What about the Barbie dolls?" Sam prodded.

"All my Ken dolls were named after Beatles or Beatle friends, and all my Barbies were named after the women in their lives. That Pattie was a real vixen. Cynthia was long-suffering. Maureen was always reassuring Ringo that he was important, too. All Paul's ex-girlfriends constantly conspired against Linda. It was very dramatic."

Since she'd told Sam her name was Jandy, she couldn't share the story of the day she asked her family to start calling her Jane instead of January. Even though her mother couldn't have known the request was prompted by admiration for Paul's one-time girlfriend Jane Asher, she was the only one who'd never gone along with the name change.

"I'd pretend all the Beatle Barbies traveled around together in a sort of perpetual *Hard Day's Night.* I tricked out my Barbie Star Traveler like it was a rock and roll bus. I *loved* that thing. When I was twelve, I was in a thrift store with Aunt Ruby and hit the mother lode: an Around the World Japanese Barbie. She was several years old by then, but she was still in her original box and looked good, and I talked Aunt Ruby into buying her."

Sam laughed and said, "She had no idea she was buying your Yoko, did she?"

"No. But just like with the real Yoko, everything went to hell after that. I had to go to camp, and when I came back, my mother had hired someone to build a shelf all the way around my bedroom about a foot from the ceiling to display the Beatle Barbies out of my reach. She didn't dare get rid of them. I'd have had a tantrum, and Grandpa and my stepfather would have found out. When I complained to her, she said I was getting too old for dolls. Which I probably was, but that made me determined not to give them up. I just got sneakier about playing with them. I had my own stereo and bought used Beatles CDs. Me and John and Yoko had a lot of Saturday morning bed-ins. Of course, I gave peace a chance by wearing headphones."

Sam was laughing again and said, "Do you still have the dolls?"

"All of them. I eventually moved them to Grandpa's house, and from time to time he reminds me that they're there. Even though I haven't seen them for years, I still know who each one's named after. I also still have all their clothes. I figure one day when I have a big enough place, I'll display them."

"Along with your Star Traveler rock and roll bus?"

"No, that's gone. I guess my mother threw it away." She blushed. "I sound so dorky. I don't know why I told you all that. I've never told anyone else about my Beatle Barbies, not even Aunt Ruby or Grandpa."

"Or your husband?"

She blinked at him, remembered her string of lies, and said, "No. Not him either."

Being in Target with twelve thousand dollars in her purse was almost a religious experience. She couldn't believe how inexpensive the clothes were, and she went back to the luggage section twice to get an incrementally larger suitcase. It would be crazy to buy one or two changes of clothes when the store had all kinds of cool shorts and cargo pants and jeans for almost nothing. And she had to have shirts to go with them. Then she needed a swimming suit, because she was sure there'd be a pool at any motels she stayed in. She also needed underwear, sneakers, sandals, and lounging pajamas.

She saw no reason to buy little travel sizes of toiletries when there were so many great oils and lotions and body washes and hair products. And it wouldn't hurt to have a few snacks, because who knew where she'd have to stay in Coventry while Grandpa's pickup was out of service?

She felt virtuous about not buying any jewelry, even though they had some good silver and turquoise pieces dirt cheap. She just added a couple of bandannas, a ball cap with a Beatles logo on it, and more hair clips, so she could continue to keep her long, heavy hair off her neck because of the heat.

After her binge of consumerism ended, her only buyer's remorse was about the digital camera with its memory card, charger, and camera case. But who knew when she'd ever drive hundreds of miles and see new places again? She should document her trip. On her way back to California, she definitely wanted to stop and get pictures of the giant boulders. There could be lots of other things to photograph, too.

She lugged everything back to her motel room, congratulating herself on how she'd evaded detection by Sam and Sue. Tomorrow when she took the suitcase down, she'd tell Sam it had been in the locked toolbox of Grandpa's pickup. If he wanted to put it back in the toolbox, they'd have a problem, because she didn't have the key. She supposed she could pretend that she'd mislaid the key overnight. Sam would believe it. He already thought she was dumb, and she was sure her confession about her Beatle Barbies hadn't changed his opinion.

She went by his room to take him a few other purchases she'd made. Sue now had a black leather collar and leash that matched her spots, a bag of dog food, two bowls, and some toys. When Sam tried to give her money, she told him to credit it against what she'd owe him for the tow.

She was about to back out of the door when he said, "If you're interested, there's a cartoon marathon on one of the channels we get. You can hang out and watch with me."

"Enticing, but I just want to take a bath and crash."

He nodded sadly and said, "I hope one day you'll correct your glaring cultural deficiency. Unlike ballet or piano, it's never too late to start cartoons."

"I'm sure it takes a refined nature to appreciate a mouse dropping an anvil on a cat."

His eyebrow slipped up again. "You've been cheating, haven't you? What would your mother say?"

She just laughed and shut the door between them. Once she was back in her room, she plugged in her cell phone to charge it while she took her bath. She could take a shower and wash her hair later.

After soaking for half an hour in the aromatic salts and oils, she wrapped herself in a towel and cut tags off her new wardrobe, folding everything and packing her suitcase. Then with a glance at the clock, she called information, got the number for the Edgewater Hotel and Casino in Laughlin, and left a message for Grandpa to call her cell number.

She rested against the pillows with the TV on. Sam must have made up the cartoon marathon. The closest thing she could find was a silly network movie about rich teenagers living in Southern California, which was about as far from her adolescent reality as she could imagine.

The next thing she knew, she was jarred awake by a ringtone warning that "instant karma" would get her. She peered at the display and saw that it was an unknown number. Since Hud would call from his cell phone and her mother wouldn't call at all, it had to be Grandpa.

"Hello?"

"Jane! You calling to get me to place a bet for you? I'm on a streak!"

"How much have you lost, Grandpa?"

"I think I just lost Ruby to some Chinese fellow," he said and gave the wheezy little laugh that she loved.

"As long as you don't bet the farm."

"I know why you're calling, worrywart. Ruby and I'll be back before Friday night. She's even bought two new outfits. One for the rehearsal dinner and one for the wedding. I told her she didn't need new clothes. It's not like anybody will be looking at her. There's no fool like an old fool."

She'd heard him say that about a zillion times in her life, and she said, "I don't know, Grandpa, I'm not old, but I can do some pretty foolish things."

There was just enough of a pause for her to realize he was debating whether he wanted to know, but he finally said, "Anything you want to talk about?"

"You and Aunt Ruby can stay in Laughlin as long as you want," Jandy said. "Hud and I decided to postpone the wedding."

"You broke it off?"

"No! We're just rescheduling."

"Cut it kind of close, didn't you? Was this your idea or his?"

She sighed and admitted that it had been hers, although she wasn't sure why she'd done it. "I know I've messed up everybody's plans—"

"You don't need to worry about that," he said. He obviously didn't want to talk about her mother any more than she did, because he said, "You ought to go to Redlands. You know where the key is. When Ruby and I get home, she can spoil you rotten. And you can help me in the grove. That's the best distraction there is: hard work in the fresh air."

"I was way ahead of you," Jandy said. "I forgot you were in Laughlin. I had to break in to your house after I sold my SUV to that guy in Palm Springs. I'm using one of your trucks. I hope you don't mind, but I've driven it to visit a friend."

"Of course I don't mind," Grandpa said. "Which truck?"

"The gold Ford."

"I hope you didn't go far," Grandpa said. "I think she's got a cracked block or something wrong with the gasket. I used some seal additive, but don't let her get too hot, and don't drive alone at night. Where did you say you were?"

"Grandpa, are you still there? I can't hear you," Jandy said, further honing her skills as a habitual liar. Maybe she should run for president. That was the ultimate temp job. "I'll call you soon!" she yelled and disconnected the call.

She checked the time. She hadn't meant to fall asleep, and now it was too late to wash her hair. It would take forever to dry, and all she wanted was to go back to sleep. At least she felt better now that someone knew where she was. Or sort of knew.

She turned off the TV, crawled under the covers, and closed her eyes. She kept seeing the road stretch in front of her and hearing the way Sam talked so affectionately to Sue. The thought of the two of them curled up on the bed in Sam's room made her feel a little envious.

You want to be cozy in bed with a man other than Hud? Pru asked.

"Of course not," she mumbled.

It would be nice to have a big dog like Sue for company. Not Sam. Although Sam wasn't really a bad guy. He was kind of adorable. She wondered if he had a boyfriend. Too bad he didn't live in L.A. She could hook him up with one of Hud's gay friends. Then again, she wouldn't recommend getting involved with anybody in the industry. Very few of them were as stable and centered as Hud.

It was a pointless train of thought. Sam didn't live in L.A., and she had other things to worry about. Only not her wedding, or Hud, or her mother. She needed a break from all that.

Break . . . broken truck . . . cracked block . . . gasket . . . seal additive. She had no idea what any of it meant, but it definitely sounded more plausible than a rotary beater or a defibrillator.

She fell asleep to the sound of her own giggling.

Chapter 4

"If all of Texas looks like this, I'll need that gun of yours to shoot myself," Jandy broke the silence the next morning. She'd never seen more boring scenery in her life. She hadn't been tempted even once to take her new camera out of her purse.

"You never said where you're from," Sam answered. He didn't seem too upset by her criticism of his home state.

"That's right. I didn't," she said.

His tendency to fight a grin whenever she was annoying was starting to grow on her. She turned around and looked at Sue, who was staring out the window with her tongue practically hanging to her knees. If dogs had knees.

"Do dogs have knees?"

"On their hind legs," he said. "But it's called a stifle, not a knee."

"Right," she said.

She wondered if his need to rename things was some kind of mental illness. He'd probably call his condition rabies. Or herpes. Or chick peas. Chick Pea Syndrome didn't sound so bad. Almost healthy, in fact.

"The scenery will get better once we're out of West Texas."

Sam's voice momentarily distracted her from her delirious interior rambling. Maybe she was suffering from whatever made people see mirages when they were trapped in the desert. Or were mirages caused by dehydration? She wasn't particularly thirsty, just numbed by the unchanging landscape.

"I don't think we'll ever *be* out of West Texas," she said and lapsed into silence again.

Silence didn't really bother her. It never had. She'd been alone so much as a kid that she was used to it. Even with her friends—Hud's friends—she preferred to stay quiet, which worked out well, since most of them liked nothing better than to be the center of attention. At least they never felt like she was stealing their spotlight.

She tried to remember if she'd ever been one of those little girls who chattered. At home, her parents mostly talked about business. Whenever she wasn't in her room, or hanging out with Aunt Ruby—who was herself quite a talker—she kept her nose in a book. She learned that as long as she drew no attention to herself, her parents wouldn't ask her too many questions or expect too much from her.

She was just as quiet at school. Even her sport had been a silent one. She'd figured out in seventh grade that swimming gave her a reason for getting out of the house before her parents' alarm went off in the mornings. The swimming coach just as quickly figured out that Jandy didn't have the competitive drive necessary for an athlete. Coach Sims didn't mind if she practiced before school with the team, though. She also didn't mind picking up Jandy on her way to the natatorium. In return, Jandy helped put away equipment and kept the locker room tidy. None of the other girls ever seemed curious about her presence. They just assumed she was one of the coach's student assistants. Nor did her parents ever question why they never got asked to swim meets. They were probably glad she didn't expect them to attend anything that would take them away from work.

It was depressing to think that her inability to find a profession that she loved was nothing more than rebellion against her parents' workaholic tendencies. She'd quit college after three semesters. She'd started court reporting school and dropped out. The same went for her attempts at retail management, paralegal training—she didn't want to think of all the programs she'd started and never finished over the past seven years. It worked out better for her to have temp positions. She could always leave when she got tired of a job or when an employer tried to hire her for something permanent.

Maybe she'd wanted to postpone the wedding because marriage had started feeling too much like a permanent, full-time job. That was a horrible thought. She loved Hud. She wanted to be his wife. It was the elaborate wedding, not the idea of marriage, that had spooked her.

She sighed. She wished she were swimming right then instead of riding through barren desert. In the water, no problem seemed insurmountable. Swimming made her feel like an efficient machine being pushed to its physical limits, and her mind cleared itself of thoughts that confused or troubled her. If only there were a way to be paid to do nothing but swim. Probably if she had to do it, though, she'd quit swimming, too.

"You've sighed about five times in three minutes," Sam said. "I've been told I'm a good listener."

"Really? I've *never* been told I'm a good talker." She was

again rewarded with his half grin. "Do you like working on cars?"

He frowned and took his sunglasses from the visor. He didn't turn to look at her when he said, "I need to make a confession."

"If you're about to tell me you're not a mechanic, that's not exactly news," she said. "Before you offer to fix my truck's Cuisinart with a pair of forceps, or whatever crazy concept you come up with, you may as well know that I'm on to you."

"Did I go too far with the defibrillator?" he asked.

"You lost me at rotary beater. If it makes you feel any better, I also have a confession."

She couldn't see his eyes, but she could tell by the way the eyebrow went up that they probably contained the good humor she'd noticed the day before.

"If you're about to tell me you don't have a husband, that's not exactly news," he imitated her.

"What do you mean?"

"Your ring. You forgot to turn it around this morning."

She grunted, frowned at her hand, and said, "Not everybody wears a—Oh, forget it. You're right. No husband. A fiancé. I didn't want you to be dazzled by the big diamond and dig too deeply inside my fake Fendi for money for the tow or the truck repair. Mechanics are always making up problems that cost a zillion dollars to fix. Especially when they think they're dealing with some gullible woman who has no husband to question the repairs or the cost."

"You won't have that problem at Revere Auto," Sam assured her.

"Is your last name even Revere?" she asked.

"Is your last name Taylor?" When she didn't answer, he smiled again. "Yes. I'm really a Revere. It was my father's business. Along with the fact that we've always prided ourselves on our ethics, it's now run by my sister. She doesn't cheat other women out of their money."

"What do you do for Revere Auto? Troll the roads looking for business?"

"I help her out with an odd job now and then. She did an engine rehaul for a vintage car collector who lives in Phoenix, and I delivered the car to him. I was on my way home when you tried to take Sue away from me."

"I have just as much right to that dog as you do," she said. "I'm the one who got food for her. And toys. Don't forget the toys."

"It's too late to buy her love. You need to accept that she adores me. We've bonded."

"I've accepted that it's you and everything you own that'll be covered in Sue goo," she said.

"Sue goo?"

"She slobbers. A lot. If you don't tow cars for a living, what do you do? Are you a botanist?"

"What gave you that idea?"

"You knew the Latin name for black-eyed susans. At least I guess it was Latin. It was Greek to me."

"Actually, I think it was named in honor of someone in Sweden. But I'm not a botanist, just a repository of completely useless information. My mother gardens. Maybe I learned that from her or one of her books."

"Not a mechanic. Not a botanist. Not a veterinarian." When he looked puzzled again, she said, "Stifle? The name of a dog's knee?"

"That one's true," he swore. "My sister works for a vet."

"She fixes cars *and* animals? That's amazing."

"Different sister. Robin is the mechanic. Swan's the vet tech. The reason *I* wouldn't have bought food for Sue at Target is because Swan will decide what to feed her. Swan believes in a raw diet for dogs."

"I don't think I want to know what that is," Jandy said.

"See? That's why I'm the right person for Sue. I won't balk at hacking up turkey necks, chicken gizzards, and beef hearts or pigs' feet—"

"Seriously, I don't want to know," she said, wondering if her face looked as nauseated as her stomach felt. "Don't tell me any more things you don't do. Just tell me what you do."

"I guess you could say I'm between jobs."

"Oh. You're in the same profession as me. Unless you won the lottery or inherited a fortune. I haven't done either of those."

"I didn't win the lottery," he said.

"You inherited a fortune?"

"Not exactly."

"Okay, one of the jobs I haven't had? Is being a dentist. Could you stop making me pull teeth?"

"I wrote a book," he said, making it sound like a shameful admission.

"It was a best seller, you made millions, and now you're retired."

"No. The book tanked. I have no idea how few copies it sold because I don't understand my royalty statements, but trust me. It wasn't a best seller."

"What kind of book was it?"

"You know the *Dummies* books?"

"Like *Auto Repair for Dummies*?" she asked.

"Yeah, or *Latin for Dummies*?"

"Uh-huh, or *Dogs for Dummies*? Why? Did you write one of those?"

"No. I wrote a parody of them called *Morality for Morons*. Apparently I overestimated the public's sense of humor."

"Maybe your next book could be *Humor for Half-wits.*"

"That's good," he said.

"I'm sorry your book tanked."

"Don't be. Someone left a copy on a plane, where it fell into the hands of someone who knows someone in Hollywood. It ended up getting optioned. They want to make it into a Will Ferrell comedy. That may never happen. I've heard those Hollywood deals often don't. But I made a boatload of money, and the publisher more than made back the advance, so everybody's happy. Except my sister, whose misadventures with immoral people I may have exploited in the book."

"Is this the mechanic or the vet tech?"

"Neither. It's Dove."

"Robin. Swan. Dove. Were you raised in an aviary?"

"I haven't even told you about my fourth sister."

"Let me guess. Goose. No, Wren. Sparrow!"

"Lark," he said. "The stay-at-home mom."

"What's with the bird names?"

"My mother's maiden name was Finch. I guess she decided to go with a theme."

"How did you manage to avoid being named Eagle? Or Hawk?"

"It's Samuel Finch Revere," he said.

"I'm sorry. So what does Dove do?"

"No one's sure. She seems to always have money but no apparent means of support. We don't ask."

"I surrender. I totally can't tell if you're making all this up."

"Every word is true," he insisted. "Now that you know I'm a failed writer and a fake mechanic, you have to tell me something equally bad about you."

"You already know too much," she said.

"I know nothing."

"You call the Beatle Barbies nothing? That's good stuff."

"That was when you were a kid. Or did you buy a new batch of Barbies at Target last night?"

"I did not."

When she didn't say anything else, he prodded, "There must be something. What would someone who knows you best say about you?"

She thought it over and finally said, "Remember how you said a woman's purse holds clues about who she is? You could be right. That novel in my purse is good, but I'm sure I'll never finish it. When I was little, Grandpa used to call me the girl who never finishes anything. He said it because I always left food on my plate—"

"You still do," Sam interrupted.

"Are you judging me on the basis of a piece of toast?"

"A piece of toast this morning. Most of your fries last night."

"Maybe I just don't eat carbs. Who's telling the story of my flaws, you or me?"

"Point taken," Sam said, and again she saw the quick smile. He really was cute. The gay ones always were.

"Anyway," she said, sounding more exasperated than she felt, "it's more than food. It's an awful trait. I've started a zillion things in my life that I never finished."

"A zillion seems to be your standard unit of measurement. I'm beginning to distrust it. Name five things you didn't finish."

"Piano lessons. Quit before my first recital. Brownies. Quit before I ever earned a single badge. Culinary school. Court reporting school. This conversation—it bores even me. What's one of your worst traits?"

"That I don't let people make me say bad things about myself. Do you think you've got attention deficit disorder?" He glanced over with surprise when she yelped.

"I *hate* that. Everyone I know is always wearing their little acronyms like they're—they're—Brownie badges that they earned. One night I was sitting with a group of my fiancé's friends and they were all, 'I'm ADD, I'm OCD, I'm ADHD, I have CFS, I've got SAD, well I've got PTSD. . . .' Isn't anyone just normal anymore? It makes me crazy."

"Maybe you've got PMS."

She glared at him and said, "That's another sad fact about me. I never come up with the punch line, just the setup."

"You came up with *Humor for Half-wits*."

"See? When you say it, it has a double meaning. You're funnier."

"Is this a competition? Like with the dog?"

"No. I'm not competitive. That's another flaw. Are we finished cataloging them now?"

"No, because you—"

"Never finish anything." She stared out the window at the barren landscape. "It isn't like I've never driven through a desert before. Just not one that never ends. It's such a wasteland."

"It's teeming with life," Sam assured her.

"Like what?"

"I have no idea. That's just what everybody says. It's all dirt, rocks, and tumbleweeds to me."

"Tell me about Coventry. I should know something about where I'm staying."

"Won't you be staying in Dallas? I assumed your husband—or rather, your fiancé—would pick you up once we got to Coventry."

The problem with telling lies was keeping up with them.

"I figured I could stay there overnight until the truck was fixed, then I'd drive to Dallas."

"I don't think even my sister can get the parts to repair your truck that fast," he said. "Also, there won't be a vacancy anywhere near Coventry until after the Fourth of July."

"That's over a month from now!"

"Coventry's tourist season is from the beginning of June until Independence Day. It's because of the Godiva Festival."

"Godiva has a manufacturing plant in Texas? I had no idea."

Sam seemed puzzled and said, "A manufacturing—oh. You're thinking of the chocolates. The Godiva Festival has nothing to do with candy, although I think both names came from Lady Godiva."

"Who's Lady Godiva?"

He glanced at her and said, "You're kidding, right?"

"No. I know Lady Madonna. Lady Diana. Lady Marmalade. I know the lady is a tramp. But not Lady Godiva."

"Lady Godiva lived in England about a thousand years ago. That's just under a zillion. She was married to a nobleman whose subjects were suffering under the steep taxes he made them pay. She took pity on them and asked her husband to lower their taxes. When he refused, saying the people didn't deserve her help, she bet him that she could ride through the streets naked and no one would shame her by looking at her. If she was right, her husband had to do as she'd asked."

"Did it work?"

"Legend has it that she rode through the town on horseback covered only by her long hair. When all the townspeople stayed inside so they wouldn't see her, her husband gave in. There's no proof that any of this happened, although Lady Godiva and her husband were real people. Another part of the story has it that one man—his name was Tom—looked at her as she rode by."

"So he was the first peeping Tom?"

"Exactly."

"What does an Englishwoman from the Middle Ages have to do with Coventry, Texas?"

"Lady Godiva was from the city of Coventry in England. Although our town's founder wasn't from there, he borrowed the name. During World War Two, we declared ourselves twin cities and sent relief supplies to Coventry, which was heavily bombed. Later, as a thank-you, someone from England sent us a replica of their Lady Godiva statue."

"What happens during the Godiva Festival?"

"All year long, the Godiva Society raises money for worthy causes. They hand out checks and honor the fund-raisers in June. The town's merchants and civic groups host medieval festivities throughout the month: music, dancing, jousting, feasts, craftspeople, artists. Even though most of that happens on the weekends, people stay in our inns and bed-and-breakfasts while they enjoy other things around Coventry."

"Like what?"

"Hiking and riding horses and bikes in the national parks. There are several lakes where people swim, ski, fish, and boat. Since people can stay in other towns in the area, hosting a monthlong festival helps draw them to Coventry. We also try to appeal to the tourists who visit Dallas and Fort Worth."

"The festival sounds a little like a Renaissance fair."

"With a few Texas twists. For instance, the kids get to rescue a damsel in distress from a dragon that's actually a very bored Texas longhorn. There's the Godiva chili cook-off. I doubt fiery hot chili was a popular dish among the lords and ladies of the English nobility. We have a dog show, hot air balloon rides, all kinds of things. The last big event of the month is the crowning of the new Daughter of Godiva at the Medieval Ball. Traditionally, something always goes wrong during the festival. Half the fun is how stories of the mishaps get embellished during the winter whenever the townsfolk get together, until the next year when we start all over again."

"Coventry must be small," she said, trying to figure out what it would be like to live in a place where everyone knew everybody else. Long Beach, where she'd grown up, not only had over four hundred thousand people, but was part of the Los Angeles metropolitan area.

"Around twenty thousand residents if you include Old and New Coventry."

She smiled; the entire town was half the size of Silver Lake, her section of L.A.

"What's the difference between the two?"

"Old Coventry is the original town. It's mostly residential with a few office buildings and small businesses. New Coventry has chain stores, newer housing developments, and apartment complexes. A lot of people like living close to a small town and commuting to work in Fort Worth or Dallas. Anyway, because of the festival, our lodging is pretty much booked until the second week of July. But I'm sure your fiancé will want you with him, even if your pickup stays in Coventry at Revere Auto."

She made a noncommittal sound, trying to figure out her next move. Not being able to stay in Coventry was a problem only because she had no way to go anywhere else until Grandpa's truck was repaired.

"Of course, I did promise to deliver you safely into his arms. Once we drop off the truck and get an idea what's wrong with it from Robin, I'll be happy to drive you to—"

"I have another confession," she interrupted. "I do

have a fiancé, but he's not in Dallas. I don't know anybody there. I was just taking a little vacation, and Dallas seemed like as good a place as anywhere. I had no idea it was a zillion miles from where you picked me up."

"As an engaged woman, you might want to be careful about saying that I *picked you up*," Sam said, keeping his eyes on the road even though his stupid grin was back.

"It's not like anyone could get the wrong idea," she said. "After all, you're—"

"Not gay," Sam said. "That's *my* second confession."

Chapter 5

Having spent the remainder of their trip to Coventry pretending she wasn't annoyed, Jandy was relieved to finally be in the town itself. She got only the vaguest impression as they drove in. A banner hanging across one of the streets proclaimed June the month of the Godiva Festival and assured travelers they'd found "The Tiny Town with the Big Heart."

She acted as if Sam's confession didn't bother her because she was dependent on *his* big heart to help her get her truck repaired and get her to the closest motel with a vacancy. She offered only the weakest protest when he pointed out that he hadn't actually told her he was gay.

"I think you did," she said.

"No, you asked how my parents reacted to the news that they had a gay kid. They do, in fact, have a gay kid who they accept without any problem. It's just not me. It's one of the birds."

"The birds?"

"That's what we call my sisters. They have bird names, remember?"

"Right," she said.

He didn't elaborate on which sister was gay, and she didn't dare assume it was the mechanic. Thinking in stereotypes was a bad idea, and she was disappointed in herself for having done it when she was sizing up Sam. If being unable to name engine parts, unwilling to shoot a gun, fastidious about a clean vehicle, and kind toward abandoned dogs made a man gay, then most of the men she knew in L.A. were gay. Which wasn't, come to think of it, altogether incorrect, except one of those men was her fiancé, and she knew he wasn't gay.

"I didn't want to leave you alone and stranded," Sam explained. "I knew you could trust me to get you wherever you wanted to go, but I didn't know if you could trust the next guy who came along. It was easier to let you think I was gay since it made you feel safer."

She shrugged and lapsed into silence again. She could have pointed out that his noble assessment of his motives was inaccurate. He hadn't known that she thought he was gay until *after* she'd slept in his truck, on his pillow, across the entire state of New Mexico. But she couldn't deny that Sam hadn't told any more lies than she had. Nor did he owe her explanations. He was just a guy who was towing Grandpa's truck. They weren't friends. After the pickup was repaired, they'd never see each other again. Whether he was straight or gay, honest or dishonest, a scheming businessman or a good Samaritan, none of it made any difference.

They pulled into the parking lot of a building with a sign that said BAILEY'S TEXACO, but there were no gas pumps. She gave Sam a curious look.

"This is the right place," he assured her. "Revere Auto moved here from its old location a couple of weeks ago. We couldn't do anything until the underground fuel tanks were removed and new concrete was poured. Now that the move's official, Robin's taking bids to get new signs installed."

Jandy had no reason to doubt him until he tried to open the door to the building and found it locked. "Isn't it hard to make money if you're closed during normal business hours?"

"Robin's probably gone to pick up a part or grab a burger," Sam said. "I'll just walk Sue while we wait."

"I need to stretch my legs, too," Jandy said. "I think I'll walk back to the town square so I can get a better look at Coventry."

Preoccupied with Sue, Sam nodded absently. Jandy grabbed her purse and began walking up Godiva Street toward the center of town. Before she'd gone a block, her mood lifted, as if the town itself were working some kind of magic on her. Except she didn't believe in magic. She took her new camera from her purse and started snapping photos.

She passed a large building with a sign that said INDEPENDENT SEVEN TOYS. Since it didn't appear to be a retail shop, she assumed it was a manufacturer. It seemed appropriate that a quaint little town with Victorian storefronts, flower-laden window boxes, and pristine sidewalks would be the location of a toy factory. It was like a fairy-tale village. Except she didn't believe in fairy tales. She decided it was more like a prototypical small town on a Hollywood back lot.

She walked through a cluster of buildings on either side of the street that signs identified as Old Towne Shoppes. Beyond them, Lady's Ryde Restaurant was across from the Brazos Inn. All the buildings looked inviting, as if just opening their doors would take her toward new enchantments.

On a whim, she went inside the Brazos Inn. An elderly

woman sitting behind an antique desk was reading *Texas Monthly*. She looked up when she heard the door chime and smiled at Jandy.

"May I help you?"

"I guess it's too much to hope that you have a room."

"I'm sorry, we're booked until August."

"Do you ever have cancellations?"

"Yes," the woman said, but she looked sympathetic as she added, "and we also have a waiting list. I wish I could give you a better answer."

"I knew it was a long shot," Jandy said. She turned to go out, then quickly turned back. "What about a job? Do you need extra help? Is there a little cubbyhole where an employee can sleep?"

The woman shook her head and said, "We're fully staffed. We usually give our summer jobs to high school students."

"Thanks, anyway," Jandy said and stepped back outside.

While she walked, the few people she passed on the street smiled or nodded. She had no idea if they were residents or tourists, but no one seemed to be in a hurry. She stopped for a minute to take photos of the lush green trees and colorful flowers. It was hard to believe such a place could be in the same state as that endless, boring desert. She found this version of Texas a lot more appealing.

"It's something, isn't it?" a woman asked as she walked by pushing a baby stroller. "Sometimes I have to stop and take it all in, too."

"It doesn't seem real, does it?" Jandy asked. She knelt to pick up a stuffed octopus the baby dropped on the sidewalk and was rewarded with a toothless baby smile. She couldn't stop herself from smiling back.

"Thanks," the woman said. "He throws that thing out every time he sees a pretty girl."

"So you've got a little flirt on your hands."

"Yes, he's a charmer. Coventry's a picture-perfect little town. If you get into conversations with the locals, you'll find they know what's going on in the world. They're just willing to let their visitors take a breather from it all."

Another woman who'd stopped to admire the baby nodded and said, "Coventry's a lovely place. I think it's special because it's not a resort built for tourists. It's a real town. I don't think I could live in a small town, but every summer for five years, it's been a good place to visit."

"Good manners and hospitality are still important here," the young mother said. She started pushing the stroller and added, "I hope you enjoy your visit."

"Thanks, you too," Jandy called after her. She crossed Oak Road to the square. Even though temporary booths and tents being set up for the festival's weekend kickoff covered the green grass, they didn't detract from the square's charm. There was a stone-and-wood church with boldly colored stained glass at the far end. On the opposite side of the square from where she stood, she could see a fountain. The sound of its gentle splash was irresistible and drew her that way.

When she reached the fountain, she stared up at the statue of the woman on horseback. She was beautiful and had long hair partially covering her nude body. Jandy realized she was looking at the statue of Lady Godiva that Sam had told her about. She took a photo.

"If you throw a coin in the fountain, your wish will come true," a girl said as she paused next to Jandy.

"I don't believe in making wishes," Jandy said, but smiled so her words wouldn't sound harsh.

The girl reached down to scratch her dog's ears—

a trim greyhound, nothing like the lumbering giant that Sam had rescued—and said, "I believe in making wishes. I'll make one for you."

Jandy shook her head as the girl tossed a coin into the water. "What did you wish for me?"

"I'll let you know when it comes true. Come on, Rip."

Jandy watched as the girl led the dog away. She felt the strangest yearning. She wanted to be a tourist like the woman with the stroller, sure of a room at the inn. She wanted to look like she belonged to the town like the girl with the greyhound named Rip. She didn't want Sam to drive her to Fort Worth or Dallas, which were probably just concrete-and-steel cities like L.A. She didn't want to worry about the truck or the wedding or where her next job would come from.

She wanted to just *be* for a while.

She looked up at Lady Godiva, thinking of the story Sam had told her, and suddenly she realized her arms were covered in goose bumps. She remembered why the city's name had seemed familiar. The year before, she'd read an article on the Internet about Yoko Ono. John Lennon's widow had dedicated two Japanese oak trees in Coventry, England, in memory of acorns she and John had planted in that city in the 1960s during one of their first peace protests.

"Imagine," Jandy said and laughed nervously. She glanced around. Seeing no one, she dug inside her fake Fendi until she came up with a fistful of coins to throw in the fountain.

She strolled back across the square to the other corner so she could examine the quaint First Coventry Church building. The sun glinted off its windows. She walked around it and took more pictures. She was sure that the pews and floors would be bathed in the colors of the stained glass. Even though in a town this small the church was probably never locked, she decided not to go inside.

Looking back in the direction she'd come, she noticed a library and a post office. Instead of retracing her steps, she went down Dresden Street in the general direction of Revere Auto. The boxy lines of the office buildings she passed were softened by trees and flower beds bursting with color. The town hall was a stately red brick building. In Southern California, brick was impractical because of earthquakes. Since she almost never saw it, it struck her as prestigious.

Reaching the end of the block, she paused in front of the Godiva Inn, wondering if she should ask about a room there, even though she already knew the answer. She glanced around and saw gold lettering on the window of a shop across the street: MOLLY'S BEAUTY SHOP.

Her hair, which she thought of as her best feature, was tightly French-braided and tucked under a clean navy bandanna. She'd now gone three days without washing it, something she never did. The prospect of having someone else shampoo it, massaging her scalp and the back of her neck, letting her sit still with her eyes closed while it was dried for her, was ridiculously tempting. Anyone who didn't have thick, curly, waist-length hair could never know what a pain it was just to dry, much less straighten and style.

She had no idea how many hours she would be in Coventry or how long it might take to find a motel room outside town, and she couldn't bear having dirty hair another second.

She crossed the street. When she opened the door, she again felt like she'd stepped onto a movie set. Two women were under retro hair dryers with hard, clear plastic hoods that lowered over their heads. Their hair was set in the kind of rollers that she vaguely remembered Aunt Ruby using many years before. The two women were speaking loudly about chili recipes until they spotted her. They broke off to regard her with friendly interest. When she smiled at them, they smiled back.

"Hi, there," a woman said, and Jandy turned to look at her. She was wearing a black apron. Her hair was dyed jet black and teased to impossible proportions, and her eyes were outlined with black eye pencil and tons of mascara. She'd paused in the middle of a foil wrap, and she and her customer were both watching Jandy with pleasant, expectant expressions. "I'm Phylura. Could I help you?"

Jandy felt a tremor of anxiety. She didn't have 1960s hair. Beatle girlfriends might have felt right at home, but all the rollers and dryers and teased hair made her nervous.

"I don't have an appointment," she said. "I just need a shampoo and blow dry."

Phylura nodded and yelled, "Evan! Can you take a walk-in?"

A tall man came from a room at the back of the shop, and Jandy relaxed. He was wearing jeans and a T-shirt that said NEVER THOUGHT I'D MISS NIXON. His blond hair was cut short and only the front part was pushed up a little. It was a style that was currently popular among some of Hud's more meticulously groomed friends. He was proof that at least one person in Molly's Beauty Shop was living in 2006.

He smiled at Jandy and said, "Hi, there. Are you in a hurry?"

"No," she said, dismissing Sam and Grandpa's pickup from her thoughts. She *needed* salon time, and she sensed that Evan was exactly the kind of stylist she needed it from. "I just want my hair shampooed and dried."

"I have to finish a cut and a comb-out, then I can take you. Sorry for the wait. We're not usually this busy on a weekday."

"And Tryphena is usually here. Tryphena is my sister," Phylura added for Jandy's benefit. "She works here, too."

"You have very unusual names," Jandy said as Evan walked away. She hastened to add, "They're pretty. Just different."

"Hon, just wacky is what they are. They suit Phena and me, I guess. They're Wicks family names that seem to skip a couple of generations, then come back. It was my luck to be born this go-round." She efficiently foil-wrapped another strand of her customer's hair while Jandy sat down to wait for Evan.

"I'm just plain Lois," the customer said with a smile at Jandy. Then she looked at Phylura's reflection in the mirror and said, "Where is Phena?"

"You haven't heard? Jay Jay—that's my brother," she explained with a quick glance at Jandy, "got Fiji—that's Tryphena's son, his real name is Fred Junior—in trouble again. See, they're uncle and nephew, but they're only two years apart. Even though Jay Jay should be setting an example, he's usually the one who starts everything."

"What did he do this time?" Lois asked.

"I can't believe Clay didn't tell you."

"You know Clay never tells me anything," Lois said.

"Well, after Mayor Murray said no fireworks from now until the official city fireworks on the Fourth, Jay Jay just had to buy some. It doesn't take a genius to figure out you can't hide fireworks. You set them off, you either get noise or a light show. Jay Jay decided he could get away with it as long as he didn't shoot them off from his own place. So he and Fiji went behind Christ Church, and the first bottle rocket? Shot right into the top of the mayor's oak tree and set it on fire. Jay Jay started running around in a panic with Mayor Murray's garden hose. He did nothing except spray water inside her open dining room window, knocking a bunch of crystal off a china cabinet and soaking her rug. Our mayor is a woman," she explained to Jandy.

Jandy nodded, eager to hear the rest of the story.

"Fiji ran inside the church kitchen, grabbed a fire extinguisher, and jammed it down his pants before he climbed the tree. Got halfway up and the fire extinguisher went off, filling his pants with foam and scaring the hell out of him. Jay Jay said Fiji hit every branch on the way down, which I guess was good. Broke his fall. The fire fizzled out by itself, but not before all the fire department and half the police department trampled Mayor Murray's flower beds. So now Phena, Jay Jay, and Fiji are talking to the mayor about a little community service for the boys."

"I'm not sure the community can take much more of their servicing," Lois said. She looked at Jandy, who was still laughing at the image of the fire extinguisher discharging in someone's pants, and said, "You must think you're in Crazy Town."

"I think it's better than television," Jandy said.

Phylura nodded philosophically, then said, "Hey, if you're thirsty—"

"Don't you dare offer her any of that liquid poison you call tea," Evan said as he settled one of the hair dryer women into a chair at the next station. He had the brightest eyes, and Jandy felt special every time he turned them on her. "I've got a spa pedicure chair in the next room. It gently massages your back while your feet soak in a hot bath of rosemary and peppermint. You can get a little pampering while you wait. And a bottle of icy cold water. My treat."

"That all sounds wonderful," Jandy said.

She followed him and took off her shoes while he got everything ready. Then he turned and said, "Did I ever introduce myself? I'm Evan Hammett."

"Jandy Taylor," she said, deciding she might as well stick with that name. After all, Jandy Taylor was on an adventure, until the person that Lois might dub *plain Jane Halli* went back to L.A.

After a few minutes of blissful relaxation, she thought about Sam waiting for her at the garage. She decided there was no hurry. He still had to get Grandpa's pickup unloaded. And his sister would need time to determine what was wrong with the engine.

She was almost asleep when Evan came back and softly said, "How're you doing?"

"I'm in heaven."

"You're easy."

"I'll bet you say that to all the girls," she said drowsily.

Evan gently removed her feet from the bath and dried them off. Then he rubbed some lotion into them and said, "Our manicurist isn't here, or you could get a pedicure on the house."

"You shouldn't be so nice," she warned. "When you see how vile my hair is, you might regret it."

"Let's go to the shampoo chair so I can assess the damage."

Once she put on a smock and settled onto the chair, Evan pulled off her bandanna and said, "Nice braid job. Do it yourself?"

"Are you making fun of me?"

"Noooo," he drawled, sounding totally insincere, which made her smile.

"I've been on the road for a few days and haven't had time to wash it."

"I've seen armadillos who were on the road for a few days and looked livelier than this," he teased. He made swift work of unbraiding her hair, then stood back and said, "Jeez. Who would have ever guessed all this was under your bandanna?"

"When it's clean," Jandy assured him, "it's my best feature."

"I believe you. Mercy. When it's not wavy from braiding, it's past your waist, isn't it? I don't think I've seen this much red hair since my last drag show in Houston. Are you one of the Daughter of Godiva contestants? You won't need a wig."

She shook her head and said, "No. I'm just passing through and didn't know about your festival until right before I got here."

"Evan! Phone!" Phylura yelled. "It's Grayson."

"My better half," Evan said with a happy smile. "I need to talk to him. I'll be just a second."

At least Evan left no doubt that he was gay. Sam could take a lesson in full disclosure from him.

She leaned back and let her hair fall into the deep sink behind her. Only then did she become aware that there was a TV suspended from the ceiling. It was tuned to *Inside Hollywood*, the most over-the-top of the celebrity gossip shows. Maybe because she actually knew a few semi-famous people, she couldn't stand the sensational approach of those programs.

She sat up and looked for a remote, found it on a cart, and stared at it with exasperation. All the print was worn off the buttons. She pointed the remote toward the TV, but instead of changing the channel, she only managed to unmute it. By the time Evan returned, she'd given up trying to figure it out and was leaning back again.

He saturated her hair with warm water. She wrinkled her nose with pleasure at the shampoo's scent.

"Chamomile and tea tree," Evan said when she asked about it. "Your hair's so heavy. Does it give you headaches?"

"Sometimes. It feels really good when you massage my scalp. You're amazing."

"I'll bet you say that to all the guys," he imitated her. "I used to have a client in Houston with hair like yours. She was an exotic dancer who came for massages and haircuts at the salon where I worked. She'd never let the shampoo people touch her hair. She said I was the only one who understood the effect of its weight on her scalp and neck."

He held up her head with one hand, closing his other hand into a fist that he pressed into the muscles of her neck. She felt like she was floating, and it took a few seconds for the chirpy voice of the TV correspondent to penetrate her consciousness.

". . . at April's Daytime Emmys with fiancé Hudson Blake . . ."

Jandy pushed Evan's hands away and said, "Can you turn off the water please, so I can hear this story?"

Within seconds, she forgot Evan and everything else as she stared at the TV with dismay. She'd seen the same footage of Hud walking with her down the red carpet many times. Hud hadn't been nominated for an Emmy award, but *Sweet Seasons* had gotten several nominations. It was the first time the awards ceremony had been in L.A. instead of New York, and since Hud was a major part of one of *Sweet Seasons'* most talked-about storylines, he'd been chosen to attend along with the show's elite group of Daytime Emmy nominees.

She'd been a nervous wreck about the Emmys until Hud's publicist, Chandra, told her about a resale shop on

Melrose where she could find a designer dress for almost nothing. Because of her red hair, the salesperson had instead directed her toward a reproduction of a Rita Hayworth gown from the 1940s. The dress's emerald beading had made her green eyes brilliant, and she'd left her curly hair down. She'd been confident that she was a presentable date for Hud until she saw his eyes. Then she knew she was a knockout. She felt like *she* was a star when she walked into the Kodak Theatre with him. It had been a wonderful night, and it was hard for her to reconcile her memory of it with the story the correspondent was telling.

"January Halli, sole heiress to the Halli real estate fortune, was last seen in a supermarket near her Silver Lake apartment. The police say there's no evidence of foul play. Sources close to the couple refuse to confirm or deny that Miss Halli is the latest in an epidemic of runaway brides."

"What?" Jandy squeaked at the television.

The footage switched from the correspondent to a video clip of Hud's friend Sorel Eisen walking away from the camera with her hand out.

"No comment," Sorel said. When the reporters began shouting questions at her, she dodged and went the other way, calling back, "I'm sure this is all a misunderstanding that Jane will clear up. Can you imagine anyone running away from Hudson Blake? That's nuts."

"I don't believe this," Jandy muttered as the next clip showed her mother and stepfather standing outside their office, the sign for HALLI REAL ESTATE DEVELOPMENT prominently featured next to them. Her mother was wearing sunglasses and a grim expression.

"I don't think the police are taking January's disappearance seriously enough," Carol Halli said. "Someone must know something. If you don't want to contact the authorities, call us at Halli Real Estate. We're offering a reward for any information that helps us find our daughter." She then turned her face into her husband's shoulder as if overcome by emotion.

"Oh, brother," Jandy said. She struggled to sit up as the segment returned to the correspondent, who began giving out phone numbers for reporting any tips or leads. When Evan kept a firm grip on her shoulder, holding her down, she said, "I need to—"

"Just wait," he warned in a low voice.

"But I'm not—"

"The TV near the hair dryers is on *Inside Hollywood*, too. Your long red hair is a dead giveaway. Let me wrap this towel around it before you get up, and my customers might not realize that they just saw you on TV. Directly behind you are stairs leading up to an apartment. You can have privacy up there. As soon as the shop's empty, I'll come up, and we'll talk about how I can help you, okay?"

"But I don't need help. I'm not a runaway bride."

"Do you *want* to be recognized and gossiped about?"

She considered Evan's words. Of course she didn't want people gaping at her and thinking she was some kind of freak. This was all just a big misunderstanding that either she or Hud could clear up with a few phone calls. She was surprised his publicist hadn't already taken care of it. Chandra knew they hadn't called off the wedding, only postponed it. Why didn't she just tell everyone that? How had the media gotten the idea that she was a runaway bride? Why did the media even care? At least Sorel had sort of stood up for her. Or maybe she'd done that for Hud, because none of his friends would want the world to think he'd been left at the altar.

And what on earth was her mother up to? Jandy knew

even if her mother hadn't listened to her voice mail, her secretary—Frida? No. Nelda—would have given her the message about the wedding rather than let her think foul play was involved. Since Chandra had taken on the arduous task of notifying everyone and canceling the ceremony, reception, and honeymoon, the only inconvenience her mother would suffer was deciding which business contacts she wanted to wine and dine on Friday and Saturday now that her schedule had opened up.

"This is insane," Jandy said, sitting up as Evan tucked a towel around her wet hair. She reached for her purse and headed for the stairs while Evan walked in the opposite direction and asked who was next.

Chapter 6

"I've never known a real live heiress," Evan said, dropping down on the sofa next to Jandy and rotating his feet. "Maybe you could make me your personal stylist and I wouldn't have to stand up all day. I'm getting too old for this job."

"I hope you don't mind that I raided the refrigerator," Jandy said, pointing to her liter bottle of Ozarka water. "Calling people all over the country has dried out my throat. You'd think if they were afraid I'd been abducted, they'd be waiting to hear from the kidnapper. But all I get is voice mail and answering machines."

"Why don't I call your parents and tell them where you are so I can collect the reward? I'll split it with you," Evan joked.

"Trust me, the only person likely to give you a reward is my grandpa if you return his truck that I sort of stole. Since he's currently gambling away his Social Security check, don't expect much."

"Damn," Evan said. "I guess I'll have to figure out a different retirement plan. So which is it? January Halli? Jane Halli? Or Jandy Taylor?"

"All of the above. But for now, I'd rather be Jandy Taylor."

"Jandy it is." He stared at her for a few seconds, and suddenly he smiled. The deep creases this caused on his cheeks gave him the debonair appearance of a classic film star: Fred Astaire to her Rita Hayworth. She returned the smile, even though her jumbled thoughts were a thousand miles away. He snapped her out of it when he said, "I can't decide if I'm coming in at the end of a story or the beginning of one."

"Me, either." She looked at him a few seconds, wondering why she wanted to confide in him. Maybe it was the kindness in his eyes, which made her realize how alone she felt.

"A lot of stories begin with 'Once upon a time,'" Evan encouraged.

Jandy grimaced and said, "Not stories like mine. Here's the beginning. About two years ago, right after I began dating a struggling young actor named Hudson Blake, he got a job on the soap *Sweet Seasons*. He decided I was his good luck charm. I don't really believe in things like luck. Hud works hard for everything he gets. All his friends say the soap is just a stepping stone to a bigger career. His publicist definitely believes that. She gives us the George Clooney speech: If George Clooney can go from *The Facts of Life* to *Sisters* to *E.R.* to A-list film actor, she's sure Hud can take that same career path, beginning with his soap. She's always trying to get his name everywhere she can. Hud—well, Hud's happy if he's working and can play as hard as he works. Last year, he proposed to me and gave me this beautiful ring."

She held up her hand, and Evan gave a grunt that might have been approval. Then he said, "Go on."

"I'm not the most romantic person in the world. I

don't go in for all that gushy stuff. But one of the places that Hud and I like to escape to is Mendocino, California, and it *is* romantic. Have you ever been there?"

"No."

"It's north of San Francisco, tucked between the coast and a redwood forest. It's a little hard to get to, which keeps it from being ruined by tourists. They filmed the TV show *Murder, She Wrote* there. That's why Hud was familiar with it. He had a tiny part in an episode of the show when he was a kid. Anyway, we decided we wanted to get married there. On the cliffs, among the wildflowers, with the redwoods behind us and just a few of Hud's closest friends there."

"What about your closest friends?" Evan asked.

Jandy felt herself blush and said, "I meant *our* closest friends. His friends are my friends, of course. Anyway, we both wanted a ceremony that was simple and sweet. But then his publicist got involved. Chandra sees a celebrity wedding as a huge bonanza of publicity that no actor can afford to pass up. Equally enthusiastic on my side was my mother."

"The real estate mogul?"

"She's not a mogul. My mother and stepfather are definitely real estate developers, and yeah, that's a lucrative thing in California. But a company that wheels and deals the way theirs does can be *Fortune* 500 one day and teetering on bankruptcy the next. All their money gets reinvested, and I'm nowhere close to being an heiress. Plus people are always suing my stepfather, Stan. Whether or not Stan's unethical, if you're perceived as having money, you can count on a few lawsuits."

"I wasn't really going to ransom you," Evan promised. "You don't have to convince me that they're impoverished."

Jandy laughed and said, "Well, hardly that. I'm just

saying that like Chandra, they had their own reasons for wanting Hud and me to have a lavish wedding. They agree that one day Hud will be A-list and hope to get a lot of show business contacts through him. So they connect that name—Halli Real Estate Development—to his whenever they can. Before I knew it, my wedding was booked into a church with musicians and five hundred guests, most of whom I've never even heard of. My dress was picked out for me by Chandra. A live band was hired for the reception—Oh, the entire thing was just out of control. Hud didn't like it any better than I did, but he just kept saying we should go along with it and it would all be over soon. And it should be over soon. It should be taking place in three days."

"But you broke it off."

"I didn't break our engagement. I still intend to marry Hud. But I just couldn't—I can't do it their way. All the excess and attention. It's not me. I think when a girl plans to get married only once in her life, she should have the wedding she wants. Even if it's not much of a wedding in anyone else's eyes."

"And you told Hud this?"

"Yes."

What she hadn't told Hud was Chandra's reaction when she'd said the same thing to her.

That's so sweet, Chandra said, *that you think this will be your only wedding. That's why you're the ideal* first *wife for Hud.*

It still made her blood boil to think of that conversation.

"And he didn't agree to scale down the wedding?" Evan interrupted her thoughts.

"He said he'd go along with whatever I wanted. So I postponed it. We'll get married later, privately, the way we wanted to in the first place. I *didn't* jilt him."

Evan stared at her for a moment and finally said, "You understand what's happening now, right?"

"What?"

"Chandra's getting Hud as much or more publicity—and your parents are capitalizing on it—as the wedding itself would have gotten. Don't you remember last year's big runaway bride story?"

"But I'm not a runaway bride! Hud's the one who told me to take a vacation. I'll admit that no one knows exactly where I am, but only because I was waiting to call them after I figured out when I'd be heading back."

"So you're not hiding out in our little hamlet?"

"No!" She explained about meeting Sam and getting towed to Coventry. "As soon as Grandpa's truck is fixed, I'll be driving back to L.A." She didn't understand the odd expression on Evan's face. "What?"

He met her eyes, and after a pause said, "If I'm out of line, just tell me to shut up. I'll admit that I haven't known any movie or TV stars. But I have known a lot of actors, and I never met one that shunned an opportunity to get publicity. People who really want to be left alone can make that happen. Like you did."

She stared at him. "You think Hud wanted the monster wedding? For the publicity?"

Evan shrugged and said, "I couldn't tell you. But I don't see how this runaway bride story would work without his cooperation."

"He'd never go for it."

"Then how come he's not on TV denying it?"

"He may not even know. I called his cell, and it went right to voice mail. The last time we talked, he was on his way to Minneapolis for a soap meet-and-greet. Everything was fine between us. We left it open when we'd talk again. He has a couple of weeks off that were supposed to be for our honeymoon. Hud's very athletic. He probably left Minnesota for somewhere that he can play golf or dive or surf."

"I'm sure you're right," Evan said.

Even though she understood that he was just saying that to placate her, it didn't bother her. Evan didn't know Hud, but she did. Hud would never go along with something as stupid as a runaway bride story just to get publicity.

"I need to call Revere Auto. Sam must be wondering what happened to me." She waited while Evan got up and found a phone book and handed it to her. "Sam said they just moved. Do you think the number stayed the same?"

"Nobody's number ever changes here. Does Sam know all this runaway bride stuff?"

Jandy sighed and said, "I'm *not* a runaway bride. Sam doesn't know about my postponed wedding. He doesn't know my fiancé is an actor. He just knows I'm engaged."

She punched the number into her cell phone. It rang several times before it was finally answered.

"Sam? It's Jandy Taylor."

"Are you hitchhiking to Dallas? At least you didn't dognap Sue."

"No, I'm still in Coventry. I'm at Molly's Beauty Shop. Did your sister figure out what's wrong with the pickup?"

"As it turns out, Robin got a root canal at the dentist today. She's home sleeping off her drugs and never came back to work. I've been calling around trying to find you a place to stay."

Jandy didn't hear what he said after that because Evan had turned on the TV, and she saw her image over Mary Hart's shoulder.

"I'll have to call you right back," she said and snapped her phone shut.

Another blonde—not Mary Hart—was laughing as she relayed the story of the latest runaway bride.

"This is crazy," Jandy said. "How do I stop it?"

Evan held up a hand when the segment flashed to Hud looking collected as he walked to a car. She assumed it was a rental, because it wasn't his silver Audi convertible. There were only a few reporters trailing after him with questions, and he turned toward them with an affable smile.

"Is there anything you'd like to say to Miss Halli?" a woman asked.

"I'm sure Jane just needs some time away to think things over," Hud said. "I'm not angry with her."

He got into his car, and *Entertainment Tonight* went back to the blonde, who then introduced the same footage of Jandy's mother and stepfather that had aired on the earlier show.

Jandy looked at Evan. "I can't tell—Is Hud actually going along with this?" She flipped open her phone and speed dialed her fiancé. When she heard his recorded greeting, she grimaced and tossed the phone across the sofa.

Evan caught it before it hit the floor. Both of them looked toward the door as they heard someone coming up the stairs.

"Oh, crap." She reached up and began twisting her still damp hair into a bun. "If that's Sam—"

She broke off as a tall man—though not quite as tall as Evan—opened the door and said, "Hey, babe." She watched as he and Evan met halfway and gave each other a hug. Then the man turned and looked at her with interest. He took off his cowboy hat and said, "Grayson Murray. And you must be the run—"

"Jandy Taylor," she interrupted. "Does the whole town know?"

"No," Evan said. "I called Gray to tell him where he could find me and why. Nobody else knows."

"Your secret's safe with me," Grayson promised.

"I hung up on Sam, didn't I?" she asked Evan.

"Sort of."

"Give me my phone, please," she said wearily. "He still has to drive me somewhere to get a motel room, since your town's stupid Lady Godiva Fest—"

"Noooo," Grayson said, covering his ears. "You'll have the townspeople clamoring outside the door with torches, ready to run you out of Coventry on a rail."

"Blasphemy," Evan agreed. "Anyway, you're not going anywhere until I do something with your hair. Or maybe you're not going anywhere at all."

He looked at Grayson, who shook his head and said, "You're the damnedest man in the world. How is it that an imaginary cousin stumbles into your shop just when you need her most?"

"I'm lucky that way," Evan said.

Jandy had no idea what they were talking about, but she said, "There's no such thing as luck. Just ask my gambling grandpa."

Two hours later, they finished the Texas-sized steak dinners Grayson had picked up for them after he retrieved her suitcase from Sam. It had taken only a little persuasion before she agreed to stay in the apartment above the shop.

"Who's Molly? Don't you have to ask if this is okay with her?" Jandy asked Evan.

"Molly used to own the shop. I bought it from her but never changed the name because you know how it is in a small town."

"Actually, I don't," Jandy said.

"I could call it Evan's, but everyone in town would keep calling it Molly's. When new people moved here, or tourists were looking for a stylist, everyone would tell them to go to Molly's, and they'd never find me. It's easier to keep her name on the window."

Grayson smiled and said, "Revere Auto could be in its new location for thirty years, but people will still call it Bailey's Texaco."

"Or they'll tell people looking for something to take Oak Road three miles out of town and turn right at Revere Auto, even though the Revere Auto building will have been gone for decades."

"I don't know how newcomers ever figure it out," Grayson said.

"People still call this Molly's apartment, even though I lived here when I took over the shop. Then I moved in with Gray. Now, because the town is overrun with tourists, everybody keeps trying to borrow it for some friend or relative. But I don't want to rent it out. I like having a place to come during the day when I need to get away from the shop."

"He keeps telling people that his cousin is coming for a visit and will need it," Grayson said. "Of course, there's no cousin, and people are starting to get suspicious. Real estate makes people crazy."

"Tell me about it," Jandy said, thinking of her parents.

"I won't actually tell people you're my cousin. But I can't help it if they make assumptions, can I?" Evan asked.

She didn't know why they were being so nice, but it made her feel like she could trust them, just as she'd trusted Sam. While they ate, she'd told Grayson the full story about her postponed wedding, her trip to Texas with Sam, and her unwelcome notoriety as a runaway bride.

"Can you believe she hopped into a truck and rode all the way to Texas with a total stranger?" Evan asked.

"She's just crazy enough to actually be one of your cousins," Grayson said.

"I'm still in the room," Jandy said. "Besides, I thought Sam was—er—a tow truck driver."

"I always thought he was gay," Evan said.

"Sam?" Grayson asked in a disbelieving tone. "Why would you think that?"

"He's in his thirties. Single. I've never seen him with a woman."

Grayson rolled his eyes and said, "I see him all the time with five women. His mother and his four sisters. They're so clannish and protective of him, they probably drive potential girlfriends away. I don't know him very well, but I'm sure he's not gay."

"Turned you down, huh?" Evan asked, but Grayson only rolled his eyes again.

"Regardless, you have to admit my instincts were good," Jandy said. "Instead of hacking me up and scattering my body parts over several states, Sam got me here safe and sound. But I really shouldn't impose on you. I should probably go to Dallas or—"

"You can't go anywhere until the pickup's fixed," Grayson said reasonably. "It would be dumb for you to stay in Fort Worth or Dallas when you can stay right here, a block from your truck."

"You won't be bothered," Evan promised. "Although normally, you'd be the talk of the town gossips."

"That description includes most of the town," Grayson said.

"But this is the best time to be incognito in Coventry. We're already overflowing with strangers. Nobody's going to notice one more."

"I don't know," Grayson said. "If they keep showing her on those entertainment shows, someone's bound to recognize her. She looks in person exactly like she does on TV."

"Great," Jandy said. "I thought I looked *good* at the Emmys. A lot better than now, with my hair flying all over and hardly any makeup on."

"It is the hair," Evan said, studying her. "You won't be able to wear it down. It's your most identifiable feature because it's so striking."

"You could dye it black," Grayson said.

She gave him a horrified look, and Evan said, "No. What's the first thing you notice about Phylura? Her jet black hair. Dyed hair looks fake against fair skin. It would just call attention to you."

"I can keep it braided and up," Jandy said. "Or . . ."

She and Evan stared at each other for a few seconds until he said, "I never, ever give a bride a drastically different cut close to her wedding date. That's a decision made out of emotion and will be regretted."

"But I'm not getting married any time soon, remember?" she asked.

"No," Evan said firmly.

"I promise this won't end up like *Bracken v. Golden Locks, Inc.*"

"Which would be what?"

"Nasty lawsuit over a bad haircut. Don't worry. I'm not litigious. But speaking of locks, isn't there an organization with a name like that? For donating hair?"

"Locks of Love."

"Is my hair long enough for them?"

"More than long enough," Evan said. He frowned at her and shook his head. "Maybe you should think about this overnight."

"It's just hair," Jandy said, surprising herself. Her hair was the one feature that never disappointed her. "It'll grow back. Let's do it."

"If you're trying not to raise suspicion, isn't it a bad idea to make Sam wonder why your hair went from long to short?" Grayson asked.

"He hasn't seen my hair," Jandy said. "It's been hidden under bandannas since we met. Sam would be hard-pressed to give a description of me, I'm sure. He's too en-raptured by that dog he got by supposedly tricking me."

"Are you *sure* he's straight?" Evan asked.

"Positive," Grayson said.

Evan turned toward her and said, "Are you *sure* you want a haircut?"

"Positive," Jandy said.

"I'm going downstairs to close the blinds. People walk by here at all hours going to the Godiva Inn or the Early Bird Café. I'll give you ten minutes to reconsider."

Ten minutes later she was in his chair. He sprayed her hair with water, straightened it while he dried it, and then braided it so expertly that she couldn't see a single random hair sticking out.

"Funny, it looks better when you do it," she said.

"That's why I make the big bucks," Evan said. "It has to be in a braid or ponytail when it's donated. This is your last chance to change your mind."

He held up the scissors so she could see their reflec-tion in the mirror. She stared at them, then at herself. Her eyes were bright, but she knew it wasn't because of tears. For the first time in weeks, she actually felt excited about something.

"I'm ready," she said.

Evan looked at Grayson, who was watching from the next chair. Grayson nodded, Evan put the scissors to her hair, and a few seconds later, he held up a braid. She exhaled and smiled.

"I'm all about change," Evan said in a tone of surrender. He put the braid in a plastic bag with the donation form she'd filled out. "Let's wash it again and condition it before I finish cutting it."

"You're going to make it even shorter?" she asked nervously.

"It has to be styled," Evan said. "It's too late to doubt me now."

"Trust him," Grayson said.

This time she wasn't in the same comatose state while Evan was shampooing her, and her thoughts were all over the place. She was still angry with her mother and Chandra for exploiting her situation. She felt uneasy about Hud. She wanted to talk to her grandpa.

"Hey," she said to Evan when she sat up. "Don't people get in trouble for causing the police to make false investigations? That thing they said on *Inside Hollywood* about the police not suspecting foul play. Should I call someone official and let them know that I'm fine? In case my mother keeps stirring things up?"

"I have no idea," Evan said as he led her back to the chair next to where Grayson was still sitting. "You remember the woman you met in here earlier today? Lois? Her husband's a cop. We could ask him."

"I thought the idea was to keep anyone in town from knowing who I am," Jandy said.

"If you're talking about Clay Gaines," Grayson said, looking up from the *Vanity Fair* he'd been reading, "he's about as honorable as they come. His wife is one of my mother's best friends. Lois always complains that the whole town knows more police business from listening to their scanners than she can get out of him."

"We'll talk to him about it," Evan said, settling her into the chair and brandishing his scissors over her head. "Now be still and let me do my magic."

"I don't believe in magic," Jandy said automatically. She cut her eyes toward Grayson and said, "What do you do?"

"He's a real cowboy," Evan said.

"Funny, my lips didn't move, yet she got an answer. That's magic," Grayson said. "I have two ranches. One in Wyoming and one here."

"Cattle ranches?" she asked.

"Horses. Arabians."

"I know nothing about horses," Jandy admitted. "The closest I've been to horses is watching them run around a racetrack."

"Now you've done it," Evan said.

Grayson ignored him and extolled the versatility of his Arabians to Jandy. Since she'd never had a passion for any job, she was always fascinated when someone talked about something he loved, and Grayson obviously loved his horses. He told her about the differences in breeding and raising horses for competition, ranch work, and pleasure riding. She also learned that a few of Grayson's horses had become movie stars, and some were used as polo horses or in police work.

She forgot all about her hair until Evan nudged her shoulder and said, "What do you think?"

She looked at her reflection without speaking, then he turned her chair and gave her a mirror so she could check out the back, which barely reached the top of her neck. She turned the chair around again and stared at herself. He'd cut her hair in short layers, blown it out straight, then styled it for height with an expertly jagged part. The tips of the front strands just brushed her jawline.

"Short hair makes your green eyes gleam. You're hot," Evan said. He didn't look a bit nervous, and she knew why.

She stood up, threw her arms around him, which surprised her more than it did him, and said, "It's great! I feel like the weight of the world has been lifted off of me. Thank you. You're—"

"A hair maestro," Evan said smugly. "Your hair is a symphony. My reputation is validated once again."

"There'll be no living with him now," Grayson said. "You're right, though. It looks great. And he's right. You're hot."

She couldn't stop smiling, as much from Grayson's praise as from her pleasure at the sight of her hair in the mirror. It occurred to her that, for once, she'd finished something: a haircut. And it had turned out fine.

"Thanks! How much do I owe you?"

In the same way that he'd evaded her earlier offer to pay him for using his apartment, Evan said, "We'll figure it out later."

While he continued to examine her hair from every angle, Jandy tried to keep her expression neutral. Experience had taught her that there was no such thing as a free lunch. If Evan wasn't willing to take her money, what did he want from her? Had he doubted her assurance that her family wasn't loaded? Was he, like so many people—including her own mother—hoping somehow to cash in on Hud's moderate fame and show business connections?

She noticed the affection in Grayson's eyes as he watched Evan and listened to him boast about his "mad skills" as a hairdresser, and her suspicion melted. Long before she'd ever met Chandra, who was always working an angle, or Hog, who took advantage of her automotive ignorance, and certainly before she became familiar with dubious lawsuits, she had memories of good people like Grandpa and Aunt Ruby. Wasn't it possible that Evan and Grayson were also good people, with no hidden motives? Maybe Evan meant exactly what he said: *We'll figure it out later.* It was also possible that he meant to show that he trusted her not to skip town without paying him.

"Have I," Evan said, breaking into her thoughts, "succeeded in turning January Jane Halli into Jandy Taylor?"

"I don't think my own mother could spot me in a crowd," Jandy assured him.

She'd worried that she might feel nervous after Evan and Grayson left her alone in the empty building, but she curled up on the couch with the TV volume on low and called Hud again, this time leaving a message for him to call her back. She considered calling her mother or Chandra, maybe even some of Hud's friends. But she didn't have the energy to talk to anyone, not even Grandpa.

She'd already unpacked her suitcase, so she went to the bathroom and brushed her teeth, again admiring Evan's work in the mirror. She'd probably never be able to make her hair look as good as he did, but he'd pointed out that she could let it dry curly for a fun look that would be easier to maintain.

After giving the claw-foot tub a scrubbing, she filled it with water and poured in some of the bath salts she'd bought on her Target shopping spree. She leaned back in the water, propping her feet against the other end of the tub, and examined her legs. She really could use some exercise; her legs looked too skinny. She examined the dusting of freckles around her knees and remembered trying to scrub them away when she was a little girl. Her freckles had long ago stopped bothering her.

She closed her eyes, thinking about Evan, Grayson, Sam, and Sue. It was strange that only a couple of days before, she'd known none of them, and now she felt like she could rely on them. Sue to make her smile. Sam to help her with her truck. Evan to keep her secret and give her shelter. Grayson, because he seemed so stable and solid that even a little praise from him made her feel like she hadn't made a disaster of her life.

She hoped she wasn't turning into one of those needy women who craved validation from men. Hud had always been generous with compliments, but they'd never had a clingy relationship. She liked his approval, but she didn't need it. Nor did she need to talk to him constantly to feel secure about him. No matter what Evan thought, she was sure there was a reasonable explanation for why she couldn't reach him by phone. She had little doubt that they'd talk the next day.

It wasn't until she was snuggled into the comfortable double bed with the lights out that she realized that not once, since her arrival in Coventry, had she heard a single reproving comment from Pru inside her head.

Maybe Sam had unknowingly kicked Pru out of his truck before they crossed the town line. Or maybe Evan had thrown out Pru with the clippings from her haircut. Jandy was just glad of the silence when she closed her eyes for her first night of sleep in her new, temporary home.

Chapter 7

Jandy was out of the apartment with her camera and walking around the square the next morning long before Evan was due to arrive at the shop. The festival was only two days away from its kickoff, and people were beginning to load merchandise into their booths. She hoped to get pictures throughout the duration of her stay that would become part of a photo journal that she could share with Hud when she went back to California.

She spotted a family placing clay bowls, flagons, and tankards in a booth. Even their kids, whose ages ranged from maybe six to sixteen, were working. She was surreptitiously taking a photo of their youngest—an adorable little girl wearing a flowered wreath that her older brother had playfully jammed on her head—when she felt something nudge the back of her thighs. She whipped around and saw Sue giving her a goofy look, her tongue hanging out.

"Good morning, Sue," she said, running her fingers over the dog's head and stroking her ears. Only then did she look at Sam. Today he was dressed in a gray T-shirt and worn jeans, topped off by a weathered straw cowboy hat with metal conchos on its leather band. He still had the stubble and the half smile. "She missed me, didn't she? That's why she tracked me down."

"Sure," he said. "I think she only slept nine and a half hours out of the last ten, she's been so worried about you."

"That's what I figured. Maybe tonight she should stay with me."

"Nice try." He seemed put out when Jandy took a couple of steps back so she could get a picture of him with Sue. Then he cooperated by squatting next to the dog.

Jandy squatted, too, and said, "Your eyes get lost under your hat if I'm not at eye level."

"There's something different about you today," Sam said. He squinted at her.

"Unlike poor Sue, I got a good night's sleep. And I'm not sweating off my makeup."

He shook his head, then shrugged. Since he'd never seen her hair uncovered, she wondered if he'd even noticed she was a redhead.

"Is there any news on my truck? Is your sister Robin back at work today?"

"Not yet," Sam said. "She will be. When you get ready to go over, Sue and I will walk with you. If that's okay."

"Of course," she said. "You can save us all time by telling Robin that I need a new baster."

"Never gonna let me live it down, are you?"

"Nope. I was planning to shoot some more pictures, if you don't mind—" She broke off when "Instant Karma" alerted her that someone was calling her cell. She pulled it from the pocket of her cargo shorts, saw Hud's number on the display, flipped the phone open, and said, "Why haven't you returned my calls before now?"

She noticed Sam slipping discreetly away as Hud said, "I've been in transit or catching up on my sleep. What's going on with you?"

"I've seen the stupid entertainment shows," she said. She looked around, wondering if anyone could overhear her, and dropped her voice. "Why is this being publicized as if I jilted you? It's making me look flighty. And mean. On one of the morning shows today, somebody called me a 'tempestuous redhead.' Does that sound anything like me? I don't think so."

After a few seconds of silence, Hud said, "I think I've been understanding about all this, don't you? Supportive of what you wanted?"

"I don't disagree," she said. "What does that have to do with—"

"I hope you'll be supportive of me, too. Chandra is paid to get me publicity. She's definitely earned her money the past couple of days. You know what they say. There's no such thing as bad publicity."

"If someone *wants* publicity, that may be true," Jandy said. "But the whole reason I"—she looked around and dropped her voice again—"wanted to change our plans was to give us back our privacy. I understand publicity for your work, but a wedding—at least my wedding—is supposed to be intimate and calm. Not a spectacle. And now instead of a bride, I'm a sideshow freak!"

"Just lay low like I plan to," Hud said. "I don't want to deal with the fallout any more than you do. I'm using my time off as a vacation from all that, and you should do the same."

"How can I when your publicist wants to turn my vacation into a circus?"

"It's not a circus," a man said, stepping around her. "Unless you count the dog show. One year that was definitely the greatest show on earth."

"You're at a dog show?" Hud asked. "Do you even like dogs?"

"Of course I like dogs. Who doesn't like dogs? Don't change the subject."

"This will all blow over; we'll both go back home; and we'll set a new wedding date," he assured her.

"Where are you?" she asked, suddenly suspicious.

"Maui."

"You went to Hawaii?" She realized how *tempestuous* her exclamation sounded, got control of her voice, and hissed, "I thought Chandra was supposed to cancel our trip."

"I had the time off and the tickets. I figured why not use them?"

"Them? *Them?* Both tickets? Is someone with you?"

"Sorel," he said.

She thought her brain might explode. "You took Sorel on our honeymoon?"

"Of course not. I changed the reservation from a suite to two rooms. It's *Sorel,* Jane. I've known her since we were both seven-year-olds missing our front teeth and pretending to eat Big Macs for the camera."

She'd been forced to watch the tape of Sorel lisping "special sauce" about a zillion times and was in no mood to take that trip down memory lane again, so she said nothing.

"You're *not* jealous. Sorel's like my sister. You know that."

"Whatever," she said. "I can't believe you're in Hawaii, and I'm . . ."

She trailed off. A man who was setting up a booth with gems, crystals, and pewter figures of dragons, knights, and wizards had turned on a radio, and the Beatles suddenly blared that she had to hide her love away.

"You're where?" Hud asked.

Was she only imagining alertness in his voice? Would

he actually tell Chandra where she was? Would Chandra leak it to a tabloid news show? Was this story really note-worthy enough to warrant any more attention than it had already gotten?

Unfortunately, she could think of dozens of stories she'd read online, watched on TV, or heard people talking about at her temp jobs that had made her think, *Why is this news?* Particularly when celebrities were involved. For some reason, people couldn't get enough gossip about anyone famous. Still, it wasn't like Hud was Brad Pitt or George Clooney, all of Chandra's efforts notwith-standing. He was a relatively unknown actor on a daytime drama.

An *ambitious* actor on a daytime drama. She didn't need Evan to remind her of that. She wasn't sure what lengths Hud would go to for publicity, but if Chandra wanted this story to gain momentum, wouldn't she have the paparazzi and tabloid journalists after Hud? Why would anyone care about January—or Jane—Halli?

She thought about Randall, Hud's friend who did stand-up. She could hear a refrain from one of his comedy routines: *If it's about a thin, young white woman, it's news.*

"Are you still on the phone?" Hud asked impatiently. "You haven't told me where you are."

"I'm . . . with a friend of mine. You don't know her. Sue," she said slowly, still trying to work out in her head whether she could trust Hud. Would he and Chandra actually set the press hounds on her trail?

She thought of the two women she'd met on the side-walk the day before and how they'd expressed their grat-itude for the secret charm of Coventry. They'd hate it if their vacations were turned into a media frenzy.

Then she looked at the people around her, who prob-ably planned all year for this month. Maybe they wouldn't

mind the publicity a runaway bride would give Coventry.
Publicity brought people; people brought money. If they
recognized her, would they provide her whereabouts to
the number that her mother was bleating all over the TV
and probably the Internet?

She reminded herself that Evan hadn't reacted that
way. He'd wanted to protect her. Or maybe he was really
only trying to protect Coventry and its sleepy, sweet
appeal, and that just happened to correspond with her
desire for privacy.

She suddenly felt unsure about everyone's motives
and tried to clear her thoughts. It was ridiculous to think
that anyone would travel a zillion miles to hunt her
down—she was nobody!—or that anyone in Coventry—
either the merchants or the tourists—would pay her any
attention at all.

Any more ridiculous than seeing your face on TV yester-
day and this morning? Pru asked. *If you didn't think being*
found and exploited was possible, why did you cut your hair?
Why don't you call your parents and tell them where you are?
Why don't you tell Hud? Shouldn't you trust the man you're
going to marry?

She sighed. The voice was back.

"It doesn't matter where I am," she said. "Have a great
time in Maui. I'll see you when you get back. Love you."

She snapped the phone shut before he could answer
and started to drop it in her pocket. Then she opened it
again and turned it off. Grandpa and Aunt Ruby should
be getting home from Laughlin in a few hours. She'd call
them because she didn't want them to worry about her,
but she also wouldn't tell them exactly where she was.
Grandpa would be uneasy about whether the truck was reliable enough to get her home. She wondered about that

herself. She turned to look for Sam so he could take her to get what was sure to be bad news from Robin Revere.

She found him watching people put barriers around an area close to the church. Sue was sitting next to him.

"Do you think I should enter Sue in the dog show?" he asked when Jandy walked up.

"It depends. Does she have to do more than drool and sleep?"

"You underestimate our girl. Beneath that . . . uh . . . placid exterior beats the heart of a champion."

She grinned at his phrasing—*our girl*—and gently nudged Sue with one sneakered foot. Sue looked up at her with an expression that reminded Jandy of a former boss who always got stoned on his lunch hour.

"A champion what?" she asked.

"I've yet to figure that out, but I don't doubt she's a powerhouse of talent and drive. However, dogs in this dog show don't have to do anything but walk and look pretty."

Jandy looked at Sue. She wasn't pretty in a fluffy, sleek, or noble way, but she had a certain appeal.

Before she could respond, a man stopped midstride and said, "Sam Revere, you decided to get a dog?"

"Nah, that's just my friend Jandy," Sam said, and Jandy smacked him on the arm, even though she'd ruined her attempt to seem mad by laughing first.

"That's Sue," she said, pointing at the dog. "I'm Jandy."

The man shook her hand and said, "Michael Boone."

He knelt down and held out a hand to Sue, who sniffed it. Jandy was surprised to see that he held a treat that Sue ate with gusto. Michael began pulling Sue's lips back and looking at her gums, which made Jandy give Sam a curious glance.

"It's Dr. Boone," Sam said. "He's the vet my sister Swan works for."

"Oh," Jandy said. "You make house calls?"

"Unfortunately, Sue won't be my patient," Michael said. "I'm a large animal vet."

"I think she qualifies," Jandy said.

Michael smiled and said, "I'm actually here to confirm the good health of Wyndmere."

"Wyndmere?"

"Wyndmere is the festival's mascot." Michael looked around and dropped his voice to say, "She's a longhorn. But don't tell anyone that. Officially, she's a dragon."

"I've heard of this dragon," Jandy said. "In fact, I know her work."

"You do?" Michael asked, and Sam gave her a puzzled look.

"Yes. I traveled over hundreds of miles of scorched earth yesterday. The most desolate wasteland—"

"We drove from El Paso," Sam explained.

"Ah, West Texas," Michael said with an understanding nod.

"Actually, we drove from Arizona," Jandy said. "That's where we met Sue. A guy put her out at a rest stop while we were there."

Michael's face seemed to tighten, and he squatted again, running his hands over Sue. She leaned into him until she lost her balance, landed in the grass, and rolled over on her back to beg for a belly rub. Michael complied, and she writhed with happiness. He examined her under the guise of petting her. He ended by grabbing her muzzle and gently shaking her head. When he let go, her lips fell back, making her look like she was grinning, then she gave his hand a quick good-bye lick as he pulled away from her and stood.

"She's a mix. I'm guessing American bulldog, boxer, maybe American Staffordshire terrier. She's probably from a litter that was bred to fight. She's got a couple of scars. One on her withers. Another on her thigh."

"You think she fights?" Jandy asked. She didn't believe it. Sue was a big, drooling, happy mess.

"I think she *doesn't* fight. That's probably why she was dropped at the rest stop." He frowned. "I assume there was no collar? No tags?"

"Nope," Sam said.

"You're planning to keep her?"

"Yep."

"She'll need an exam. Heartworm test. Immunizations. When you run her into Dr. Townshend, have him check her for a microchip."

"It's not like I intend to return her to the dumbass who dumped her," Sam said.

"No, of course not. But if she's chipped, maybe Arizona can be nudged into checking up on her previous owner to see if he's fighting dogs. Or breeding them for fighting." When Sam nodded, Michael turned to Jandy with a smile. "It's a good thing you two did, rescuing her. Tomorrow night, my wife and I are having a few people over for a cookout. If you don't have plans, you should join us. Sue's welcome to come, too. Around six."

Before Jandy could answer, someone called for the vet; he gave them a brief wave and walked away. She turned to Sam and said, "I don't know why he assumed that you and I are—"

"We did say we'd been traveling together," Sam said. "You can straighten it out when you see him tomorrow night."

"I can't go to his house. He only invited me because he thought you and I are . . . whatever."

"Do you have plans tomorrow night?"

"Well, no, but—"

"There's no reason we can't go as friends, is there?"

She eyed him for a few seconds and finally said, "We're not really friends. We hardly know each other."

"True. But it takes so long to say, 'This is Jandy. She's a total stranger who I drove nine hundred miles to a fiancé who isn't where she said he'd be.'"

"Be sure and add how you did that after you cheated me out of a dog and lied about what's wrong with my truck," she said.

"See how complicated that would be? It's easier to say we're friends." He smiled. "You'll like his wife, Keelie. You've already met her best friend."

"I have?"

"Evan Hammett."

"Oh. Do you think Evan and Grayson will be at the cookout?"

"I imagine so."

After a few seconds, she said, "I'd like to go. As friends."

"Good." He looked down at Sue, who was biting her leash. "She's bored. If you're ready, we'll walk you to Revere Auto."

Everyone they passed nodded or said hello. Sam's responses were brief because he was busy pointing out buildings to Jandy. Independent Seven Toys was, as she'd assumed, a toy manufacturer. He said the two men who owned it would probably also be at the Boones' house the following night. He then pointed out a historic school building that was now a daycare center, some offices, and the grocery store, which was on the same block as Revere Auto.

Jandy shook her head as they read a note on the door that said Robin would be back in one hour. "I'm starting to think your sister doesn't exist."

"So am I. You want to go to Dr. Townshend's with me?"

"No. I'll stay nearby in case your mythical sister puts in an appearance. I can wander around and take more pictures. Are you coming back here after you see the vet? I want to know how Sue's checkup turns out."

"Yeah. I'll be back," Sam said.

She watched as he and Sue got into a black Jeep and drove away. She then walked back to the Early Bird Café, thinking she might as well have a cup of coffee while she waited for Robin Revere.

The only other patrons in the café were three women sitting at a round table in the corner. Apparently they'd wanted to avoid the light coming through the large front window, but Jandy welcomed the sunshine. The table by the window also afforded her a view of Revere Auto's parking lot.

After a waitress brought coffee, Jandy took her Jennifer Weiner book from her purse. It had been so long since she'd read it that she couldn't remember any of the details. She went back to the first chapter and started over. Then she realized that she had no idea what she was reading because she was furtively checking out the women at the corner table.

One of the women was wearing khaki shorts and a chambray shirt. She was winding a strand of her shoulder-length brown hair around a finger, letting it go, then doing it again. She'd pushed her chair a few inches from the table. That and her frown as the other two women talked made Jandy think she didn't really want to be there.

The woman with her back to Jandy had closely cropped brown hair and was wearing blue scrubs. She was leaning forward and gesturing with her hands a lot. Her voice was too low for Jandy to hear what she was saying, so she shifted her gaze to the last woman at the table.

One of these things is not like the others, Jandy thought.

The third woman had blond hair piled on top of her head. She was wearing a tight black shirt, a black linen pencil skirt that would probably reach midcalf when she stood, and black heels. Her body language made it look as if she were restraining herself, like she wanted to do something but couldn't. That behavior was familiar to Jandy as typical of a person who craved a cigarette. The woman was probably a smoker. She was the type who would look elegant with a cigarette in her hand. In fact, she reminded Jandy of the Patsy Stone character from the British comedy *Absolutely Fabulous*. She certainly had Patsy's deadpan expression.

Patsy Clone, Jandy thought and smiled at her joke.

"I think," Patsy Clone said in a voice loud enough to rise over Scrubs, "you're overestimating her importance."

"No," Chambray disagreed, "she's right. This is the first time he's shown interest since Daisy died. I think this could be the one."

"He just feels sorry for her," Patsy Clone said.

"Maybe at first. But didn't you notice that he couldn't stop talking about her? He's got that infatuated look in his eyes. I think he's finally getting over Daisy."

"It *has* been eight months," Scrubs agreed.

Jandy wrinkled her nose and looked down at her book. It seemed a little heartless that a man's wife or girlfriend had died and they thought he should have gotten over her in eight months. Aunt Ruby's husband had died over twenty years ago, and she still missed him.

"Once Sam makes up his mind about something, there's no changing it," Chambray said.

Sam? Jandy's senses went on full alert.

"It's only been a couple of days," Patsy Clone said. "We'll see."

Jandy dropped her head even lower as she tried to work

out what they were talking about. It wasn't necessarily the same Sam. But the three women . . . The one in scrubs could be his sister Swan, who worked for Dr. Boone. Chambray could be Lark, the stay-at-home mom. And Patsy Clone, with all that teased hair and artfully applied make-up, would be Dove, the one with the mysterious source of income.

It's only been a couple of days. . . . She and Sam had met two days ago, and he'd been awfully vague about whether there was a woman in his life. At first she'd thought it was because he was gay, but he'd corrected that assumption. But if he had a girlfriend, he probably wouldn't have asked her to go to Dr. Boone's cookout with him, even as friends. She thought of how persistent he'd been and felt her face get hot again. Could she really be the woman that his sisters thought might be helping him get over the loss of Daisy?

No, she assured herself. *He knows I'm engaged.*

Why should he believe that after all the other lies you told him? Pru asked.

Chambray's voice rose over the others. "The question is not whether he wants her, or even if she's right for him. After all, she could just be a temporary way to fill the emptiness left by Daisy's death. It's not like he went looking for her. He picked her up at a rest stop. That's enough reason for me to keep her away from the boys until we know more about her."

"I agree," Scrubs said. "She could have diseases or genetic abnormalities. She could be pregnant. She could even be—"

Jandy slammed her novel down on the table and yelled, "Engaged!"

Patsy Clone and Chambray stared at her, and Scrubs turned around and said, "Pardon?"

"I've heard that you're protective of your brother, but I'm not some skank Sam picked up at a rest stop. My truck broke down, and he helped me out because he's a nice person. I didn't know about Daisy, or that she was dead, but he has no romantic interest in me. I'm engaged to another man. Could you please stop insulting my parentage and questioning whether I'm good enough for him?"

Chambray and Scrubs had the decency to look appalled, but Patsy Clone maintained her deadpan expression in silence for what seemed like forever. Then she actually cracked a smile and said, "Unless you're a real bitch weighing about seventy-five pounds who has a black eye and goes by the name of Sue, we weren't talking about you."

Chapter 8

Jandy emerged from Revere Auto with even more information than she'd dreaded learning about gaskets and engine blocks. Robin had wanted Jandy to understand that she wasn't ripping her off. She painstakingly explained the labor costs and the expense of the parts. She also couldn't promise when the job would be done, since she had to check all over the country for the right parts at the best prices.

As a mechanic, Robin was at least a lot more agreeable to deal with than Hog. She was perky from her upturned nose and her blond ponytail that was pulled through the back of her baseball cap to her toes encased in work boots. She had one of those faces that managed to look pleasant even when she was delivering news that would deplete Jandy's hidden stash of money by several thousand dollars.

That money was supposed to be going toward a new car for her, and she knew Grandpa would never want her to spend so much on repairing his truck. She had no choice, though. It had been her decision to take the pickup in the first place, driving it farther than it should have been driven. Now it would have to get her safely back to California, and Robin's thorough explanation and upbeat attitude made Jandy believe that would happen. She'd just be poorer when she got there. One day she'd be able to tease Hud in front of their grandchildren about marrying him for money instead of love.

Robin hadn't questioned whether Jandy could afford the repairs, but she had seemed curious about how she'd ended up in Coventry with Sam. Jandy made it clear when she told the story that theirs had been a simple business deal. If Grayson was right, and Sam's sisters were protective of him, Robin would probably spread the word that there was nothing romantic going on between Jandy and their brother.

After giving a go-ahead for the repairs, Jandy walked outside Revere Auto to find Dove sitting in a gray Mini Cooper convertible, smoking and listening to her radio. Dove spotted Jandy, waved her over, flipped her cigarette out the far window, and said, "Bad?"

"Not good," Jandy admitted.

"Nothing worse than feeling stranded and screwed. Not in the good way. My morning's free. Any errands you need to run? I'll drive you. Or would you like a tour of your port in the storm?"

Jandy almost said no to Dove's offer. She still felt stupid about the misunderstanding at the café, and she suspected that Dove was the second sister checking up on the woman Sam had brought to town. But since she had no idea how long she'd be stuck in Coventry, it wouldn't hurt to know a few people with transportation.

She reached into her purse and pulled out her digital camera. "Would you happen to know where I could pick up another memory card for this?"

"Let's jet," Dove said.

It was hard for Jandy not to stare at Dove while she drove them out of Coventry. She was wearing what Aunt Ruby called "granny" sunglasses: thin frames and round, brightly colored lenses that were too small to conceal the thick coating of black mascara on her lashes. Her dark lipstick was expertly applied. She seemed to have forbidden her big pile of blond hair to get windblown. Her hands rested on the steering wheel in a way that showed off her flawless manicure. Her nail polish was the same bronze as her lipstick.

Jandy was startled to hear herself say, "You look like a movie star."

"My sisters say I look like a hooker," Dove said, her face still expressionless. Jandy wondered if Dove used Botox. "I probably shocked you. Should I apologize now or wait? I'm likely to shock you again. Maybe I'll do one blanket apology when I drop you back in town."

"You haven't shocked me," Jandy said.

"I'm not, by the way."

"A hooker?"

"A movie star." Her mouth twitched. One thing Dove had in common with her brother was a fleeting, impish smile.

Thinking it might be better if she changed the subject, Jandy said, "I'm an only child. I imagine growing up with a brother and three sisters was a lot of fun."

"It had its moments," Dove said. She cast a quick glance Jandy's way and said, "Sam must have given you an earful."

"Not really. He just told me that you all have bird names. He said that Lark has kids, Swan works for a vet, and Robin fixes cars. Do your parents live in Coventry, too?"

"Not in the summer."

Jandy wasn't sure what that meant, but she was a little

intimidated by Dove so she didn't ask questions. She feigned an interest in their surroundings, which had gone from a rural road lined with trees and an occasional house, to residential developments that could have been anywhere, with generic names like Oak Crest, Oak Terrace, and Oak Shadows. Then New Coventry was upon them, and familiar signs flashed by: The Gap, Starbucks, Eddie Bauer, Pier 1, Banana Republic, Foot Locker, Bombay, Tuesday Morning, Olive Garden. She knew it was politically correct to deride the homogenization of America, but it would have been hypocritical of her to do that. The profits from such developments had fed, clothed, and housed her, as well as sent her to private schools and provided all those extracurricular activities that she always lost interest in almost before she began them.

Just past the mall, Dove whipped the Mini into the parking lot of an Office Max and said, "They have memory cards. I'll wait." She held up her cigarette pack to indicate that she wanted to smoke.

"I'll only be a minute," Jandy said.

"No hurry."

Inside, Jandy went to a kiosk with camera supplies and resolutely ignored the lure of the computers she could see across the store. It would be so much easier if she could just download her photos to a laptop. But even if she ended up in Coventry for two or three weeks, as Robin had warned her she might, her reason for being there—repairs to Grandpa's pickup—reminded her that she had to be careful about expenses.

She paid for a memory card and went back outside. Two men were standing next to Dove's car, but as Jandy approached, they said their good-byes and hurried inside Office Max.

"Find what you needed?" Dove asked as Jandy fastened her seat belt.

"Yes, thank you. I really appreciate your driving me here." Somehow her tone sounded more prim than she'd intended.

Dove tossed her cigarette, started the car, and said, "I'm not a hooker, either."

"I didn't think—"

"I went to school with those two old boys. Billy Mac and Bobby Ray. They saw you when you went in the store and wanted me to hook you up."

"With *both* of them?" Jandy asked.

"They're enlightened," Dove said. She gave a throaty laugh when she saw Jandy's expression and said, "I'm kidding. They'd let you pick which of them you found the most irresistible."

"What did you tell them?"

Dove spared her another quick glance and said, "You made it pretty clear that you're taken."

Embarrassed to be reminded of her outburst in the café, Jandy sank lower in her seat, not an easy task with long legs in a Mini Cooper.

"How long does Robin think you'll be stuck here?" Dove asked.

"She said anywhere from two weeks to a month."

Dove's furrowed brow satisfied Jandy's curiosity about whether or not she was Botoxed.

"That seems like a long time. Robin's usually so efficient."

"It's a matter of getting parts for the truck, I think," Jandy said. "It's thirty years old."

Dove made a noncommittal noise and said, "A month. And you're staying here the whole time? What about your fiancé?"

"He understands," Jandy said vaguely.

"You'll be here most of the tourist season," Dove mused. "I don't suppose you'd be bored enough to—never mind."

Jandy suspected that Dove thought her engagement was imaginary, and she quickly said, "I don't think my fiancé would be quite as understanding if you fixed me up with Billy Ray."

"Mac. Billy Mac. *Bobby* Ray. Like I told them, I don't do fix-ups." She pointed toward an apartment complex called Oak Manor. "This is where I live. Do you mind if I stop for a minute?"

"Of course not," Jandy said. "It's not as if I have anywhere to be."

After they got out of the car, Jandy followed Dove, trying to figure out how some women were able to pull off such a distinctive look. From her artfully disheveled hair to the efficient click of her high heels on the brick walkway, Dove was a put-together package. For no discernible reason, Jandy pictured Sam's sister with Hud. They'd make a stunning couple.

After she walked through a wooden door that Dove held open, Jandy looked around and gasped. The apartment buildings surrounded a huge courtyard filled with lush plants and ornamental trees. Tons of flowers spilled out of pots arranged around a large pool. It took all of Jandy's self-control not to hurl herself into the water.

"What?" Dove asked, casting a wary look around.

"I never would have guessed all this was hidden here," Jandy said. "No offense, but the complex itself is pretty generic."

"I never paid much attention," Dove said. "To the building or the pool. It's just where I live on the way to someplace else."

"If I lived here, I'd be in that pool all the time," Jandy said. "I love to swim."

"Not me. Chlorine turns my hair green. You're welcome to use the pool anytime as my guest. No one's ever in it during the week. On the weekends, it's party central. I think most of the people who live here are single."

"Thanks," Jandy said. "But since I don't have a car—"

"If you've got a cell, I'll give you my number. I know what it's like to be stuck someplace where you don't know anybody. My wheels are at your disposal."

"Thank you," Jandy said. She took out her cell phone and put in the number as Dove recited it, but she doubted she'd take advantage of the offer.

When Dove opened the door of a ground floor apartment, Jandy managed to stifle a second gasp. Except for a chair, a TV, and a small computer desk, the living room was empty. Dove definitely traveled light.

The only thing that alleviated the boring blankness of the wall was a single print, Jandy's gaze was drawn to it. While Dove disappeared somewhere inside the apartment with a murmured, "Be right back," Jandy crossed the room to look at the poster-sized, black-and-white photo of a fountain. It reminded her of a similar fountain on the campus in Long Beach where she'd had her brief flirtation with college.

When Dove returned, Jandy asked, "Did you take this photo? It's very good."

"Yes," Dove said. "It's the Wortham Fountain in Houston. I had it blown up to remind me that I'm not stuck here. I have a plan."

Jandy didn't want to be nosy, but she couldn't resist saying, "And that would be . . ."

"The style is called dandelion," Dove said. "There are

dandelion fountains all over the world. I intend to visit all of them."

While Dove stared at the photo, Jandy scrutinized her. For the first time, she realized that Dove's blasé attitude and sophisticated appearance were a kind of veneer. Beneath that was someone who was a little like her. They kept things temporary because they felt like they were on their way to somewhere else. Dove, however, at least had some kind of plan.

"Tell me where some of them will take you," Jandy gently urged, wanting to spend more time with this version of Dove.

"New York, San Francisco, Minnesota, Indiana. Sydney, Australia. Christchurch, New Zealand. Donetsk, Ukraine. Vancouver. Frankfurt. Stockholm. The Netherlands. Yorkshire."

"It sounds like an adventure just to track them down," Jandy said. She didn't mention the multiple dandelion fountains on her old campus; she couldn't remember if she'd ever told Sam the truth about where she was from. "It'll be fantastic to actually travel to all those places." When Dove nodded absently, Jandy decided it was a good time to pump her for more information. "What were you hoping I'd be bored enough to do?"

It was as if a door slammed, returning the bored expression to Dove's face, but she said, "If you really want to know, I'll show you."

A few minutes later, she was pulling the Mini into a NO PARKING space in front of the Godiva Inn. Jandy glanced across the street and noticed that Evan's salon looked busy. She had a lot to tell him, and she wanted to hammer him with questions about the Revere family, especially Dove.

Dove got out of the car and lit a cigarette. Jandy followed a little more slowly and said, "Won't you get a ticket for parking there?"

"I'll just toss it in the glove box with the rest of them," Dove said in a bland voice. "The town and I have an understanding. I pay for my parking spots about every six months, and they don't boot my car or haul me to jail." She jingled her key chain until she found the key she was looking for, then she led Jandy inside the Hannah Herren Gallery next to the inn. She turned on the lights after she opened the door, and a sweep of her arm took in the entire room as she said, "My friend Tori's mother owns this. All the work is by local artists."

Jandy was a little overwhelmed by the sheer number of paintings, vases, and other art objects. Overcrowding didn't display them to their best advantage, although a couple of the paintings caught her eye.

"Tori lives in San Diego. Hannah spends the winter months with her and comes back to open the gallery during tourist season. That's when she makes most of her sales. But Tori's first baby is due any day, and her mother wants to be with her. Hannah hired someone to run the place while she's gone. That woman flaked on her. I was supposed to be keeping an eye on things." Dove looked around. She didn't seem upset when she added, "As you can see, I haven't done a whole lot with either of my eyes. Would you like a job to help you pay Robin for your truck repairs? Of course, it's only temporary. And it only pays ten dollars an hour, but it's up to you how many hours you work. Even noon to six would be better than the place being closed all the time, right?"

"Temporary is what I do best," Jandy said, trying not to smile as she compared the amount to what she made as a temp in L.A. Ten dollars an hour wouldn't even begin to pay for the truck repairs, but it would keep her from spending her secret stash on anything else. She looked around, thinking it over, and said, "I *could* make things more presentable."

"You're hired," Dove said.

"I've never sold art. How will I know how much everything costs?"

"It's all catalogued," Dove said, sounding tremendously bored. "The artists set their own prices. You'll just make a record of anything sold. Hannah will eventually take her commission and pay them. It's painfully simple. No checks accepted. Cash or credit cards only. If you've ever used one of those credit card things—"

She gestured toward a terminal and Jandy said, "Yes."

"I can show you how to do the bank deposit. Central Coventry Bank is on the square. Have you been to the square?" Jandy nodded, and Dove went on. "Don't overexert yourself on the job. To be honest, Hannah doesn't derive a lot of income from it. She does it for the artists. You'll be doing all of us a favor, and possibly preventing your own death from boredom." She looked around the room and added, "Or accelerating it. It's your call."

Jandy thought it unlikely that she'd get bored in Coventry. She was still too enthralled by its quaintness. But after a few days without a car or a computer, she might change her mind. Working in the gallery would not only give her a chance to meet people, it would make her feel like she belonged in Coventry. Tourists might even mistake her for one of the locals. Until the silly runaway bride publicity died down, that would be a good thing.

"When do I start?" she asked.

"Now is good," Dove said and took out another cigarette.

"No smoking in my gallery," Jandy said firmly.

In spite of Dove's expressionless face, Jandy sensed from a certain gleam in her eyes that she was amused.

"The alarm code is 1776. Where are you staying? I'll get another set of keys made and deliver them to you."

"The apartment above Evan's shop," Jandy said. When Dove gave her a blank stare, she added, "The beauty salon?"

"Oh," Dove said. "Molly's. I'll bring the keys there later."

Jandy altered the slant of the blinds against the noon sun heating the front window of Molly's Beauty Shop. She returned to her stool to continue reading *Cosmopolitan*. She was waiting for Evan to take a break. The shop was busy, so she wasn't sure how long that would be. She finished reading "Marry Me! The Truth About Why Men Will or Won't Pop the Question" and closed the magazine.

"Damn," she said, looking at the cover. "Claudia Schiffer's had work. She looks ten years younger."

"Nine years," Evan called. When she gave him a puzzled look, he said, "Look at the date."

She looked, giggled, and said, "July 1997. Have you thought about getting more current material?"

"Nobody reads the magazines at Molly's," Evan said. "Come here. I want you to meet someone."

The stocky woman that Evan introduced as Elenore Storey had piercing eyes. Although her expression was kind, she made Jandy feel a little like she did in a doctor's office: overly scrutinized and nervously hopeful that everything would turn out okay.

While Evan began trimming her straight, white hair, Elenore said, "Evan tells me that Sam Revere practically kidnapped you and dragged you to Coventry."

Jandy gave Evan a scolding look and said, "My pickup

broke down, and Sam towed it here and put me in Robin's hands."

"And capable hands they are," Elenore said. Her eyes twinkled a little. "He also told me that Dove has put you in charge of Hannah's gallery, and you're curious about the Reveres. Evan knows that I don't gossip—"

"Please," Evan said and rolled his eyes.

"—but if you're planning on staying in town, you'll hear plenty of stories about the family. Occasionally one of them may even be true."

"Those Reveres are all batshit crazy," another customer said. When Elenore shook her head, the woman swatted Phylura's hands away from her hair so she could lean forward. "I ought to know. Their property abuts mine, so I've had a front row seat for thirty-five years."

Jandy saw Evan give her a little wink before he said, "I don't know much about them. They must all get their hair cut in New Coventry."

The woman snorted and said, "Swan surely gives herself that crew cut. When Sam was a boy—poor lamb, his hair is dark now, but it used to be blond—his mother, Rachel—she's not *from here*, you know—didn't get his hair cut until he'd already started school. I think he was in first or second grade. He had long curls just like Robin. People who didn't know them thought they were twin girls."

"Are you talking about the Revere kids?" another woman asked as Phylura's sister, Tryphena, led her to a chair. "I swear I never saw any of those kids in a pair of shoes unless they were in school."

"Oh, come now," Elenore said. "They were always dressed warmly in the winter. They were just like any other kids, spending all their time outside in warm weather. Back then, we just accepted that kids would be barefooted and dirty. We weren't always scrubbing them with antibacterial soap and organizing every hour of their days."

"Children were better off then, too," another woman chimed in. "The Revere kids always seemed happy and healthy to me."

"But their mother is so *peculiar*," Phylura's customer said. "You know she dropped out of some college up North to get married. There never could have been a more mismatched couple than Rachel Finch and Hop Revere. He worked in his daddy's garage before he was even as tall as a tractor wheel. Rachel came flitting into his life like a radical butterfly—"

Everyone began talking at once, and Jandy couldn't keep up with who was saying what. She met Elenore Storey's amused eyes and thought, *She's a devil. She doesn't have to gossip because everybody else does.*

She grinned knowingly at Elenore, who grinned right back at her and whispered, "Now you understand why nobody reads the magazines here."

"Rachel's a pagan, you know. She grows herbs and—"

"Oh, she is not. She has the best vegetable garden in the county, and her flowers do better than anybody's, too. There's nothing wrong with growing herbs."

"I grow herbs," an ancient woman warbled from the shampoo chair. "Just because Rachel let Sam's curls grow and the girls dressed like ragamuffins doesn't mean Rachel is a witch."

"Dove never dressed like a ragamuffin," someone said, and all the chattering stopped.

"Well, Dove," the woman said and dropped her voice, "has always taken care of Dove."

"All the girls are named for birds," Tryphena's customer said to Jandy, who was acting like everything they said was news to her. "Robin, Dove, Swan, and Lark. Robin was the only one who showed any interest in tinkering with engines. Swan works for the horse doctor. Lark got married right out of high school to Jimmy Whiteside."

"Don't they call him James now?" someone asked.

"He'll always be Jimmy to me. Jimmy and Lark have two little boys. I think Lark is the prettiest of the Revere girls."

"But she was always such a worrier," Tryphena said. "Even as a little girl."

"What was Dove like when she was little?" Jandy asked just to see what would happen. As they had before, everyone got quiet.

"Dove was a bit of a princess," one of the women finally said. "The boys used to call her Goosey Lucy because of her long neck. She usually walked around like she was holding up the weight of a crown that no one else could see. The other Revere girls—"

"That Lark is an angel. I won't hear a word against her," Phylura's customer warned.

"Lark's okay. I was just going to say that Robin and Swan were tomboys."

"Tell *me*," a woman said. "Swan beat up my son Jeffrey at least once a week for years."

"Jeffrey *was* kind of a pain," Tryphena's customer said.

"Yes," Jeffrey's mother agreed. "He got better, thanks to Swan's whaling on him. I always figured I'd end up with Swan as a daughter-in-law."

"Well, if Jeffrey had been a *girl*," one of the women said in an arch tone. When Evan paused with his scissors and gave her a cautionary look, she said, "Relax, Evan. I didn't say there was anything wrong with Swan's romantic temperament. Except she won't make the time to find herself a nice woman and settle down. She's too busy taking in every stray and wounded animal in the county."

Jandy silently congratulated herself for not having assumed that it was Robin the mechanic who was Sam's lesbian sister and said, "Sam just picked up a stray dog, too."

"Swan's probably already taught it to sit, stay, and heel," Jeffrey's mother said. "She's a bossy thing. But she does love animals."

"All those kids are alike," Phylura said. "They can't turn away from anything or anyone that's sick or injured or helpless."

Jandy frowned, wondering if Sam had thought she was helpless.

"If you're chasing Sam," a woman piped up from the waiting area, "you'd better prepare yourself for Rachel Revere to come down on you like a ton of bricks."

"I'm certainly not—"

"Dove hired Jandy to take care of Hannah's gallery," Evan's explanation cut Jandy off.

It occurred to her that he meant to stop her from telling everyone she was engaged, in case they made the connection between Jane Halli, runaway bride, and Jandy Taylor, mystery visitor.

"You can bet that whatever Dove Revere does, she's the one who benefits most from it," a woman said in an acid voice as she walked out of the pedicure room, stepping gingerly around a pile of Elenore's hair to protect her freshly polished toenails.

"You know why she left Dallas, don't you?" Tryphena's customer asked. All conversation ceased as everyone turned their attention to her. "She worked for a man who owned an import company. One of the things he imported was precious stones. My cousin's husband was flying business class on Delta to New York, and Dove happened to be in the seat across the aisle. He said she seemed very nervous about a small cosmetics case. The old-fashioned kind that looks like a box and has a couple of latches. Dove was constantly checking it, then tucking it between her feet, then checking it again. At one point when it was open, the plane hit turbulence, and a velvet bag bounced out. Dove almost fell out of her seat grabbing for it. The drawstring wasn't pulled tight. My cousin pretended to be sleeping, but he kept his eyes cracked. He saw Dove nervously sift several dozen loose stones through her fingers before she tightened the bag and put it back in the case. Not just any loose stones, mind you. Diamonds."

"She was probably delivering them to someone for her boss," Elenore said in a tone meant to squelch further speculation.

"The boss turned up dead," the woman said. "At first the police said it was foul play, but later it was ruled a heart attack. But Dove didn't come back to Texas for months."

"You think she killed her boss and stole a bag of diamonds?" Evan asked, his eyebrows nearly reaching his hairline.

"I don't think Dove's capable of murder," another woman said.

"Of course she is. However, I suppose she could have stolen the diamonds, then her boss got the blame, and somebody whacked him."

"You've been watching too much HBO," Elenore said.

Another woman nodded and said, "The only part of that story I believe is that Delta flies from Dallas to New York. Especially if the cousin's husband you mean is Kenny Fair. He was riding with a bunch of boys to Falfurrias one night and fell out of the Jeep. They were all too drunk to know it, and Kenny swears it was Elvis who picked him up and drove him to the closest emergency room. That boy's not right."

"Was it fat Elvis or young Elvis?" someone asked, but apparently no one knew the answer.

"If none of it's true, why didn't Dove go back to her home and her job in Dallas? Why did she show up here months later driving a new car and dressing like a model? She doesn't work. How does she pay rent? Afford gasoline? Buy groceries?"

"Shhh," somebody hissed. "Sam Revere just crossed the street with a big white dog, and it looks like they're coming in here."

Sam seemed a little bemused when he opened the door of the shop to be greeted by dead silence and endless sets of eyes. He doffed his cowboy hat, a gesture Jandy had never seen outside of a movie, and scanned the room until he saw her. He smiled, and Jandy could feel the entire room turn electric as the women tried to decide what was going on between them. She suspected they were probably also trying to remember every word that had been said about the Revere family in front of her.

"Dove asked me to deliver a set of keys to you," Sam said. "And I figured you might want to hear about Sue."

Jandy slid off the stool and said, "I do!"

She ignored Evan's muffled laugh as he heard her say the words she hadn't been willing to repeat in front of a minister, a groom, and five hundred wedding guests. After casting a sweet smile toward the women in the shop—with only a brief pause to acknowledge Elenore's mischievous grin—she crossed the room to leave with Sam and Sue.

Chapter 9

Jandy hadn't intended to go back to Hannah's until the following morning. But after telling her about Sue's good report from the vet, Sam volunteered his services if she wanted to hang paintings or move items around. She supposed he was bored; he'd told her he was between jobs.

"I appreciate your help," she said, "but shouldn't you be looking for a paying position somewhere?"

"I've got a couple of things lined up in the fall," he said.

She wondered why he was being cryptic, but she let it go. She could hardly expect him to confide his every secret to her when she was keeping so many of her own.

While they worked in the gallery, they talked about Sue. Dr. Townshend hadn't found a microchip to help them identify her former owner, but he was less inclined than the rest of them to judge the man who'd dropped Sue at the rest stop.

"He said most dogs that won't fight are killed," Sam explained.

"Put to sleep, you mean?" Jandy asked.

"Not exactly," Sam said.

"I don't want to know," Jandy said, dropping to her

knees and hugging Sue. When Sue leaned into her, she almost toppled over, which wasn't surprising. Sue had been weighed at the vet and was only thirty-five pounds lighter than Jandy.

"At least that guy who dumped her gave her a chance at life," Sam conceded. "If we hadn't been there, some-one else would have picked her up. After all, she's a beauty."

Jandy looked up and saw that Sam was watching her and Sue with an odd expression. He quickly looked back at the painting he was hanging. His sisters were right; Sam clearly was infatuated with the dog. It made her wonder about Daisy, the dog he'd lost.

"I'm sorry I keep joking about who Sue belongs with," she said, standing up and brushing dust off her shorts. She looked around. She hoped for a vacuum cleaner but would have settled for a broom. When she saw neither, she shrugged and went back to her de-cluttering efforts. "She's better off with someone who's been around dogs all his life. You know about stuff like raw food. And your sister trains dogs. Considering your family's tendency to take in strays, Sue couldn't have landed in better hands."

Sam was quiet for a few seconds as he used a level to make sure the painting was straight. He finally said, "So they *were* talking about my family in the beauty shop, huh?" When she didn't answer, he laughed. "It doesn't bother me. I hope it wasn't all bad."

"What makes you think any of it was bad?" Jandy asked. Her eyes got wide as she moved a box of paper and spot-ted a computer monitor. "Now this could be good news. If it's actually connected to—" She squatted down and sighed with happiness when she saw the computer tower. She flipped a switch on the power strip, then hit the com-puter's ON button, smiling when she heard the hum.

"I know what you're up to," Sam said.

She gave him a nervous look. Did he know that she was hoping the computer came with an Internet connection? Had someone told him that she was the so-called runaway bride? Did he suspect that she wanted to find out whether her face and story were all over the Internet?

"I want to download my photos," she said, trying not to sound defensive. "Then I can burn them to a CD. Otherwise, I'll have to keep buying memory cards, and those suckers are expensive. I need to economize. I have a several thousand dollar rotary beater to pay for."

Sam shook his head and said, "You're using that computer to change the subject. Or maybe in your case, you don't want to *finish* the conversation."

"I see how you are. I confide one of my flaws to you, and you throw it back in my face the first chance you get. What conversation? What subject?"

"My eccentric family. Don't believe everything you hear."

She met his eyes and said, "I know my track record with honesty isn't so great. But the truth is, I liked hearing them talk about your family. So what if you're not conventional? Try being an only child."

"Try being the only boy with four sisters."

"Hey, I gave up the dog. At least let me have a worse childhood than you did."

He pretended to think it over and finally said, "All right. If you'll stop pestering me about Sue."

"She'd be good company for me while I'm working for your sister. For very low wages, I might add."

"I'm working for you for free," he reminded her.

"You call this work? You're just standing around talking. Soon you'll be demanding coffee breaks and health insurance."

"You'll be hearing from my union rep."

They kept up the banter for hours while they worked. Jandy was surprised by how much they accomplished. All she needed was a good broom from Evan's shop and a few more hours to arrange things and she'd be ready to open for business on Saturday, just in time for the tourists who'd be in Coventry for the kickoff of the Godiva Festival.

That night, Jandy tried not to consider what it meant that the apartment over the beauty shop was beginning to feel more like home than either her own place in Silver Lake or Hud's Los Feliz mid-rise. There wasn't anything special about it, unless she was just becoming fond of the oversized claw-foot tub. The tub was good for soaking muscles she'd forgotten she had until they began rebelling against all the uncustomary walking she'd been doing, as well as the physical labor of getting the gallery ready to open.

She finally dragged herself out of the tub and got ready for a good night's sleep. But first she had a phone call to make.

"I've been wondering when I'd hear from you," Grandpa said after she told him hello. "I want to know how that truck made it all the way to Dayton."

"Dayton?" She had no idea what he was talking about. "As in Ohio?"

"Ruby and I figured out that's where you are after we watched the news. She says you probably left the truck in airport parking and flew to Dayton."

"Back up," Jandy said, rubbing her temples against the early warning signs of a headache. "I was on the news? The real news? Not one of those tabloid shows?"

"Your mother was on the news," Grandpa said. "She's still saying you're the victim of foul play. But the reporter

said he learned from 'a reliable source' that you're staying
with a friend known only as 'Sue.' Ruby remembered that
you once had a roommate named Susan. She said Susan
lives in Dayton now, so we put two and two together—"

"And came up with the wrong zip code," Jandy said.
She didn't know what news her grandpa had been watching, but she did know the "reliable source." Hud was the
only person she'd told that she was staying with a friend
named Sue. She couldn't believe how quickly either he
or Chandra had fed information to the press. Jandy felt
like her fiancé had betrayed her.

"If you're not in Dayton, where are you?"

"Grandpa, can you just trust me? I'm fine. The truck
is fine. My friend Sue's . . . aunt has offered me a job. It's
just a short-term thing while someone's having a baby,
but I think I'll enjoy it. I'm sure Hud's publicist is the one
who's keeping my name in the news. It's silly. You know
I'm not a runaway bride. So does Mother. But since this
story keeps the Halli name and business in the news,
she's going along with it. I guess it doesn't matter. It isn't
like anyone's bothering me. But if I don't tell you where
I am, you won't have to lie to her."

"If she asks me where you are, I'll just tell her it's none
of her damned business," Grandpa said. "It's none of my
business either, Jane. You just enjoy yourself with your
friends and come home when all this has blown over.
Hold on." She waited while he had a muffled conversation with Ruby. Then he said, "Ruby says hello."

She wondered what Aunt Ruby had really said. He obviously wasn't going to tell her, which probably meant
Aunt Ruby was doling out advice that Grandpa thought
she didn't need to hear, either about her mother or Hud.

"Tell her hello. I may be away for about a month,
Grandpa. My rent is paid through August, so that's not a

problem. And Hud and I haven't set a new wedding date yet. We'll do that when I get back."

"You promise to call if you need anything?"

"Of course. And you have my cell phone number. You can always call me," she reminded him.

She brooded after they hung up. It had been a long day, beginning with her conversation with Hud. She didn't want to call him and end her day with an equally frustrating second conversation. Whatever Hud and Chandra did to keep his name in the news, she was safe in Coventry. Any doubts she might have had about staying were evaporating in the warmth and kindness of people like Evan and Grayson, the fun of the gossips in the beauty shop, and the hospitality of people like Dr. Boone. Besides, she not only had a job, but she'd just begun to scratch the surface of the Revere family's mysteries. Like how Dove made money. Or where Hop and Rachel Revere went in the summers.

As she hugged her pillow tight and turned on the TV to make sure any new pictures of January Halli looked nothing like Evan's version of Jandy Taylor, she remembered there were also plenty of things she didn't know about Sam, other than that he was nice to dogs and could make her laugh.

"It looks good in here," Evan said when he brought a broom to Jandy the next afternoon. "You must have the Capricorn devotion to hard work."

"Why would I? I'm not a Capricorn," Jandy said, shooting a photo of Evan while he stood in front of a four-foot by four-foot painting that was her favorite. She'd never thought a lot about art. She'd once gotten bogged down by all the dates and details of an art history class and dropped it. But as she was arranging and scrutinizing the canvases in the gallery, she found herself drawn to those that were more abstract.

"Aquarius?" Evan asked, turning so she could get a shot of what he obviously thought was his best angle.

"Libra," she said. "I was born in October."

He faced her with a confused expression and said, "You are really Jane Halli, right?"

"Yes."

"Jane which is short for January?"

"Oh, I see. You're not the first person to make the assumption that I was named for my birth month. That's not why my mother chose January. My full name is January Day Taylor. Taylor was changed to Halli when she married my stepfather and he adopted me. I think the name 'January Day' was meant to be a dire warning about the consequences of carelessness. I was the unplanned result of her fooling around one January day."

Evan frowned and said, "You're making that up, right? Nobody ever actually called you a consequence."

"Not in so many words. But I don't think my mother was ever married to my biological father. He moved away before she knew she was pregnant. I doubt she was thrilled by the baby news. No one can say my mother doesn't learn from her mistakes. Her life hasn't left much room for screwups since then. *She* works hard—day and night. She'd consider what I'm doing right now dabbling. Anything that doesn't make a lot of money is dabbling. Or a hobby."

Evan ignored her when she reached for the broom.

"You don't have to help me clean," she said.

"I'm all about beautification." He began sweeping with a thoughtful look on his face and finally said, "Would you say you had an unhappy childhood?"

To avoid his eyes, she flipped through a set of vintage

Coventry photographs that she was thinking of display-
ing and said, "One time I was with Hud's—*our*—friends,
and everyone was talking about their childhoods. When
I tried to explain that things were never bad for me as
much as lonely, Sorel called me a poor little rich girl. She
didn't say it in a nice way."

"Sorel's a hag," Evan said.

Jandy giggled and said, "Kind of, but she and Hud
have been friends for a zillion years. I don't think of
myself as a poor little rich girl. Like I told you, we weren't
rich. My parents worked all the time, but my aunt Ruby
was there. She's actually my grandpa's sister, so she's my
mother's aunt. My great-aunt. We had a housekeeper who
cleaned once a week, and a handyman who took care of
other things, including our yard. But it was Ruby who
looked after me and cooked our meals. I love Aunt Ruby;
she's a lot of fun. The best times from my childhood were
the weekends that Ruby and I went to Grandpa's in Redlands. We also spent almost the whole summer there every
year."

"Tell me about your grandpa."

"Grandpa's wonderful. He and Ruby grew up on a
farm in Minnesota. When his parents died, they had to
sell their farm. Ruby was married then, so Grandpa and
his wife loaded up all their stuff in a truck and headed for
California."

"Like the Clampetts," Evan teased.

"Except the Bagbys didn't make it all the way to Beverly Hills. Grandpa went to work for an orange grower
in Redlands, and they had my mother. When other
landowners sold their groves to real estate developers, the
man Grandpa worked for, Mr. Tilden, held on to his. He
didn't have any family, so when he died, he left everything to my grandparents. Grandpa kept up the groves

as long as he could, but he said agriculture was a dying venture. It cost more to grow oranges than they made selling them. Then my grandmother died, and he sort of lost interest in the groves for a while. He ended up selling most of the land. A lot of the other groves got sacrificed for tract housing, but Grandpa held out for affluent, noncommercial buyers, who put up mansions on estate-sized lots. Grandpa continued to own enough of the land to keep distance between himself and his rich neighbors. The money he made from his real estate sales sent my mother to college. Eventually, Grandpa also provided the loan she used to start Halli Real Estate Development with my stepfather."

"That's a little ironic," Evan commented. "Your mother chose the profession that took away your grandpa's livelihood."

"It's probably how she got the idea," Jandy said. "She saw where the money was. My mother hated growing up on a farm. She hated having to do chores in the vegetable garden or the grove. She still won't eat oranges. Mother likes to forget her humble beginnings. It doesn't go with the successful, urban image that she and my stepfather project."

"And in true rebellious fashion, you like the groves."

"I do. I used to play in the irrigation ditches when I was a kid. The branches of orange trees are allowed to grow low, so under every tree was a private little world where I'd sit on a blanket for hours and play with my dolls. I love the smell of orange blossoms and the taste of Grandpa's oranges, which I think are the best I've ever eaten. He has a few hundred trees left, and thanks to organizations that help preserve the remaining groves and find markets for his oranges, he still sells them. But he really lives off his Social Security, and his investments from the real estate sale. Aunt Ruby has a little money, too."

"How did your aunt end up in California?"

"When her husband died, she moved to Long Beach to take care of me. Sometime after my twelfth birthday, Mother said I didn't need a nanny anymore. I think she and Aunt Ruby probably fought because of me, so Mother asked her to leave. Aunt Ruby moved into Grandpa's old cottage at one end of the grove. Grandpa lives in Mr. Tilden's house. A lot of the original orange growers built elaborate mansions, but Grandpa's is kind of a rambling old farmhouse. I think it's about the most heavenly place on earth. Grandpa and Aunt Ruby always remind me that the land will eventually be mine. I hope that's a long time away, but I'm sure when it happens, my mother will want to sell it for me."

"Would you sell it?"

"Never," Jandy vowed. "Even if I end up with one orange tree, I'll keep the land and the houses. They're a part of the area's history, not just my history. They should be preserved. How did I get started on all that?"

"Who cares?" Evan asked. "It's fun getting to know you." She stopped fidgeting through photos and stared at him. "What?" he asked.

"Why are you and Grayson so nice to me? You don't really know anything about me. In a few weeks, you'll never see me again."

"Do you want me to give you some flippant answer or tell you the truth?" Evan asked.

"The truth."

Evan paused, lost in thought, and finally said, "I guess it's sort of a truism that gay men make families of their friends. Grayson's mother—the town mayor—is a really good person, but Grayson's father disowned him for being gay. Because of that, Grayson left town when he was young. He went to your part of the world—California. He made a lot of friends, including the man who became his business partner on his Wyoming ranch. After Grayson's father died, he came back here to keep an eye on his mother. She's the only biological family he has. His friends are his real family."

"What about your family?" Jandy asked when Evan fell silent.

"It's big, but most of them live in a little town close to Houston called Edna."

"Is Edna like Coventry?"

"I'm not sure any place is like Coventry, but I could be wrong. If *you* went there, you might find the same kind of welcome as the one you've gotten here, but it was never that way for me. My family's very straitlaced, and needless to say, I didn't fit in. Especially when I got older." He smiled. "I have an aunt, too, though. Aunt Ninny. They started calling her that when she was little because she was simple."

"Simple?"

"Not exactly mentally handicapped, but not real bright," Evan explained. "She isn't book smart at all, but she understands people. She's the kindest person I've ever known. Whenever I had trouble at home, I could always go to Ninny's Hill."

"She lived in the mountains?"

"If you knew Texas geography, you'd know anything close to Houston is flatter than flat. Unlike your coast, ours has no cliffs or mountains anywhere near it."

"I know plenty about *West* Texas geography," Jandy muttered bitterly, thinking of those endless miles of boring landscape.

"My grandmother had an expression that all of us grew up hearing: Everybody has to go over fool's hill."

"What did she mean?"

"Everybody has to be foolish at some point in their lives. If we don't do it when we're young, we do it when we're older. I suppose it's another way to say that we should sow our wild oats as teenagers and get all that out of our system. Since Ninny wasn't bright, she was sometimes called a fool by other kids. It all got mixed up in her head, and she told her family that she wanted her own hill. So every time anyone cleared land, they'd dump tree limbs and stumps, rocks, or loads of dirt next to an area of the old Hammett place that was mostly pine, oak, and pecan trees. Eventually, Aunt Ninny had a tiny hill next to the woods that she and her brothers, including my father, landscaped with ornamental trees, flowers, and rocks. They put up a tree house and hung some hammocks for her. For at least twenty-five years, Aunt Ninny has spent most of her time there, adding birdfeeders and wind chimes, watching birds, deer, coons, and squirrels. Ninny's Hill was my refuge, and she's the only real friend I had in Edna."

"Ninny sounds pretty smart to me," Jandy said.

"What all this has to do with your question," Evan said, leaning on the broom handle and staring at her, "is that like a lot of gay men, Grayson and I grew up feeling different and cut off from our families. So we made new families out of our friends. Having good friends got us both through a lot of miserable times. When you showed up two days ago, it seemed like you'd hit a rough patch and could use a friend."

"I could just be some crazy runaway bride, like the TV tabloid reporters say."

"Who says crazy runaway brides can't be fun friends?

Didn't you see the Julia Roberts movie? Or *Smokey and the Bandit?*"

"Julia, yes. Smokey, no."

"That one was Burt Reynolds rescuing Sally Field so she wouldn't have to marry a bubba," Evan said. "And Ginger Rogers ran out on a few bridegrooms in a golden oldie called *It Had to Be You.* Even if you don't need friends, by hanging out with you, Grayson and I can at least count on some wacky high jinks and maybe a car chase or two."

"I'm not a runaway bride," Jandy reminded him. "I never said I didn't want friends, but I don't want you to think I'm taking advantage of you. And *nobody* needs to rescue me from anything."

"I'm just the supporting cast in your movie," Evan said. "It's Sam Revere who crossed state lines with you and will have to answer to an irate groom one day."

"Sam!" Jandy said, looking at her watch. "I'm going to a cookout with Sam and Sue tonight."

"At Michael Boone's?"

"Yes."

"Gray and I will be there, too. You'll get to meet one of my favorite people, Keelie Boone. We were friends when we lived in Houston. Both of us fell in love in Coventry and moved here about the same time. Me to be with Grayson. Keelie to be with Michael."

Jandy was about to ask questions about Keelie when she noticed the speculative look Evan was giving her. "What? Do you think I shouldn't go with Sam? Does it look like a date? He said people wouldn't assume—"

"Who cares what people assume?" Evan asked. "This will be your first social thing in Coventry. I think the haircut will keep people from recognizing you. But it just occurred to me that you could dodge a lot of uncomfortable questions if you weren't wearing that rock on your finger."

Jandy looked at her engagement ring and suppressed an internal quiver. It wasn't as if the ring hadn't been removed since the night Hud gave it to her. She usually took it off when she washed dishes, bathed, and slept. But this seemed different, as if removing the ring was like cheating on her fiancé. Then again, Hud was on their honeymoon with Sorel. In separate rooms, but still . . .

He'd also told Chandra that she was staying with a friend named Sue.

She took off the ring, and Evan said, "Let the high jinks begin."

Chapter 10

Jandy never had a problem going into a new temp job and meeting a group of people for the first time. She was confident that she'd be able to do whatever work was asked of her, and any mishaps on her part could always be defended with that old standby, *I'm just a temp*. If she didn't get close to people in the workplace, that was all for the better. She was hired to work, not make friends. She certainly didn't want to end up in a messy situation like the temp in *Hardaway v. Melton Manufacturing, Inc.* (Alameda County Superior Court), who misinterpreted the friendliness of her managers as an offer of permanent employment and considered the failure of a permanent job to appear the consequence of a coworker with a grudge. Although Jandy usually liked her coworkers, she didn't want to get mired down in the politics and rancor that people trapped in the same place for eight to ten hours a day so often did. Being a temp meant making a clean break from office drama and tension when a job ended.

She'd approached her first meeting with the Foundlings with much the same attitude. She and Hud hadn't been dating long, and she had no reason to believe they weren't in the temp territory of relationships. If his long-time friends didn't rave that she was the best thing since airbrushed headshots, she didn't think that would affect her one way or the other.

As her role in Hud's life transitioned into girlfriend, she found that she cared a little more about the good opinion of his friends. She also found it increasingly difficult to crack their code. The Foundlings had been friends for so long, and their relationships were so entwined, that they were able to communicate in a verbal shorthand. For a long time, their conversations made her feel stupid. Eventually, however, she became annoyed. She sometimes thought that they liked having an outsider among them, as if it confirmed their cohesion as a group.

Another thing that put her on the outside with the Foundlings was that they were all connected to the entertainment industry. It wasn't as if Jandy longed for deep conversations about politics, religion, or any of the other so-called forbidden topics. But she did wonder if Hud's friends knew there was a world outside the boundaries of show business or if it ever crossed their minds that their incessant discussions of deals, ratings, agents, auditions, publicists, and who was screwing whom—more often figuratively than sexually—might actually be boring.

Even as she grew tired of feeling like she was slamming her head against the impenetrable wall of their clique, she realized that her own friends and roommates had left for various schools or jobs, gotten married, or simply dropped from her radar. She supposed that was just the natural course of growing up.

At her loneliest times, she wondered if she was the problem. Maybe she just didn't know how to be a friend. Maybe lacking a passion for something—a job, a volunteer group, a cause, or even a hobby—had made her too uninteresting to befriend.

Hud had never seemed to be bored with her. Then again, Hud never really had time to get bored. When he wasn't working and she was with him, they were either running his lines, hanging out with his friends, attending functions where Hud could be seen and photographed, traveling, or spending time between the sheets. He'd never complained that she didn't measure up in her roles as arm candy, girlfriend, or lover. Nor did he seem to mind or even notice that everything in her life seemed to hinge on what happened in his life: when she worked or didn't work; when and where she took vacations; the people she knew and spent time with.

In fact, Hud always seemed surprised anytime she did something that didn't include him, like visiting Grandpa and Aunt Ruby or going alone to movies or plays that she knew he wouldn't enjoy. She'd begun to suspect that Hud liked it that she didn't have a lot in her life that would draw her attention away from him. Like his friends, maybe Hud just wanted an adoring audience.

One reason she'd wanted a small wedding with no wedding party was because she had a recurring mental picture of a church aisle getting longer and longer as she walked down it. One side of the church—Hud's—was packed with people. On the other side, she saw row after row of empty pews, with her parents, Grandpa, Aunt Ruby, her landlord with his unpronounceable name, and Pam, her contact person at the temp agency, huddled together in the front. Meanwhile, at the altar, the groomsmen and bridesmaids were jockeying for positions next to Hud while fielding calls on their cell phones throughout the ceremony. There'd be no one to hold her bouquet, push back her veil, or help with her train.

The simple ceremony she and Hud had planned with only a couple of friends in Mendocino had allowed her to breathe again. The anxiety attacks stopped. Then her mother and Chandra went to work, and suddenly all she could envision were five hundred guests whose names she didn't know, *couldn't* know because they were nothing more than business contacts of Halli Real Estate Development or Henry Hudson Blake, Actor, all gaping at her and wondering how she'd managed to snag one of daytime TV's hottest hunks.

Those thoughts, expressed in the voice of her old adversary Pru, careened through her brain as she sat in the passenger seat of Sam's Jeep while Sue panted behind her. She was about to meet another group of strangers, and her only credentials were: *Sam towed my pickup truck to Coventry, Sue likes me, and Evan is letting me live over the beauty shop.* Even if she could somehow parlay her job at the gallery into something interesting to talk about, she'd have to weigh every word she said before it came out of her mouth. Otherwise, if Michael Boone's guests hadn't already recognized her as the so-called runaway bride, she'd give herself away sometime during the night by making a reference to Hud, the postponed wedding, or jobs she'd had in California. It made her want to beg Sam to turn around, take her back to Molly's Beauty Shop, and never look at her friendless face again.

Not long after arriving at the beautiful old rock house that was the Boones' home, she couldn't believe she'd ever been worried. There were two or three dozen people and almost as many dogs scattered around their big backyard. People sat in groups on the grass and in Adirondack chairs, or they stood around a barbecue pit that offered a tantalizing aroma of wood smoke. Next to the grill was a teenager who Jandy recognized as the girl with the greyhound whom she'd met at the fountain on her first day in Coventry. Sam told her the girl was Michael and Keelie's fifteen-year-old daughter, Jennifer.

A little confused, Jandy said, "I got the idea from Evan that Michael and Keelie were practically newlyweds."

"Keelie's her stepmother," Sam explained. "Jennifer's mother died a few years ago."

Jennifer and a few of her friends were in charge of cooking. Apparently Jennifer was on her way to becoming a chef, but that didn't stop most of the men standing near her from offering her advice that she either ignored or laughed at.

Keelie was a petite blonde with a big smile. Coming from the house with a tray of vegetables and dip in her hand, she spotted Jandy standing with Sam. She put down the tray and greeted them with warmth, patted Sue on the head, directed them toward the drinks and the other appetizers, ordered Sam to make sure Jandy was introduced around, and promised to sit down for a real talk after everyone was stuffed with food.

As Jandy and Sam walked toward a cooler, Sam asked if something was bothering her. When she said no, he said, "You seem jumpy. I know you don't want people to get the wrong idea, but there are worse things than being mistaken as my date. Like maybe a root canal."

"Don't be ridiculous," she said. "I would never compare a date with you to a root canal. They give you *great* drugs during a root canal to take away the pain. Just ask Robin."

He suppressed his smile and said, "All right, worse things like a bad toupee."

"There's no such thing as a good toupee."

Sam pointed to his high hairline and said, "Are you sure? Because I've been thinking maybe—"

"Don't do it," Jandy said. "There's nothing wrong with

your hair. If you get to the point that you think you're
losing it, just shave it off. Shaved heads are sexy."

Their discussion was taken up by several people standing nearby, and before she could say "Jean-Luc Picard," the
group was debating the merits of shaved heads versus
comb-overs and hair plugs. As Jandy sipped a beer and
added a comment now and then, she felt a flush of gratitude for people like these. She was among them, as if she'd
always been there. No one was staring at her or asking her
uncomfortable questions. There was none of the stiffness
that had marked her parents' few social occasions. There
was certainly nothing like the "Who are you?" "What can
you do for me?" attitude that was typical of many of the parties she went to with Hud.

As people talked, Sam murmured an occasional aside
so she'd know who they were. A striking black woman
named Vanessa, who agreed with Jandy that shaved heads
were sexy, was married to one of the men at the barbecue
pit, Terry Bowen. Terry was co-owner of Independent
Seven Toys. His partner, Carl Taylor, was throwing horseshoes with his wife, Faith, in a game against Evan and
Grayson.

"I wonder if you're related?" Sam said.

"What? Who?"

"Carl Taylor. Jandy Taylor."

"I don't have any relatives in Texas," Jandy said, sti-
fling Pru's smug reminder that this was what came of
lying about her name.

Vanessa's father, Isaac Phillips, was also among the
men at the barbecue pit. Jandy recognized him because
he owned Phillips Hardware Store. She'd gone there to
get more wire and nails for hanging paintings and photographs in the gallery. Isaac was a big man with a boom-
ing voice. As soon as she'd told him she was going to be

managing the gallery, he'd put everything she bought on Hannah's account at the hardware store and talked to Jandy like she'd lived in Coventry all her life.

When Sam apologized for not knowing Jennifer Boone's friends' names, Jandy shrugged and said, "They're teenagers. I'm sure as soon as the food's done, they'll race away from all us boring old people."

In any case, she couldn't keep up with all the names he did know. At best, she could remember that Sam pointed out a couple of people who worked for Dr. Boone; a dentist and her husband; three attorneys and their dates or spouses; a woman who owned the buildings that the Old Towne Shoppes were in; a man who did something at City Hall; a group of nurses from Coventry Hospital, which had recently opened in a big, modern building in New Coventry; and some other business owners. A small group of men were playing some kind of game at the far end of the lawn, which was bordered by an unfenced pasture. They looked like cowboys, and when she asked about them, Sam told her that they were ranchers whose cattle Michael vetted. The game they were playing was bocce ball. Apparently a couple of them had learned it from someone they met on a fishing trip, and it had been popular at get-togethers all spring.

She noticed that almost all of the men, Sam included, wore cowboy boots and jeans. A few of them, including Evan and Michael, and most of the women, like her, were in shorts, although several women wore summer dresses. Everyone looked relaxed and happy, like they should on a perfect summer night.

Just beyond the horseshoe pit, thick, dark leaves on a line of tall trees were rustling in the light breeze. When Jandy asked what the trees were, Sam said, "Magnolias.

They're old. Probably not as old as the house, though. It dates back to just after the Civil War."

"Since you're the plant guy, what are those flowers?"

"Who said I'm the plant guy?"

"You knew the Latin name for black-eyed susans," she reminded him.

He looked around and said, "Lantana, Mexican heather, and I'm sure you recognize roses when you see them. Michael had those planted for Keelie this past spring. If you're really that interested in flowers, I'll have to show you my folks' place."

"I'd like that."

She fell silent, rubbing Sue's belly and listening to Vanessa tell a story about her daughter. She glanced up as a shadow fell across her and smiled at Jennifer, who was holding out a plate of deviled eggs.

"I remember you. The lady who doesn't believe in wishes."

"Jandy Taylor," Sam said, taking one of the eggs. "Jennifer Boone."

Jandy took an egg, too, and said, "I don't suppose your wish was for me to stay in Coventry for a while, was it?"

Jennifer's smile was enigmatic when she said, "Not exactly. Is this your dog?"

"Mine," Sam said before Jandy could answer. "Sue."

"She's a big girl." Jennifer handed off the tray of deviled eggs to Keelie as she walked by, then squatted to check out Sue much the way her father had when he'd met the dog. "I hope you guys are hungry. I've cooked about a zillion steaks, hot dogs, and hamburgers."

"A zillion, huh?" Sam asked, with a meaningful grin at Jandy.

Jandy pretended not to hear him and said, "Sam told me that you're planning to be a chef."

Jennifer nodded, and Sam said, "Sometimes she gives cooking classes. I failed soufflés."

"You didn't fail as long as you learned *something,*" Jennifer disagreed.

"I learned that I can't make a soufflé."

"Did it by chance require a rotary beater?" Jandy asked, and it was Sam's turn to fake deafness.

"I don't remember. What kind of soufflé did you cook?" Jennifer asked.

"I *attempted* a chocolate soufflé," Sam said.

"Then yes, he used a rotary beater," Jennifer said, looking mystified when Jandy snickered.

"She's just having a little joke at my expense," Sam said. "I'm sure *your* idea of cooking is figuring out how to turn on the microwave."

"Shows what you know," Jandy said. "Maybe one day I'll let you taste my frozen orange soufflé."

"Do you make the one that calls for Grand Marnier?" Jennifer asked. When Jandy nodded, she said, "That's delicious. On Tuesday nights, all summer, I'm doing a pastry class in the kitchen at Christ Church. Please come if you want to. All you have to pay for is your ingredients."

"I actually went to a few classes at culinary school, but I dropped out. It wasn't the career for me. But I do like to cook. I'm sure I'd enjoy your class."

"You can drag him along, too," Jennifer said, pointing a finger at Sam. "He needs more confidence in his kitchen skills."

One of Jennifer's friends called her name, and Jennifer gave Sue a final ear scratch and smiled at Jandy before she left them.

"I believe she thinks I'm your girlfriend," Jandy said apologetically. "You don't really have to go to cooking class with me."

"You're afraid I'll out-cook you, aren't you?"

"Not if you have the same skill under an oven hood that you do under the hood of a pickup."

"Just because I couldn't immediately identify the problem with your old clunker of a truck—"

"That truck is a classic," Jandy said. "And I've already told you, I'm not competitive."

"Damn," Evan said, bending over to squeeze her shoulder, "I'm all about competition. I came to ask if you and Sam wanted to pitch horseshoes."

"I don't understand the allure of hurling horseshoes around," Jandy said.

"The same as any other game you can play while holding a beer," Sam said.

"Pitching horseshoes takes a lot of skill," Evan said.

"How hard can it be to throw a piece of iron at a stick in the ground?" Jandy asked.

"Also known as a stake," Sam said. "If it's that easy, you should be able to whip us all."

"I might need a little instruction first, but I don't see why I couldn't," Jandy said.

"Oh, no, you're not at all competitive," Sam said.

She walked with them to the horseshoe pit and nodded when Grayson said, "You and me against Yosemite Sam and Evan the Terrible?"

"Anyone have a coin to toss to see who goes first?" Evan asked.

As Sam reached for the pocket of his jeans, Jandy said, "I don't think so, Mr. Heads I Win, Tails You Lose. Grayson?"

Grayson took out a quarter, Evan called heads, then Grayson tossed it and said, "Heads it is."

Evan took his place next to Grayson, and she and Sam stood at the opposite end of the pit.

"You can throw from that line," Sam said, nodding toward what looked like part of a railroad tie about ten feet away. "Women throw from twenty-seven feet. Men from thirty-seven."

"I see you guys have this down to a science," she said, checking out the weight of the horseshoe she picked up.

"Evan and Grayson will each throw two shoes," Sam said. "Then we'll take our turns. You can go last so you'll have a chance to watch our form."

"Yes, oh great horseshoe mentor."

He flashed his impish grin and said, "After we've all played and counted our points, we'll change places. That way we share equally in any disadvantages like the sun in our eyes or the direction of the breeze."

"How do you count points?"

"Three points if you ring it. Two points if it's a leaner."

"A what?"

"The shoe leans against the stake. One point if the shoe lands within six inches of the stake or is touching the stake but isn't standing up." He looked at Evan and Grayson and raised his voice to ask, "Are we playing count-all or cancellation?"

"Count-all," Evan said. "We wouldn't want to make Jandy cry over her dead ringers."

"You guys mock me all you want to," Jandy said. "It can't be that hard."

"Each player gets a total of ten pitches—five rounds of two pitches," Sam said. "The team with the most points at the end wins."

As Evan and then Grayson pitched their horseshoes, Sam maintained a running commentary, telling her to take note of their stances, the way each man brought his left leg forward as he pitched with his right hand, and to watch the arc of their arms as they released the horseshoe.

"You make it sound so complicated," Jandy said, frowning a little as Evan made three points and Grayson only made one.

"It's not something a person can just do," Sam insisted. "Professional horseshoe players practice for hours every day. There are horseshoe tournaments and champions like in any other sport. It's not as glamorous as golf or tennis, so you aren't aware of it."

"You don't know that. I could be a horseshoe groupie. C'mon, try me. Test me on the Tiger Woods of horseshoes. Or that, er, Federline guy."

"Britney Spears's husband is an athlete?" Sam asked, picking up two horseshoes.

"Not him. That guy who won Wimbledon."

Sam cracked up and said, "Federer. Roger Federer."

"As a horseshoe groupie—actually, we call ourselves shoeies—I can't be expected to know players from lesser sports."

Sam rolled his eyes, got into position, and focused on the opposite stake. She watched the trajectory of the horseshoe as he released it, frowning again when he got a ringer.

"A lot of it's in the wrist," Sam said. "You want to release at just the right time, letting your shoe sail about seven or eight feet off the ground. Your shoe should have a good wobble to it."

"Uh-huh," she said.

His second horseshoe didn't garner him a point. She took her two horseshoes to the line he'd indicated, flinching as her first pitch landed short and skidded to the right. Sam came up behind her and said, "Do you mind?"

She glanced back at him, unsure what he wanted. He took her right hand and showed her proper finger placement on the horseshoe.

"You want to stay loose, knees bent a little," he said. "Keep your toes pointed forward, but let your right knee relax a little toward your left. That way, when you bring your pitch forward, you won't hit your leg."

"Uh-huh," she said again, a little unaccustomed to having a man other than Hud standing so close to her.

He put his left hand on her waist and his right hand around her wrist from behind. Then he made her move her arm in a fake pitch.

"You don't snap your wrist at all," he said. "Keep it straight, and let the shoe naturally leave your hand as you bring your arm up, right about this point."

He was still holding her wrist, and his breath was warm against her bare neck. She blushed as she realized that she'd just discovered one of the advantages of really short hair. She hoped Sam didn't realize that she was enjoying his closeness a little more than she should be. She glanced at Evan and Grayson, but Grayson was petting Sue, and Evan was saying something to him. Both of them were obviously fine with Sam's giving her a pitching lesson.

"Okay, pitch your second shoe," Sam said, stepping away from her.

Get a grip, Pru scolded. *You are* not *falling for an unemployed whatever it is he doesn't do when he's not driving tow trucks.*

"Of course I'm not," she said.

"What?" Sam asked.

"I said—I don't know what I said. It's the horseshoe groupie chant for luck. Stop distracting me."

"Sorry. I wouldn't want to ruin the moment when a shoeie goes pro," he said.

She released the horseshoe, scowled as it went beyond the stake, and said, "Don't know my own strength."

"I think you should be aware that you just quoted Bullwinkle," Sam said.

"Is that the squirrel or the coyote?"

"The moose. Actually, you do have good upper body strength," Sam added as they changed sides with Evan and Grayson.

"No worries," Grayson said when he passed her. "We're just getting started. We'll kick their butts."

"In your dreams," Evan said.

"Swimming," Jandy said, while Sam wrote his points on a little chalkboard next to the pit.

"What?"

"I'm a swimmer. That's why I have good upper body strength."

"Ah," he said.

She got a little better with subsequent pitches, and when she got her first ringer, she did a little dance and held up her hand for Sam to high-five.

"Hey, Sam," Evan called, "you do realize you're play-ing *against* her, right?"

Although Grayson did his best, he couldn't overcome what Evan gleefully called his "Jandy-cap," but Jandy re-fused to apologize for their abysmal loss, saying, "Just wait until next time."

"Right," Evan said. "Even Sue couldn't bear to watch the massacre."

Jandy looked around and spotted Sue running and playing with other dogs. A Doberman darted toward the pasture and grabbed one of the balls the ranchers were using in their bocce game.

"Damn it, Seig," one of the men yelled. "Come back here!"

The chase was on, with people and dogs running in circles. Sue's lumbering ecstasy as she joined the chase made Jandy smile, and she got Sam's attention and pointed. His eyes crinkled with affection as he watched the dogs. It occurred to Jandy that if he ever looked at a woman that way, he wouldn't be stuck bringing a dog and someone else's fiancée to a cookout.

"Maybe we just haven't found your game," Grayson said, and in a hopeful tone asked, "Do you play pool?"

"'Fraid not," Jandy said.

"It's just as well," Keelie said, stopping to shoo them toward the serving tables. "Grayson cheats at pool, and I can still beat him."

People were already filling their plates with food, and Jandy went inside with the others so they could wash their hands in the kitchen. Grayson kept up the questions.

"Golf? Tennis? Badminton? Softball?"

"Nope," Jandy said sadly.

"Ping-Pong? Hackey sack? Chess?"

"I play a mean game of jacks," Jandy said. "Oh. And hide-and-go-seek."

"Tag!" Evan said.

"Freeze tag," Sam said.

"Red rover," Jandy said. "Hopscotch."

"If we were all ten years old, you'd be the queen of the neighborhood," Grayson assured her.

"Only if her mom had a freezer full of Fudgsicles," Sam said.

Jandy laughed inwardly at the idea of her mother having a freezer full of anything. Her mother's idea of dinner was whatever she and Jandy's stepfather picked up on the go. After Aunt Ruby had moved out, Jandy cooked her own simple meals and ate alone in the kitchen with a book in front of her. In fact, she could only remember two occasions when their dining room had been used in all the years she lived at home. Both times were open houses for clients, with hors d'oeuvres provided by a caterer.

Sue spotted them when they went outside and ran at full speed toward them. She'd apparently taken a detour through some vines, and they were trailing from her collar, green leaves fluttering.

"Brace yourself," Jandy said. "Here comes her majesty."

Sam bent in a goalie stance, and Evan said, "Maybe one of the Daughter of Godiva contestants should try that outfit."

"Bad idea," Grayson said as Sam made a lunge for Sue and ended up holding only vines as she took a hard left. "I think that's poison ivy."

"She's *your* dog," Jandy reminded Sam, edging away from him.

"Are you sure?" he asked. When she nodded, he dropped the greenery in a trash can and said, "Too bad you gave up so quickly. It's harmless Virginia creeper, not poison ivy. On the bright side, you finally finished something: this argument about who Sue belongs with."

"Four sisters," Evan said, a sad expression on his face as he shook his head at Sam, "and you still don't know women. No argument is over until *they* say it's over." Sue ran back and fell in an exhausted heap at Jandy's feet, prompting him to add, "I rest my case."

Chapter 11

As Jandy had predicted, Jennifer and the other teen-agers vanished sometime after they began eating. Keelie noticed it, too, and said, "They're afraid they'll get stuck cleaning up. Cooking is fun to them. The rest of it's drudgery."

But Jandy noticed that even though everyone complained about being too stuffed to move, the one thing that didn't happen was the women getting stuck cleaning up while the men went back to their horseshoes or bocce ball. All of the Boones' guests pitched in until the un-eaten food was put away, the dishwasher was running, and the yard was clear of trash. Then the ranchers sat near the grill talking and smoking, as if huddled around a campfire, and a couple of them brought out guitars to strum. A few people took advantage of the last few min-utes of daylight to pitch horseshoes or toss a Frisbee.

The rest of them sat in the chairs or on the grass nearby to talk. Jandy noticed that Sam was as quiet as she was, apparently content to listen. As conversations about stem cell research, gas prices, the future of hybrid cars, politics, the war, and global warming went on around her,

Jandy felt as if she were a zillion miles from L.A. Not only did the Boones' guests not avoid hot topics, but they didn't mention a single celebrity or anything about show business, unless she counted a brief discussion of who planned to see *An Inconvenient Truth* when it came to New Coventry's movie theater sometime during the summer.

When one of the women linked high gas prices to Katrina, the hurricane that had struck the Gulf Coast the year before, wiping out whole towns in Mississippi and causing the levees in New Orleans to fail, Faith Taylor looked at Sam and said, "Have you heard from your parents? How are they?"

"They're doing well," Sam said.

Keelie looked at Jandy and said, "Has Sam told you about his parents?"

"No," Jandy said.

"He's being modest," Terry Bowen said. "Usually in the summers, they go up North where it's a little cooler and build houses with Habitat for Humanity. This summer, they took an RV to New Orleans to help with cleanup and anything else they can do."

Jandy looked at Sam and said, "You must be really proud of them."

Sam nodded. As the conversation moved into a discussion of New Orleans and good times some of them had enjoyed there in the past, Jandy stared at the grass. She wondered what it would be like to have parents who thought there was something more important than making a multimillion dollar deal or beating out a competitor to develop a piece of commercial real estate.

You wouldn't like it, Pru jeered. *Imagine having to live up to virtuous parents like that.*

Jandy looked at Sam, who gave her a rueful smile. As

if he'd read her mind, he said, "You're probably thinking I should be there with them."

"No way," she said. "I'm too selfish. If you'd been in New Orleans, who'd have rescued me from death under the Arizona sun? Who'd have saved Sue from my less-than-adequate care?"

"You'd have been fine," he said.

"Didn't you tell me that no one needed to rescue you from anything?" Evan asked.

"Hush," Jandy said and became excessively interested in a box that Vanessa and Faith had just brought from Vanessa's car.

Vanessa began removing dolls from the box and passing them around for everyone to look at, saying, "This is our new line."

"We call them the Look Back Girls," Faith added.

"They're a little like Barbies, but younger," Jandy said when the first one got around to her. "They remind me of Barbie's cousin, Francie."

"You know the Francie doll?" Vanessa asked. "You can't be old enough to remember her."

"I have a couple," Jandy said. "I got them at resale shops. Don't they still make Francie?"

"Not since the mid-seventies," Vanessa said. "Here's a bit of trivia for you. Mattel actually made a black Francie, but they didn't change the head, so she had the same features as the white Francie. She can't really officially be called the first black doll in the Barbie family."

"The first truly black Barbie was Christie," Faith said. "Then they made black Barbie."

"Who became African American Barbie," Vanessa said. "Now there are many ethnic Barbies. Barbies of color. Shani. Simone. Nikki. Treasures of Africa Barbies."

"DeeDee and Cara," Faith added. "There was even a black Midge."

"You two really know your Barbies," Jandy said. "I've never heard of most of these dolls, and I love Barbies."

"Barbies attract fanatical collectors," Vanessa said. "Check them out online sometime. You may have picked up a used Barbie that would auction for a chunk of change on eBay."

"I doubt that," Jandy said, realizing that even if it were true, she could never get rid of one of her dolls. It would break up her extended Beatles family.

"The Look Back Girls aren't fashion dolls," Faith said. "There won't be black and white and Asian copies of each doll, because only one doll will fit the character she's based on. Keelie is writing a series of novels, each of which has as its main character a girl in the twelve- to fifteen-year-old range."

"They're fictional stories," Keelie said, "but the girls are true to the times they lived in. I just write about their lives, but Vanessa is the one who researches all their clothes to make them authentic. Faith designs their clothes and accessories."

"The point of the dolls is to encourage girls to read," Vanessa said. "While they're enjoying a novel that features the character a doll is based on, they're also learning about other times and places. Even after the book ends, when they make up their own stories for the dolls, they may incorporate what they've learned."

"And also learn to empower themselves," Faith said. "The girls in Keelie's stories usually have some sort of hardship to overcome, related either to their environment or their personal circumstances. But they'll always be stronger in the end."

It struck Jandy that what they were saying wasn't so different from what she'd done with her own dolls. She'd learned a lot of sixties and seventies pop culture in order to make up the Beatle Barbies' melodramatic stories. She felt somehow validated, as if she hadn't been just a silly girl using dolls to create a connection to a father who loomed over her life with the same mythic stature as rock stars.

"I'm awed by all of you," Jandy said. She looked at Keelie. "I can't imagine writing a book. I once took a creative writing class, and I couldn't even finish a short story."

"I can't say that it's easy, but I love it." Keelie paused, and Jandy dreaded the question that would most likely follow: *What do* you *do?*

"It took Keelie a while to start writing, but sometimes I think people are better off if they live a little before they settle on a career," Evan said.

"I agree," Michael said. "I always knew I wanted to be a vet, but I've known a lot of people who got the careers they thought they wanted, only to find out they were miserable or ill-suited for them."

"Right on," muttered one of the attorneys.

"Oh, you like your job," his wife said. "You just hate lawyer jokes."

The conversation shifted to the variety of jobs they'd all had in their lives. No one put Jandy on the spot with questions, and she could have bitten off her tongue when she threw pari-mutuel teller into the mix and Michael's head snapped her way.

"Horses or greyhounds?" he asked.

"Horses," she said faintly, wishing the ground would swallow her up. In her panic, she couldn't think of the name of any racetrack other than the one where she'd worked: Hollywood Park.

"Don't let Michael get started on dog racing, or we'll be here all night," Evan said with a subtle wink at Jandy when she gave him a grateful look.

"It's a good thing I don't have your conscience, or I'd have a hard time selling horses," Grayson said.

"I'm not entirely opposed to greyhound racing," Michael said. "Most owners and trainers take good care of their dogs. I've got a problem with irresponsible breeding and the fate of dogs who don't make the cut. And you," he said, pointing at Grayson, "not only don't breed thoroughbreds and quarter horses, but you don't sell your horses to the limited market for racing Arabians."

"True," Grayson said.

One of the ranchers drawled, "Lucky for me your affection for animals didn't bother you when you were eating that steak."

Michael nodded with a somewhat rueful expression and said, "But you don't mistreat your cattle. Humans and animals have always had a symbiotic relationship. Sometimes we work together. Sometimes we're their food. Sometimes they're our food. I don't mean to sound like an old parson in a pulpit. I've just seen the downside of overbreeding animals."

"I've seen the downside of overbreeding gamblers," Jandy said. "I didn't work at the track for very long. It was making me dislike people too much."

Another of the ranchers laughed and began singing a song about a Kentucky gambler. The last sliver of sun dipped below the horizon, and garden path lights cast a soft glow over everything. Jandy stretched out on the grass, using one arm as a prop for her head and draping her other arm over Sue. She wished she had her camera with her; the rancher's weathered face appealed to her. There was *life* on that face, much like her grandpa's. But she supposed it would be rude to spend the evening aiming a camera at people, especially when they didn't know her.

After he finished that song, the man sang other country songs that she didn't recognize. By then, more guitars had come out. Some people sang along; others shared quiet conversations.

Jandy smiled appreciatively through a few blues songs, then Terry Bowen sang a song by the Grateful Dead that she recognized. She felt drowsy and contented and thought, *I could stay right here, in this moment and place, forever.*

Before she had time to examine that thought, someone passed a guitar to Sam and said, "You may as well do one of those protest songs your mama taught you when you were too young to know better."

"You play the guitar?" Jandy asked. She didn't know why it surprised her, since she'd been acquainted with him for only a few days.

"There must be a *zillion* things about me you don't know," Sam said and tuned the guitar.

She was eager to hear his voice, but as soon as he began singing along to his guitar, she had to lower her head and pretend to kiss Sue's nose. She was actually hiding her face in case anyone was watching her, because she was unaccountably moved to hear him sing "And I Love Her."

She remembered that she was supposed to be at her rehearsal dinner, on her last night as a single woman. She was to have eaten at an expensive restaurant with her family and Hud's, being toasted and giving presents to all the people in their wedding party.

Instead, Hud had probably gone to a luau with Sorel, while Jandy had eaten a grilled hamburger, had badly played a game of horseshoes, and was sitting on the grass with two dozen strangers, most of whose names she couldn't remember. But instead of feeling miserable and alone, she felt comfortable and, in an odd way, special. Because Sam had deliberately chosen a Beatles song, making it a connection between them that no one else could know.

Regardless of all their bickering about Sue, the more she learned about him, the more she appreciated Sam's kindness. He hadn't used the discussion of the Look Back Girls as an opportunity to tell everyone about her Beatle Barbie obsession. He'd teased her about her lack of horseshoe skills, but he hadn't picked on her about quitting her cooking class when she was talking to Jennifer, her writing class when she was talking to Keelie, or her job at the racetrack when she was talking to Michael.

He couldn't know, of course, that he'd chosen one of her favorite Beatles songs. It was probably the only one he knew how to play. But it was still a sweet moment and left her eyes bright with unshed tears.

Maybe there was such a thing as magic. Maybe it was okay to sometimes believe that fate brought people together for a reason. Maybe she should just enjoy the possibility instead of adamantly denying it. And maybe she could let down her guard just a little, unlike her habit with her coworkers at her temp jobs, even if, in the end, it would be only temporary, this permission she gave herself to experience the magic of Coventry and the people who lived there.

* * *

Catastrophe, not magic, was the first word on Jandy's mind when she awoke just before dawn on Saturday morning and realized that it was raining. She wondered what the festival organizers planned in case of bad weather. But the whisper of rain against the glass windows of her apartment was so softly comforting that she had only seconds to worry about it before she was lulled back to sleep.

The next time she woke up, she'd have believed she dreamed the rain if, while brushing her teeth, she hadn't looked out her bathroom window to see the way the sun turned water droplets on the trees into diamonds. She opened the larger windows in the living room and felt how the rain had cooled the air. It was going to be a gorgeous day.

Your wedding day, Pru reminded her, but Jandy shook off the annoying inner voice. She would remain true to her promise to enjoy her time in Coventry without constantly thinking of the real life waiting for her in California.

She took a quick shower and silently thanked Evan again for the easy styling of her hair. Even without his skill, she could make it look good. She shoved money in her pants pocket, put on a pair of sunglasses, and grabbed her keys and camera. She could pick up breakfast later. For now, she just wanted to be on the square and to see every moment leading up to the opening festivities, before she unlocked the gallery and started trying to sell art to tourists.

Although there were a lot more people on the sidewalks than she'd anticipated, she maneuvered her way through them to the square. The booths weren't open for business yet, but Jandy was able to get plenty of shots of people in their medieval garb. They were happy to pose for her, and several of the men made her smile by telling her what a fine wench she was.

A group of children near the fountain were getting their faces painted by Faith Taylor, who smiled and waved as if they were old friends. Jandy was about to join them to take some photos when Elenore Storey called her name. She joined her next to the street.

"If you want to get the best pictures of the procession, you should stand by the church. But if you want to get closer to everyone, the fountain corner is where they all end up."

"Thanks," Jandy said.

"There's a computer at the gallery, isn't there?"

"Yes," Jandy said, "but I haven't used it yet. I'm hoping I can download my photos to it and save them to disks."

"You ought to pick up one of those flash drives," Elenore said. "They take up a lot less space than disks." When Jandy gave her a surprised look, Elenore laughed and said, "Didn't expect an old lady to know about computers, did you? Here's a card with my e-mail address and the address of my blog. I don't have a digital camera. If you get some good shots that you don't mind sharing, e-mail them to me, and I'll give you a photo credit on my blog."

"I wouldn't mind at all," Jandy said. "Is there anything in particular you want me to shoot?"

"Whatever interests you as a newcomer to Coventry is good enough for me," Elenore said. "The opening of the festival through eyes that never saw it before."

Feeling like she had an assignment made Jandy more

discerning with the photos she took. It was hard not to shoot everything, because the town and everyone in it seemed to shine with happiness and health. But she tried to do as Elenore suggested and capture a tourist's perspective.

The procession began with a group of men in period costumes leading Wyndmere around the square. If the longhorn minded the way a papier-mâché dragon head had been artfully positioned on her horns, she gave no sign of it. Children's squeals of delight as they saw her were lost in the noise of the high school's marching band that came next. Then Grayson drove by in a convertible carrying his mother, Mayor Murray, followed by a pickup truck with members of the town council sitting in the bed and playing an unrecognizable song on kazoos.

After that, came group after group of horses and their riders. Because she knew nothing about horses, Jandy had no idea what the differences were. She took photos of the banners listing group names as well as the types of horses so she could later ask Grayson about Tennessee Walkers, Missouri Fox Trotters, American Saddlebreds, Quarter Horses, Arabians, Appaloosas, and Florida Cracker Horses. Although the sizes of the horses intimidated her, she found their faces as fascinating as those of the people and dogs she'd discovered that she liked to photograph.

An antique pickup truck following the last group of horses billed itself the official transportation of "Cow Pie Clowns" but the bed was empty, as all the clowns were on the street entertaining the crowd with exaggerated gestures of dismay as they cleaned up after the horses. A few minutes later she understood why it was important to clean the streets; the next group of people walking in the procession wore elaborate Renaissance costumes. They were followed by the King of the Godiva Festival being pulled in an open carriage.

Jandy forgot to take photos after the king went by. A costumed group of men billed as the "Godiva Goliards" sang chants as they walked ahead of at least twenty girls on horseback. All the horses were white, with flowers woven into their manes. The girls were dressed in white flowing dresses and sitting sidesaddle. All of them had hair even longer than hers had been before Evan cut it. She wasn't sure if their hair was real or wigs, but she understood that she was getting her first look at the contestants in the Daughter of Godiva pageant. They seemed so young and innocent as they smiled and waved that her eyes filled with tears.

Another carriage pulled by a team of four white horses was the final part of the procession. It carried the currently reigning Daughter of Godiva, who reminded Jandy of pictures she'd seen of Vanessa Williams the year she won the Miss America pageant. She was regal in a lavender gown, and she was wearing a head wreath of tiny purple and yellow flowers, with a mixture of iridescent and silver ribbons trailing down her back. Although growing up on Hollywood's doorstep had inured Jandy to gorgeous women, she was still dazzled by all the girls in the pageant.

"Maybe they're so beautiful," she said to Evan later as they took turns pulling meat off a fried turkey leg, "because they're real."

"It's not like movie stars are aliens," Evan said, using his napkin to wipe a smudge of grease from her face.

She batted his hand away and said, "They kind of are. They're plucked, lasered, injected, lifted, tucked, tightened, liposuctioned, and peeled. They have weaves, spray-on tans, permanent eyeliner, fake lashes, fake nails, fake breasts, and fake résumés. And just in case all that doesn't make them look flawless, their body fat and blemishes are airbrushed off of them on magazine covers."

"Thank goodness," Evan said, "because they send the rest of America's women into salons like mine. Trust me, when the Godiva girls get out of bed in the morning, they're not flawless either."

"I never said they were flawless," Jandy defended herself. "I just said their beauty seems more genuine."

"Your problem," Evan said, "is that you have a crush on Coventry. During the infatuation phase, you can't see that it's like any other place."

She stared at him for a few seconds and finally said, "Do you really believe that?"

"No," he confessed. "That's why I moved here. It certainly wasn't for the cuisine."

She laughed as he tossed the turkey bone into a trash can.

"I thought you moved here for love."

"That, too," he said and stood. "Back to work."

"Me, too. I need to get that gallery open and sell something so Hannah won't regret paying me."

"Hannah's loaded," Evan said. "Tell yourself you're doing it for art, not commerce."

Jandy was surprised by how many people not only came in, but bought things. The vintage photographs she'd hung went first. Then a few of the smaller canvases and several pieces of pottery. She was glad she'd found a detailed book of instructions from Hannah that Dove hadn't mentioned, because Hannah was very firm about not letting buyers haggle over prices.

We are not one of the festival booths on the square, Hannah had written. *Our artists have set their prices, and their work shouldn't be undervalued.*

Hannah had also left information about how to charge for packing and insuring items to be shipped. Once the gallery cleared, Jandy was carefully bubble wrapping a raku-fired vase when an elderly man walked in and waved his cane in her direction.

"I need to sit," he barked between taking in gasps of air.

Jandy pushed the chair from Hannah's computer desk to him and said, "Are you okay? Should I call someone?"

"I'm fine. It's just damn hot, and there are too many people crowding the sidewalks," he answered in a querulous tone. When she gave him a worried look, he added, "You could get me a cup of water. Cool. No ice."

She hurried to do as he asked and came back to find him staring at the large painting she and Sam had hung as the gallery's focal point.

"What do you call that?" he asked.

She stifled a grin and said, "Art. From the abstract expressionist school."

"Somebody should have fired the schoolteacher. How much does something like that go for?"

"It's actually quite a steal at twenty-two hundred dollars," Jandy said gamely.

"It's robbery, all right." He took another drink of water and turned his bushy eyebrows and steely eyes her way. "Now who are you? I don't believe I've seen you before."

"I'm Jandy Taylor. I'm taking care of the gallery while Hannah's with her daughter in California."

"I know where Hannah is," he snapped. "Jandy! Sounds like a name for a horse."

"It's short for January," she said, sure that this old

goat was the last person in town she had to worry would connect her to the January Halli of the TV tabloid shows. "What's your name?"

He seemed not to hear her. Instead of answering, he looked at the painting again. For whatever reason, it apparently had gotten under his skin because he said, "You think it's worth twelve hundred, do you?"

"Twenty-two hundred," she said loudly.

"There's no need to bellow at me, young woman. I've got the hearing of a twenty-year-old man."

"Oh," she said. "Selective."

He cut his eyes at her as if trying to decide whether his hearing was as good as he thought, but merely said, "Would you pay that for it?"

"Not on my salary," she said. "But if I were able to afford it, sure."

"As an investment?"

"No," she said. "I happen to love this painting. That's why it's featured so prominently in the gallery."

"What's to love about it?"

"The bold colors. The energy. It's called *Trail Ride,* so it makes me think of the pioneers and cowboys who settled Texas. Can you imagine what they must have endured to live here when it was still wilderness?"

"If they'd found the place full of tourists, they'd have kept going."

There was something about the cantankerous old man that appealed to her, even though he was nothing like Grandpa, who enjoyed nothing better than a good laugh.

"Would you like some more water, sir?" she asked.

He absently handed over the empty cup, his eyes on

the painting again, and said, "Who's responsible for that nonsense?"

"I'm afraid I don't know the artist's name," she said. "I can look it up for you."

"You do that," he said.

Before she went behind the screen that hid Hannah's desk, she gave him a full cup of water. He grunted something that might have been a thank-you. Then she went to the book where all the works were listed and found the entry for *Trail Ride*. She'd remembered the price correctly, and the artist's name was Wayne Plochman. But when she went around the partition to give that information to her visitor, all she found was an empty cup sitting on an empty chair.

She shook her head with exasperated amusement, picked up the cup, and threw it away. She had no idea how the old man had slipped out without making a sound. If she saw him again on the street sometime, she hoped she'd remember the name Wayne Plochman so she'd have a reason to strike up a conversation with him.

She went back to the desk, glanced at the computer, and for a moment considered checking online to see if she and Hud had become yesterday's news. Since it was the day of their non-wedding, she somehow doubted it. By the time the weekend was over, however, she was sure something new would replace them on the gossip circuit.

As she began filling the empty places left by all the items she'd sold with new pieces of pottery and additional paintings, she glanced again at *Trail Ride* and thought of her visitor. His ornery appeal was proof that Evan was right: She was falling in love with a town.

She searched her mind for a legal case that could serve as a warning to her, but came up with nothing. The best she could do was accept the probability that her feelings were intensified by knowing that she would eventually leave the town behind. Parting might be difficult at first, but once she was back on the road, on her way to L.A. and Hud, Coventry would become a pleasant memory, less tangible even than those photos that had sold so quickly.

Chapter 12

A couple of years after she graduated from high school, sometime between her jobs at Disneyland and Hollywood Park, Jandy lived with two roommates who were in their early thirties. They'd believed that having a decade on her gave them the right to impart wisdom and life lessons. This was particularly true anytime they had a few shots of tequila and played a game they called "Do Over."

Rather than taking offense, she always laughed at their examples of things they'd do over if they had the opportunity.

I wouldn't have dated that guy from William Morris who made me dress up as Captain Janeway and tell him how much I admired his manly phaser. . . .

I wouldn't have turned down the chance to go with my grandmother to Europe just because she's an old bitch. . . .

I wouldn't have dyed my hair green on the first St. Patrick's Day it was legal for me to drink. . . .

I would have agreed to go with my friend to lay down some backing vocals for a mystery band that ended up with a Rolling Stone cover and a Grammy. . . .

I wouldn't have told my boss to shove my annual review up his butt. . . .

I would have gone out with the securities analyst just so I could drive his Ferrari. . . .

Those stories always ended in drunken giggles and the conviction that it was okay for Jandy to make mistakes because they'd give her plenty of conversational material in years to come.

In fact, however, as people and jobs came and went, Jandy found there were rarely many things that she wanted to do over. She stuck by most of her decisions even when her mother and the voice of Pru let her know how disappointing she was.

By the end of her first Sunday in Coventry, she had a colossal headache and an overwhelming desire to do one thing over. If she'd known what she was getting into, she'd never have gone to the gallery, locked the doors, pulled the shades, made herself a pot of coffee, and used Hannah's computer to get online. It was her intention to create a new e-mail address and send festival photos to Elenore, but by the time she shut down the computer, those photos were the last thing on her mind.

January Halli had become the cause célèbre of the Internet. Her vanishing act was being debated on blogs. There were sensationalists: Was she alive? Was she dead? Had she been murdered? Who had killed her? There were also cynics: Was this all a ploy to get coverage because her fiancé was rumored to be slated as the central character of a new *CSI: L.A.*? Or wasn't he being cast as the man who'd break up Carrie and Big in a possible *Sex and the City* movie? Or would he be playing the love interest of Jennifer Aniston in a sitcom under development at NBC?

On YouTube, someone had interspersed the only

footage of her he could find—her walk on the red carpet at the Daytime Emmys—with scenes from *Runaway Bride*. YouTube also had clips of jokes about her from talk shows. She learned what a viral video was when the term was used for "Roman Halli-Day," a five-minute film consisting of quotes about her from various tabloid news shows juxtaposed with photos of people who were purported to be her in disguise. It was meant to be funny. Jandy wasn't amused.

It had been only six days since she'd told Hud she wanted to postpone their wedding. Regardless of the way the media portrayed her as part of a runaway bride phenomenon, she knew it was a story that would never have gotten any attention had Chandra not started spinning it almost as soon as it happened.

However dismaying it was to find that Hud's publicist had turned her into a headline and a punch line, that was nothing compared to the horror she experienced when she read people's comments about her on blogs, news stories, and videos. How was it possible that someone who'd never sought any kind of fame, whose life was boring, who'd never accomplished much but had managed to stay out of any kind of trouble, was suddenly the object of scorn, ridicule, pity, and lies?

On various sites, she saw herself described as a hooker, an opportunist, a transvestite, a drug addict, and the mother of at least two secret children by a number of actors and musicians whom she'd never even met. Every new accusation made her reach for her cell phone, then she remembered that the people who she should have been able to count on to protect and console her—Hud and her parents—were almost certainly the ones responsible for her blazing notoriety.

She felt angry, alone, and hurt. She didn't want to call

her grandpa because she hoped that he and Aunt Ruby were oblivious to most of the publicity. At the very least, they had no computer and couldn't read what people said about her on the Internet.

She wasn't tough enough to laugh off the lies and jokes. As she left the gallery, she couldn't stop herself from casting a cringing look around, waiting for paparazzi to leap from the shadows and take photos, or for microphones to come at her from every direction while bright lights illuminated all of her flaws.

Then she remembered that this was Coventry, where only a few people knew her as a girl named Jandy Taylor. She was more likely to be confronted by a friendly squirrel than an aggressive photographer.

She climbed the stairs to her apartment and, without undressing, crawled between the covers and lay in the dark. She was sure she slept at least a few hours, but when she finally got up, her appearance made it seem that she hadn't. After her shower, she put on makeup, covered her hair with a black bandanna, dressed in the drabbest of the clothes she'd bought at Target, found her largest pair of sunglasses, and walked to City Hall, where she followed signs to the police department.

A man in uniform behind a desk looked up and said, "Let's see. Lost dog? Towed car? Misplaced purse?"

She shook her head and said, "Is there a policeman here named Clay something?"

"Clay Gaines. But he's not on duty yet." He gave her a curious look. "Is there anything I can help you with?"

"Do you know when he'll be here? Could I wait for him?"

"Sure you can wait. As for when he's coming in, I can radio him right now if it's an emergency."

"It isn't an emergency," she said, even though it felt like one to her.

She declined his offer of a cup of coffee and sat down to wait. As a few people came in and out, bringing papers or just passing through on their way to somewhere else, she made herself as small and inconspicuous as she could.

The man behind the desk had a huge cinnamon roll on a plate. She watched as he used a plastic knife and fork to cut it, then ate one tiny piece at a time. She'd never seen anyone eat pastry that way. She wondered if it was a Texas custom or just his own quirky habit. If he was married, was that the kind of thing that his wife would see as endearing or annoying over time? It seemed like a pretty harmless thing—nothing like helping thrust your fiancée into an undeserved cyclone of publicity.

She didn't know if the officer had radioed Clay Gaines, but it was less than twenty minutes before a man who looked about forty was standing in front of her and introducing himself with his hand held out. She shook it and studied his face, noting that he had wide-set eyes and broad shoulders, a combination that made him seem at once kind and strong.

"I'm Jandy Taylor," she said softly. "Grayson Murray suggested that I talk to you about a problem I'm having. Can we talk somewhere that we won't be overheard?"

"Hey, Cesar, is anybody using the interview room?"

The man behind the desk gave Clay a disbelieving look and said, "Yeah, we had a sudden spike in crime last night. Somebody was looking in old lady Sullivan's window, and she shot him dead with her pellet gun. They're roughing her up in the interview room now."

"Everybody's a comedian," Clay muttered and motioned for Jandy to follow him.

He offered her coffee, which she again turned down,

then he poured himself a cup. He sat across from her as she told him her story, offering no comment and keeping his expression blank. When she finished, he sighed.

"People," he said, "are idiots. So your current residence is in Los Angeles County?"

"Yes. And if I knew any cops in L.A.—but I don't. I'm also leery of just randomly calling there. In the first place, they have better things to do than get involved in such a ridiculous situation. And then I worry that . . . Well, what if . . ."

"They leak to someone where you are?"

"It's so crazy," she said. "I'm nobody. Why does anyone care?"

"You do have a famous fiancé," he said.

"Have *you* ever heard of him?"

"Well, no," Clay admitted. "But I'm not much of a TV watcher. Especially not soaps. And by the way, those *CSI* shows aren't all that realistic."

She smiled weakly and said, "Hud's not really being considered for a show like that. I don't even know if there is such a show in the works. I know as little as anyone else about show business. I'm just a woman who didn't want a big wedding. I'm not a celebrity. And even though it seems crazy to think that anyone would hunt me down in Coventry, Texas, six days ago I would have told you that Googling my name wouldn't have gotten a single hit on the Internet. All I can think about is the way that real runaway bride got in trouble for lying about the details of her disappearance. I don't want to end up paying for an unnecessary police investigation. I also don't want to be bothered by tabloids."

"I don't know any cops in L.A.," Clay mused. He smiled. "But that's not a problem. I can get the information to the right person in L.A. and do my best to protect your privacy. I do need you to tell me one thing."

"Okay."

"Just in case your parents are sincerely worried about you"—when she started to protest, he held up a hand to silence her—"tell me something only you and your mother would know about. So she'll know it came from you."

Jandy thought it over for a few minutes and finally said, "When I was a kid, Laura Ingalls Wilder's book *The Long Winter* murdered my pet turtle, Martha."

"Sounds like a cold case," Clay said.

Jandy stared at him, wondering if he was making fun of her, and again saw only kindness in his eyes.

"I had Martha out while I was reading," she explained. "I got called away to do something, and when I came back, Martha was missing. I searched everywhere and couldn't find her. A few days later, I opened the book to see if the blizzard on the prairie had ever ended, and there was my poor turtle, dead between the pages."

"I'm sorry," Clay said.

"It was twelve years ago. I've recovered."

"You're very brave," he said, and even though this time she knew he was teasing her, it still didn't seem mean-spirited, and she laughed. He handed her a card and said, "If anyone gives you any trouble at all while you're in Coventry, you call me. Day or night. We may be a small town police force, but we take care of our guests."

"Thank you for helping me," she said. "At least it may stop the rumors that I've met an untimely end." She could see that he was suffering to keep himself from saying anything, so she said it for him. "Like Martha."

"I'm trying so hard to wait until you're gone."

"It's okay. I'm sure it would help Martha rest in peace knowing she brought hilarity to your Monday morning."

* * *

By Wednesday morning, most of the TV gossip shows had aired a clip of someone from the LAPD making a statement; he said that January Halli had contacted the department to say that she wasn't a victim of foul play and was out of state visiting friends. There were no new clips of her mother and no new statements from Hud or his publicist.

Over the next few days, Jandy forced herself not to do any more online searches and hoped that a lack of new information would make the story die a natural death. She was checking her voice mail periodically but not getting any messages from her mother, Hud, or Grandpa, so she turned off her cell phone and stopped taking it everywhere she went. It seemed like an umbilical cord connecting her to the life she was trying to take a break from.

She sent her photos from the first weekend of the Godiva Festival to Elenore Storey, which began an e-mail correspondence between them. Although she was at first a little uneasy to see photo credits to "Jandy Taylor" on Elenore's blog, she reminded herself that there was no longer a reason for anyone to be looking for her; and even if they were, it wouldn't occur to them to search for her by that name.

Just in case the story and her image were still familiar to Coventry's tourists, she didn't go to the square on the second weekend of the festival. It wasn't really a sacrifice to spend all her time over those two days in the gallery. She liked meeting the people who came in, and enjoyed their assumption that she was a Coventry native. If they asked questions about the town and the area and she didn't know the answers, she made quick calls to Evan. By the end of the weekend, she realized she needed him less because most tourists asked the same questions.

She closed the gallery early the next Tuesday afternoon and went by the grocery store, where a cashier directed her to a list of the ingredients needed for Jennifer Boone's pastry class. That night, she walked to Christ Church's kitchen, where she joined three young married couples, two middle-aged women saying they needed a night away from their husbands, five single women, and three single men.

She sensed at once that the single women were edgy about her presence, but they relaxed when she found ways to hint that she was already involved with someone. The cooking class was clearly their way to meet men, and Jandy enjoyed watching the interplay between the women as they competed for the men's attention. From time to time, she met Jennifer's eyes and realized that although she might be fifteen, Jennifer saw everything and was as amused as Jandy. Jennifer was also a good teacher. Jandy was able to give Evan, Tryphena, and Phylura a batch of mouthwateringly good peach pastry pillows on Wednesday morning.

"You know," she said to Evan when they had a moment alone, "I've been talking about how funny the singles were to watch, but I probably should have paid more attention to the married couples."

"How come?"

"I need to figure out more things that Hud and I can do together. He has too many interests, and I don't have enough. Now that I think about it, we've never tried to find something that both of us want to do and have time for."

"Do you think he'd take a cooking class with you?"

"Not a chance. That doesn't matter. I only went to last night's class because it was something to do and kept my mind off the runaway bride stuff. Plus I think Jennifer Boone's kind of adorable, and she invited me. I have no idea what Hud and I could do together, but there has to be something."

Evan was busy rearranging a display of hair products. His voice sounded a little distracted when he said, "I guess I never thought too much about a hobby to share with Grayson. The weird thing is, everything we do together ends up being fun, so it doesn't matter that I don't ride horses or know a lot about them. Or that shopping and having lunch with Keelie isn't Gray's idea of a great way to pass a day."

"I always have fun with Hud, too," Jandy said, but she knew her words sounded defensive even without Pru's saying so. It was a little weird how infrequently Pru was sounding off lately, but Jandy didn't intend to complain about it.

The topic was still nagging at her later when she locked the gallery. Instead of going back to her apartment over the salon, she walked aimlessly toward Revere Auto. It had only been a week or so since Robin began working on Grandpa's pickup, so she had no reason to check on things. It was just that the Reveres were among her few acquaintances in the vicinity other than Evan.

Dove was getting into her Mini Cooper when Jandy walked into the parking lot. She waved and said, "I'm on my way back to my apartment. Feel like a swim?"

"Yes!" Jandy called. "Can you give me about ten minutes? I need to grab my suit."

"I'll pick you up in front of Molly's. I'll be the one illegally parked," Dove said, looking as inscrutable as ever behind her granny sunglasses.

After Jandy's swim, she agreed to Dove's suggestion that they have a pizza delivered and watch a movie. Although they ate from the delivery box with a roll of paper towels on the floor between them, Dove did make one concession to fine dining by pouring their beers into glasses. They were both still stuffed and stretched out on the floor of the barren living room when *Sliding Doors* ended.

Jandy rolled over on her back, thinking about the parallel lives Gwyneth Paltrow's character, Helen, experienced after catching or not catching a train, and said, "Do you ever speculate about things like that?"

"The 'what if' factor?" Dove asked. When Jandy nodded, Dove said, "I'm not big on second-guessing myself. You?"

"Maybe sometimes. But I've never believed in things like fate or destiny. I think we shape our own lives. You know, instead of just existing at the whim of random events."

Dove nodded and said, "Shit happens, but really, wasn't Helen ultimately in control?" Her expression didn't change, but she sounded interested when she went on. "Sure one guy was a jerk, and one guy was nice. One life was a little classier, and the other was a little harder. But Helen made the best of things in both lives because it was her nature to rise above the bad stuff."

"Right," Jandy said. "I guess we could all stand to be a little more like Helen." She sighed. "You know what gets on my nerves about most romantic comedies? The myth of the soul mate."

"You don't think there's one right person for everyone?"

"Not really. People who keep looking for that one perfect person are missing the point."

"What's the point?" Dove asked.

"A real relationship is not something that just falls in

your lap when Mr. Wonderful shows up. Yeah, you should be attracted to each other. But a relationship is something you build over time. Together. It doesn't always start with a big moment and become some sweeping romance. It can be quieter and . . . I don't know. I'm not sure what I'm trying to say."

"That you're bored with your fiancé?"

"No! Not at all. But don't you ever wonder when you're watching a movie what happens to the couple after the credits roll? When she finds out he tells the same stupid jokes over and over? Or he has to deal with her when she's hormonal? Lots of times I never even make it to the end of a movie because I know it's going to come to some totally implausible, sappy conclusion. Do I sound cynical?"

"As if I'd judge you," Dove said. "Lots of times I haven't made it to the end of *dates* if I know how they'll turn out."

Jandy laughed and said, "I'm so glad I never have to go on another bad date. You haven't smoked the entire time I've been here. Did you quit?"

"I never smoke in my apartment. I like smoking in public because I enjoy the expressions on people's faces when they see me fire one up. I swear I could get less disapproval walking stark naked down Godiva Street than I do when I light a cigarette."

"Well, it is *Godiva* Street," Jandy said. "Though I don't think there'd be only one peeping Tom in your case."

Dove almost smiled, then said, "Smoking is one of the last legal things I can do that works people up. Now you know too much about me. What were we talking about?"

"Love, I guess." Jandy glanced at the print of the fountain on Dove's wall and asked, "Which is more real? To fall in love with a man who says that he can't think of anything more exciting than traveling the world looking for dandelion fountains with you? Or to be alone at one of those fountains, meet a stranger's eyes through the mist, fall in love, and live happily ever after?"

"Which man's rich?" Dove asked. "International flights aren't cheap."

Jandy laughed again and said, "It's possible you're even less of a romantic than I am."

As she lay in bed later, Jandy applied her thoughts about the movie to her relationship with Hud. They hadn't fallen madly in love on their first date. They hadn't had a whirlwind romance. And maybe they didn't have a lot of common interests. But as she'd said to Dove, those were things that developed over time. She and Hud had something solid. Marriage would take it to another level. Over the years, they'd grow together and find new ways to connect and relate to each other.

She felt a little smug at the way her vacation was allowing her to figure things out. Not having the elaborate wedding had been a good decision. Her head was clearer now, and she knew she and Hud should become husband and wife the way they wanted to, not according to anyone else's wishes.

In a way, she was getting a do-over. When she got back to California, she wouldn't let Chandra, her mother, or anyone else coerce her into doing anything she didn't want to do. Hud would be impressed at how determined she could be when her mind was made up. She was in control of her own future and needed no silly romantic illusions to make her happy.

Now that her plans for her love life were squared away, she could spend the rest of her time in Coventry figuring out how to fix her other problems. In all of L.A., there had to be people like those in Coventry, with whom she could feel a connection, the way she did with Evan and Grayson, or even Dove and Sam. She intended to get involved in something that would bring new people into her life. Hud could adapt himself to her friendships for a change. Maybe they could even find new friends together.

She also needed to think seriously about what she wanted to be other than a wife. It was time to get off the temp merry-go-round and find work that satisfied her.

I'm too sleepy to figure that out now, she thought. She rolled over to the other pillow and wondered if Hud was back from Hawaii. *That's another thing. I never really wanted to go to Hawaii anyway, even before Hud went with Sorel. I'll pick our next honeymoon destination. It won't be somewhere that Hud spends all his time being Mr. Sportsman while I languish around a pool. We'll embark on an adventure that's new for both of us. . . . Something. . . . Somewhere . . .*

"My parents' house," Sam said when he walked inside the gallery with Sue.

Jandy took a nail out of her mouth and said, "What about it?"

Instead of answering, Sam cocked an ear and said, "I must have some strange magical power to trigger Beatles songs wherever I go."

"I agree that you're a little strange, but I don't believe in magic. That's Hannah's *Abbey Road* CD I have on the sound system."

"Would you like for me to hang that painting for you?"

"Considering that we're listening to a song about a sociopath who uses a silver hammer as a weapon, I don't think so. Again, I ask: What about your parents' house?"

"I have to drop off something there, so I thought it would be a good afternoon for you to see the gardens at the Revere estate. And by estate, I mean regular old house in the middle of nowhere. But it does have at least a *zillion* varieties of flowers."

"Keep on mocking me, Utensil Man." She looked down into Sue's gaping mouth as the dog yawned and said, "Good grief. I think I just saw my birth father crossing a street in Japan."

"Nah, that's just my nephew's Shrek action figure that Sue ate this morning."

She held up a hand in a *stop* gesture and said, "Animation. Talking donkeys."

"You break my heart."

"Whatever. Is this painting straight?"

"Looks fine to me."

"Good. Let's get out of here."

She had to fight Sue for real estate in the front of Sam's Jeep, then she watched the countryside with interest as he drove in a direction she hadn't been before. He pointed to a turnoff that went to Grayson's ranch, and another that led to the Storey house. The road they were on took so many twists and turns that by the time he turned onto a gravel road, she felt completely disoriented. He stopped his Jeep at the top of a hill, made a sweeping gesture with his arm, and said, "There it lies before you. The Revere ancestral lands."

Jandy frowned and said, "If I thought for one minute that profits from Hog's garage provided anything like this, I would be so bitter."

"Who? What?"

"Never mind."

She drank in the sight of the rambling white house that reminded her of her grandpa's place. It was nothing fancy and adhered to no particular style of architecture. In fact, she was sure that it had begun as a modest home, with additions tacked on as its family expanded. But it had a big front porch, green shutters against white wood, window boxes dripping vines and color, and paths through endless flowers that led to a barn and to woods behind the house.

As Sam drove down the hill and into the driveway, Jandy said, "Are your parents back?"

"No, they're still in New Orleans."

"Do any of your sisters live here? It looks like someone's taking care of it."

"I do most of it," Sam said. "Although sometimes I can get Lark or Swan to help in the vegetable garden."

"You live here?"

"Temporarily. I'm sort of displaced from my current home," he added, sounding a little rueful.

Jobless and homeless, Pru said. *Hard to believe some lucky girl hasn't snatched him right off the market.*

"Shut up," Jandy muttered.

"It's not as bad as it sounds," Sam said. "I'm not one of those thirtysomething men living in his parents' basement and eating nothing but Cheetos."

"There is no basement," Jandy said.

"And I prefer barbecue Fritos." He grinned and got out of the truck with Sue close on his heels. He opened the back of his Jeep and began pulling out flats of plants.

"What are you planting?" Jandy asked.

"See the little rock wall on that drop over there?" he asked and pointed. When she nodded, he said, "Mom wants me to put zinnias along that border. Before I do that, how'd you like a tour of the house?"

"Yes, please."

As they went through the first floor, she wasn't sure if it was Sam's detailed descriptions or just the number of things she tried to quickly take in that left her tongue-tied. Sam said that the home's original builder had moved there from an area known as Texas Hill Country, and he'd used a lot of the building materials and ideas already familiar to him. She admired the long leaf pine floors set off by braided rugs, the bead board ceilings, and the Early American and Shaker furniture. Collections of pewter dishes and stoneware jugs were scattered throughout the house, and folk art tapestries and paintings hung on the walls.

"It's pretty simple," Sam said.

She wondered if he misunderstood her silence and said, "I think it's wonderful. It's so warm and—I guess cozy. Welcoming." She looked at him. "What I'm trying not to say is that it's completely different from my parents' house, which always felt like no one lived there."

He cut off whatever he'd been about to say when the phone rang. While he went into another room to answer it, she walked to a built-in bookcase in the den to look at family photos in plain black frames. She smiled at younger versions of the Revere kids mugging for the camera. She remembered women from the beauty shop talking about how they were always outdoors in bare feet. They did look a little bedraggled, but they also looked like happy, healthy kids. Even Dove, who apparently had smiled more often as a child.

"I'm sorry," Sam said when he came back. "Robin needs me to tow in a car from Mineral Wells. I'll drop you in Coventry on my way."

"Actually," Jandy said, "if you'll show me where the gardening tools are and exactly where your mother wants the zinnias planted, I'd be glad to do that while you're gone."

"I'm not going to stick you with a job like that."

"I used to work with Aunt Ruby in Grandpa's vegetable

garden all the time. I don't know why you always think I'm some helpless female."

"Trust me, I think you're anything but helpless." He looked her over. "I'm not sure you carry enough hand sanitizer in your purse for this job, and Texas dirt doesn't really go with your nail polish."

"That's what gloves are for. Lead me to your garden tools. Of course, if you don't trust me alone in the ancestral home, you can always leave Sue to keep me company."

"Good effort. The dog goes with me."

"It's a sign of insecurity when you won't let the object of your affection out of your sight."

"I was only thinking of *Manthey v. Donaldson,* when a man had to sue a friend to get his dog back."

"Hey, don't steal my material," Jandy said, wondering exactly how often she'd cited legal cases in their conversations. "You just made that up."

"I'll leave you in suspense. With a *zillion* zinnias, a shovel, and no dog."

Chapter 13

Jandy was pulling another bag of soil from the barn in the garden wagon when she came face-to-face with Swan. Both women shrieked, then started laughing.

"Sorry, but I wasn't expecting anyone to be here," Swan said. "Especially not my mother."

"Your mother?"

"The hat. The gloves. The trowel in your hand. From a distance, you could be mistaken for Mom. Of course, close up," Swan added hastily, "you don't look old enough to be *anybody's* mother."

"Nice try," Jandy said.

"What are you doing? Did you bury Sam under the rose arbor?"

"Yes. I'm taking out your family one at a time because I want this house."

"Then you should know that the attic door sticks, the city refuses to run septic lines this far, and the field mice are out of control in winter."

"Because you've shared this information, I'll let you live longer," Jandy said. "I coerced Sam into letting me plant the zinnias your mother wanted in one of the flower beds. Want to help?"

"Sure," Swan said and fell in line behind the yellow wagon.

Jandy continued to dig out a place for the plants, and Swan gently extracted them from the flats, put them in the ground, and packed soil around them. After a few minutes, Jandy said, "It's the weirdest thing. I feel like a black bird over on that fence is supervising our every move."

Swan looked up, nodded, and said, "That's the family crow."

Jandy thought Sam was lucky he hadn't been named Crow and said, "Your family has a pet crow?"

"I wouldn't call him a pet exactly. I found him a few months ago with a broken wing and helped him get well. Mom helped, too, by making sure none of the cats that wander through here got him while he was disabled."

"And he stuck around even after he could fly again?"

"Crows can be very affectionate when they're young, and they've bonded with humans. Come September, he'll hook up with other crows and forget all about us."

"It sounds like one of those summer romance songs," Jandy said. She stared at the crow for a few seconds. "He's definitely watching us."

"They say crows like shiny things and will steal them, though I've only seen this one steal food. He could be noticing the glint from the ring on the chain around your neck."

Jandy self-consciously checked her ring, which she'd worn hidden under her clothes since Evan had talked her into taking it off. "I didn't want to get my engagement ring dirty. It seems sad that you take care of the crow when he's a baby, then he just flies away."

"That's the natural thing he'd do with his crow mother,

isn't it?" Swan asked. "They have to leave the nest. In any case, it's against the law to keep a crow in captivity."

"It always makes me sad to see a bird in a cage," Jandy said. "Or any animals, actually. I never liked zoos. Did you always know you wanted to work with animals?"

"I guess," Swan said. They'd finished planting the zinnias, and she sat back, staring thoughtfully at the crow as it strutted up and down the fence, still keeping a close eye on them. "At various times, I think we all took in some kind of stray. If any animal that Sam or one of my sisters brought home was injured or sick, it usually ended up with me. I liked taking care of them. And just like with the crow, I knew not to get attached to anything that should be wild. I think that may have been why they turned them over to me, because they had a harder time letting animals go. Emotionally, I mean."

"What were some of the animals you took care of?"

"Lots of baby possums and raccoons, because their mothers were roadkill. Injured birds. One time an injured bat. I didn't think Dove was going to forgive me for that, because she doesn't like bats. At all. A few snakes. A fawn that was orphaned. A goat or two. The occasional rabbit. I suppose the biggest animal was an abused pony that Robin discovered on somebody's farm. We turned him over to animal control, and he lived out a happy and sheltered life with one of their staff members. Then there was Daisy, who got Sam in trouble."

Jandy had been watching the crow, and her head snapped around as she said, "Daisy? That's the dog who died?"

"Yeah, not long before Christmas last year. She was thirteen, which is a good age for a yellow lab. She'd been with Sam since he was eighteen. She got him kicked out of his dorm his freshman year of college."

It was amazing all the things she didn't know about Sam. During their conversations about the many classes she hadn't finished, he'd never mentioned that he went to college.

"How did she do that?"

"You have to understand the way we grew up. We didn't have a lot of things. What we had was a lot of freedom. We were outside all the time. We roamed the countryside. Knew every inch of the woods. We also had chores outside, like weeding the garden, taking care of the animals, cutting grass, whatever. But we played outside, too. Other than Saturday morning cartoons, I don't remember watching a lot of TV except sometimes at night for an hour or so. Occasionally we played together. Other times we went our separate ways. We all fished, hiked, and canoed as we got older. But even as kids, we got so much fresh air and exercise that there was no malingering at bedtime. Looking back, I think we were all pretty good kids, even if we didn't have a lot of rules and restrictions."

"It sounds idyllic," Jandy said.

"Truth is, we got in trouble from time to time, and we didn't always get along. We all have strong personalities. And our mom can be a bit inflexible at times. But, yeah, I think it was a great childhood. Anyway, when it was time for Sam to go to college, the last thing he wanted was to live in a dorm. All those rules and people confined in a small place looked like prison to him. He'd always worked—we all did—and since he had a scholarship, plus my parents were helping with his expenses, Sam thought he should be able to spend his own money on an apartment. Even sharing a house with a couple of friends sounded better to him than a dorm. But Mom was sure he'd just end up partying all the time, so he got stuck in a dorm. He was totally miserable. When he was home for

Christmas break, he was out walking one afternoon and he came across a group of boys with a puppy. He had no proof that their intentions were bad, but he talked them into handing her over."

"That was Daisy?"

"Uh-huh. He knew there was no way my parents would let him keep the puppy since he had to go back to school, so I kept her with me until he went back in January. For a while, he and his roommate were able to hide her. But puppies aren't known for being quiet and well behaved. They got caught, and Sam either had to get rid of Daisy or move out of the dorm."

Jandy shook her head and said, "And your parents let him get away with that?"

"This is where my mother's craziness kicks in. Have you heard stories about her?"

"Not really," Jandy said evasively.

"Which means you have, but you're too polite to repeat them. Mom was from Michigan and went to school at the University of Michigan. She was a hippie and involved in the antiwar movement. Her roommate was from Coventry, and she came home with her one summer. I think they planned to agitate or hoped to ferret out oppression in a small Texas town. Instead, she met my dad, fell head over heels, and never went back to Michigan."

"How romantic," Jandy said, trying to imagine the courtship of a radical activist and a small-town mechanic. It seemed so improbable.

"Lucky for Sam, old hippie habits die hard. When it was Sam versus my parents on the dorm issue, no way could Sam win. But when it was 'the establishment' trying to dictate the right of her son to have a dog, even though keeping a dog was against all the rules, Mom was on Sam's side. Good-bye dorm; hello off-campus housing."

"Lucky for Daisy," Jandy said.

"Sam and Daisy would have melted even the hardest heart, and no one's ever accused my mother of being heartless. For as long as he had her, Daisy and Sam were inseparable. She outlasted all his girlfriends. She was his best friend. This may sound awful, but when she got sick, I was glad she went fast and Sam didn't have to make any hard decisions. She died in her sleep. She's buried in one of Sam's favorite places in the woods."

Jandy looked toward the woods. It probably wouldn't be tactful to ask Sam to show her where Daisy was buried, but she felt a sudden longing to put flowers there, or sit there with Sue. Which was crazy. It wasn't like she had any connection to Daisy.

Swan went on. "Sam mourned Daisy so much that I wondered if he'd ever get another dog. Then Sue showed up, and she must have been the right one at the right time. Once Sam knows what he wants, nothing will stop him from trying to get it."

To keep Swan from guessing that she was on the brink of tears, Jandy began briskly putting the gardening supplies and tools in the wagon.

"I'll help with that," Swan said.

"I've got it," Jandy said. "Thanks for helping me plant."

"I like getting my hands in the dirt," Swan said.

"Me, too." She noticed Swan's dubious expression and said, "My grandpa farms and gardens, and I always liked helping him."

"I get the idea you're a lot tougher than you look," Swan said. "I might have prematurely written you off as a girly girl."

"Like Dove?" Jandy asked.

Swan snorted and said, "Don't kid yourself. Dove can kick ass if she needs to."

"I don't doubt it for a minute," Jandy said.

"Do you want a ride back to town?"

"No. I'll put this stuff away, then wait for Sam to get back. I want to see him admire the results of our labor. He thinks I'm a girly girl, too."

Swan just laughed and waved as she walked off. She turned back and yelled something, but Jandy wasn't sure she heard her correctly over the rattling wagon. It sounded like she said they should go out for a Guinness sometime. Jandy nodded and waved. It would be fun to share a beer and more conversation with Swan. Sam's sisters were so different from each other, but they were all likable.

She did a little weeding in the vegetable garden, then put the gardening tools away. After she cleaned up and drank some water inside the house, she fought the temptation to explore the rooms that Sam hadn't had a chance to show her. It seemed like an invasion of the Reveres' privacy, something she wasn't inclined to do after her recent experiences of feeling like her own privacy had been violated.

She sat on a rocker on the front porch for a few minutes, then decided to walk toward the woods.

You aren't *going to look for that dog's grave,* Pru said. *When did you turn into such a sentimental fool?*

"It's just too hot to sit on the porch when the sun is setting," Jandy defended herself. "I'm sure it'll be cooler in the woods. And you know, I really have to stop talking out loud to you. Even the birds are giving me strange looks."

A group of fifteen to twenty birds walking toward her from the woods did seem to be eyeing her with suspicion. She wasn't sure what they were. They looked like turkeys, but she didn't think turkeys were gray with white dots. As the distance between them narrowed, she began to wonder anxiously if they weren't actually planning to collide with her.

Like a game of chicken, she thought with a nervous giggle.

She was surely imagining that their pace had picked up. Just in case, she decided to step off the path and take another route toward the woods. When she did, the birds veered off course as if to intercept her.

"Oh, come on," she said. "They're not actually trying to head me off. That stupid crow made me paranoid, like I'm in the first few minutes of a Hitchcock movie."

She turned and walked a little faster in yet another direction. When she looked back over her shoulder, the birds were not only in pursuit, but they were gaining on her. She gave a little shriek and broke into a jog, slipping between the rails of a fence. She hoped she hadn't just traded a flock of birds for a bull, but since she didn't see any cattle in the pasture, she decided to take her chances.

When she turned back again, her mouth dropped open. The birds *were* chasing her. They'd followed her right into the pasture.

"Leave me alone," she begged. "I've done nothing to you! Do you want me to stop eating chicken? Join PETA? Boycott KFC?"

"Have no fear," Sam said, appearing beside her. "Your mighty steed is here. And your valiant canine defender, Super Sue! Hop on!"

She began to giggle hysterically. The birds had stopped to give Sue a perplexed look as the dog began sniffing at something in the pasture, fell down, and started rolling in it.

"What's her super power? Odor?" Jandy asked between laughs. As ordered, she climbed on Sam's back, holding on to his shoulders while he caught her legs before charging toward the birds.

"Excelsior!" he yelled.

"What does that even mean?" Jandy asked.

"I don't know. Isn't that what they always yell? What would you yell?"

"Scat?" she suggested.

"Scat!" Sam repeated at the birds.

They stared at him without blinking for a few seconds. When they finally realized that he didn't intend to stop trotting toward them with their intended victim on his back, they turned as a group and began a strange, rolling gait toward the barn. Jandy couldn't catch her breath from laughing.

Sue finally got up and trotted along as Sam ran the birds all the way back to a little shelter built against one side of the barn. With an assortment of clucks, chirps, and squawks that made Jandy think of what rusty bed springs must sound like, the birds went inside the shelter and began pecking at food that had been left for them. She slid off Sam's back so he could close the gate to the fenced-in area around the shelter.

"I can't believe I had to save you from a flock of guinea hens," he said.

"Is that what they are? I thought they were a variety of turkey. I won't even attempt to deny that this time, I needed rescuing. Those birds are thugs."

"Look how sweet they are," Sam disagreed as the hens began settling themselves down for the night on a specially built perch. "Don't call them thugs. Even Sue knew they meant you no harm."

"I saw a thirst for blood in their beady little eyes."

"They're good watch birds," Sam conceded. "Possibly Sue could learn something from them."

Jandy looked at Sue, who was nosing the dirt without a care in the world, and said, "I think those birds could eat her alive. Vicious, horrible creatures."

"Harmless little chickens," Sam disagreed.

"I know chickens. I grew up around chickens. They never paid any attention to me unless I was feeding them. These birds are a menace, and I can't imagine why anyone would have them. Do they lay eggs? Do you eat them?"

"Yes to both, but that's not why my mom keeps them. They eat the bugs and beetles that go after the vegetables and flowers in her gardens. And they don't eat the vegetables or damage her flowers." Sam looked at Sue and added, "They also think ticks are delicious. Which makes them not only useful to dogs and cats, but a barrier against Lyme disease."

"Whatever," Jandy said. She suddenly smacked her head and said, "Guineas! That's what she said." She noticed Sam's puzzled expression. "Swan was here. When she was leaving, I thought she yelled something about going out for a Guinness sometime. Now I think she must have been warning me to watch out for the guineas." She gave the birds a disdainful look. "If they eat all those bugs, why do you still feed them?"

"To entice them into the coop at night so the foxes and coyotes don't get them."

"I'd put my money on that bunch against a predator any day. Sue knows not to mess with them, and she was bred to be a fighter."

Since at that moment Sue seemed to be chasing her own tail, Sam made no comment. He began walking around the house, and Jandy followed.

"Nice job on the zinnias."

"Thanks. Swan ended up helping me, so we got done faster than I expected. I did a little weeding in the vegetable garden, too."

"With that kind of work ethic, I might have to persuade Robin to delay repairs on your pickup. This place never runs out of things that need doing."

"Whoever does the work around here, it's paid off." She looked at the flowers and inhaled their mingled scents. "It reminds me of my grandpa's place. If it were mine, I'd never want to leave it."

"It could be said," Sam mused, "that one advantage of leaving a place is the pleasure of coming back to it. I guess a home can be a little like a relationship that way. Probably the way you'll feel when you see your fiancé again."

"Is that a fountain or a bird bath?" Jandy asked, spying a basin among a profusion of bushes with tiny blue flowers.

"Fountain. I can turn it on if you want me to."

"Please?"

While Sam walked around the side of the house, Sue followed Jandy to the fountain. Beyond the bushes was a grassy area. Jandy sat on the grass, and Sue fell down next to her, nudging Jandy's hand for an ear rub. The fountain came on with a gurgle followed by a delicate splash.

"Nice," Jandy said when Sam joined them.

He nodded and stretched out on the grass, staring at the wash of colors the sunset was leaving across the sky. Neither of them spoke for a long time. Jandy wasn't sure what Sam was thinking about, but she was trying to remember the last time she'd felt so relaxed. She was also wondering if she should feel guilty because, contrary to Sam's conjecture, her reunion with Hud wasn't something she'd been thinking much about.

To keep herself from stressing out about the life she

was neglecting in California, she said, "I didn't realize until Swan mentioned it that you'd gone to college. You almost never talk about yourself."

"My life is an open book," Sam insisted. "Unlike *Morality for Morons,* which seems to have stayed mostly closed all across America."

"Did you major in English? Did you plan to be a writer?"

Sam snorted and said, "I picked an even less practical major: sociology."

"What do you do with a degree in sociology?"

"According to my parents, you stay in school forever."

"You haven't graduated?"

"I graduated. A couple of times."

"I don't get it," Jandy said, shifting so she could get Sue's head off her leg, which was falling asleep.

"I'm working on my dissertation," Sam said.

"You're getting your doctorate?" When Sam nodded, she said, "You don't have to look so apologetic about it. I don't expect everyone else to be an underachiever just because I am. Let me rephrase my question. What do you do with a doctorate in sociology?"

"I haven't decided. See? You and I aren't so different after all, except you've been making money while you're trying to figure it out, and I've only been spending money."

"You're patronizing me. What does a dissertation involve?"

"Doing a bunch of research, pulling together what's probably a lot of useless information, and trying to draw some conclusions from it. Boring, right?"

"It's vague."

"Let's hope my dissertation isn't."

"Seriously, I'm interested."

"Last fall and spring, I worked in the field. You know

the RV my parents took to New Orleans?" She nodded, and he went on. "That's actually been my home for a long time. When I'm in Coventry, there's a pad for it, with water and waste hookups, on the other side of those trees. Since I needed to do a lot of paperwork, I decided not to travel this summer. The timing worked out for my parents, too. I'll be back in the field in the fall, then I'll finish my writing in the spring."

"You live in an RV? That's so cool!"

He flashed his quick grin and said, "Spoken like someone who's never suffered a lack of closet space or a stopped-up black tank."

"I think it would be a blast to travel around in an RV. Where do you go? What kind of research are you doing?"

"Don't say I didn't warn you that it's boring," he said. "I'm observing the differences and similarities in behavior and demographics of random groups of people at attractions, whether natural or built."

She crossed her eyes, which made him laugh, and said, "What does that mean?"

"How people interact with each other or form groups at a natural attraction—Old Faithful, for example—versus a fabricated tourist spot like Disney World."

"Okay. Other than just the pleasure of traveling around under the guise of research, what's the purpose of gathering such information?"

"An environmentalist could use my findings to develop ways to minimize the impact of tourism on the environment. An urban developer could use the research to identify shifting population trends. The tourism industry could project earnings and identify investment opportunities. Someone in crime prevention could study habits of at-risk populations in unfamiliar environments. You, for example, would fall into that last category."

"Me? How?"

"I met you at a natural attraction—Texas Canyon in Arizona—where you did something you probably would never have done in an urban setting. You voluntarily got into a vehicle with a stranger and turned over control of your well-being to him."

"Hmmm. I'm not so sure I like being a research subject. Especially when I realize how stupid that makes me sound."

"But you weren't stupid. You weighed the risks and drew a conclusion. For example, I was kind to a dog. I didn't do or say anything to make you feel threatened. I didn't approach you; you approached me. My vehicle identified me as someone whose livelihood depends on towing people, not hurting them. And you decided I was gay. Those things all made leaving with me seem less hazardous than staying under the sun, inside a nonfunctioning vehicle, and worrying about unknowns—like who or what might become a threat to you the longer you left yourself vulnerable."

"When you put it that way . . ."

"Tell me this. Would you have gotten in the white Jeep with the guy who dropped Sue? Even before he abandoned her?"

"No."

"Why not?"

She thought it over and finally said, "He sped into the rest stop, which seemed a little reckless. He spit when he got out of his car, which was gross. And yeah, I guess you're right. He wasn't driving a tow truck. I'd have been more suspicious of him if approached me, even with an offer of help. Maybe I'm not as dumb as I feel right now."

"You're not dumb at all. Anyway, you're not a research subject. I have no objectivity where you're concerned."

She met his eyes and felt a blush move upward from her throat to her face. Although she was a little afraid of the answer, she said, "Why not?"

"Because you're not just some woman that I provided roadside assistance to."

"What am I?" she asked. She felt a little light-headed. She moved her hand to her throat, so he couldn't see evidence of her racing pulse. Her fingers touched the chain around her neck and slid down, catching her engagement ring. Its flash caught Sam's eye, and his expression became less intense.

"You're a fearless horseshoe opponent, a fighter of guinea hens, and Sue's best buddy," he said.

She wished she didn't understand her disappointment at his words, but she did. A little like Swan's crow, she'd been dancing on a fence, flirting with something that would end. She was infatuated with Sam's dog, his town, his sisters, his friends, his family home, and because of all that, with him. She didn't feel guilty on Hud's behalf, because she knew nothing would come of it. Nor did she have to worry about Sam. He'd grown up understanding that crows always returned to their own when it was time.

Swan's stories had made Jandy think the crow was lucky to be taken in by the Reveres until his broken wing was healed. She hadn't expected to sympathize with how the bird would feel on the day he finally flew away.

It's not a Disney crow, Pru reminded her, but Jandy wasn't so sure that mattered.

Chapter 14

Jandy closed the gallery early on her third Saturday in Coventry. She felt a little guilty, since she'd been busy all morning and could no doubt sell more in the afternoon. But she was hungry, had a headache and the cramps, and felt generally moody, so she took advantage of the first lull to pull the shades and lock the doors. She updated Hannah's ledgers, took a deep breath, then turned on her cell phone and hit speed dial.

"Hi," she said when Hud answered his phone. "I assume you're back in L.A."

"Yes," he said. "I've left you messages every day. Haven't you been getting them?"

"I haven't checked my messages. *You* were the one who told me to take a break from everything, so that's what I've done."

"I start taping again on Monday. I'd hoped to have a little time alone with you before then. Are you at your apartment?"

"No. I'm not in L.A."

After a pause, Hud said, "I'm still not sure where you are. You never told me."

"With my friend Sue."

"I don't know where Sue lives."

"Texas."

"You're in *Texas*?" She didn't answer, and he finally said, "It's just as well you haven't tried to go back to your apartment. Your landlord made your parents empty it."

"He *what*? Why? My lease goes through August."

"The neighbors complained about the news trucks."

"What news trucks?"

As if he hadn't heard her, he went on. "And also the rest of the disruption to the area."

"What kind of disruption?"

"Have you not been watching the news, Jane?"

"I just told you that I'm taking a break from everything. Didn't the whole mess go away when the LAPD let the world know I was alive?"

"No. If you wanted it to stop, you should have surfaced. Instead, your vanishing act turned everything up a notch or ten. You've got your own gawkers and wannabe stalkers keeping vigil outside your apartment, my building, your parents' house, and even your temp agency. Right now, I'd say you're probably the most famous invisible, non-celebrity I know. I'm sure if your weird following knew where your parents had your stuff stored, they'd be hanging out there, too."

She wanted to scream. Instead, she took another deep breath and said, "I can't believe this. It's so stupid."

"Then come home and put an end to your fifteen minutes of fame."

"I can't. I accepted a temp job; it's not over yet. You know, none of this would be happening if it weren't for your publicist. Let her fix it."

"She works for me, not you. That's keeping her a little

busy right now. Especially because she has to distance me from you in the public's mind."

Jandy rubbed her hand over her aching forehead and said, "But the only reason I was ever news, no matter how stupid, is because of you. And she's the one who made that happen."

"The runaway bride thing got the focus on me, but then it shifted to you. We have to fix that. Have you ever heard of Eddie Ringer?"

"No."

"He's a character in a series of detective novels set in Chicago. There's a movie in development. Rumor has it that I'm their first choice for Eddie Ringer. And get this. They want Julia Roberts to play against type as Eddie's hard-assed boss, and Scarlett Johansson would play Eddie's partner and potential love interest. This is huge, Jane. It could be my Danny Ocean or Jason Bourne role. To go from *Sweet Seasons* to film—that would be amazing. Chandra says the best thing we can do now is get my personal drama out of the news and emphasize my acting skills."

"Does Chandra have a plan for that?"

"Yes," he said, sounding relieved that she'd asked. "You come back. We get some stories out there about how we're working things out. We reconcile, have the wedding, and whenever I make public appearances, you'll be at my side showing the world how happy we are. And don't worry. Chandra has convinced your mother that a splashy wedding has now become a bad idea. Our ceremony will be private. Although Chandra has negotiated a lucrative deal with *People* for exclusive photos when the wedding takes place."

"I see."

"Everybody wins. You get the small wedding you wanted. Instead of getting publicity as a jilted groom or a suspect in your mysterious disappearance, I take my career in a new direction that smells like success. And the public is finally satisfied that instead of being the victim of foul play or a runaway bride, you're my blissfully happy wife."

"And all this depends on my coming back to L.A. and going along with it."

"That's a weird way to put it. It was your decision to postpone the wedding so you could plan a smaller one. This is what you wanted. I guess if you've changed your mind and you want the big wedding now—"

"No, I definitely don't want that. I'll do it your way. Or Chandra's. But not for another couple of weeks."

"I don't get it. What kind of job is so important that you'd keep this media insanity going? Seriously, Jane, when have you ever cared about any job this much? You know how much my career means to me and how hard I've worked. Is what you're doing as important to you? This is nuts."

"You're right," Jandy said. "I'd never do anything to hold you back or interfere with your success. Let me talk to some people and see what I can do about getting back to L.A. sooner."

A couple of men in coveralls were working at Revere Auto when Jandy arrived. She didn't recognize them, and one of them told her that Robin had gone to the square to check out what was happening at the festival. She at least had the satisfaction of seeing Grandpa's pickup elevated on a lift with parts spread out underneath it. If Robin was almost finished repairing it, she could be home within three or four days. The thought didn't really improve her mood, but at least Hud would be satisfied.

She trudged to the square, determined to find Robin

so she could encourage her to finish the job as quickly as possible. She was in such a bad mood that, unlike the other times she'd walked around the festival booths, she paid little attention to the tourists or the vendors. Her stomach was growling. She wanted to grab something to eat, go to her apartment, and curl up in bed with a heating pad on her back, reading her Jennifer Weiner novel until she fell asleep.

She finally found Robin among a group of children watching two jugglers. Robin's face was transformed by her customary big smile when she saw Jandy.

"I don't mean to bother you," Jandy said, "but it seems I need to leave earlier than I originally thought. I was wondering when the pickup would be ready for me to get back on the road?"

Robin's face fell, and she said, "The last part I ordered shipped out yesterday. I didn't realize you might need your truck sooner, so I had it shipped ground. It might not be here before Friday." When she saw Jandy's frustrated expression, she added, "Once it's here, I'll only need about three hours to finish. You could be on the road by Saturday morning for sure. Will another week be a problem?"

"I guess I don't have any choice," Jandy said. "I'm not all that eager to leave, but I'm messing up someone else's plans."

She felt like she was on the verge of tears, and Robin reached out to pat her back and say, "You look all done in. Are you sick?"

"Not really. I'm just having one of those days."

"Have you eaten?"

"I had half a muffin at breakfast."

"Let's go over to Lady's Ryde Restaurant. My treat."

"It's bound to be full of tourists—"

"Don't worry about that. Mrs. Cherry will find a place

for us. I fix her cars, and my mother's always giving her produce from the garden."

Jandy shrugged and allowed Robin to lead her down the street to the restaurant. She'd never been there, but she'd heard good things about it. She wasn't sure if it was the prospect of a nourishing meal or Robin's buoyant personality, but she was already feeling better, in spite of the bad news she'd have to give Hud later.

The lighting inside Lady's Ryde was subdued, even with candles flickering on every table. It took Jandy's eyes a few minutes to adjust, then she looked around with admiration. The walls were covered with murals featuring a radiant version of Lady Godiva. On one wall, she was obviously pleading with her opulently dressed husband on behalf of the taxpayers of Coventry, England. She'd been painted wearing a green velvet dress that set off her strawberry blond hair.

Other murals depicted her actual ride. Like the contestants in the parade that had opened the Godiva Festival, she was riding a white horse with ribbons in its mane. Her long hair was down and flowing and was artfully arranged to preserve her modesty. A final painting showed her in a gold gown being cheered by a crowd of townspeople as her husband held some kind of rolled parchment, obviously a declaration lowering their taxes.

"These paintings are wonderful," Jandy murmured.

"Mr. Plochman did them about thirty years ago," Robin said. "Last year, the murals were cleaned and the colors touched up a little. They look better than they did the whole time I was growing up."

"Plochman? Wayne Plochman?" When Robin nodded, Jandy said, "We have a painting by him at the gallery, but it's nothing like this."

"Yeah, these were done when he was young," Robin said. "Aren't his paintings more abstract now?"

"The one at Hannah's is. I love it, but I love these, too."

A plump woman came toward them with a big smile and said, "Hello, Robin. We're just clearing your favorite table for you."

"Thank you, Mrs. Cherry. Have you met Jandy Taylor?"

Mrs. Cherry beamed at Jandy and said, "I've heard about you. You're the one who takes the pictures Elenore Storey puts on her blog. You two girls sit right over here. I'll be glad to give you a menu, but I have to tell you that you'd be crazy not to order the chicken pot pie. My pastry chef is the best in all of Texas."

"That sounds wonderful," Jandy said. After they sat down, she looked at Robin. "I'm going to miss Coventry's comfort food when I leave. I think I've gained five pounds since I got here. Of course, if I hadn't been doing so much walking, not to mention swimming at Dove's apartment, it would be ten pounds. I don't know if I'll still be able to get into my wedding gown."

"It's so weird to think that you have a whole life that I've never heard you talk about," Robin said. "What does your fiancé do?"

"He's kind of a doctor," Jandy said vaguely, pretending to be engrossed by the dessert menu. It wasn't really a lie. Hud played a doctor on *Sweet Seasons*.

"Kind of a doctor," Robin repeated. "Like Sam. Although my parents are sure he's never going to finish school. They always say they couldn't get the rest of us in college, and they can't get Sam out of it."

"I think Sam's research sounds interesting, though," Jandy said.

She paused while salads were set in front of them by a waiter who couldn't have been more than sixteen. He was covered in freckles and his ears stuck out. He looked like he'd just stepped out of a Norman Rockwell painting, and Jandy couldn't stop herself from grinning at him. He turned beet red and almost tripped over his own feet when he walked away.

"I think you've made another conquest," Robin said.

"I doubt that. He probably thinks I'm an old woman. And what do you mean, another conquest? It's not like I have men falling at my feet."

It was Robin's turn to blush, and she said, "I just meant—I don't know what I meant. Anyway, what were you saying about Sam's research?"

"You know," Jandy said slowly, "sometimes I get the idea that the Revere girls think something's going on between Sam and me. You know there isn't, right? I'm engaged. I wouldn't be disloyal to my fiancé, and I definitely wouldn't lead Sam on."

"Oh, I never meant to imply that," Robin said, looking stricken. "You've never given any of us the impression . . . It's just that Sam . . . You know what? Let's talk about something else. Your truck. While I had everything taken apart, I realized that all you needed to make your air conditioner and heater work was a new fan. I actually had one in stock that came off a wrecked truck, so I replaced yours."

"Thank you," Jandy said. "That'll make my drive back home a lot more comfortable. Just add it to my tab."

"I'm not charging you for it. The fan wasn't doing me any good and didn't cost me anything. Plus I didn't get your okay."

"I'll pay for your labor," Jandy insisted.

"Don't worry about it, really. It's no big deal."

"You're not like any mechanic I've ever met. How old were you when you started working on cars?"

"I hung out in the garage from the time I was just a

little thing," Robin said. "I was such a daddy's girl. When I graduated from high school, my parents made me go to college. I got awful grades, and I was miserable. I didn't have the nerve to tell them I just wanted to work at Revere Auto until I got my fortune told by Madame Vorjean."

"You what?"

"Have you seen her tent? She's on what Sam calls Charlatan Row. It's where all the fortune-tellers, tarot card readers, palm readers, witches, and wizards are. You'd think with all the Bible thumpers in Texas that the new agers' presence would be a problem, but every year theirs are some of the most popular booths at the festival."

"I don't believe in psychics and fortune-tellers," Jandy said. "You're not honestly saying that you do, are you?"

"All I know is that Madame Vorjean told me to stop trying to be something I wasn't. So I finally told Daddy that all I wanted to do was work with him at the garage. And look at me today."

Jandy managed not to roll her eyes, saying only, "A good career counselor could have told you the same thing."

"But they didn't. Everybody always acted like I had to go to college. Madame Vorjean was the first person who told me to be what I wanted to be."

"She told you to be a mechanic?"

"Well, no—"

"Exactly," Jandy said. "So-called psychics tell you the most generic things, and you're the one who applies their words to your life. Someone else might have heard the same advice and decided to be an astronaut. Or a homeowner. Or a mother. Whatever it was they wanted to be in the first place. Those frauds don't really tell you anything specific because it's all a bunch of hogwash."

Robin flashed her irrepressible smile and said, "I

think you should let Madame Vorjean tell your fortune. Then you can prove she's a fake."

"That's backward," Jandy said. "I don't have to prove she's a fake. She has to prove that she's not."

"So you'll do it?"

"Of course not. I'm not giving my money to some fake psychic."

"I'll pay for it."

"No thanks."

"You're scared of her, aren't you?" Robin asked.

"I've never even seen her! That's like asking me if I'm scared of the Loch Ness Monster."

"You believe in Nessie, but you don't believe someone can tell your fortune?"

Jandy squinted at Robin and said, "If this is the way you argue, it's no wonder your father handed over the keys to the garage. You wore him out."

"At least you don't have a business to lose. Just a few minutes of your time. Come on. Even if you don't believe in it, do it for fun."

"Fine," Jandy said. "I'll see your Madame Vorjean. But *only* to get you out of my hair."

As they wandered through booths on the square later, Jandy stopped to watch a craftsman shape a dragon out of spun glass.

"Stop stalling," Robin said. "Madame Vorjean may have a good fortune for you."

"Yeah? Well, I'm not buying it."

The glass spinner overheard her and said, "It's not finished anyway. Perhaps one of the finished dragons would suit you."

Jandy gave Robin an abashed look, and Robin giggled.

The two of them walked to the other side of the booth where the finished glass pieces were displayed.

Robin looked at a group of hanging dragons. "What about the purple one?"

"I'm not much of a purple person," Jandy said. "Purple's not a redhead's color."

"Really?" Robin stared at Jandy's hair. "I guess I never thought much about it."

"Because you're a blonde. Blondes can wear anything."

"I can't wear yellow," Robin disagreed. "Not that I ever do. What colors *can* you wear?"

"Browns. Earth tones. Moss and olive greens. It's very boring."

"Here's a dragon with green wings," Robin said.

"The problem is," Jandy whispered, "I never wanted a dragon at all."

"I knew you were just trying to weasel out of seeing Madame Vorjean," Robin said. She gripped Jandy's arm and slowly backed them away from the booth. Once they were out of the glass spinner's sight, Robin began walking purposefully toward another area of the square.

"Seriously, I'm not stalling. I'm stuffed with chicken pot pie. If you don't slow down, I'll get a cramp."

"You are what you eat," Robin said, but she slowed down. "I guess you can tell by looking at me that I don't know much about colors and fashion. That may be one reason why I never get a date. I look like a girl who's better at fixing a man's carburetor than dressing up for him." She looked at Jandy's crisp white blouse and khaki shorts. "You're like Lark. Feminine and classy."

"Oh, come on," Jandy said. "I got these clothes at Target. Anyway, I think a man should appreciate you for exactly who you are, whether you're in jeans and a football jersey, a dress, or in coveralls lying on one of those rolley things under a pickup truck."

"Rolley things," Robin said and giggled. "I think you mean a creeper."

"Sam would probably call it a lazy Susan," Jandy said. "My point is, the right man will love you for who you are."

"Is that the way your fiancé is?" Robin asked. After a long silence from Jandy followed, she said, "It's none of my business."

"Actually," Jandy said slowly, "it bothers me that I didn't say yes as soon as you asked the question. It's not that he's ever tried to change me. Or even criticized me. He's not like that. But I'm starting to wonder if he knows the real me. It's only been lately that I've started feeling like I know myself. Which is way more information than you wanted. Sorry."

"No, don't be sorry," Robin said. She seemed about to say something else, then she stopped short and stared at a booth with black velvet drapes pulled shut and said, "Look! This is Madame Vorjean's spot."

Jandy scrutinized the booth, trying to figure out how Robin knew. Before she could ask questions, the curtain was pulled back by a ring-laden hand.

"Come in. Sit down."

At least the fortune-teller's voice wasn't full of omens. She sounded normal. Nor was she wearing a turban or lots of shawls with fringe. As Madame Vorjean pulled the curtains shut and lit more candles, Jandy studied her. She was wearing a sleeveless batik dress with a scooped neck on a body that could carry it off. The dress's light blues, greens, and plums provided an upbeat contrast to the dark velvet draperies inside the booth. Madame Vorjean's hair reminded her a little of Dove's: lots of blond in a messily attractive pile on top of her head.

An electric fan was situated so that it cooled Jandy but didn't blow out the flickering candles. It was hardly the dark, mysterious place she'd expected, despite the candles and black velvet.

Madame Vorjean sat across from Jandy and said, "Give me your hands."

Jandy placed her hands, palm to palm, against Madame Vorjean's, and before she knew it, her bad habit reasserted itself, and she thought of *Langley v. Stewart* (Los Angeles County Superior Court). Langley claimed that "Bubbles" Stewart, Psychic to the Small Business Owners, had bilked him out of thousands of dollars by cracking open eggs to figure out who was embezzling money from Langley Roofing and Construction.

Madame Vorjean smiled and said, "There isn't anything wrong with being skeptical, dear. There's absolutely nothing I can tell you about your situation that you don't already know."

"I tried to tell Robin that, but she insisted that I see you. Since you have no advice for me—"

"I didn't say that. Maybe you'll listen to me, because you're certainly not listening to yourself. Sometimes if you hear the truth in someone else's voice, you're more likely to pay attention. Much like the voices we hear inside our heads." When Jandy jerked her hands away, Madame Vorjean smiled and said, "We *all* have them. Usually more than one. We just have to find the one who tells us the highest truth."

Silence fell between them. Jandy was determined not to give the woman a single bit of information that would allow her to make up some bogus predictions.

"You're not wearing an important piece of your jewelry," Madame Vorjean finally said, while lightly tapping Jandy's ring finger. "It's a pity. I can often pick up a lot of information by holding a person's ring or necklace. No matter. You lost something when you were very young. Someone who loves you will return it to you, but the gift comes at a price. Only you can decide if the price is right."

Great, Jandy thought. *My life has now become a game show. Come on down!*

"You'll need to be brave enough to listen to the right voice," Madame Vorjean was saying. She smiled and patted Jandy's hand in a gesture of dismissal.

"That's it? That's the big truth you have to tell me?"

Madame Vorjean gave her another enigmatic smile, and Jandy wanted to kick herself for asking. It made her sound like the price she was willing to pay was belief in the whole fortune telling thing. But she had no faith whatsoever in Madame Vorjean's ability to intuit truths about her life. She was just creeped out because the woman seemed to know about the voice of Pru and about her engagement ring. But as Madame Vorjean herself had said, everyone had inner voices. And everyone owned jewelry, so the fact that Jandy wasn't wearing any was noticeable, especially to someone like Madame Vorjean, who was dripping with rings and bracelets.

If the fortune-teller had said, *Put your engagement ring back on and stop trying to fool people about who you are,* that would have shown she was psychic. Or that she watched tabloid TV shows.

"What happened?" Robin asked eagerly when Jandy walked out and blinked at the sunlight. "Did she tell you anything interesting?"

"Yes," Jandy said. "I'm now more certain than ever that I know exactly who was stealing money from Langley Roofing and Construction."

"I don't get it," Robin said with a blank look.

"Maybe not, but Bubbles sure did," Jandy said.

* * *

Jandy was relieved that night when Hud didn't answer his phone and she could leave a message. She chose her words carefully to make him feel like she was giving him a lot of information, while still keeping him from being able to tell Chandra or anyone else where she was.

"I tried to arrange to get back sooner, but there's something I haven't told you. I sold my SUV to that man in Palm Springs, and I drove one of Grandpa's pickups to Texas. I had a little problem with the truck, and it can't be repaired before next weekend. Since I committed myself to the temp job through the end of June anyway, I may as well finish. If nothing else goes wrong, I'll see you a week from Tuesday."

Later, when she was getting ready for bed, she took the chain from around her neck and held the diamond ring to her eyes, moving it around. She was mesmerized by the way its facets caught the light. Suddenly her own words, the words that she'd thought should have come from Madame Vorjean, came back to her: *Stop trying to fool people about who you are.*

"It doesn't matter," she said out loud. "Being Jandy Taylor instead of Jane Halli doesn't affect anyone in Coventry one way or another. Who cares if I'm fooling them? It's a lot more disturbing that I'm sitting alone in a borrowed apartment talking to myself. That's something to worry about."

She turned on the clock radio next to the bed. It was tuned to an oldies station, and she gave the radio a smug smile and said, "If there was such a thing as magic or fate or weird portents, you'd have been playing a Beatles song instead of 'Wooly Bully.' No deep, significant message there. And now I'm talking to the radio."

She put her engagement ring away and applied herself to practical tasks like brushing her teeth, putting on moisturizer, and dragging Jennifer Weiner's novel to bed with her. But she stared at the words without comprehension as she mulled over the consequences of misleading people. Maybe it wasn't deceiving the good citizens of Coventry that she should be worried about. Maybe it was the people she knew in California with whom she'd been less than honest.

She thought about her conversation with Robin. Was it possible that Hud didn't really know her? Had there been some part of her that understood that even before she postponed her wedding and took off in Grandpa's truck? Driving away had seemed random, but maybe she'd instinctively known she needed a little journey to find . . . What?

There's absolutely nothing I can tell you about your situation that you don't already know. You'll need to be brave enough to listen to the right voice.

She slammed her hand down on the radio's OFF switch when it began to blare Gary Lewis and the Playboys' "This Diamond Ring."

"Oh, brother," she muttered out loud before Pru had the chance to say it inside her head. "When did you become so pathetically susceptible to such ridiculous things?"

Chapter 15

During her time in Coventry, Jandy had quickly made one discovery. Monday was her least favorite day of the week. Things were always slow at the Herren Gallery because many of the tourists from the weekend were leaving town, and a new group was just arriving. Visiting an art gallery wouldn't be on their agenda until after they'd enjoyed some of the other activities and sights in the area.

In addition to her own slow day, Molly's Beauty Shop was closed on Mondays, and Evan usually didn't come into town from the ranch. Any other day, if Jandy got bored or things were slow in the gallery, she could walk across the street and have an entertaining visit with Tryphena and Phylura, both of whom could chatter without ever committing a hair-don't on their clients. She loved listening to the Wicks sisters volley good-natured barbs at each other. Even on busy days, when she couldn't pass the time in the beauty shop, she and Evan stole moments to visit and gossip over a cup of coffee or a hurried lunch.

On Tuesday evenings, she had Jennifer Boone's cooking class to look forward to. And several afternoons a week, she went swimming at Dove's. But for some reason, there never seemed to be much to do on Mondays once she'd downloaded photos from her camera to the gallery computer and e-mailed them to Rook Drugs for printing. The process wasn't exciting, but staying on top of it meant that when she went back to L.A., she'd be able to easily access all her memories of this time in her life.

This particular Monday, however, held a certain poignancy for her. It was her last one in Coventry. By next Monday she would be on the road. She intended to savor each day of her final week in the town, because she couldn't imagine any circumstances that would allow her to come back in the future. The area's natural attractions wouldn't be exciting enough for Hud, and even if he agreed that the town was charming, it wouldn't satisfy his passion for adventure the way his vacations usually did.

After she showered and dressed, she decided that since she didn't have any photos in her camera and didn't need the computer, she wouldn't open the gallery at all. Dove certainly wouldn't care. She'd made it clear that under Jandy's oversight, the gallery had already exceeded anyone's expectations for the month of June.

Taking her camera with her when she left the apartment, Jandy made her first stop at Independent Seven Toys. She was just in time to join a group touring the facility. Although she wasn't allowed to shoot pictures, she enjoyed seeing the design areas and the actual plant where the Look Back Girls were manufactured. When she got back to California, she planned to start a collection, buying each of the dolls as it was released.

Afterward, she took a stroll through some of the historical homes that had been built in the 1800s when wool was manufactured on the site. Somewhere along the way, she realized how odd it was that she wasn't hearing Pru's voice disparaging everything she was doing. Instead, she frequently found herself considering what Hud would think of it all, and her conclusion was disappointing. He would be bored out of his mind.

She finally bought a sandwich and some chips and sat at the Godiva Fountain to think things over. If Hud's career took off the way he and Chandra wanted it to, was she really ready to be Mrs. Movie Star? She felt uncomfortable in the limelight, and she certainly didn't want to spend the beginning of their marriage being publicized as the runaway bride who came crawling back to her groom.

She assured herself that she was overestimating her importance. Her return would be a non-story because there was nothing salacious about it. Once they were married, she'd have little public appeal as merely the wife of Hudson Blake. Celebrity spouses were nonentities unless they were themselves celebrities. Not that she found the idea of being a nonentity particularly comforting, either.

Stop, she ordered herself. *You've already committed yourself to finding a profession and some friends when you go back to L.A., and you'll undoubtedly have plenty of time to fill if Hud has the kind of success that Chandra's predicting.*

She sighed, thinking that was just what every bride wanted. A new husband who wouldn't be around. A relationship that had to be fit into *his* free time. Which brought her right back to the uncertain state of mind that had caused her to postpone her wedding in the first place.

She walked to a trash can and threw away her unfinished lunch. As she did so, she spotted Tryphena and Phylura sitting on a distant bench, their heads close together as if they were trying not to be overheard. It was a silly assumption on her part, since the square was noisy with families and vendors, and anyone who passed near them would be within range of their voices for only a few seconds.

Still, they did look conspiratorial, and Jandy was intrigued. She wouldn't really be snooping if she just stopped by to say hello. It wasn't as if she intended to lurk unnoticed and eavesdrop on their conversation.

The sisters glanced up as she approached them and immediately smoothed their faces into bland expressions that could have come straight from lessons with Dove. That made Jandy even more suspicious, but her voice was cheery when she said, "Isn't it a gorgeous day to be out and about? I'm hoping to get a lot of good photos today. What are you two up to?"

"Up to? We were just—"

"Talking about the dog show," Tryphena interrupted Phylura. "Do you know if Sam's going to enter Sue?"

"If he is, he hasn't said anything to me," Jandy said. "Of course, it isn't as if we talk every day." She was dismayed by how guilty she sounded. Even if she and Sam did talk every day, it wasn't like that was something she needed to hide.

Before she could continue in a less defensive tone, Isaac Phillips, the proprietor of the hardware store, stopped at the bench and said, "Are you trying to solve the mystery, too?"

"What mystery?" Jandy asked, noticing the way Phylura's face went blank again, while Tryphena's turned a deep red.

"We've lost our dragon," Isaac said.

"Dragon? You mean Wyndmere?"

"Yep. She vanished in the dead of night. Everyone thinks she escaped. Funny thing is, if she did, she managed to turn around and close the gate of her stall behind her. That's one talented longhorn."

"Maybe Doc Boone found something wrong with her and took her to his clinic," Tryphena said.

"Nope. He's looking for her, too."

"I hope no one mistreats her," Jandy said, feeling anxious for the longhorn.

"Maybe it's just a prank," Phylura suggested. "I'm sure she'll be back safe and sound before you know it."

"My grandbaby Rochelle has talked about nothing except the rescue of the fairy princess from the dragon," Isaac said. "Bound to be a lot of disappointed kids on Saturday morning if Wyndmere doesn't turn up. Not to mention a very annoyed owner."

"Maybe they can find another longhorn to play the part of the dragon," Jandy suggested.

Isaac laughed and said, "If only the festival organizers had thought to have an understudy waiting in the wings all these years. I'd better be getting back to the store. You ladies have a good day!"

Jandy watched him walk away, then she turned back in time to see Phylura and Tryphena exchange a worried glance. She narrowed her eyes and said, "You two know something, don't you?"

"About what?" Tryphena asked.

Before Jandy could say anything, Phylura said, "I wonder if the dragon head disappeared, too? I don't see why another longhorn couldn't take Wyndmere's place. The cow is led into everything she does by handlers dressed as knights. It's not like she's actually acting or even knows what she's doing."

"Why don't we just call the local Rent-A-Longhorn and ask for one?" Tryphena asked.

"Maybe you should, since it's *your*—" Phylura broke off with a wary look at Jandy.

"I knew it!" Jandy said. "You think Tryphena's son

had something to do with Wyndmere's disappearance, don't you?"

"Of course not," Tryphena said with a sniff. "Fiji knows better than to get in trouble again. He's already spending every Saturday doing community service. The flower beds around City Hall and Mayor Murray's house have never looked so good. I'm sure that's how he got all that mud on his sneakers."

"Are you kidding yourself or just trying to fool Jandy?" Phylura asked. "Maybe she could help us solve the mystery. In those detective shows, it's always the stranger who comes to town who figures things out."

"I'd love to help," Jandy said. "Although in movies, doesn't the new woman in town usually end up dead?"

"Only if she's a hussy," Phylura assured her. "You're not a hussy, are you? Anyway, in all these years, Fiji and Jay Jay haven't killed anyone. Yet."

"You don't even know they had anything to do with this!" Tryphena said.

"Phena, you know darn well it's just a matter of time until the entire town has the same suspicions we do. That's why Isaac Phillips was just running his mouth to us. He already suspects Fiji and Jay Jay. Who else would do something so silly as to kidnap Wyndmere?"

"I don't know. Maybe this is just the first strike from a ring of cattle rustlers."

"Somebody better call Wyatt Earp," Phylura said, and Jandy giggled. "Here's the problem, Jandy. We know Jay Jay's at work, and Fiji's helping pick up litter out on the highway. I'm sure wherever they have Wyndmere, they're checking up on her in the evenings. Phena and I were going to split up, and each of us tail one of them. But that's a little hard to do when they know our cars."

"And I don't have a car," Jandy said. "If only my pickup had already been repaired."

"See? There's no way she can help us, and now she knows too much."

"I guess *I* have to kill you," Phylura said.

"You can't. I'm not a hussy," Jandy said. "What if I borrowed Dove's car?"

"Speaking of hussies?"

"Oh, my God, no! I didn't mean that at all."

"I'm just teasing you. But I think the boys might notice that little tin can following them all over the place."

"Would you two stop messing around?" Tryphena demanded. "We need a plan."

"You know," Jandy said thoughtfully, "it seems to me that Robin's got some responsibility here. She's taking so long to fix my truck that she should at least offer me a loaner. Especially for a good cause."

Both women gasped, and Tryphena said, "You can't tell Robin what we're up to! That's all we need is the Revere family thinking an animal's in peril. You know how they are. They'll call Mayor Murray and Clay Gaines, and before you know it, the entire town will be after my brother and my son."

"I don't have to tell Robin why I need a vehicle," Jandy said. "Trust me. I'm sure I can get something to drive for a night. Just tell me where I should meet you later."

"Oh, dear Lord," Tryphena said when she and her sister met Jandy behind the vacant building where Revere Auto had once done business. "Is that the best Robin could do?"

"I asked for this," Jandy said, looking proudly at her ride. "It's got plenty of room for one or both of you to hide. And do you think either your brother or Fiji would ever expect you to be tooling around town in a hearse?"

"I don't know what to say," Phylura muttered. "I'd rather it be a couple of decades before I'm laid out in the back of one of these things."

"What on earth is Robin doing with a hearse? I don't recognize it from any of Coventry's funeral homes."

"It belongs to a rock band from Fort Worth. Robin had to put a new carburetor in it. She wanted to loan me her truck, but this was the one vehicle I knew Fiji and Jay Jay wouldn't recognize as belonging to anyone. Robin called the hearse's owner, and he said he didn't care if I used it for a few hours. People in Texas are so generous."

"I reckon," Tryphena said. She looked at her sister. "If it belongs to a band, at least there haven't been any bodies laid out in it lately."

"Not dead ones, anyway," Phylura conceded. "Oh, what the hell. You're right, Jandy. A hearse might get noticed, but nobody would think it was following them."

"Nobody would *want* to think it was following them," Tryphena said.

"That's why I think it'll work," Jandy said. "Fear trumps reason every time. Who's riding with me?"

"Not me," both women said in unison.

"Somebody has to go with me," Jandy insisted. "I don't know what the boys drive. And I don't know the area. Would you really let me get lost in rural Texas in a hearse? I'm envisioning myself as the stranger who gets chainsawed again!"

Tryphena looked sullen and said, "If I do it, *you're* doing it."

"Fiji's *your* kid."

"We're wasting time," Jandy said.

"Fine. We both do it," Phylura said. "Jay Jay's probably

at the Early Bird Café getting some supper. Do you know where Fiji is?"

"His daddy was picking him up and taking him home. I left their supper on the stove and told them you and I were going to the mall in New Coventry."

"I wish you'd brought some of that supper for me," Phylura said.

"Get in," Jandy ordered. She couldn't wait to start tailing someone. Maybe she'd found her calling. She wondered if detectives went to school to learn their trade. It could be an exciting new career to attempt and quit. Of course, her real pleasure was in driving the hearse. How many people ever got to do that? Maybe she should get a job hauling bodies for a funeral home.

Perry v. Sweet Repose Funeral Home (Superior Court of Orange County) flashed through her brain. Ugh. What could be worse than picking up the wrong dead body and burying it in another family's plot?

Picking up the wrong live *body and burying it in another family's plot,* Pru answered.

"Go to the café, I guess," Phylura said. "But take the long way around so you can go through the Whataburger drive-through. I'm starving."

Later, as Jandy and Phylura slouched in the front seat and watched the door of the Early Bird Café while they ate, Tryphena spoke from the back. "I don't know how you can eat inside this car." When neither woman answered her, she said, "You could at least offer me some of your fries."

"I thought you didn't want to eat inside a hearse," Phylura said.

"I can't help it. The smell makes me hungry."

"You can have my fries. I never finish a whole order," Jandy said and passed them back. "Do you want half of my burger?"

"Does it have mustard on it?"

"For heaven's sake, Phena, remind me never to go on a stakeout with you again," Phylura said.

"That's him! That's Jay Jay! Duck!" Jandy ducked instinctively, causing Tryphena to add, "I didn't mean you. You have to drive."

"That red pickup is his? That's the one I'm following?"

"Yeah. But not too close," Tryphena said.

"You just stay down and leave the driving to her," Phylura ordered.

"You're the one who'd better keep that big head of hair out of sight."

Jandy looked in her mirror, but Tryphena was presumably stretched out in comfort, hopefully not with her hands crossed over her chest. If anyone passed the hearse, looked inside, and saw her in that pose, it might cause an accident.

Phylura was now hunched down in the passenger floorboard, covering the seat with napkins so she could use it as a table for her Whataburger combo. Jandy reached over and snagged a fry, then shifted her gaze back to the truck ahead of them.

"He's definitely heading out of town," she said. "In the direction of the Boones' house."

"Let's just hope he's not going to see one of his girlfriends. I don't much cotton to sitting outside a house if my brother's inside fooling around."

"How many girlfriends does he have?" Jandy asked.

"Who knows?"

"This is kind of comfortable," Tryphena said from the back. "It might not be so bad, owning one of these."

Phylura looked at Jandy and rolled her kohl-lined eyes. Jandy grinned. She wondered what Hud would think if he could see her at this moment. He'd probably dismiss her whole adventure as silly. Maybe it was, but Jandy was having fun. She was willing to bet that if the sisters had been willing to let him come along, Sam would be having fun, too. She didn't believe he'd get all wigged out about Wyndmere, even if he was an animal-loving Revere. He was more likely to see himself as upholding a family tradition by rescuing the longhorn.

"Oh, crap," Jandy said.

"What?" both sisters screeched.

"He's pulling off the road. I think to talk on his cell phone. At least he has it up to his ear. I can't stop behind him without looking suspicious."

"Go past him," Phylura ordered, crouching even lower.

"You'd better drive fast so he doesn't get a chance to see me lying here looking like Evita," Tryphena said.

"You told me you didn't see that movie," Phylura said.

"What'll I do after I drive past him? Don't you think he'll notice if I show up behind him again later?"

"I *didn't* see the movie. Everybody saw pictures on the Internet of Madonna in that glass coffin. Those were some weird pictures."

"Yeah, they were. I liked the movie, though."

"Apparently, I'm in this on my own, but don't cry for me, Tryphena," Jandy said, breaking into the women's conversation. "Fortunately there's a church right here. It won't be suspicious for a hearse to park next to it. Maybe he won't figure out that we're tailing him."

"I don't think I'd like a glass coffin," Phylura said.

"It's a little too Snow White for my taste," Tryphena agreed.

"What? Snow White was in a glass coffin? And that's a *kids'* movie?" Jandy asked.

"You never saw *Snow White*?" Tryphena's tone made it

sound as if Jandy had just told her she drowned kittens for a living.

"You're kidding, right?" Phylura asked.

"No."

"What little girl doesn't see *Snow White*? That's crazy."

"You're skulking around in a hearse to spy on your brother and rescue a cow. And you think it's crazy that I never saw a Disney movie where someone's in a glass coffin?"

"She has a point," Tryphena said.

"He's on the move again. What should I do?" Jandy asked.

"Tell me when he's out of sight," Phylura said. As soon as Jandy let her know, Phylura popped up to look around, and Tryphena stuck her head over the seat.

"I'll bet I know where he's going," Tryphena said. "Terry and Betty Fields's house."

"What makes you say that?"

"Betty told me they'd be in Redfish Bay this week. The boys could hide Wyndmere in the Fields's barn, and no one would ever know."

"Then we stay parked right here," Phylura said. "Either he drives by again, and we check the place out, or we wait until after dark, sneak onto the property, and see if we can find Wyndmere."

"Can I have the rest of your fries?" Tryphena asked.

After an hour had passed, Jandy was regretting her giant Coke from Whataburger. Phylura finally climbed through an open window on the back side of the church and unlocked a door. Each of the women took turns in the bathroom. Right after Jandy had settled back into the driver's seat, Jay Jay drove by going toward town.

She followed Tryphena's directions and approached the sprawling ranch house with trepidation. "Are you sure they're out of town? I don't want to get shot at."

"Lord, child, even if they were here, why would they shoot at us?"

"They might be a little put off by the hearse," Jandy pointed out.

"Fine. We'll park at the house and knock on the door. If no one answers, we'll walk down to the barn."

"What if Wyndmere's not in the barn?" Phylura asked.

"Let's cross that pasture when we come to it," Tryphena said.

After no one came to the door, Jandy's nervousness vanished. She walked to the barn with the two women and helped Tryphena open the doors. The longhorn was standing in a stall, looking at home and completely contented as she chewed on something.

"Oh, thank goodness," Phylura said. "I *knew* those boys were behind this. I'm going to skin Jay Jay alive."

"You don't actually have proof that Fiji did anything," Tryphena said. "Anyway, you can see she's been taken care of. She's happy as a clam."

"I wonder why they say clams are happy?" Phylura asked.

"Um, I don't mean to be difficult, but what's the rest of the plan? Because I don't think Wyndmere will fit inside the hearse," Jandy said and watched realization cross the Wicks sisters' faces. She sighed. "All right, ladies. I'm taking you back to your cars. You're going to forget you were here. You're going to forget Wyndmere is here. By tomorrow, she'll be back on the square, preparing for her big moment on Saturday."

"What are you going to do?" Phylura asked.

"The less you know, the better. At least if I end up like

the hussy who comes to town in the movies, I already have the lead car in my funeral procession."

"Good grief," Keelie said. "I'm staggering around like a blind dog in a meat house. Point that flashlight over here, Evan."

"Don't let Wyndmere hear you talking about a meat house," Evan warned. "I still don't understand how you found out the longhorn was here." Before Jandy could answer, he said, "All right. I remember. We're working on a need-to-know basis."

Jandy had intended to get Dr. Boone's help in transporting Wyndmere back to the town square, but he was out on an emergency call. Instead, she'd found Keelie and Evan blending mocktails in the Boone kitchen. After hearing only the most basic details, they'd jumped at the chance to help her pick up Wyndmere. Fortunately, Evan was driving one of Grayson's trucks, but it took the three of them quite a while to hook up the livestock trailer, especially since they kept stopping to laugh at their ineptitude. The sun had set long before they got back to the Fields' barn.

"It's a good thing stealth isn't important," Jandy said. "It must sound to Wyndmere like an entire herd of cattle is coming to rescue her."

"I know how Jandy found Wyndmere," Keelie said smugly.

"How?" Evan asked.

"She tractor down."

"If either one of you makes another farm or cow joke—"

"Aw, come on, Jandy, we have to milk these jokes for all they're worth," Keelie said.

"She's so bossy," Evan said.

"If our jokes offend you, just turn the udder cheek."

"Now I know why Texans carry guns," Jandy muttered.

"What would Wyndmere be if she could hear all our cow jokes?" Evan asked.

"What?" Jandy asked with dread.

"Laughing stock," Keelie and Evan answered in unison and cracked up.

"Wyndmere's riding in the cab with me," Jandy said. "You two can ride back to town in the moooo-ving van."

Chapter 16

The morning after Jandy's adventure in cattle rustling, she arrived at the gallery to find Dove there ahead of her. Dove had placed a painting that Jandy hadn't seen before on an easel and was studying it with her enigmatic expression.

"I'm surprised to see you here this early," Jandy said. "Or were you worried that I wouldn't show up because I didn't open the gallery yesterday?"

"You didn't?" Dove asked, still staring at the painting. "I didn't even know. Every time I think of Hannah trusting me to manage things here, I wonder if she might be in the early stages of dementia."

"Delegation is one of a good manager's strengths," Jandy said.

"Where did you hear that?"

"Could have been at any of a zillion temp jobs."

"Employee retention is another one," Dove said. "I guess you haven't run across many good managers."

"Where'd the new painting come from?"

"Do you like it?" Dove asked.

Jandy contemplated the painting. The artist had used

a twelve-by-twelve-inch canvas, but the vibrant colors and impression of motion made it seem larger.

"Abstracts are my favorites," she said, "even when I'm not sure what they're meant to convey. I see a lot of movement in this one. I love the colors: those coppery hues and the greens."

Dove glanced at her, an eyebrow raised, and said, "Don't those colors seem at all familiar to you?"

Confused, Jandy said, "Should they?"

"You see them in the mirror every day when you look at your hair and eyes."

Jandy looked again at the painting and said, "Huh. You could be right."

"I know I'm right," Dove said. "I had dinner with the artist last night. When he turned the painting over to me, he told me its title."

"What is it?"

"The title is *A Horse Called Jandy.* He said you inspired it."

"What? Who painted it?"

"You don't recognize the style?" When Jandy shook her head, Dove pointed toward *Trail Ride* and said, "Wayne Plochman did both paintings."

"Are you nuts? Why would Wayne Plochman say I inspired a painting? I've never met the man."

"You met him. Maybe he didn't tell you who he was."

"Oh," Jandy said. She supposed he could have been any of the men who'd come into the gallery. "I don't remember talking to anyone about horses. That's weird."

She puzzled over it for a few minutes. Maybe Wayne Plochman was one of the people who'd been at the Boones' cookout, and Sam had failed to point him out to her. She remembered horses had been among the topics discussed that night, and she'd admitted that she once worked at a racetrack.

"I hope you like it," Dove said, breaking into Jandy's reverie. "He asked me to make sure you got it."

"Got it? As in understood it?"

"As in it's a gift to you from him. He painted it of you and for you."

Jandy was aghast. "I can't accept that kind of gift. I know what his paintings sell for."

"You can't turn down someone's work when it was done for you. Not without offending him. He meant for you to have it."

"I've got to see who this guy is," Jandy said, walking toward the computer. "Do you think there are photos of him online?"

"Bound to be," Dove said. "I'm going outside for a smoke."

Jandy nodded absently, her attention already focused on starting the computer. But she flinched as soon as Hannah's default welcome screen, a news site, appeared on the monitor. She saw her own face looking back at her over the question *January Halli: Runaway Bride or Crime Victim?* She glanced toward the window of the gallery and saw that Dove was almost finished with her cigarette. She'd have to read the article later. Or maybe she wouldn't. Why upset herself? She pulled up a search engine and put in Wayne Plochman's name just as Dove came back inside.

"Oh! It's the grumpy old man," Jandy said when she saw a photo of the artist.

"Walter Matthau or the other one? Jack Lennon."

"Lemmon," Jandy said. "Jack Lemmon. It's *John* Lennon."

"What about him? Did he die?"

"No. I mean yes. They've all been dead for years. I'm talking about Wayne Plochman."

"He's very much alive. I told you I had dinner with him last night."

"No, I mean *he's* the grumpy old man."

"I don't have a clue what you're talking about."

"The first day I opened the gallery for business. An old man came in here complaining about the crowds and demanding a chair and some water. Then he insulted *Trail Ride*. His own painting!"

"I guess he was having a little joke at your expense," Dove said. She cracked one of her rare smiles. "Wayne's an old family friend. Quite a character. And you definitely made an impression on him. He told me that you're cheeky, and he likes that. So he did the painting for you."

"He did tell me that Jandy sounds like a horse's name."

"Now you know why he gave your painting that title."

"I guess." Jandy stared at the painting again. "I really do like it. Are you sure I should keep it?"

"Of course. *Always* accept gifts that will appreciate in value."

Jandy was grateful that Dove stuck around after the gallery opened. They were uncharacteristically busy. She had to admit that Dove could be quite a salesperson when she wanted to be. It didn't hurt that her personal style made her look like someone who knew about art.

They worked through lunch. By two, the gallery had emptied out, and Dove said, "I think we've done enough damage for one day. Let's take advantage of this lull and close."

"You're the boss," Jandy said. She looked at her painting and said, "Do you think it would be okay if I left this here?"

"This is probably the best place for it until you leave town. I hope that's not anytime soon."

Jandy grimaced and said, "My departure date depends on Robin, but it'll either be Sunday or Monday."

"*This* Sunday or Monday?" Dove asked.

Jandy was gratified by Dove's stunned expression. She was definitely showing emotion now. "The pickup will be fixed, so it's time to head back to the life that's waiting for me."

"Right," Dove said, still looking a little dazed. "These weeks flew by. It seems impossible that this is the last week of the festival. The gallery will definitely experience a drop in foot traffic."

"I guess that's not so great for the artists, but it makes me feel better to know I'm not abandoning you when things are at their busiest."

"I'm not worried about the gallery. You know how little of myself I've invested here. I just hate to see you go. It's been fun having you over to swim and watch movies and eat food of questionable nutritional value with me. I'll miss you."

"Thanks. I'll miss you, too." Jandy hesitated for a moment, then said, "I've got a stupid question."

"You want to know my source of income?"

"No! If I left Sunday, and five hundred miles later, my pickup broke down again, would you be concerned if I called you?"

"Concerned? I'd jump in the Revere tow truck and come get you," Dove said.

"Even if you wouldn't really, it means a lot to hear that," Jandy said, remembering how alone and friendless she'd felt before she met Sam at the big rocks of Texas Canyon.

"But I would," Dove assured her. "And if you didn't want me to come in the tow truck, I'd show up in the

Mini, and we could put the top down and cruise anywhere you wanted to go."

"We could be like Thelma and Louise."

"But with a happier ending."

Instead of automatically insisting that she didn't believe in happy endings, Jandy said, "We could go on a
quest for dandelion fountains."

"It's a date," Dove said. "Not that I want your truck to
break down, of course. Seriously though, I would rescue
you. So would Evan, I'm sure. And Sam and any of my
sisters."

Rather than making her usual protest that she would
never need rescuing, Jandy said, "That's so nice. Although I don't know about Lark. I've never spent any
time around her."

"You haven't? Lark's my baby sister."

"I know that."

"What I mean is that Swan always looked after Robin,
and I looked after Lark. It's amazing how well she
turned out, considering. Probably because she's completely different from me." Dove glanced at her watch.
"Are you hungry?"

"Ravenous."

"Let's go to my parents' place. Sam told me I need to
get some of their tomatoes, because apparently the vines
are producing like mad. We can kill two birds with one
stone—which is not a phrase I usually like, as you might
guess. Lark is there, and we'll get her to make us her
famous tomato sandwiches. Have you ever had a sandwich
with homegrown tomatoes?"

"I've had BLTs."

"Not the same thing. Let's go."

* * *

"How can this be so good?" Jandy asked between enthusiastic bites of her sandwich.

She and Dove were sitting at a worn oak table in the Reveres' breakfast room. Lark had been working on something there, but cheerfully pushed it all aside to serve sandwiches to them.

While Jandy had watched her prepare them, she realized that from the first time she saw Swan, Dove, and Lark at the Early Bird Café, she'd been more intimidated by Lark than the others. Robin was open and sunny. Swan might be a little brusque, and Dove might seem beautifully aloof, but Lark was the most unreadable of all the sisters. She was quieter than the others, and she also looked the most like Sam, with her dark hair and blue eyes. If *Sweet Seasons* had been casting a soccer mom, Lark would have been hired on the spot. She was attractive, poised, and crisply dressed, as if she'd just stepped out of a Gap ad.

"I don't know why they're so good," Dove said. "This is the only time I eat white bread."

"The sandwiches have to be on white bread," Lark said, sitting down with them after she finished cleaning the kitchen counter. "White bread, vine ripe tomatoes, Hellmann's mayonnaise, and salt and pepper."

"And it has to be Hellmann's," Dove said. "I hope you're not one of those Miracle Whip people, Jandy."

"I don't know what Miracle Whip is," Jandy said.

"Apparently, it's big in the Midwest. Mom grew up eating it, but our father took her away from all that. He lives by the slogan 'Bring out the Hellmann's and bring out the best.'"

"That's the commercial for *my* mayonnaise," Jandy protested. "But it's 'Bring out the Best Foods and bring out the best.'"

"You must be from the other side of the Rockies," Lark said. "It's Best Foods out West, but it's Hellmann's in the rest of the country." She reached for the project she'd been working on before they interrupted her.

"What's all that stuff?" Jandy asked quickly to forestall quizzing about where she lived when she wasn't visiting Coventry.

"My scrapbooking."

"She's obsessed," Dove said.

"No, I'm not." Lark rolled her eyes at Jandy. "I started scrapbooking when my oldest son was born. You'll have to come by sometime and see their books. Mom said I could go through our family photos and make scrapbooks for all of us. So far, I've only finished Swan's, which she has at her apartment. I'm working on Sam's now."

"May I see?" Jandy asked.

She pretended not to notice the eye play between the two sisters as Lark pushed the pages toward her. After all this time, she was surprised to think they might still suspect there was something romantic going on between Sam and her.

"I haven't done much yet," Lark said. "Mostly I've picked out the paper and some of the photos."

"This is so cute!" Jandy exclaimed. "I guess I didn't understand what scrapbooking entails." She was looking at a photo of Sam as a kid, holding a fishing pole while standing on the end of a pier. The background paper was covered with fish, and Lark had added little stickers that said "Gone fishin'," and also a tiny little fishing pole and a line with a glittery fish on the end of it. "How old is he here?"

"Seven. I can always tell, because that was the summer Swan knocked out his two front teeth. He didn't smile for pictures again until the gap was filled in with his permanent teeth."

"Poor thing. Don't you just want to squeeze his little cheeks?"

"Whose?" Sam asked.

Jandy blushed and looked up to see Sam coming through the open back door. Sue was behind him, slobber dripping from her hanging tongue. Jandy hoped she didn't look like Sue when she stared at Sam. Whatever he'd been doing made him look hot in a good way. He was holding his straw cowboy hat and pushing his hair off his forehead into that cute style he wore. He looked a little scruffy and a lot adorable.

Suddenly aware of his sisters' watchful eyes, she pointed to Lark's scrapbook pages and said, "I'll bet you were a terrible child who always picked on your siblings."

"It's like you were there," Lark said loudly to drown out Sam's denial.

"No way!" Sam insisted. "Swan was always whaling on me, and Robin and Lark were constantly snitching on me for something. Usually things I didn't do. Dove just pretended like we weren't related."

"I did that to all of you," Dove said with a sniff. "Still do."

Sam looked around and said, "You made me a tomato sandwich, right?"

"Are your arms broken?" Lark asked.

"See how they treat me? I've been toiling in the fields since sunup—"

"Oh, please," Dove said.

"—and I can't even get a morsel of food."

"It's tragic," Jandy said and stood. "I'll make you one."

"Don't wait on him!" Lark said.

"I just want to see if I can master this sandwich."

"Yeah, it's pretty tough," Sam agreed. "Good thing you've been going to Jennifer Boone's cooking classes."

He rinsed a tomato and handed it to Jandy, then filled a glass of water and drank it. "Where are the boys?"

"Jimmy's bringing them later," Lark said. She looked at Jandy and said, "Sam's babysitting tonight. Tomorrow's my wedding anniversary. My husband's taking me to Dallas for dinner, then we're spending the night there at the Adolphus."

Dove saw Jandy's questioning look and said, "Very elegant hotel. Queen Elizabeth once stayed there."

"And U2," Sam said.

Jandy threw away the tomato peel and washed the knife while Sam munched on his sandwich. All of them looked toward the door as Sue began to bark. Swan walked in and said, "Oh, tomato sandwiches!"

"I'll make it," Jandy said, determined to prove to Sam's sisters that she didn't cater only to him.

"I'll never turn down a sandwich," Swan said. "As long as there's no meat on it."

"You're a vegetarian?" Jandy asked.

"Meat is murder."

"Tasty, tasty murder," Sam said.

"It's so pathetic that you get your philosophy of life from a T-shirt," Swan said.

"Jimmy has friends who really do seem to have learned everything they know about life from T-shirts," Lark mused. "Life's a bitch. Mean people suck. Skate or die. Use the force."

"Frankie Says Relax," Sam suggested.

Jandy giggled, then said, "Everything I need to know about life I learned from Beatles songs." She put Swan's sandwich on a plate and handed it to her.

Sam said, "Everything I know about life I learned from—"

"Moonstruck," Dove finished Sam's sentence with him, and they smiled at each other.

"'It's Johnny Cammareri,'" Swan quoted in a singsong voice between bites of sandwich.

"'A wolf without a foot!'" Lark said.

"'Don't shit where you eat,'" Dove chimed in.

"Good grief, do all of you know every line in the movie?" Jandy asked. They all turned to stare at her. She was reminded of Wyndmere's bovine gaze. "What?"

"Please don't say you haven't seen *Moonstruck*," Lark said. "It's the Revere comfort movie."

Jandy stared back at them, one after the other, until she got to Sam. Her mouth twisted into a smile and she imitated Cher's accent when she said, "'I don't believe in curses.'"

"'Atta girl," Sam said. "Of course, you did manage to find the one quote in the movie that falls in line with your own worldview."

"Turn up the radio!" Swan barked.

Jandy watched, bemused, as Sam cranked up the Doobie Brothers singing "What a Fool Believes." Swan, Dove, and Lark all danced around the kitchen, following one another's leads while they did dance moves Jandy had never seen.

"It's another Revere family tradition," Sam explained. "Our mother always plays classic rock, and there are certain songs that make the birds get dance fever."

"Shopping cart!" Lark said, pulling Sam into the dance line. Jandy laughed when Sam mimed taking things off of shelves and dropping them into the invisible grocery cart he was pushing. She remembered when they'd met how she thought he was cocky, but now she realized his attitude was meant to be a spoof of cockiness. A single female would have accepted it as flirting and played up to it. But she wasn't single. And he wasn't flirting.

Dove grabbed Jandy's arm and forced her to join them as they laughed their way through the twist, the locomotion, and the slide.

"You're all a little crazy," Jandy gasped when the song ended and she collapsed onto a chair.

"We had to make our own entertainment on the farm," Lark said, plopping back down to stare at her scrapbook supplies.

"I envy you," Jandy said before she could stop herself. She blushed. "It must be so great to have each other. To share the same memories. Enjoy the same things. You all get along so well."

"We're just showing off for you," Swan said. She put her plate in the kitchen sink and laughed. "And we don't always get along. Remember when we went to Italy?"

"Don't listen to them," Sam warned Jandy. "They always drag out this story to make me look bad."

"That trip was the biggest thing that had ever happened to us," Swan said, ignoring her brother. "Our parents planned and saved for it forever. We did all this touristy stuff in Rome, then we rented cars to go to Florence."

"That's two hundred and thirty miles," Lark said.

"Kilometers," Swan corrected. "It's about one hundred and fifty miles."

"And Lark, being a complete loser, made us stop to eat at McDonald's," Sam said. "In Italy!"

"I was a teenager!" Lark defended herself. "When we continued our journey, Sam was driving the car with Jimmy and me in it. We weren't married then; he was just my boyfriend. Mom and Dad were in the car ahead of us with all the luggage. And Robin was driving Swan and Dove behind us."

"So we get to a fork in the road—"

"There's *always* a fork in the road," Jandy said.

Lark nodded. "Mom and Dad went to the right. Of course, Sam followed them. A truck had gotten behind us, and Robin—"

"Who won't admit to this day that she wasn't paying attention," Sam interjected.

"—went to the left. I tried to get Sam to turn around and go after her, but he wouldn't. He asked me what I would do if I were in Robin's place. I said the first thing I'd do, once I realized I was lost, was turn around and go back to McDonald's."

"But Sam said noooo, Robin would never do that," Swan drawled.

"You weren't in my car," Sam reminded her.

"He asked me what else I'd do, and I said I'd try to call Mom and Dad. They had our only cell phone in those days."

"One of those huge ones," Swan said, and Dove rolled her eyes and nodded, as if their parents were the last word in archaic.

"Which I thought was ridiculous," Sam insisted. "How would Robin ever manage to call a U.S. number from a pay phone in a country where she didn't speak a word of the language?"

"So I told him that next I'd cry, and after that, I'd try to find someone who could give me directions to the hotel where we were staying that night."

"So what happened?" Jandy asked.

"Mom and Dad pulled up to the hotel, and we drove up right after them. They got out and nearly had heart failure when they realized the birds weren't behind us.

Sam tried to weasel out of responsibility. They were all still arguing when Robin pulled up behind us less than ten minutes later."

"Sam was all smug, and he asked Robin what she did when she realized she took a wrong turn. And she said that *first* she went back to McDonald's." Dove paused until Jandy stopped laughing. "After that, she tried to figure out how to call the cell phone. Then she sat on a bench and cried until an old man stopped and asked in broken English if he could help us. Between his smattering of English—"

"And our broken Italian, we managed to get directions to the hotel, and Robin hauled ass until we jerked to a stop behind them as they all stood around wondering if they'd ever see us again," Swan finished the tale.

"What a great story," Jandy said after another outbreak of giggles. "Sam, you could have just tossed a coin to make your decision about whether or not to go after a carful of sisters."

"You make us sound like nuns," Dove said.

"Now you can see how horrible Sam is, and how things aren't always hearts and flowers in the Revere family," Lark said.

"Yeah, I'm so horrible that you dump your kids on me every chance you get," Sam said.

"I don't bring them over here because of *you*. I want them to occasionally be in an environment where they have to use their imaginations the way we did when we were kids. You know," Lark said with an imploring glance at Jandy, "instead of having everything done for them with video games and DVDs. I'm probably fighting a losing battle, especially against TV. I don't think there's any way to win against television."

"Yet you watched cartoons when you were a kid, right?" Jandy asked.

"So what? *Everybody* watches cartoons," Lark said.

"I never did."

Sam smiled at his sisters' shocked expressions and said, "I've tried to enlighten her in the ways of animation. She resists."

"Never?" Lark sounded dumbfounded.

"Nope."

"So if I told you that we call my sons Heckle and Jeckle, you wouldn't get it?"

"Are they the chipmunks?"

"That would be Chip and Dale," Swan said.

"Heckle and Jeckle are two blackbirds," Lark said.

"More specifically, magpies," Sam added. "Regrettably, the bird theme is continuing into the next generation."

"Those aren't your sons' real names, are they?" Jandy asked apprehensively.

Lark laughed and said, "No. My five-year-old is Seth, and my three-year-old is Shane. Basic normal names. Stick around and you can meet them."

"Stick around and you can help me babysit," Sam said. "Or at least watch cartoons with us."

"Dove's my wheels," Jandy said. "I leave when she does."

"Why don't we pick up your PJs, toothbrush, and a change of clothes, and we can have a slumber party?" Dove asked. "I have nothing to do tonight."

"I'm in," Swan agreed. "We can make s'mores."

"We'll see if Robin's free and make a family night of it," Dove said.

They're matchmaking, Pru warned, but Jandy just smiled and said, "Sounds fun. The only slumber parties I ever had were with my aunt Ruby. Although we had a great time," she hastened to add. "We'd watch old movies, pop corn, paint our toenails—"

"I draw the line at popcorn," Sam said firmly.

* * *

Jandy had never been around children, so she was a little shy with Seth and Shane. With so many aunts, an uncle, and a big dog like Sue around, they weren't lacking for attention and seemed barely to notice when their parents left for the night. Robin brought pizza. After they ate, they settled into the family room, where Sam kept the cartoons coming courtesy of old videotapes.

She forgot all about the kids as she found herself rooting for a coyote, giggling over an amorous skunk, and marveling at the clever humor of the moose and squirrel she'd heard so much about. She wondered why her mother had denied her such simple entertainment as a child. She couldn't stop herself from brooding a little about it, barely noticing when Sam's sisters began yawning and drifting upstairs.

Sam had made up the sofa bed in the family room for the boys. Jandy was lying among pillows, quilts, and empty juice boxes when Shane crawled toward her from the foot of the bed and nestled against her. She was surprised, but automatically put a protective arm over him, much the way she did whenever Sue stretched out next to her. She breathed in the scent of his hair—a mixture of baby shampoo and little boy sweat—and something seemed to flip over deep inside her stomach.

I want this, she thought, and was shocked. She and Hud had occasionally talked about children as something that might happen in the distant future, when his career was more stable and she'd figured out what she wanted to do with her life.

But what if this is *what I want to do with my life? What if I want to be a mother? Not according to some vague timetable, but now?*

She felt guilty, as if every woman who'd ever fought for her right to a career was about to rise up and come after her, zombielike, until she sold her soul to a forty-hour workweek with benefits and a 401k. She tried to shake off the sudden yearning that had wrapped itself around her heart more comfortably than the soft old quilt that brushed her skin. Being stirred that someone else's three-year-old had entrusted himself to her so easily was hardly a reason to want a baby. She might not know much about them, but she'd seen enough children acting like brats in public places to make her grateful that there was such a thing as birth control pills.

But Lark's boys aren't like that, she silently debated. They were funny and cute and well-behaved. Seth had helped Robin throw away paper plates and pizza boxes, and Shane had crowed with delight when Sue gently took torn bits of pizza crust from his hands.

"I think he's asleep," Sam whispered, and Jandy was jerked back to reality. "Do you want me to move him? Is he crowding you?"

"No. I'm fine."

"Shhhh," Seth ordered. "This is one with Marvin the Martian."

Sue let out a groan, and Sam said, "Was that you or the dog?"

"The dog. I *like* cartoons. But why can't the coyote ever win?"

"It's the question of the ages," Sam said.

"Shhhh," Seth hissed again.

Sam tried not to look smug and failed miserably. She stretched her arm to flick him with her thumb and middle finger. He stopped her by catching her hand in his. She shifted her eyes back to the TV, pretending not to notice that he didn't let go. She liked the way his hand felt around hers: big, warm, not at all clammy. She was glad his sisters weren't there to exchange glances fraught with speculation. She was comfortable; that was all. She certainly wasn't imagining what it would be like to be part of a couple with Sam, or daydreaming that the two children lying between them were theirs.

Ah ha, Pru said victoriously. *See what happens when you watch cartoons? You're just a few episodes short of losing yourself in some silly fairy-tale fantasy. This isn't real. In a few days, you'll be back to reality with Hud.*

She closed her eyes, willing herself to think about what kind of wedding she and Hud would salvage out of the mess they'd made. When she opened them, the TV was off. The only light in the room was the grayness that came just before the sun rose and bathed the world in white gold. She was still lying on the sofa bed, and Sam was stretched out opposite her. His breathing had the regularity of sleep. Seth had somehow gotten twisted in the covers, and all she could see of him was one foot sticking out and resting on Sam's shoulder.

Shane was still lying against her. His weight on her arm had left it completely numb. She eased it out from under him, shaking it a little to fight off the stinging needles as her circulation returned. She yawned and turned to look toward the grandfather clock. She didn't even blink when she saw Lady Godiva standing next to the stone fireplace. Years of interior conversations with Prudence had left her unflappable when faced with the specter of Coventry's legendary horsewoman.

She waved her tingling fingers at the apparition, and Lady Godiva looked amused and waved back. Jandy closed her eyes with a smile. It was nice to dream of Lady Godiva watching over them all while they slept. Somehow it took away a tiny bit of unease she felt about having just spent a night in bed with a man who was not her fiancé. Lady Godiva knew she and Sam were just friends. . . .

The next time she woke up, shafts of sunlight were falling across the bed. Sam and the boys were gone. She stood, stretched, and walked down the hall to a bathroom. When she came out, she was drawn by the aroma of coffee toward the kitchen, where she was sure to find one of the Revere girls or Sam. But when she walked in, she gasped, remembering her dream. Lady Godiva once again stood there watching her. The brilliant sun behind her gave her an ethereal glow.

Jandy rubbed her eyes and muttered, "I must be losing my mind."

"Then you should fit in around here," Lady Godiva said.

"Look, I don't believe in ghosts or poltergeists or whatever you are. You've done a good job of dressing like a modern woman, but I'd feel a lot better if you stayed on the walls of Lady's Ryde Restaurant, where I first saw you. Because this is a—"

"Good morning," Sam said, fighting Sue to be the first one through the back door. "I see you two have met."

Jandy frowned at him. Surely she and Sam couldn't be having the same vision. That would be almost like *Hart v. Barker* (Los Angeles County Superior Court), when Hart said hysterical visions suffered by his three children occurred after their nanny, Sarah Barker, told them late-night tales of ghosts and goblins.

She and Sam *had* watched that stupid Casper cartoon with their stomachs full of pizza the night before.

Lady Godiva extended a hand toward her and said, "You must be Jandy. I'm Rachel Revere. Sam's mother."

Chapter 17

"Is she as scary as everyone says?" Evan asked as he studied Jandy's reflection. He grabbed his scissors and began snipping at random wisps of hair.

Jandy was sure Evan was faking an excessive interest in her hair to keep from laughing at her. She didn't blame him. She felt pretty ridiculous for not realizing that Rachel Revere was flesh and blood rather than a dream or a ghost.

"You've never met her?"

"I've seen her from a distance here and there," Evan said. He threw the takeout containers from their Early Bird Café breakfasts into the trash so he could lean against the counter and check her hair again. "I don't know why I never put it together that she was the model for the murals of Lady Godiva at Lady's Ryde Restaurant. I guess I never studied them that intensely. I go for the food, not the art."

"As she pointed out when I brought it up," Jandy said, blushing at the memory, "she posed for those several decades ago. She's a lot older now and usually wears clothes."

"Did she pose *nude* for Wayne Plochman? That dirty old man."

"He was a lot younger when he did those paintings," Jandy pointed out. "Also, I think Rachel and Sam's father were already married then. She was probably just his model, not his lover. I'll bet it's an interesting story, all the same."

"I'm all about interesting stories," Evan said. "Back to yours. Was she appalled to find you in bed with her son?"

"I was not!" Jandy yelped. "We were both fully dressed with two kids and a dog snoring between us. It's not like she walked in on some romantic tryst. Anyway, she seemed to already know all about me, including the information that I have a fiancé."

"She probably saw you in her crystal ball. Half the town thinks she's a witch—"

"She knew about me from her daughters."

"—and the other half thinks she's a bitch. What did *you* think?"

Jandy paused, considering, and finally said, "I guess I was a little dazzled by her. Sure she's older than when she posed for those paintings. But you know how you get an image in your head of someone? She's the mother of five children. She has to be, I don't know, in her midfifties? If I thought about her at all when the birds or Sam talked about her, I pictured her as matronly. She's a grandmother! I thought she'd have dyed brown hair cut in that dowdy old lady style—"

"Good thing the salon isn't open yet," Evan interrupted. "You'd offend some of my regulars."

"I envisioned her as a little plump, with glasses hanging from one of those chains like you always see librarians wear. Instead, she has this mass of strawberry blond hair that she stacks on her head—"

"Now you see where Dove gets her style."

"She has a few freckles and some lines around her eyes,

but her skin looks like cream. You've seen her. Even from a distance, you already know that her figure's trim, and she's tall because she has long legs. She's really lovely."

"You could be describing yourself. Except for the lines around the eyes," he hastily amended.

Jandy blushed and said, "Isn't it funny that none of the Reveres ever mentioned that their mother's a redhead? Usually people I meet immediately tell me about other redheads they've known. Especially when they're about to describe our alleged personality traits."

"Like a bad temper?"

"Which is so untrue," Jandy said. It was her turn to frown at her reflection. "Do you think I'm looking a little shaggy around the ears?"

"It's a new style. All the cool kids are wearing it. I call it the Yorkie." He grinned and trimmed a few unruly hairs. "You're right. I know how she looks. But what's she like?"

Jandy frowned again, no longer seeing her reflection as she hesitantly said, "I liked her. In fact, I'm going back to the Revere house tomorrow to help her can tomatoes." She rolled her eyes at the skeptical expression on Evan's face. "I used to help Aunt Ruby make orange marmalade and put up fig preserves. Rachel said that Sam has been too zealous with her tomato crop. According to her, there's an old rule that the rabbits get a third, the bugs get a third, and she gets a third. Apparently, Sam has let the insects and rabbits go hungry." She spun her chair around, and said, "Stop fussing with your scissors. I can't afford to have my hair styled by you all the time."

"I've charged you nothing," Evan said.

"I'm running a mental tab. I don't take advantage of my friends."

"Don't try to divert me. Damn it, I've been warned

that this woman is a dragon, and all I get from you is that she's lovely and likable."

"Maybe she's like Wyndmere: a make-believe dragon."

"But you take no stock in make-believe," Evan reminded her.

"Is that another lame attempt at a cow joke?"

Evan shook his head, put down his scissors, and picked up a large brush with soft bristles to sweep bits of hair from her shoulders.

"You're right," she said slowly. "I don't do make-believe. Or fantasy. Or magic. Or ghosts! I have to get out of this town before I turn into Miss Cleo or Sylvia Plath."

Evan snorted and said, "You mean Sylvia *Browne*. Unless you're worried about turning into a suicidal poet. Either way, you can't leave until after the weekend. You have to see Sue in the dog show. You have to be there when a new Daughter of Godiva is crowned. You've stuck it out this long. May as well see it through to the finish."

"The finish," Jandy repeated absently. Then she met Evan's eyes and said, "Thanks for dealing with my hair once again. I don't know what I'll do without you when I go back to L.A."

"Please. You can't swing a hair extension without hitting a stylist in that town. Speaking of hair extensions, now that your return to your fiancé is imminent, how do you think Hud will react to your shorn head?"

"It's really nothing to do with him, is it?" Jandy asked primly.

Evan tactfully changed the subject to some of the Daughter of Godiva contestants and last-minute disasters they always had with their wigs, weaves, and hair extensions. When he opened the shop for his first customer, Jandy left. Instead of going directly to the gallery, she walked to the square, wondering why she felt so out of sorts. It wasn't like her to snap at Evan.

A group of boys were playing on the sidewalk near the bench where she sat. She watched them for a while, then took out her cell phone and called Hud. She wasn't sure whether he'd answer; she'd lost track of what days he taped. Even if he wasn't taping, chances were that he'd be doing something with one of the Foundlings. She was surprised when he answered.

He sounded groggy, and she said, "Did I wake you? I'm sorry. I forgot the two-hour time difference. I guess I messed up your day to sleep in."

"That's okay," he croaked. "I programmed the coffee-maker last night. Just let me pour a cup so I can start waking up. What the hell is all that racket?"

"Some kids near me are playing with cap guns."

"They still make those things?"

"Apparently they still make them in Texas."

"I thought Texans gave their kids real guns."

"Maybe these are tourists."

"That explains it." She heard him gulp his coffee, then he said, "I thought you might be calling to tell me you were already on the road. That your truck got fixed early or something."

"No. I'm still planning to start back on Sunday. I just wanted to say hello."

"Hold that thought. I've got another call."

She gritted her teeth. She'd almost forgotten his habit of taking every call, as if he didn't have voice mail on all his phones.

"Back," he said and yawned. "I'm glad you called. Wait. The land line's ringing."

She sighed and watched the kids as someone—maybe the father of one or two of them—walked up and handed them what appeared to be breakfast burritos. An exchange was made, and the man ended up holding the cap guns. The kids sank to the ground, carrying on an animated discussion about cowboys between bites of burritos.

"Sorry, that was Chandra. What were we talking about?"

"When do you suppose we'll have a baby?" Jandy asked, watching the kids on the sidewalk and thinking again of the yearning she'd felt when Lark's little boy had settled so comfortably within her embrace.

There was silence from Hud. She wondered if he'd taken yet another call, but he suddenly said, "So that's it."

"What?"

"Are you pregnant? Were you worried about how I'd react? That's why you're staying away, isn't it? I'll admit a baby isn't in the plan right now, but I'm not that hung up on schedules, Jane. You know me better than that, right?"

"I guess. But I'm not—"

"Chandra may die of happiness. Having a baby bump under a wedding dress is practically de rigueur these days."

She felt her entire body get hot, then cold, then hot again before she managed to say, "In the first place, nobody outside the fashion industry uses the phrase 'de rigueur' in casual conversation without sounding silly. In the second place, a baby is not a bump, and it also isn't a freaking ruse to get publicity. In the third place, I am *not* pregnant. And right now, I'm thinking that I never want to be."

"Don't hang up!"

"Can you not see that the exact issues that made me postpone our wedding in the first place are cropping up again? Everything is about *the wedding*. How you guys can spin it for positive publicity. How important it is for me to come back soon so you can capitalize on the timing. This will be the third time we've planned this, and every time, it becomes some gigantic thing that consumes everything else. What happens after the wedding, Hud? What am I supposed to do with myself while you work and play with your friends? Who, truth be told, couldn't care less if I ever come back, much less marry you."

"That's not true. They ask about you all the time."

"I ask about global warming; that doesn't mean I like it. Hud, I understand the thrill of living in the moment and being ready to take off on an adventure at a moment's notice. But maybe you and I don't have the same idea of what adventure is. Or maybe I want my adventures to be part of something bigger than just the moment. I know I'm not making sense. I'm still trying to figure things out. I probably should have stayed and let you figure them out with me. But whenever I tried, I always ended up feeling like I was in a relationship with Chandra, not you."

After a long silence, Hud said, "Maybe what you really need to question is what's happening right now. Why you've been inventing reasons not to come home. You act like you're the only one affected by all this. You're not in it alone. I'm half of the equation."

"Your math sucks. You're a third. You're leaving out Chandra."

"And you're blowing Chandra's place in our lives way out of proportion."

"Maybe you'd like to call off the wedding altogether."

"Is that what you want me to do? So you don't have to do it? I'm not the one who wouldn't go through with it. I'm not the one who ran away. Think about that."

She snapped her phone shut when she realized he'd disconnected the call. She took a few deep breaths. Before she could organize her thoughts without the annoying voice of Pru butting in, the man holding the cap pistols ambled up and said, "Howdy."

She spotted his kids, guns and burritos apparently forgotten, running toward a woman in medieval costume handing out helium-filled Mylar balloons near the Godiva fountain. She gave their father the weakest of smiles, wishing he'd follow his kids and leave her alone.

"You see 'at dog over air?" the man asked in an accent that she assumed was from a part of Texas even more rural than Coventry.

Jandy looked in the direction he indicated and saw a dog sitting a few feet away. Its fur was mottled shades of bluish-gray, and it had a white patch on its head. The dog's pointed, upright ears and bright brown eyes gave it an alert, intelligent look.

"What about it?" she asked.

"'At's a Australian cattle dog."

She wasn't sure how she was supposed to react, but he seemed to expect something. She tried to look impressed and said, "It herds cows?"

"Mine don't. Ain't got no cows. But he's gotta trick. Wanna see?"

She sighed. Maybe if she agreed, he'd go away and leave her alone. "Sure."

"Beau," he yelled, and the dog stood, looking like he might explode out of his thick coat of fur. The man nodded toward the square, said, "Git 'er," and fired one of the cap guns. Beau was a flash of gray as he took off. Jandy had to turn quickly to keep him in sight as he hurled himself toward the children's petting zoo, which hadn't yet opened for the day. The dog easily slipped between the fence rails and landed on a large pig who was lying on its side to soak up the early morning sun. The pig didn't budge or react as Beau, lacking only a flag to look like a proud conqueror, stood on top of it.

"'At's my hawg dawg trick," the man said. "You ever see anythang like 'at?"

"No," Jandy said. "I can honestly say I never saw anything like that."

"He'd jump onnit even if it'uz standin' up. He'd ride 'at hawg if he had to!"

"That's quite a dog," Jandy said.

"Yup," the man agreed. With a nod of his head, he left to get Beau, and maybe to find his kids. Jandy shook her head and laughed, her mood lifting a little. She slouched on the bench and jammed her Beatles cap on her head, disregarding Evan's recent efforts to freshen her haircut. She didn't want to turn the color of that pig—*hawg*, she corrected herself—sizzling under the sun.

She stared at the square as vendors began opening their booths. It was hard to believe that, in a few days, everyone would be gone, including her. She would never see the square when it wasn't covered with tourists. She'd no longer be greeted every day by merchants selling fried turkey wings, grilled ears of corn that dripped butter down to her elbows, geodes advertised as dragon eggs, and ceramic statues of Lady Godiva on horseback.

The realization of how much she would miss Coventry made her heart ache. But she had her own life to get back to, and Hud was clearly getting impatient about resuming it. She didn't know what was wrong with her. Of course, she might miss him as much as he seemed to miss her if they could have a single conversation without his bringing up Chandra and her relentless quest for publicity.

Jandy shrugged off her thoughts. She wasn't leaving for four more days, and in the meantime, she had a gallery to open and paintings to sell. She was eager to get another look at the painting Wayne Plochman had given her. She'd been trying to figure out where she wanted to hang it in Hud's apartment. Its vivid colors would finally add a bit of interest to the place.

As she got to her feet, the Revere Auto tow truck slid to a stop next to the curb. Sue's head was hanging out the passenger window, her jowls trailing streams of slobber. Jandy rubbed the dog's ears and peered inside the truck at Sam.

"I have to pick up a crippled Dodge from New Coventry," he said. "Want to go along for the ride?"

Unlike her, Sam didn't seem to feel at all awkward that she'd awakened after spending a night with him to find his mother in the kitchen. Then again, since nothing had happened between them, he had no reason to feel awkward. Nonetheless, she thought it might be best if she stopped giving his family reasons to speculate and matchmake.

"Sorry. As much as I'd like to hear you explain to the owner of a Dodge that his nine iron is stripped, I have a gallery to open."

"You must not have talked to Dove," Sam said, pretending that she hadn't once again mocked his mechanical skills. "Seems she spotted a giant rat at the gallery and has to get it taken care of before you can open."

"She called an exterminator? You mean there's an animal the Revere kids won't defend and protect?"

"I'm sure Swan already has a catch-and-release team on the way to rehabilitate the rat. Or at least give it a hot meal and a bus ticket out of town. Meanwhile, it could be a fun morning for me and you and a dog named Sue."

"Better not," Jandy said. "I have a ton of laundry to do before I pack to leave on Sunday. I'll take this opportunity to get started on it."

She couldn't tell if Sam was frowning or squinting at the sun when he said, "You're really leaving town, huh? You must not have heard that Jennifer Boone's next cooking lesson will be artichoke fritters. Sounds awfully tempting."

"It does. But my own frittering has to end as soon as Robin gets the truck fixed."

"How about this. We'll toss a quarter and—"

"The only quarter I want to see from you is one I can use in the dryer at the Scrub and Pub."

Sam's eyebrow slipped up. "If you step into the pub side, by tonight the whole town will be talking about your drinking problem *and* how often you change your underwear. I always thought it would be Dove who ruined your reputation."

"I wonder why people talk about Dove so much," Jandy mused.

"Because she wants them to," Sam said. He put on his sunglasses. "Sue and I will be on our way. Enjoy your suds."

She felt a little pang as the truck drove off. It would have been fun to ride around with the two of them. But for all she knew, the grapevine was already buzzing about how she hadn't spent the previous night in her apartment. She had to stop giving people reasons to gossip about her. She was supposed to be keeping a low profile, not drawing attention to herself.

She cut between the buildings of the Old Towne Shoppes and skirted the playground, intending to get to Old School Road and the gallery without running into anyone who would delay her with conversation. She was hoping if Dove was still there, she could talk her into giving her and her laundry a ride to the apartment complex. She could swim laps while she used Dove's laundry room.

But as she came around the corner of the school, she froze at the sight of a van parked in the street midway between the gallery and Evan's shop. An exterminator's truck wouldn't have a mast and a satellite dish on top of it. Nor would it have a TV station's call letters painted on the side.

Not everything is about you, Pru scolded. *They're probably doing a news segment on the festival. Or interviewing Daughter of Godiva contestants.*

"Of course," Jandy said. Nonetheless, she slowly backed up until she was behind the school again.

She wasn't sure which way to go. Even if the news team was in town for the festival, there was no reason to take a chance on being recognized. She reached into her pocket only to realize that she didn't have her cell phone and couldn't call Evan to find out what was going on. She tried to remember what she'd done with it after talking to Hud. She'd been distracted by the hog dog man. Had she left her phone on the bench? Dropped it near the playground?

She was immobilized by indecision. The people from the TV station could be anywhere, so she was afraid to go back to the square to look for her phone. But she needed to find it before anyone else did. It had all her information in it, along with everyone's numbers in L.A. Evan would help her, but for all she knew, an entire news team was in his shop, since he was the official hair stylist of the pageant.

Think, she ordered herself.

A lot depended on how long Dove had been at the gallery before she saw the rat, and whether she'd run out after seeing it. The first thing Dove always did, over Jandy's objection, on those rare occasions when she came to the gallery in the mornings, was to open the windows in the back to air out the space. Jandy argued that the air might damage the paintings and lamented the waste of electricity and money by running the air conditioner with the windows open. Dove maintained that the gallery could only benefit from letting in a little fresh air.

If Dove was there long enough to open the windows, Jandy thought, *maybe she ran out without closing them when she saw the rat. Do I want to go in there if a rat's racing around? It's probably a perfectly nice rat. . . .*

A nice rat. That was what came of watching stupid cartoons with Sam. No doubt the rat and all his friends were singing while they swept out the gallery and straightened the paintings on the walls, just waiting for her to come in so they could ask why Prince Charming had hung up on her.

She skulked close to the back of the school and quickly crossed the area visible from the street until she was behind the gallery. She nearly sobbed with relief when she saw an open window. Making as little noise as possible, in case the rat was in the gallery or Swan had come to rescue it, she moved a heavy plastic bucket under the window. She climbed on it, then began pushing herself through the window. She was halfway in when she heard voices. Once again, she found herself paralyzed by indecision. She didn't know which option was worse: explaining to Sam's sisters why she hadn't come through the gallery's front door, or lurking in the alley until she could make sure the coast was clear for a dash to the beauty shop.

The bucket made the decision when the edge of her foot pushed it sideways. She pulled herself the rest of the way through the window, relieved, as she lowered her legs, that she and Dove always closed the lid on the toilet. She brushed paint chips from her clothes. All she had to do was wait until the girls were gone before she called Evan and begged him to find her cell phone and tell her when the news van was gone. She hesitated before walking through the bathroom to make sure a giant rat wasn't about to charge her. Just before she could step into the gallery, she heard a man's voice and stopped.

". . . station manager got a call from a friend who said January Halli sold her a raku pot, whatever that is, from this gallery."

"Those are raku pots behind you. They get their name from a firing process, which I can explain. I can't explain why you were misinformed about this Holly Whoever—"

"January Halli."

"Right," Dove said in her familiar bored tone. "Hannah Herren owns the gallery. I'm running it while she's out of town. Nobody named January Halli works here."

"A couple of tourists next door at the Godiva Inn told me a redhead works here. January Halli is a redhead."

"Oh, they're talking about Jandy," Dove said.

Jandy winced. She might as well just go out there and get her secret out in the open before some second-rate newshound did it for her.

"And Jandy is?"

"Jandy Taylor. Evan's cousin."

"Who's Evan?"

"Evan Hammett. He owns Molly's Beauty Shop across the street. You can see it through the window. Jandy's probably there. She usually is, if she's not here or out with Billy Mac or Bobby Ray."

Who? Jandy wondered.

"Who?" the reporter asked. "Wait. Let me take some notes. You're saying she's got a couple of boyfriends?"

"Oh, probably more than that," Dove said with a rude snort. "She's been this way ever since she was a majorette in high school. Not just any majorette, but one with flaming batons. Ask anybody about her. She ended up losing the Daughter of Godiva pageant the year she set the tent on fire. I think she's also set a few backseats on fire from time to time, if you know what I mean. I personally didn't want her at the gallery, but Hannah insisted that we get help. Not that Jandy's ever here. She's as likely to lock up the place and leave on a date with a male customer as she is to sell him a painting. And I use the term 'date' loosely."

Is she nuts? Jandy thought. *What is she talking about?*

"This woman was certain that she saw January Halli working here."

"I don't know what to tell you. Maybe your source mixed up where she saw this woman. Or she could have seen another tourist visiting the gallery, because I've lived in Coventry all my life, and I never knew anyone named January Halli."

"You never heard of January Halli," the man said, his tone indicating that he felt dubious about Dove's ignorance.

"I already said that."

"The runaway bride? She's been all over the news for the last month."

"Oh. I vaguely remember hearing about that. Didn't she go back to Georgia or something?"

"You're talking about last year's runaway bride. January Halli is Runaway Bride 2006."

"You're free to search the gallery for wilted bouquets, stashed veils, or hidden flower girls," Dove said, sounding bored again.

"I think I'd rather talk to this Evan guy. The cousin."

"Right across the street," Dove said. "Remember while you're in town to enjoy some of our fine restaurants and attractions."

"Yeah, I'll do that," the man said.

Jandy heard the door close, and she stepped into the gallery space. Dove had her back to her as she stared out the window with her cell phone to her ear.

"Evan? A vulture has landed. I told him she's your cousin. I also went with the majorette story because every good story has a majorette, doesn't it? Right, and a dog. Okay. I'll call her."

Jandy cleared her throat. Dove obviously didn't hear her, because she began punching another number into the phone.

"Keelie? We're on vulture alert. Make your calls. Yes, from a Dallas TV station. The slutty majorette who's Evan's cousin."

This time when Dove closed her cell phone, Jandy said, "Excuse me?"

For once, Dove lost her composure as she shrieked, spun around, and said, "How long have you been standing there? Where did you come from?"

"I came in through the bathroom window," Jandy said. Dove blinked at her, perhaps thinking, as Jandy was, of the Beatles. "I'm not—Did you—Am I to understand that you lied to that man on purpose? That you know who I am?"

"January Halli? Or Jane Halli? Yes," Dove admitted.

"Did Evan tell you?"

"Oh, Jandy," Dove said, her mask of world-weariness slipping over her face. "I've known almost since your first day here. We all have."

"All? Your sisters?"

"Yes."

"Sam, too?"

"Basically, everyone with access to a TV who's over the age of five and isn't canine," Dove said. "Don't worry. You may be a runaway bride, but you're *our* runaway bride, and we're not giving you up to anybody."

"I am *not,*" Jandy said from between gritted teeth, "a runaway bride."

Chapter 18

It hadn't occurred to Jandy that the downside of being in a town where everyone knew her by her name—or at least her assumed name—was that becoming invisible wasn't an option. After Dove's revelation, she wanted nothing so much as to move with anonymity through the town until she could find a place to think. A place where no one would smile with recognition or ask after her health or wonder if there was anything they could do for her, and all the while she'd be wondering, *Do they know? Did they know all the time?*

Dove seemed to understand that Jandy had gotten not one but two shocks. She shrugged out of her cobalt blue linen blazer and tossed it over, saying, "Put on my hat and my sunglasses. My keys are still in the door. The Mini's parked illegally in front of the school. Take it and make yourself scarce."

"The last time I escaped in a vehicle that wasn't mine, I broke it and ended up a zillion miles from where I started," Jandy said.

Dove waved her hand indifferently and said, "If that's what you need to do."

"Why would you trust me after I've been lying to you and your family for weeks? Or even if you don't trust me, why are you so nice to me?"

Dove almost cracked a smile as she said, "When I ran afoul of the bingo mafia, I learned what it's like to be hunted."

"The what?"

"Just a little incident in Ohio. We'll save that tale for another day. Your jeans are almost the same as mine. If you wear the hat and affect an indifferent saunter, anyone seeing you from a distance will mistake you for me. Now go, before that stupid reporter person comes back to his van."

"Thank you," Jandy said, jamming Dove's straw hat with its four-inch brim on her head.

Dove winced slightly and said, "My dear. No crisis merits poor fashion." She reached out to make a quick adjustment to the hat. "Don't forget to lock the door when you leave, in case anyone's watching. Not that I always remember to lock the door. Do you ever wonder why Hannah hasn't been robbed blind?"

"If I lock the door, how will you get out later?"

"Maybe I'll go out the way you came in. Or maybe I'll sit right here and balance the books or catch up on the gallery's correspondence. Just don't tell anyone and ruin my slacker reputation."

"Your secret's safe with me," Jandy said.

"Likewise."

Jandy turned to go, then turned back. "Aren't you afraid of being trapped in here with the rat?"

"The rat?"

"Sam told me not to come to work because you spotted a rat in the gallery. He said Swan's on her way with some kind of catch-and-release device."

"That Sam. What a kidder. He was probably trying to divert you. I think the rat he was talking about works for a Dallas TV station."

"Oh." Somehow that news didn't make her feel any better. It was so weird to think that Sam had always known her secret.

She locked the gallery door behind her and tried her best to imitate Dove's walk as she headed for the Mini. She considered turning in the opposite direction when she saw Clay Gaines, looking starched and official in his cop uniform, standing next to Dove's car. Before she could dodge him, he spotted her. Annoyance covered his features. Then he did a double take, smiled, jammed his ticket book in his back pocket, and walked away.

"At least that's something I did for Dove," she muttered as she crammed her long legs into the Mini. She bumped her knee, grimaced from the pain, and swore about people who drove toy cars. But once she was out of town, she pushed a button to lower the top and stopped complaining. The car was just plain fun, and if her thoughts hadn't been careening through her brain at about five times the speed she was driving, she'd be having a good time behind the wheel.

She was out in the country before she realized what direction she'd taken. How lame was it to be racing toward the Revere house? Did she expect Rachel Revere to take her in and soothe her agitation? Rachel wasn't her mother, after all. She'd be more likely to scold her children for inviting duplicity inside and serving it tomato sandwiches.

Jandy refused to believe for a second that she wanted to see Sam. In the first place, she wasn't in the habit of running to some man just because she felt bad. In the second place, she didn't want to face Sam knowing that he thought she was some flighty runaway bride. In the third place, Sam was out in the tow truck picking up some-body's stupid Dodge instead of being at home with Sue.

Actually, it was *Sue* she wanted to see. There was noth-ing like a dog to make a person feel better.

But really, she wondered, *what do I have to feel so terrible about?*

How about lying to everyone in Coventry, Pru suggested.

She was tired of going through the same argument about whether or not using a different name and being discreet about oneself constituted lying. She had her answer. Not knowing that everyone else had known the truth—that felt like they'd been lying to her. It definitely didn't feel good, but it was exactly what she'd been will-ing to do to them.

Her face flamed red as she thought of the women in the beauty shop. The people in Jennifer's cooking classes. The check-out clerk and bag boy at the grocery store who always chatted her up. Mr. Rook at the drug-store and Mr. Phillips at the hardware store who treated her like their best customer. The Boones' guests. Michael and Keelie Boone themselves. Reverend Black at First Coventry Church and Reverend St. John at Christ Church. Tryphena and Phylura. Probably even those mis-creants Fiji and Jay Jay, who she'd had the audacity to bust for cownapping. It was a little hard to walk cockily across her moral high ground when she'd been spreading manure over it for weeks.

She groaned and pulled over to the side of the road as the slide show continued through her brain: a proces-sion of the friendliest, kindest faces she'd ever known. Every one of them had been aware that she was January Halli, or Jane Halli, or Hudson Blake's missing fiancé, or

Stan and Carol Halli's daughter. She wasn't sure what was worse: being a really bad liar or a first-class idiot.

She suddenly remembered telling Robin, who had to be the most guileless person she'd ever met, that Hud was a doctor. Robin hadn't even blinked.

Maybe she should stop tormenting herself with every lie she'd told Sam's sisters. They had a few things to answer for, too. They'd gone along with whatever she said while they were scheming to hook her up with their brother. At least she'd *always* told them she had a fiancé, even if she had played loose with a few other facts.

"I've been watching you for five minutes, and you had no idea I was here. You seem like a woman with a lot on her mind."

Jandy gave a little shriek and looked toward the fence, where Grayson Murray was sitting astride a horse.

"You could give a person a heart attack, sneaking up like that," she said.

Grayson looked a little perplexed as he stared down at his horse, which was making a big ruckus as it snorted and pawed the ground, obviously eager to move on or at least get as far as possible from the mysterious metal box sporting wheels and an oblivious redhead. "I'll try to remember that. Car trouble?"

"No. Just trying to find a quiet place to think." She realized how rude that sounded. "I mean, not that you—"

"I got off the phone about half an hour ago after getting an earful from Evan. Conrad Schaeffer—you probably know him; he delivers mail to the gallery—found your cell phone on the square and took it to Evan. Dove told Evan you wouldn't be working today, so he said he'll get it to you later. Also, your intrepid reporter has left town, convinced by everyone he talked to that Jandy

Taylor was born, raised, and trained to twirl her fire batons right here in Coventry, Texas."

"So the news thinks Jandy's a slutty ex-majorette."

"That may have been the perspective Dove gave him, but the rest of the town thinks you're aces."

"Fabulous."

Grayson grinned. "It is, actually. I don't think I've seen the town this single-minded since the year a handful of outside agitators tried to make us put clothes on the Lady Godiva statue. You've turned into the town's mascot. You're even bigger than Wyndmere. And by bigger, I mean more important of course. Because you're not actually—"

"So you're confirming that people not only know who I am, but they've been actively conspiring to protect my identity if I was tracked down?"

"Yep. They've been protecting you all along. They tried to keep you busy and having too much fun to know there were days when your face was on CNN or Fox every thirty minutes. You've been talked about on Letterman, Leno, Conan, Larry King, Jon Stewart, and *The View*. If it weren't summer, Lindsay Lohan would be doing skits about you on *Saturday Night Live*. The cashiers at the grocery store started putting the tabloids under the counter if they saw you come in."

"It's like *Ricker v. Rucker* in the Second District Court of Appeals, when Rucker impersonated Ricker to bilk old people out of their life savings. I'm living in hell."

"Nope. Just Coventry, where your impersonation has neither fooled anyone nor cheated them out of money. In fact, a vote taken at Coventry's best-attended city council meeting in the town's history was unanimous that you deserved all the privacy and quiet you wanted while you're visiting us. That was even *before* Wayne Plochman's offer."

"Him? Again? What offer?"

"Old Mr. Plochman took a liking to you. He said you're plucky. He pledged that if we kept your presence in Coventry a secret, he'd donate a substantial sum to the Daughters of Godiva Benevolent Fund. There was quite an uproar after that announcement."

"Because someone wanted the reward money that my mother offered?"

"Because everyone was insulted by the implication that they needed to be bribed to keep your secret. You became the town's cause, Jandy. Plochman intends to donate the money all the same. If nothing else, feel good about that. It'll probably buy equipment for the new hospital."

"That's the silver lining to my personal humiliation?"

Grayson gave her an exasperated look and said, "No. Your silver lining is the way a town full of people who were strangers to you a month ago have made themselves your friends and champions."

She considered that a few seconds and finally said, "I feel even lower than the snake I felt like for lying to everybody. Now I'm the dirt on a snake's belly." She sighed. "Grandpa would say I need some good, hard work to clear the cobwebs out of my soul."

"If that's all it takes, I've got two ranch hands out sick and stables needing attention."

"You're on," she said. "Unless their tenants are in them." She gave his horse a wary look as it impatiently tossed its head again.

"No, the horses are being exercised. I wouldn't dream of letting you muck stalls, though. It's a hard, dirty job."

"I want to. Seriously! I'd love to work myself into a state of complete exhaustion. And not get back to town until it's dark, everything's closed, and I don't have to face anybody."

Grayson shook his head but said, "I guess I've got some work boots and gloves that'll fit you. But don't cry to me when you're covered with blisters and wanting to die tomorrow."

"Just tell me which roads and turns to take, and I'll meet you there. I don't mind getting dirty, and I'm a lot tougher than you think I am."

Once Grayson turned over her training to Devon, a teenage boy who was working on the ranch for the summer, Jandy found that she wasn't at all repulsed by the things she had to do. It was hot in the long gloves and Wellingtons that Devon found for her, but she appreciated their protection as she banked unsoiled straw against the sides of the stalls. Then she had to rake out dirty straw and shovel manure into a wheelbarrow. Devon kept a radio blaring and didn't seem inclined to talk whenever he came to haul the wheelbarrow out to dispose of her treasures. That suited her. She needed time to herself and mindless work to mull over the day's revelations.

She suppressed her discomfort about Sam and everyone else in Coventry. It was too late to regret her attempt to deceive them and pointless to be embarrassed about how that attempt had failed. Those were things over which she had no control.

What she could control was her future and what she did next. She still hadn't figured that out when Grayson came back. He handed over her cell phone, which he'd picked up from Evan. She put the phone in her pocket and showed off her progress.

"You don't have to do the rest of the stalls," Grayson said. "I thought you'd quit long before now."

"This is one time I'm determined to finish what I started," Jandy insisted.

Grayson shrugged and left her alone again after pointing out—for the second time—where she could find drinking water. Her muscles began to ache from shoveling, but true to her word, she didn't slow down until she'd finished mucking out the last stall. Devon showed her where to wash up and yet again pointed out where she could get water to drink. It was obviously a ranch obsession.

She finally left the stable and walked to a circle of live oaks near Grayson's cabin. She was relatively sure she wouldn't have to worry about stampeding horses or cattle that close to the house. Then she chided herself for imagining she was living in the kind of stupid old TV westerns that her stepfather left on while he snored in his recliner late at night.

She wasn't sure what she intended to say when she called Hud's cell phone again, but once he answered, his voice a little frosty, the words came tumbling out.

"I know you're not going to understand this. I don't understand it myself. But it's the way I feel, and I owe you honesty, if nothing else."

He didn't say anything, a sure sign that he'd reached the end of his patience with her. Her resolve almost failed her, then she took a deep breath and continued.

"What I said before is true. I resent the way our wedding plans keep being hijacked by someone else's schemes. I get so upset by it that I start thinking maybe I don't want to be married at all."

"To anyone? Or just me?"

"I don't know. I don't know if I really even feel that way. What I do know is that I'm not willing to come back and put on an extravaganza of a wedding for anyone else's benefit. Even yours. Even for the sake of your career. I'm sorry. But in that regard, I'm very sure of how I feel."

"We can talk about this when you get home on Tuesday."

"Hud, please try to understand. This is the first time in my life that I don't feel weighed down by someone else's expectations. Or rather, by not being able to live up to their expectations. I'm tired of feeling like I can never measure up. My parents wanted a Beverly Hills kid. Someone who'd be an asset to them. But I wasn't popular. I was nothing special. I didn't go to college and pledge a sorority or become a socialite. The first thing I ever did that got their approval was saying yes to your proposal."

"Is that why you said yes?"

"No. I fell—I thought I fell—I loved you."

"Loved? As in you don't feel that way now?"

"That's not what I meant. I'm not expressing myself very well."

"I think I'm hearing you loud and clear."

"Maybe you're hearing things I'm not saying. I only know that I don't want a monster wedding, and I do want more time to sort through my feelings. Part of me thinks I'm entitled to that time, and that you have no right to make demands. But I did agree to marry you, so maybe you do have the right to expect more from me. If you're tired of waiting and dealing with my indecision, if you want to call the whole thing off, I'll understand."

"Are you trying to get me to end this so you don't have to?"

"No. I'm saying I'll understand if you want to move on with your life. The media thinks you already have. Your fans are probably inundating the network with hate mail about me. If I just fade away—"

"The problem is, you're not fading away. For some

reason, your stupid disappearance is all people want to talk about. Even if you don't want to get married, if you want to call the whole thing off, could you just please come back to L.A. and show your face? Because you're knocking the usual suspects off the front pages of the entertainment rags with regularity. Last week, your photo on the side of *People* was bigger than Madonna's. *Madonna*, Jane. It's insane."

"You almost sound jealous."

"Yes. That's it. I'm jealous, because the only way I'll ever get more space than Madonna is if I confess to killing you and throwing your body off the Hoover Dam."

"Then maybe it's better if I don't turn up at all unless I can do it as a corpse," she said.

"I'm sorry I said that. I just don't get what's going through your head. Why you had to go all the way to Texas in the first place. What's keeping you there. And don't say a job. We both know that isn't true."

"When I got here, I realized that all I wanted was some time to just be. Not do anything. Not meet anybody's expectations. Or let them down. Just be me for a little while. But if I wasn't me in California, then who was I? And when I come back, will I be able to mesh the new things I've learned about myself with the person you know?"

She heard Hud's frustrated exhale before he said, "Jane, you talk like you have multiple personality disorder. Just come home, and let's get on with our lives."

"No."

"What?"

"I said no."

"Ever?"

"Of course not. I'll come back when I'm ready. I'm not coming back just because you told me to. And if you can't live with that, don't. You have choices, Hud, but so do I."

"I have a meeting to get to. I can't argue in circles. Will you at least tell me where you are? Don't you think it's weird that you won't do that much?"

"A town called Coventry. Satisfied?"

"Thrilled," he said. "Call me when you feel like sharing your itinerary."

There was nothing like getting hung up on two times in one day. She'd wanted to have a decent conversation with her fiancé. She'd hoped he could help her work through some of her confusion. Instead, the longer she stayed away, the less either of them seemed to be able to communicate with the other. He was probably right. It was time to go back to L.A.

She leaned against the broad tree trunk. Her shoulders and arms were aching from the shoveling she'd done, but it was a good ache. Grandpa was right about the value of hard work. Unlike her ongoing argument with Hud, physical labor made her feel cleaner somehow, which was crazy, since sweat was drying on her skin and she probably smelled a lot like the ass-end of a horse.

But there was a nice breeze blowing, and she felt cool in the shade of the trees. Somewhere she could hear the voices of men calling to each other, and the nickering of horses. The smell of freshly mown grass was almost enticing enough to make her leave her shelter. She felt like running through a meadow, perhaps coming to a clear pool of water where she could tear off her sweaty clothes and dive in. Swimming, as always, would wash away her guilt and uncertainty. Maybe she should have gone to Dove's apartment, after all.

She waited for the voice of Pru to tell her what a jerk she'd been to Hud. When nothing happened, she said,

"Even you're tired of my crazy moods and self-absorbed whining, huh?"

"Talking to yourself?" Grayson asked, sinking down next to her. She smiled but didn't answer. "I wish I could make you feel better about things. I suppose all of us—even Evan and me—thought that protecting you and keeping your presence in Coventry a secret was a kind of game. It's probably not much fun to you. Real feelings drove you here. Real feelings kept you here. I just hope when it's time, and you go back to California, you'll believe that the people you're leaving behind genuinely care for you. What it comes down to is that Coventry really did want to be the tiny town with the big heart."

When she started crying, Grayson didn't say anything. He reached over and pulled her against him. It didn't matter to her that she smelled like livestock or that the temperature was steamy even in the shade. She only thought of how strong he seemed, how safe. It was easy to understand why Evan had fallen in love with him.

"I hate crying," she said when he handed her a clean bandanna from his jeans pocket. "Redheads don't cry well. We get all blotchy and ugly."

"You look all right," he vowed.

"Liar." She gave a trembling laugh. "I suppose I'm the last person who should accuse anyone of lying."

"People in Coventry don't think you're a liar, anymore than they think you're a person named January Halli. You're just Jandy to us. We assume you have your reasons for doing what you do. We respect them."

"I'll feel like such an idiot now when I work in the gallery or walk through the beauty shop, knowing that everyone is fully aware that I've been lying since the first day Sam drove me into town. I'm not ready to go back to L.A., but as soon as Robin tells me Grandpa's truck is safe to drive, I'll find somewhere else to hide from my responsibilities and troubles."

"Now you sound silly and sorry for yourself. I wasn't sure about your plans, but the reason I walked over here in the first place was to make you a job offer."

"That's sweet, but all my bragging aside, I don't think I'm tough enough to shovel manure everyday."

"You nut. I'm not talking about that. You probably won't believe me, but this isn't some spur-of-the-moment idea. Every night, Evan and I read Elenore Storey's blog as a way to unwind. Both of us have commented lately on how much more we're enjoying it now that Elenore's including photos."

"My photos?"

"Yeah. They add so much to her blog. You really have done what she wanted you to: shown us the town through new eyes. Your pictures don't just complement her posts. We think you're actually inspiring some of them. As if she wasn't sure what she would be writing about next until she checked out whatever photos you gave her."

"Thanks, but what does this have to do with anything?"

"You're a good photographer, and I've got work for you, if you want it. It's nowhere near as exciting as turning your camera on Wyndmere when she has a pensive look on her face, or on Fiji when he dumps soap into the Godiva fountain, but it does pay well."

"What would I be shooting photos of?"

"My horses. I use a software program to maintain information on all my horses, and those records include photographs. I also use photos when I list horses for sale. Before you decide that I'm creating work for you, understand that I pay someone to do this on a regular basis. I pay well, as a matter of fact, and I'm willing to hire you at the usual rate. I do think you'll need a better camera than the point-and-shoot you've been using. Evan and I bought a digital SLR when we went on vacation last year. I don't understand half the things the damn camera does, but you could probably have fun with it. It comes with a manual, if you can make sense of it. I never had the patience."

"Are you sure this isn't a sympathy job?"

"The only reason I didn't talk to you about it before was that I thought you wanted to go home as soon as your truck was fixed. But if you're planning to stay for a while, why shouldn't you earn money for something you're good at? I'm sure I pay better than Hannah does at the gallery. You can't be getting rich there."

"No," Jandy agreed with a smile. "But I don't want us to end up like *Kaba v. Goldstone.*"

"What happened to them?"

"Kaba was supposed to paint a portrait of Goldstone's debutante daughter. Kaba insisted that she be allowed to work in complete privacy, so no one saw the portrait until it was unveiled at the Beverly Wilshire on what was meant to be the happiest night of Miss Goldstone's life up to that point. Unfortunately, Ms. Kaba was a follower of the cubist school, and Mr. Goldstone was more of a Renoir man."

Grayson laughed and said, "It would be a problem if you made Picassos of my Arabians. I'll keep a close eye on your work." He paused for a few seconds, then went on. "I have another proposition. Unlike with the job, I am coming up with this on the spot. Now that you know you're not exactly incognito in Coventry, if you want to move out of town, I've got a couple of empty cabins out here. I use them when I take on temporary help."

"My specialty," Jandy said with a tiny smile.

"They're not much. One large room for living, sleeping,

and cooking, plus a separate bathroom with a shower, sink, and toilet. No air-conditioning or heat. Nobody could endure them in winter, but with a few strategically placed fans, you should be comfortable enough. You'd have lots of privacy. You'd be close to your work."

"As long as I don't have to sleep with the horses. I'm sure it's obvious I'm a little afraid of them."

"Handlers will take the horses wherever you want to shoot them on the ranch. Well, not *shoot* them. You know what I mean. Anyway, if loving and understanding horses was a prerequisite for being out here, Evan would still be living over his salon. I long ago gave up on making a cowboy out of him. He barely knows a horse's head from its ass."

"At least I'm ahead of him on that score."

"Because you used to work at a horse track?"

"No. Because I've seen *The Godfather* about thirty times."

"Really? I like movies about violent crime families as much as the next guy, but I would never have suspected it of you."

"It's not me. It's Hud. He'll watch any movie with the blessed trinity."

Grayson gave her a puzzled look and said, "The Father, Son, and Holy Ghost?"

"Brando, Pacino, and De Niro," Jandy corrected him. "Hud says the *Godfather* movies are better than acting class."

"Huh. The most significant thing I learned from *The Godfather* was Clemenza's recipe for spaghetti sauce."

"Not a bad lesson," Jandy said. "I don't suppose you've got a pot of it simmering in your kitchen, by any chance? I feel like it's been forever since breakfast."

"No spaghetti sauce, but I've never yet let one of my employees starve to death. I'm sure we can find something."

"I haven't said yes to your offer yet. I need to figure out if I'm really ready to stay here and further strain my relationship with Hud."

"Take all the time you need." He stood and held out his hand to pull her up.

"Ow," she said. "You were right. Mucking stalls is tough on the muscles."

Grayson nodded. "Compared to that, photography is a snap."

"Coventry: the tiny town with the bad puns," Jandy said and pretended to be groaning about that instead of her aching muscles. "Instead of eating, what I really need to do is get Dove's car back to her and spring her from the gallery."

"If there's one thing in life I'm sure of," Grayson said, "it's that Dove Revere will never be trapped anywhere she doesn't want to be."

As they walked toward Grayson's cabin, Jandy said, "You're an only child, too. Do you ever envy big families like the Reveres?"

"I definitely used to wish I had a brother or sister," Grayson said. He gently took Jandy's arm to lead her around a tree root she hadn't seen. "That's the thing about growing up and making friends, you know. You get to create the family you always wanted."

She thought about Hud and the Foundlings and their close relationships. She'd tried so hard to merge herself into their created family. Maybe the problem was that they hadn't chosen her and she hadn't chosen them. Probably if they'd met any other way except through Hud, they wouldn't have become friends.

If she actually lived in Coventry, she was sure the friendships she'd begun would grow into something deeper, more lasting. Part of her reluctance to go back to California was giving them up; she didn't want to.

But I will for Hud, she thought quickly, before Pru could lecture her about her fiancé. *I'll find other friends as funny, generous, kind, and interesting.*

Lots of people moved and started over, forging new relationships in new places. When she'd started her adventure, she'd thought being Jandy would make her more fun. Maybe going back to California as Jandy, instead of Jane or January, would attract people who were more like those in Coventry.

I can think of my return as another adventure, she reassured herself.

Chapter 19

Jandy drove Dove's car back to the gallery after a dinner of Tex-Mex with Grayson and Evan. The food was another attraction she could put on her list of things she would miss about Coventry, especially a sausage queso dip that was Evan's specialty. She'd eaten so much that she had to unbutton her jeans.

Dove wasn't at the gallery, but Jandy found a note taped to the easel where *A Horse Called Jandy* was displayed.

Unexpected trip to San Antonio with a friend to pick up paintings from Dorcas Laughton. Back Saturday. Before you leave on Sunday for sure. Drive the Mini all you want. Just remember to park in a loading zone now and then so it doesn't miss me. D.

Jandy tried to suppress her selfish irritation. A Coventry artist, Dorcas Laughton had broken her back while on vacation in San Antonio and was stuck in traction at the house of a friend. But really, what kind of martyr continued to paint when she was in traction? Jandy's remaining hours with Dove were being squandered on someone who painted grotesque dead fish with yellow roses arranged around them.

Grandpa would not stop laughing when she complained about it—minus some details that would place her in Texas—the next morning on the phone. "I really need to get me one of those paintings."

"Trust me, you can't afford it," Jandy said. "Anyway, for you, she'd probably want to paint a dead fish on a bed of orange blossoms."

"I hope it's not a dead rockfish," Grandpa said. "They've about disappeared, you know."

"It's not like it's a photograph, Grandpa. No fish would actually have to die. She could bring attention to the plight of the—" Jandy broke off when she heard his wheezy little laugh again. "Are you making fun of me?"

"Would I do that?" he asked. "So tell me the plan."

"Your old truck will be home on Tuesday," she said.

She wouldn't tell him about the work on the truck until she actually handed it over to him. She knew he was going to want to repay her, which she wouldn't allow.

"I don't miss the truck. I miss you, Jane. I don't know who'll be happier to see you, me or your fellow."

She could have answered, but didn't think he'd like what he heard. Instead she said, "I feel like I've been gone a zillion years. I'll probably feel disoriented for a while. At least the stupid runaway bride publicity died down." She hoped he wouldn't tell her otherwise. When he didn't say anything at all, she said, "Grandpa? Are you still there?"

"I was just waiting for you to apply a legal case to your situation. You know how you always do that."

"It would be a criminal court case," she said. "As in *State of California v. Halli*, wherein a tormented young woman thrashed her grandfather with a dead rockfish."

"Better not let the Department of Fish and Game get wind of that."

"Don't you mean downwind of that?" She smiled as he wheezed again, then said, "Grandpa, I've missed you so much. Sometimes I think if it weren't for you and Aunt Ruby, I'd just get on the road and keep driving."

"You might not want to share that news with your fiancé or your mother," Grandpa said. His voice sounded more serious when he went on. "If you ever had a reason to stay away, I wouldn't want you to come back just for me, Jandy."

She got tears in her eyes, chided herself for still being weepy the way she'd been the day before with Grayson, and said, "It makes me feel like a little girl when you call me that."

"I always thought it suited you better than either of the other names," he said.

"I did, too, Grandpa. In fact, sometimes I still do."

"I think," Jandy said haltingly, "that my mother had higher expectations for me than I had for myself." She hadn't realized she'd spoken the words aloud until Rachel Revere turned from the dishwasher with a quizzical expression. Jandy blushed and said, "I didn't mean to say that out loud. I was sort of answering a question you *didn't* ask about an hour ago."

Only the two of them were in the kitchen. When she'd arrived in Dove's Mini at the Revere house that morning, Rachel said that her kids always disappeared whenever time in the kitchen might involve sweating instead of eating. Jandy knew she wasn't serious. Swan and Robin were at work. Lark had her hands full with her two boys. As for Sam, Jandy wasn't sure if he was avoiding her or just doing whatever he usually did to occupy himself. There was no sign of Sue, either. Maybe the two of them were taking a crash course in obedience before the Godiva Festival's dog show the following afternoon.

"You're too young to worry that you haven't lived up to your potential," Rachel said. She pulled more sterilized jars from the dishwasher and frowned. "Scratch that. I was much younger than you when I felt like I'd failed to live up to people's expectations. I know your feelings are real."

Jandy wiped perspiration from her face with a paper towel. Rachel turned up the setting on the fan, and the two of them worked in silence for a while. Jandy was remembering how she'd learned years ago, from Aunt Ruby, to lift the hot jars from the canner with the grabber tongs. Her experience was proving useful. Rachel had taught her how to blanch tomatoes, and they were also experimenting with creating salsa instead of just canning whole and diced tomatoes.

"I think we could use a water break," Rachel finally said.

Jandy nodded and poured them both tall glasses of water from the dispenser in the refrigerator door. They might be using generations-old methods for canning tomatoes, but there were some things improved by technology, and one of them was having filtered water with crushed or cubed ice at one's fingertips.

"Tell me about New Orleans," Jandy said as the two women sat where the oscillating fan would cool first one, then the other.

"Have you ever been there?" Rachel asked. When Jandy shook her head, she said, "Hop and I go every year. Never in the summer; it's too hot. We're usually in Wisconsin by this time of year. And never during Mardi Gras;

it's too crowded and crazy for us. We usually meet some of our friends in New Orleans between carnival season and summer. Just like this year, but with a big difference. We all took campers and RVs so we wouldn't use up rooms needed for contractors and other people who're coming in to clean up, repair, and rebuild. It's not very easy to get work done on your house when so many houses need it. And contractors from out of town are limited because there's no place to stay. People are living in cars that were abandoned under overpasses during the evacuation. You can look down the street of a neighborhood, and every house has a blue tarp on the roof and a camper out front where the former owners are living until their houses can be cleaned of mud and mold. Nobody knows when that will be, because insurance companies aren't paying claims yet, and FEMA is bogged down in red tape. Businesses are closed because there isn't anyone to work in them. Some of the stores that are open have limited hours. It's depressing if you know anything about the way New Orleans used to be."

"Do you think things will ever get back to normal?"

"Well, as my kids could tell you, I'm an idealist. I'm convinced that eventually, they'll be even better than before. That doesn't mean the city isn't suffering now." Rachel looked pensive. "We decided not to make our Midwest trip this summer. There's too much work we can do on the Gulf Coast. We didn't want to keep Sam from being able to use his RV, though, so we brought it home. We plan to buy our own so we can go back to New Orleans."

"I think it's amazing, what you're doing," Jandy said. "It has to feel good to know you're making a difference."

"Is that the problem? Does your mother expect you to make a difference, and you feel as if you're failing her?

Excuse me if my questions are rude. It's another thing the kids could have warned you about."

"You can ask me anything," Jandy said. If she were to blurt out the whole truth, she'd have to admit that she was as smitten with Sam's mother as with his sisters. Rachel's air of confidence, her willowy movements, and her efficiency in the kitchen overwhelmed Jandy. "Unlike you, my mother isn't an idealist. I guess she might call herself a pragmatist. Isn't that the nice way to say that, for her, making money is the most important thing in the world?"

"So you failed her when you didn't choose a lucrative profession?"

"I haven't chosen a profession at all. I'm still trying to figure out what I want to be when I grow up."

Rachel smiled faintly and said, "Are you looking for some motherly wisdom?"

"Am I that transparent?"

"Do what makes you happy. That may change several times in your life, but it's your life, so who cares?"

"Is that what you and your husband told your children?"

Rachel smiled. "Hop worked from the time he was a kid. While he thinks there's value to that, he wanted our children to have chances he didn't have. I just wanted them to be happy. It didn't bother me at all when Sam was the only one who finished college. The girls knew the opportunity was there. They knew we'd help. But Robin loved the smell of auto grease and the way engines are put together, so she dropped out to work in the garage. Swan could have gone to vet school, but she's happy working for Dr. Boone. She says she has all the fulfillment and none of the headaches of working in his practice. She makes enough money to take care of her needs, has a little fun now and then, so she's happy. Lark went to UT for one semester and was utterly miserable. The day she married Jimmy, she practically danced down the aisle. I've never seen a happier bride."

"What about Dove?" Jandy asked quickly, wanting to talk about anything but weddings and brides.

"Dove was always too pretty for her own good. People made things easy for her because of it. I've always admitted that Dove intrigues me more than the others. I never know what she'll do next, but I also never doubt that she can take care of herself." Rachel stood to refill their glasses. "Have the birds told you about when I met their father?"

"Not really."

"I was in college, where I was majoring in rebellion and minoring in what would come to be called women's studies. This wasn't at the beginning of the women's movement, but for many of us, it was all very new and abrasive and man-hating at that time. Which is just silly, because that isn't at all what feminism is about. Nor," she added, with a stern look at Jandy, "was it about anything so ridiculous as burning bras, which *none* of us ever did."

"Me, either," Jandy said in an attempt at solidarity.

"My parents were dismayed by my politics. Mine are ancient stories, but believe me, I understand parental disapproval. When I came to Coventry with a college friend, I fell in love with Hop. My socialist friends were delighted that he was a genuine member of the working class. My feminist friends felt betrayed. I dropped out of school, started growing my own vegetables, and began popping out babies. My family was thrilled. They thought these were my first signs of normal behavior. Of course, when I went through my metaphysical phase, they revised their opinions."

"Is that why people call you a witch? Maybe I shouldn't say that."

"It's not news. Who knows why people say half the nonsense they do? No matter what choices you make, someone will always disapprove of you. So what? The only companionship guaranteed you in this life—for your entire lifetime—is your own. As far as I'm concerned, the only approval you need is your own. Your mother might not see it my way. But the whole point of feminism, as we envisioned it in my day, was that a woman should be free to choose the life she wanted." She stopped talking and smiled. "Frankly, any woman over forty defines feminism as whatever validates the choices she's made. But really, who is anyone to judge what's right for someone else? If you're madly in love with your young man and what you want most in the world is to marry him and have a family with him, then it's really nobody else's concern. It's *your* life."

"Right," Jandy said thoughtfully. She finally lifted her eyes to meet Rachel's gaze. "The problem is, I'm not too sure about that, either."

Rachel stood, looked at the sky through the back door, and said, "I think we may get a thunderstorm later." She turned around. "How did you and—what's his name? Hub?"

"Hud. Short for Hudson."

"How did you meet?"

"I was temping for an attorney who's in the same building as his publicist. She wasn't there when he was supposed to meet her for an appointment, and his cell phone battery was dead, so he came into our office to make a call."

"And he asked you out?"

"No. I guess he flirted a little, but I figured—Well, Hud's got movie star looks. I'm not in his league. I thought he was just being charming so he could use our phone. A couple of weeks later, he was back to see Chandra again, and we ran into each other in the elevator. He asked for my phone number. I'm not sure which of us was more shocked when he actually called and asked me out."

Probably Chandra, Pru suggested.

A crease marred the nearly unlined skin on Rachel's forehead as she said, "Who taught you to sell yourself short? Your mother?"

"I'm just being honest. I have almost nothing in common with Hud's friends or the girls he dated before me."

"You're the one he wants to marry," Rachel said.

"That's true," Jandy said and jumped up to check on the jars of tomatoes in the canner. When she turned around again, she said, "I don't believe in love at first sight, by the way."

"I don't either," Rachel said.

"But you just told me that you and your husband—"

"One reason some people call me a witch is because I do believe in past lives and karma. I think we make certain choices before we're born. As the man I chose, Hop was my destiny."

Jandy stopped herself from insisting that she didn't believe in destiny, either. Instead, she said, "How did he get the name Hop?"

"Like my kids, he started hanging around the garage when he was just a toddler. A car ran over his foot."

"How awful."

"He recovered. But while his foot was healing, he hated using crutches, so he hopped. One of his brothers gave him that nickname, and it stuck."

"Did Sam ever have a nickname?" Jandy asked. "Or did he manage to escape childhood accidents?"

"I think the worst calamity to befall Sam may be a very

recent one," Rachel said. She blew wisps of her strawberry blond hair out of her eyes and began filling more jars with sauce so Jandy could put them in the canner.

"You mean when he lost Daisy? I heard about that."

Rachel glanced at her for a moment, then slowly said, "It wasn't as easy as I made it sound to give up my old life when I fell in love. For a while, I had a foot in both worlds. I finally realized that no matter where I was or what I was doing, everything would be better because Hop was with me. I don't know if that means anything to you, but that's all the advice I've got."

Before Jandy could answer, she heard someone coming in the back door. She and Rachel both turned around, and Jandy tried not to gape at the man who was undoubtedly Rachel's husband. She'd expected him to look like Sam, or to be tall like Dove, or maybe stocky like Swan. What she hadn't expected was that he'd be at least four inches shorter than his wife and extremely thin. His hair was even darker than Sam's and Lark's, almost black, but his eyes were the same color blue as theirs. They crinkled at the corners when he smiled at Jandy. She smiled back, thinking that he was so adorable that she wished she could carry him around in her pocket.

"Hop, this is the young lady the girls have been talking about, Jandy Taylor."

"Hop Revere," he said, holding out his hand.

Jandy shook it and said, "It's nice to meet you, Mr. Revere."

"Mr. Revere's my father. At least he was before he died. But I've got two older brothers who can fight over the title. I'm just Hop. Has Rachel made you sick of tomatoes?"

"Not yet," Jandy said. "Since meeting your family, I

have a new appreciation for them. Lark taught me how to make a tomato sandwich."

"Just remember to use Hellmann's."

"This is a long-standing family dispute," Rachel said. "Don't get dragged into it, Jandy. If you want to put *mustard* on your tomato sandwiches, feel free."

"That's disgusting," Hop said.

"No more disgusting than your disrespect of Miracle Whip."

Hop ignored his wife and said, "When the kids were youngsters, Rachel always tricked them into doing dirty jobs by telling them how well they did them. Swan was the best duster. Dove was the best dish washer. Sam was the best weeder. She's not pulling that on you, is she?"

"She did praise my blanching skills," Jandy said and laughed at his knowing nod. "Seriously, I used to help my aunt Ruby put up preserves. I'm not a complete novice at this."

Hop made a fresh pot of coffee, then all three of them maneuvered around each other. Sam's father pitched in without complaint, reminding her a little of the way Sam helped whenever he came to the gallery.

While they worked, the Reveres asked Jandy questions about her aunt, and she ended up telling them more stories about Grandpa, Aunt Ruby, and her childhood than she'd shared with anyone in Coventry, even Evan.

"I'm sorry for babbling," she finally said, feeling embarrassed. After the work they'd been doing in New Orleans, she was sure they had more important things to talk about than her lackluster life story.

"You sound a little homesick," Rachel said.

"Not really. I do miss Grandpa and Aunt Ruby a lot. It'll be good to see them again."

Hop and Rachel exchanged a glance that seemed to

mean something. Jandy realized she hadn't said she missed Hud, but it was too late to add his name without sounding awkward and forced.

Rachel nodded, and Hop said, "I reckon you could be seeing them sooner than you thought. Take a look at what's in the driveway."

Jandy walked over and looked out the window, as much dismayed as surprised to see Grandpa's truck. "It's fixed? I thought Robin didn't expect the part until tomorrow."

"It got here early. I fixed the truck myself," Hop said. "Robin said you were planning to leave Sunday, but if you want to go earlier, now you can."

"That's great," she said weakly.

"It's time," Rachel said. When Jandy gave her a startled look, she added, "It's time to take the jars out of the canner."

"Right," Jandy said. Before going back to the stove, she smiled at Hop and said, "I really appreciate your work on my truck. When I get back to town, I'll settle up with Robin."

"No hurry," Hop said. "I doubt you plan to slip out in the dead of night without paying your bill."

As she lifted out the jars of tomatoes, Jandy thought that slipping out in the dead of night sounded appealing. No long good-byes. No sad promises of reunions that might never happen. Just a letter to Evan thanking him for everything and including cash for the haircuts and the use of his apartment. A note for Grayson thanking him for his offer of work but saying it was time to go home. A letter to Dove thanking her for so many things. Maybe letters to all the Reveres telling them what they'd meant to her. And a note to Jennifer Boone . . .

The more she thought about it, the more notes she

needed or wanted to write. Maybe not five hundred, like with her wedding gifts. But so many people in Coventry had been good to her.

She couldn't believe the weight on her chest. She felt like she was about half a second from sobbing, and it didn't help when she thought of never seeing Sue again. A dog wouldn't understand a note.

She squared her shoulders and said, "Anyway, I definitely won't leave until after the dog show."

After a restless night, Jandy dragged herself out of bed at six o'clock on Friday morning and stared wearily at the water as it circled the drain while she brushed her teeth.

It's a metaphor for your life, Pru warned. *You need to pack your truck and hit the road. All these excuses to stay are nothing more than another case of pre-wedding jitters. You life is in California with Hud. Stop dawdling.*

She could be in L.A. by Sunday. No. She could be in Redlands by Sunday. She'd already told Hud she wouldn't be there before Tuesday. She could spend a couple of days with Grandpa and Aunt Ruby to ease out of her Jandy Taylor persona and become Jane Halli, Fiancée, again. Not to mention January Halli, Daughter.

She'd gone by Revere Auto and paid her bill the day before. Evan wouldn't be in the beauty shop for almost three hours. She'd done her laundry and cleaned the apartment. It wouldn't take long to pack.

"Just do it," she snapped at her reflection.

Forty-five minutes later she was showered, packed, and sitting on the bed to write her notes. She put cash in Evan's envelope along with letters to him and Grayson. She gave Dove Hud's address so she could mail her last check from the gallery, and added little notes to Sam,

Swan, Robin, Lark, and their parents. Then she put the keys to the apartment and the gallery with the letters on the kitchen table.

After taking her suitcase and a few bags of other things she'd accumulated to Grandpa's truck, she stood in the middle of the apartment for a last look around. It was impossible to believe that it had been her home for only a month. It seemed like she'd been there forever.

"And it may take forever to forget it," she said.

Don't think about Sam. Don't think about Sue. Just go.

By the time she cranked the pickup, her sense of urgency was intense. Now that her mind was made up, she didn't want to run into anyone. But she couldn't just leave without some kind of good-bye to the town itself. She drove around the square, but instead of heading out of town, she did it again, this time parking close to the Godiva fountain. She was sure neither Clay Gaines nor any other officer would be out this early to give tickets. The festival's vendors hadn't even begun to arrive yet.

All the stores were closed. The sidewalks were empty. In the distance, she saw a couple of people who she didn't recognize running with their dogs. Another car drove slowly through town but kept going.

She sat on the edge of the Godiva fountain and looked up at the serene face of the woman on horseback.

"I'll miss you and your town. Thank you for giving me a safe harbor for a few weeks." She dug in her pocket for change, tossed it into the fountain, and said, "And let Sue win the dog show. Not that I believe in wishes or anything."

She felt better once something had been said that felt like good-bye. After she reached the 20, which would take her through that barren desert to the 10, which would get her all the way back to L.A., Pru was finally silent.

Because I'm doing the right thing, she thought. *I'm living up to my commitments. I'm going back to where I came from, the way I should.*

Then why did her spirit feel so heavy? Why did she feel like she was leaving something unfinished?

That's just me, she thought. *I'm the girl who never finishes anything. Just keep driving. Don't think. Don't remember. Don't look back. Don't—*

"My painting!" she said. Fortunately there were no other cars anywhere near her, since she veered across the right lane to get to the exit ramp. She turned left on the overpass, then got back on the freeway heading east.

By the time she got into Coventry, the town was coming to life. Shopkeepers swept the sidewalks in front of their stores. People mingled near the square as the festival merchants got their booths ready to open.

Even if it hadn't been too early for the gallery to be open, Dove was in San Antonio, and Jandy had locked herself out of Molly's Beauty Shop. She went to the Early Bird Café and got a cup of coffee and a bagel to go. She ate her breakfast in the cab of the pickup while she waited for Tryphena or Phylura to show up and let her in.

But it was Evan and Grayson who pulled into the parking spot next to her. They smiled at her as she got out of her pickup.

"You're out and about early. It has to be fun to finally have your own wheels again," Evan said.

"Uh-huh," Jandy agreed. Neither of them seemed to notice her suitcase in the bed of the pickup. "I locked myself out."

The three of them walked into the shop together, then Jandy went upstairs to retrieve the keys to the gallery. She could get her painting, put it inside the pickup, and take the keys back to the apartment. She wondered when Evan would figure out that she wasn't coming back. When he'd go upstairs and find the letters.

Don't turn this into another Beatles song, Pru warned. *You wrote a beautiful good-bye in your letter. Evan will understand why you left. Just get back on the road.*

When she went downstairs, Grayson was making a pot of coffee while Evan pulled up the shades and examined the windows to see if any smudges needed to be wiped clean. Grayson smiled at her and said, "Have you made a decision about my offer?"

She met his eyes, which held nothing but kindness and expectation. How would his eyes look when Evan told him that she'd left without telling them she was going? Would he understand?

"I can't do it," she said.

"That's okay. I knew it was a long shot."

"No, I mean I can't—something's just holding me—"

She couldn't even finish a sentence, and both men stopped what they were doing to look at her with concern.

"Are you okay?" Evan asked.

"I think so. I know Hud's not going to understand. But I just can't leave here yet." She looked at Grayson's eyes, now full of worry, and gave him a tremulous smile. "Yes, Grayson. I'll move into your cabin and shoot your horses. So to speak. My stuff's already loaded in the truck. I just need to run up and get a couple of things I left on the table."

"That's great," Grayson said. "I'll ride out with you and hand over our camera. You can use it for your festival pictures if you want to. It'll give you the chance to get familiar with it."

Evan put his arm across her shoulders, gave her a quick squeeze, and said, "It'll be weird not having you upstairs, but I've already done a few things to make the cabin more cozy for you. You know I'm all about creature comforts."

She was back on the square that afternoon in plenty of time to watch the preparations for the dog show. She'd never seen so many dogs in her life. She was glad she had her camera and Grayson's, along with an extra memory card. Maybe she'd create a blog of her own just to publish her best dog-and-owner photos.

A chorus of howls and barks sounded after the speakers set up by the radio station began broadcasting feedback squeals. Then Elvis's "Hound Dog" boomed across the square, followed by other dog songs, though she didn't recognize most of them except "Puppy Love" and "Black Dog." She smiled when they played "Me and You and a Dog Named Boo," remembering the way Sam had changed Boo to Sue when he quoted the song.

She hadn't seen either Sam or Sue, but she kept looking. She was taking photos of a little girl holding a beagle when the Beatles' "Martha My Dear" began playing. Her head whipped around. She assumed that few people knew the song was about Paul McCartney's Old English sheepdog, but Sam did. She remembered telling him that she'd named her pet turtle Martha after the dog. She wondered if he'd requested the song for her.

She heard the sounds of people laughing and turned in the opposite direction to see a dachshund with a rope toy trying to outrun a black Lab. The Lab kept overshooting the dachshund when the smaller dog made abrupt direction changes.

"Something always goes wrong at the dog show," a man next to her said.

"If that's all that happens, it'll be a dull year," his companion answered.

At that moment, Jandy spotted Sam leaning against his Jeep with some men she didn't recognize. Sue was at his feet, and both of them were watching the dachshund. Sam was laughing, and even though Jandy couldn't hear him over the noise of the music, the crowd, and the persistent barking of dogs, her memory of the sound of his laugh made her smile.

She forgot her cameras and everyone around her while she memorized the sight of him, as if she really was leaving that night, or the next day, or the next. Jeans, black Chucks instead of the usual cowboy boots, black T-shirt, and the same old straw cowboy hat, his sunglasses hanging, as usual, from the collar of his T-shirt.

She was torn between wanting to cross the square to him and wanting to stare at him from a distance. It was hard, watching him, to admit that she'd been lying to herself for weeks. She could blame his sisters for putting ideas in her head all she wanted, but she couldn't blame anyone but herself for the funny way her heart felt.

There was nothing she could do about it, though. She loved someone else. She'd made a promise to someone else. She was sure she'd be attracted to men other than Hud over the years. Attractions were natural. That didn't mean she had to do anything about them.

But the things she'd already done—staying in Coventry, accepting Grayson's offer, calling Hud and Grandpa and telling them she wasn't coming back quite yet—had she done those things because of Sam or for herself?

As she was trying to figure it all out, her attention was caught by a flash of color to her right. She looked over and saw Wyndmere being led onto the square, the big dragon head resting on her long horns. Simultaneously, she saw

Jay Jay and Fiji in the street. She grinned, thinking of their attempt at cattle rustling and the way she, Keelie, and Evan had helped Tryphena and Phylura thwart them. It was the kind of tale she could tell her—

Before she could finish that thought, Fiji put a match to a string of firecrackers that Jay Jay was holding. Jay Jay tossed them away from the crowd as they began popping. Everything seemed to happen in slow motion—some people pulling away from the noise, others looking in that direction to find out what was going on. Jandy saw a flash of blue-gray go past her, then Beau the Australian cattle dog was on Wyndmere's back.

For a moment, Wyndmere seemed too stunned to move. But she wasn't like the hog in Beau's earlier version of that trick. Wyndmere's rehearsals for terrorizing a damsel in distress had never included being conquered by thirty-five pounds of canine fury. She swung her horns, her eyes became rimmed with white circles, and she took off toward the assembly of dogs and their owners.

Beau jumped down, looking proud of himself, and Jandy began to laugh as dogs and people scattered in all directions, turning over crates and kennels and toppling pedestals. She looked again at Sam, who held tightly to Sue's leash while he watched and laughed at the chaos. Their eyes met, and before she knew what she was doing, Jandy began walking toward him through the bedlam.

Sam and Sue met her halfway. She wasn't sure which of them made the first move, but Sam's free arm went around her, and she held Grayson's camera behind her as she tilted her head to avoid his cowboy hat. It could have been a friendly kiss or a happy kiss, but it was a different kind of kiss, the kind that sent a shock wave down her spine, then radiated out to every nerve of her body.

Between one moment and the next, she forgot it was

broad daylight and that most of the population of Coventry and all of its tourists could get an eyeful if they were so inclined. She forgot Pru and caution and her fiancé in California and lost herself in the kiss that she hadn't allowed herself to want or dream about for four weeks.

Chapter 20

One thing Jandy had learned from Sue over the long days of July was the value of sky gazing. She couldn't remember doing that as a child. When she'd been in the orange grove, she'd loved the secret space the trees provided, and their foliage had been too dense to show much sky. At her parents' house, she was almost never outside. Playing was reserved for adults and teens with golf clubs or tennis rackets. Because of her fair skin, she'd been unable to spend much time lying on beaches and squinting at the clouds rolling in from the Pacific.

She knew a state as big as California must provide lots of places to lie in lush grass and stare at the sky. But proud Texans would no doubt agree that the Lone Star State seemed to provide a larger vista of sky than anywhere else on earth. It definitely offered a lot of variation. She couldn't remember experiencing such crashing thunderstorms even when she and Hud had vacationed in various tropical paradises. Other days were cloudless, the sky so blue it hurt her eyes. And sometimes, the infinite variety of clouds billowing across the sky provided the perfect panorama for her thoughts, worries, and daydreams.

Her life seemed unchanging from one serene day to the next. She knew she was in a holding pattern, but it suited her state of mind. She liked being lulled by the landscape and the heat into a kind of mental lethargy. She tried not to think about her problems. If she thought about anything, it was all that had happened to her since she'd arrived in Coventry, including the day of the dog show. Especially the day of the dog show.

After that incredible kiss from Sam at the height of canine madness, they'd taken Sue and snuck away to Rook Drugs. The drugstore was empty; everyone was outside enjoying the Mad Cow show. Nelson Rook made them cherry Dr. Peppers, then went out to the sidewalk, leaving them alone with Sue.

"Is she allowed in here?" Jandy asked.

"Technically, no. But you don't think I'd let her pick up bad habits from those ruffians who've taken over the square, do you?" He ignored his Dr. Pepper, keeping his eyes fixed on hers so that she couldn't look away without seeming guilty of something. Finally he said, "Let's not pretend it didn't happen."

"I'm not. Although maybe I forgot it. Maybe you could do it again to help me remember."

His gaze fell to her lips. His impish grin came and went, then he said, "You're still wearing that ring."

"I know. You probably have a lot of questions, don't you?"

"Nope." His expression became serious. "From the beginning, you told me what you thought I needed to know. Although I'll admit other people might have given me an earful from time to time. It's not easy to avoid advice when I'm not courting a runaway bride."

"So all that charm and attention you haven't lavished on me was because you're not interested?"

"That's not what I meant. I couldn't court what doesn't exist. You were never a runaway bride, were you?"

She shook her head. "I'm still not. I'm an undecided bride. For a month, I've tried every way I could to pretend this thing"—she motioned to the air between them—"doesn't exist. Because the place where it's happening isn't real, Sam."

"What do you mean? It feels real to me."

"Have you ever heard people say how superficial L.A. is? That nothing or nobody is genuine there?"

"That's a common impression, yes."

"It's not true. California natives understand that the mythical part—the entertainment industry—that's just another business. Maybe crazy money gets thrown around and people are successful for unusual reasons, but it's no different from anywhere. One little part of the population has too much. Most people's lives are just average, and some people don't have enough. People go to their jobs, raise families, try to get by. Whatever. L.A. may stretch from the sublime to the gritty, but it's real. This—Coventry—it's not real."

He made a noncommittal noise.

"Here," she went on, "everything's as idyllic as the towns Hollywood invents. The people are nice. Everyone's a neighbor. Everyone's ready to help a friend or even a stranger. I don't remember one awful thing happening since I've been here. I've never even seen a dead squirrel in the road."

Sam reached over and brushed the line of her jaw with his thumb. "Nobody likes to hear that she's wrong, but you are. People think L.A.'s prettier than Cleveland. Cleveland's prettier than somewhere else. Old Coventry has been kept quaint and charming on purpose. But like you said, people are the same everywhere. Good and bad. We wouldn't have doctors, lawyers, therapists, auto mechanics, plumbers, and cops if people and things didn't break down. The difference between Coventry and every place else at this moment in time is you. You're infatuated with a town, so you don't see its flaws."

She was annoyed to realize that her eyes were filling with tears. It was so nice to be taken seriously, even if he didn't agree, that she didn't know how to react. He slid off his stool, stepped over Sue, and put his arms around her. She liked resting her face against his chest.

"I keep telling myself that I've fallen for your dog, your town, and your family. I want your family. I have all these feelings, but how do I know if they're because of you or because of all that you have? You probably don't even realize what you have."

"Sure I do."

"I'm so hungry for it all. It's better than the Beatle Barbies." She was relieved when he laughed with her. "I do love Hud. I never intended to leave him or stay away from him this way. Can a person love two people? Do I just feel obligated to him? Or am I just infatuated with you?"

"Depends. Do I have any flaws?"

"Dozens," she said.

He pulled away to look down at her, his eyes still serious but affectionate. Everybody should have eyes like his.

"What are your immediate plans?" he asked.

"I told Grayson that I'd stay a while and photograph his horses. I'll be living in one of the cabins on his ranch. I told Hud I need more time. In a way, I think he's relieved. His manager or publicist or whatever she calls herself this week is negotiating a big deal for him. Before, she wanted me to come back so she could get me out of the news. Now I think some other story has made me old news, because she and Hud aren't pushing so hard. Why didn't you tell me you knew about the runaway bride nonsense?"

"I already explained: I don't know that person on the news. To me, you're just Jandy. The woman who makes me laugh. Makes my heart beat faster. Won't get out of my head when I'm trying to work or sleep or think about my future."

She couldn't do anything after that except kiss him again. It was just as good as the first time, and he was the one who pulled away.

"Tonight, Mom, Dad, and I leave for Okalahoma. Robin has a lead on an RV for them that sounds like just what they need, and the price is right. We'll probably spend a couple of nights in Tulsa, then take our time driving it back so they can get used to it. It's a little bigger than mine. I agreed to do it because I thought you were leaving this weekend. I figured being on the road was better than moping about that."

"Would you really have moped?"

"I had a big helping of moping planned, with a side dish of regret."

"And now I'm not leaving."

"So you said."

"It sounds like you don't believe me. Do you think I'll also be a runaway girlfriend-if-only-she-could-figure-out-what-she-wants?"

"I hope not. That's harder to say than runaway bride. I've got an idea. If you're not leaving town, why don't I leave Sue with you? You have to feed her raw meat, but I could give it to you already portioned out. You have to promise you won't get all woozy if you find a chicken head or foot."

"If you tell me those are dead guinea hen parts, I'll give them to her with pleasure," Jandy vowed. "How do you know this won't be my big chance to steal your dog?"

He shook his head and said, "You wouldn't do that."

"Haven't you watched the news? I'm not stable."

"Why would I believe that story? After all, sometimes they say you're dead, and you seem pretty alive to me. Although I could check again." After their third kiss, he said, "Anyway, you're talking about Jane or January. Not Jandy."

"They're all three me," she said. "But you're right. Even though by rights, that dog is just as much mine as yours, I won't run off with her."

And she hadn't. Instead, she'd spent the rest of that weekend taking photos at the crowning of the new Daughter of Godiva and at the Medieval Ball. She'd attended the ball in a costume gown loaned to her by Elenore Storey, whose granddaughter had worn it so long ago that no one remembered it. At the ball, when Jandy wasn't tormenting everyone with cameras, she danced and ate and had a fantastic time, although she did wonder wistfully what it would be like to dance with Sam. Watching some of the other men, she also wondered what Sam would look like in a kilt. She was pretty sure he could carry it off.

Then the festival was over, with the Fourth to look forward to. Sam had returned from Oklahoma, but asked if she could keep Sue a few more days. His parents were ready to go back to New Orleans in the new RV, and he and Swan were following in his RV. Dr. Boone had given Swan time off so she could help with a mobile vet lab. Chances were that she and Sam would be transporting a few dogs and cats to an animal rescue group in Dallas.

Jandy and Sue had helped them pack Sam's RV with crates and cat carriers. She didn't mind that she had no opportunity to be alone with him. She was still mulling things over. That was why watching clouds came in handy.

In the mornings, Devon helped her set up photo shoots in various places on the ranch. One of the hands always brought the horses and stayed with them. She remained a little wary of her equine subjects and wished she had Sue's instincts. The dog seemed to know which horses didn't mind having her around and which ones were too high-strung to tolerate her. Jandy never worried about her because she realized Sue didn't go far. She could almost always see her, a big lump in the grass that looked like a white boulder. Jandy liked to imagine that Sue kept an eye on her for Sam, but she knew the dog was probably just snoozing.

Whenever a shoot ended, Sue would appear as if she'd never left, and the two of them would find a place to eat, then they'd lie in the grass or rest under the branches of a live oak and sky gaze. Even though the days were hot, there always seemed to be a breeze to bring the sounds of bird calls, the buzz of bees, the lowing of cattle from a distant ranch, and the nickering and whinnying of horses.

Jandy knew the peaceful afternoons were lulling her into a false sense of well-being. She knew that all the problems and decisions she was avoiding were still there. But by the time she walked to Grayson's and Evan's cabin every night and helped them cook dinner, or even on the night she went to the Boones' house for a cookout and fireworks, Jandy felt as if the clouds had come down from the sky to cloak her, buffering her from her own worries as well as other people's curiosity and speculation.

She still went to the beauty shop and gossiped with

the Wicks sisters. She sat at the counter at Rook Drugs, drank cherry Dr. Peppers, and remembered the afternoon with Sam that she'd never allow herself to call magical because she didn't believe in magic. She went to Dove's apartment and swam, and sometimes they'd pick up Robin and visit Lark, Jimmy, and the boys.

Hannah Herren came back from San Diego and thanked her profusely for her work in the gallery. Jandy felt like the job had given her far more than she'd given it, and not just because of Wayne Plochman's painting, although it was the first thing she saw when she woke up in the morning, and the last thing she looked at before she turned off the light at night. She'd asked Dove if she could be formally introduced to the irascible old artist, but apparently he went to Vancouver every July.

"Stick around until he gets back," Dove suggested.

Jandy just smiled, reminding herself that a few blissful moments with Sam didn't keep her time in Coventry from having an expiration date. The only thing she could promise was that she wouldn't leave until Sam came for his dog. She certainly wouldn't attempt another exit without telling him good-bye.

She and Sue went to town one day to pick up a few necessities. After visiting Molly's Beauty Shop, they walked to the square. Jandy was down on her belly in the grass, taking her zillionth photo of Sue, when she saw a pair of feet in colorful sneakers and four unfamiliar paws stop next to her. She looked up to see Jennifer Boone and Rip the greyhound staring down at her.

She laughed and said, "This is almost where I entered. Do you remember that day?"

Jennifer nodded and said, "I made your wish for you."

"You wished for me to come to your cooking classes,

didn't you? You may have gotten what you wanted, but I still don't believe in wishes."

"You're so silly," Jennifer said. "I would never waste a wish on that."

"Then what was it?"

Jennifer flashed her dimples. "Since you don't believe in wishes, I don't have any reason to tell you."

"So it didn't come true, and you won't admit it."

"Keep telling yourself that," Jennifer said. She waved good-bye, then she and Rip went on their way.

"This town is crazy about superstitions, fortune-telling, and other such foolishness," Jandy said to Sue. "You and I are practical girls. We know the real magic life offers is an unending supply of dog biscuits and—" She broke off, struck by a sudden realization. After a few moments' thought, she said, "And the mysterious disappearance of Pru. Do you think she's haunting someone else? Maybe she found a way to get back to California. Maybe Pru and her new host are planning to marry Hud. If there could only be *two* of me, wouldn't life be easier?"

After a quiet Sunday morning of downloading photos to Grayson's computer and putting them in the software he'd taught her to use, Jandy nudged Sue with her foot and said, "You're getting too lazy. Didn't you used to do a lot more when Sam was around? An idle dog is the devil's workshop."

Evan yawned from the sofa and said, "Grayson and I were thinking of driving to New Coventry to catch a movie. Want to join us?"

"Sue and I will guard the ranch," Jandy said. "She should be doing something to earn those raw turkey necks."

"I'm all about canine health, but I'll pay you if you don't mention her diet again," Evan said with a squeamish expression.

One useful thing about Sue was that sometimes, if she was really sleepy, she'd lie still enough to provide a good pillow for Jandy's head while she sky gazed. It was nearly dusk, and they were doing exactly that when Sue, who wasn't normally much for speed, jumped up so fast that Jandy's head hit the ground.

"Ow! Why'd you do that?"

She sat up and saw why Sue had begun to bark and run in circles. Sam was riding one of Grayson's horses, although she now knew enough to recognize it as a working quarter horse instead of one of the pampered Arabians. Even from a distance, it looked huge, and she stood nervously and brushed grass from her clothes as horse and rider approached.

"Do I look like a desperado who's come to claim his woman?" Sam asked.

"If I'm the woman in question, you'd have been smarter to bring your Jeep. Or even the tow truck."

"You don't have to be afraid of him. He's gentle."

"He weighs a zillion pounds. He might crush me. Even if he did it accidentally, I could sue Grayson. It would be like *Cooper v. Meddars*, Orange County Superior Court, when Meddars' ferret accidentally bit off Cooper's pinky finger. You don't want me to sue Grayson, do you?"

"If I promise that you'll be safe, will you ride with me?"

"Sue and I can just walk alongside you. Really. We like that better."

He nodded toward Sue, who was already halfway back to the cabin in her zeal for chasing fireflies, or lightning bugs, as Evan called them.

"Traitor," Jandy muttered.

"You once trusted me enough to get in a truck on Interstate 10 with me."

"*The* 10. That's how we say it in California."

"You told me your childhood secrets. Who else knows that you have Yoko Ono stashed in your grandfather's attic?"

"She's in a closet," Jandy said, but she smiled in spite of herself. "Don't get off the horse. I'm not getting on it unless you're holding the reins."

He leaned over with his hand out. She put one foot in the stirrup, let him help her up, and settled on the saddle in front of him.

"You can relax," he said. "I won't go too fast."

She considered his words as the horse began a gentle pace. Wasn't it going too fast if someone who'd known you for less than two months thought he was falling for you? Wanted you to fall for him? Wanted you to go back on your word to another man for him?

Or was he the soul of patience because, feeling that way, he had never pressured her? He acted as if they had all the time in the world. He made her almost believe it, too.

It felt so good to lean back against his chest. How was it that this man could amuse her, annoy her, and make her want to forget there was anything in the world other than the moment and place they were in? It wasn't rational.

"What are you thinking?" he asked.

Because she wasn't facing him, she found the nerve to say, "There's a part of me that wants nothing more than to get in your RV with you and Sue and head for—where's the next place you're going?"

"Old Faithful."

"It would be," she muttered at the reminder that she was someone's faithless fiancée. "I want to go to Old Faithful and take photos while you make people tell you why they attract and repel each other. I can't think of anything more enticing than spending every new day on the open road with you. Until we both decide it's time to settle down. Then we'll live in the RV in the woods near your parents' house—"

"I can promise to do better than that when the time comes," Sam said.

"Hush. This is my fantasy. I don't do this often; you should savor the moment. Your parents will retire to Palm Springs—or wherever Texans retire to—and we'll move into the Revere ancestral home and start filling the rooms with girls who look like Dove and boys who don't like to ride horses."

"I like a big family, but exactly how many of those are you planning on?"

She ignored him. "You'll be eccentric old Professor Revere, with those elbow patches on your tweed blazers. And I'll be Jandy, the crazy lady with the zillion dolls and the ever-present camera."

"That fantasy works for me. What does the other part of you want?"

"I want to live up to the promises I made to Hud. For once in my life, I want to finish what I started. I want my mother to look at me without that pinched expression of disappointment on her face."

They were at her cabin. Sam pulled up on the reins and slid easily off the horse, then helped her to the ground. When she saw his expression, her heart sank. She tried to remember if she'd ever seen Sam angry before.

"I guess it's really bad taste to talk to you about him, isn't it?" she asked.

"It's not that," he said. He met her eyes. "If you love him, if you want to marry him, that's what you should do. What pisses me off is that the person you keep trying to please is someone who doesn't even know you."

"He knows—"

"Not *him*. Her. I'm sorry your mother got left by a man who may or may not have existed anywhere except in your aunt's imagination. I'm sure it was scary as hell to be alone and pregnant at her age. But what kind of woman cheats a girl out of her childhood? Nobody has to believe that fairy tales are real, Jandy, to appreciate imagination and whimsy and, yes, magic. Look around; the world is full of it. The stupid grin on Sue's face and the lightning bugs she chases. A random pile of rocks that draws two strangers to the same place. A place neither of them expected to be, but both of them needed to be. Because all their lives, they may have been moving toward that moment. Friendships are magic. And the way a ripe tomato fresh off the vine teases your taste buds. Or the laughter of a girl, as if she just discovered laughter for the first time. And maybe she did, because the person she should have been able to count on never let her watch a cartoon, or believe in a miracle, or put her faith in herself to be okay no matter what."

He stopped talking, and they stared at each other. She was afraid if she said anything, she'd start crying, then he might hold her, and she might let him hold her, for all the wrong reasons.

"Just be happy, Jandy. That's all."

She didn't try to stop him as he got on the horse and set off at a brisker pace than they'd taken when she was in the saddle with him. Sue ran beside him. Even though it was killing Jandy to watch them both go, she had to smile at the way Sue loped, ecstatic in the moment, with no thought of what she was leaving behind.

"A person can learn a lot from a dog," Jandy said and went inside the cabin.

Jandy didn't see Sam again over the next week. Nor did she hear from any of his sisters. She remembered her early days in Coventry, when people had talked about how protective the Reveres were of one another. She tried not to think too much about it. Instead, she worked twice as hard on her project with Grayson's horses.

She was at his computer on a Monday morning when Evan sat next to her and said, "Do you want to talk about what's bothering you?"

"I'd rather do anything but talk about it."

"Go into town with me," he urged. "I have to pick up my laundered towels from the Scrub and Pub and drop them at the salon. We'll have lunch at the Early Bird Café and gossip about whoever walks by. Hang out. See if we can get into some trouble."

"It's not like the old days, is it, when we took on the cattle rustlers and won?"

"Don't forget your slutty past as a majorette."

She giggled and said, "Okay. I'm in."

They kept the conversation neutral on the drive into Coventry. She would have been okay if John Lennon could have kept "Ticket to Ride" out of it. If they'd been in her truck she would have turned off the radio, but since they were in Evan's car, she had to endure it.

"I'm so tired," she finally said.

"It's the heat."

"It's my brain. And my indecision."

"Do you mind if I sound like an annoying old uncle?"

"Go ahead. Please."

"You're trying to figure out your entire future, and you've been at it less than two months. It takes some people longer than that to choose a hair color."

"Maybe I should color my hair."

"Or take Japanese."

"Or switch to a macrobiotic diet."

"Or go to trade school."

"Or become a folk singer."

"Stop," he begged. "You're scaring me."

When he parked in front of the beauty shop, she said, "I think I'll take a walk around the square. When should I meet you at the café?"

"Give me thirty minutes," he said.

She nodded and took Grayson's camera with her when she got out of the car. Instead of going up Dresden Street, she walked by the gallery. Looking through the window, she saw Hannah on the phone. They both waved, but Jandy kept walking. She looked toward Revere Auto but didn't turn that way. She didn't have enough time for a good conversation with Robin, and she didn't want to ask about Sam. She wondered if he and Sue had left for Old Faithful yet.

She cut behind the school and dodged the limbs of a tree as she walked across the grass next to the library. She stopped to take a picture of a pair of cardinals, then turned toward the square and froze at the tableau before her.

Four black Lincoln Town Cars parked on Oak Road were between her and the statue of Lady Godiva. All their doors were open. Chandra stood outside the first car with two people Jandy didn't know. All three of them were on cell phones. Her mother was sitting half in, half out of the backseat in the next car. She was on her cell phone.

Her stepfather stood by the hood of the car, also talking on his cell phone.

Sorel stood next to the third car. She was bending over, looking in the side view mirror as if checking her makeup.

At least she's *not on her phone,* Jandy thought. As if on cue, she heard a chiming sound, and Sorel reached into the car, pulled out her cell phone, and answered it.

Meanwhile, three more of the Foundlings were circling the last Town Car as if guarding it. It seemed absurd, but all three of them had phones to their ears.

Where is he, she thought, impatient for a look at her fiancé.

At that moment, Hud emerged from Sorel's car. He looked so handsome that he left her breathless. How could she have forgotten his toned body, broad shoulders, and gorgeous skin? He was dressed in cargo pants. Although they were a little baggy in the rear, it was impossible not to see how sexy he looked from the back as he walked toward the Godiva statue. His tight black shirt accentuated the muscles on either side of his spine. She shivered at the memory of all the times she'd gripped those muscles during passion.

He stopped at the fountain, but he didn't look up at the woman on the horse. Instead, he was looking down at his cell phone.

Jandy smiled, pulled her phone from her pocket, and waited. After a moment, "Instant Karma" began playing.

"Hello," she said.

"Hi. Don't be mad."

"About what?"

"You seem to love Coventry, Texas, too much to leave it. Instead of trying to lure you back home, I figured out a way to make us both happy."

"What's that?" she asked, still watching him from the shadows cast on the side of the library by the trees.

"I brought the wedding to you, Jane. To Coventry. I've got a best man and two groomsmen. Sorel's here to be your maid of honor. I know you've made some friends here. Like Sue. Isn't that her name? She can be a bridesmaid. Stan's here to give you away. Chandra and your mother are here to put everything together."

"I see," she said, watching her mother as she did something on her BlackBerry while she continued to talk on her cell phone.

"Are you mad? Did I screw this up?"

"No, Hud," she said, smiling again. "I'm not mad at all. I can't think of anything I want more than a Coventry wedding. You did exactly the right thing."

Epilogue

It was the perfect late-August morning for a wedding. The slant of light and the cool breeze gave Jandy her first sense of the coming autumn. Having grown up in a place without winter, she liked the idea of seasons that changed. She leaned from the window and stared at the brilliant blue sky with its puffs of clouds. She couldn't have hoped for a better day to say her vows and begin a new journey with the man she loved.

The sound of a violin warned her that she should stop daydreaming. She backed away from the window and appraised her reflection in the full-length mirror. Her hair looked fine; Evan had seen to that. She wondered if she'd ever let it grow long again.

Someone tapped on the door and said, "Jandy? Are you ready?"

She considered not answering. She knew that outside, her guests were holding their collective breath, wondering if she would ditch yet another wedding. No matter how many times she insisted that she'd never been a runaway bride, she feared the label would haunt her for the rest of her life.

Get on with it then, Pru said.

"Oh, go away."

Sounding a little injured, the voice—Tryphena's? Phylura's?—on the other side of the door said, "I was just going to ask if you need anything."

"I'm fine. I'll be right out," she called.

She checked the mirror one last time to make sure her dress was okay. She wasn't wearing the elaborate gown that her mother and Chandra had agreed on when they were planning the ceremony she'd canceled. Nor was it the simple dress she'd picked out for her Mendocino wedding. It was a tea-length, ivory dress, A-lined and sleeveless, with tiny pearl beading scattered over its outer layer of lace. It had a simple elegance that she loved. After her future mother-in-law had worn it at her own wedding decades before, it had remained packed in a sealed box until it was taken out and cleaned for Jandy.

She was surprised to find the hall empty when she stepped out of the bedroom. If they thought she was a flight risk, it seemed like they should have someone stationed at each escape point along the way. She wondered if everyone had taken their keys out of their cars and trucks. She had a vision of Dove pulling up and offering her Mini as a getaway car. That picture would have been better if Jandy had been wearing a veil to fly behind her as they sped away with the top down.

But she wasn't wearing a veil, and Dove wasn't at her wedding. Dove had left a few days ago for New Zealand on a quest to see the dandelion fountain at Christchurch. Jandy had hugged her good-bye and put her copy of Jennifer Weiner's *Good in Bed* in Dove's hands.

"Is this a how-to book?" Dove asked. "If it is, I don't need it."

"No. It's a good novel, but every time I try to finish

it, something crazy happens to stop me. Maybe you'll have better luck with it."

"I think I'd rather have crazy," Dove answered, but she tucked the book inside her carry-on bag.

As much as she loved imagining Dove flying around the world on adventures, Jandy remembered that she had her own adventure to get on with. She went downstairs and found Grandpa waiting for her just outside the door.

"I wondered if you were going to show up," he said.

"I don't have anything better to do today," she said airily.

He grinned and said, "You're almost as pretty a bride as your grandmother was. I hope you're as happy."

"If she was half as happy at her wedding as I am today, she was the luckiest woman in the world. Not that I believe in luck," she hastily added.

Grandpa just shook his head and led her around the arbor, which was the signal for the processional music to begin.

Jandy stopped short to look at the array and color of the flowers that stretched in front of her. They surpassed even her first vision of walking through the wildflowers of Mendocino on her wedding day. She looked down at her bouquet, which contained a mixture of the flowers that grew all around the winding path that she and Grandpa would be taking. Among them were black-eyed susans—*Rudbeckia,* she corrected herself. She smiled, thinking of the day she'd met the dog who was named for the flowers. Sue and Sam had forever changed her by driving her to a town that would remain a part of who she was no matter where her future might take her. She would always be grateful for that.

"Jane!" Grandpa hissed, and she realized the musicians

and vocalist were staring at her, their eyes bugging out a little.

"Do I look like I'm going to run away?" she whispered back. She made a rolling motion with her free hand, and the vocalist began singing the Beatles' "Here, There and Everywhere."

Grandpa nudged her on. She looked toward the first row of chairs and saw Aunt Ruby beaming at her. Her stepfather was facing forward, so she couldn't see his expression, but her mother was looking down, her mouth set in a narrow line. Jandy wasn't sure if Carol Halli was annoyed with this version of the wedding, so different from the one she'd once planned for her daughter, or if she was just having her usual sour reaction to the music of the Beatles.

If I believed in magic, Jandy thought, *I'd tell myself that somewhere in the world, Thomas Taylor, who doesn't realize he has a daughter, much less that she's getting married, is also listening to Beatles songs, maybe even this song.*

"It could happen," Jandy whispered.

"What?" Grandpa asked.

"Nothing."

She smiled at the people who were watching her as she walked closer to the latticed arch that served as the wedding altar. She'd once feared that she would have to face rows of empty seats where her guests should be. Now that she was actually getting married, she was surrounded by friendly faces. Not just friendly faces, but actual friends. Like Keelie, Dr. Boone, and Jennifer. The night before, at the party the Boones had given in honor of the wedding, she'd sought out Jennifer and asked again about the wish she'd made at the Godiva fountain.

"I thought you had the saddest eyes," Jennifer said.

"I wished that you'd find happiness while you were in Coventry."

Fine; now and then, wishes do come true, she thought as she recognized shopkeepers and ranchers and lawyers and Daughter of Godiva contestants. She saw Elenore Storey and her husband, whose name Jandy couldn't remember; Devon, her favorite stall mucking teacher and photography assistant; Tryphena and Phylura and even Fiji, whose expression clearly showed he was plotting something. She needed to warn someone to keep an eye on him. The millisecond she faltered because of that thought sent an apprehensive current through her guests. She lowered her head for a moment so no one could see her smile.

Imagining her birth father somewhere in the world listening to Beatles music, getting married in Coventry, Texas, having chairs full of people who wished her well—those things were no more or less strange than the idea that Henry Hudson Blake, instead of waiting for her to finish this wedding march, could be sitting in an office signing his name on a three-movie deal to play a character named Eddie Ringer. Or that he could one day decide that it had been Sorel Eisen, not Jane Halli, that he'd loved all along.

But there was no reason to think about all that when the man she loved was holding out one hand to her as Grandpa let her go. His other hand was holding the leash of a big, white dog who was looking up at her as if to say, *What took you so long?*

She smiled at Sam, who quietly said, "What I love about a woman who doesn't finish things is that the journey we start today won't ever be over."

"What I love about you," she said, "numbers in the zillions."

It hadn't been easy to face Hud and confess that not only was she not cut out to be Mrs. Movie Star, but she'd fallen completely, irrevocably in love with another man. Hud had been surprisingly decent about it. Maybe he was relieved that she would no longer present a public relations dilemma for him. Chandra hadn't even blinked. She'd just gone to work planting blind items in the tabloids about Hud's new, unnamed love interest. In Chandra's world, brides came and went, but show business was forever.

The music stopped, and the guests again sat on the chairs that covered the Reveres' lawn. Jandy's eyes filled as Robin, Lark, and Swan stood next to her, all of them smiling a welcome into their family. Evan, Grayson, and Jimmy were smiling, too, but looked a little less certain that she wouldn't suddenly bolt down the path, jump in Grandpa's pickup, and head for the hills. She gave them a reassuring glance, then watched as Grandpa led Shane and Seth back to their grandparents after Reverend St. John had taken the rings from them. Hop was watching the boys, but Rachel was looking at Jandy with understanding.

In a physics class that she'd dropped before the first test, Jandy remembered learning that nature abhorred a vacuum. She would never be able to change her mother, and her mother didn't want to change anyway. But nature had finally stepped in to give her Rachel. Jandy looked forward to years of getting to know her mother-in-law; how many brides were lucky enough to say that?

Fine; maybe there is such a thing as luck, she admitted.

She turned around as Reverend St. John began the ceremony. Jandy tried to listen, but she was thinking again how much she liked it when Sam held her hand.

From the day they'd met, her senses had understood what her mind refused to admit. The scent of him on the pillow that rested under her head in the tow truck. His breath on her neck and his hand on her arm when he taught her to pitch horseshoes. The night they watched cartoons and he held her hand, just like now. Riding on horseback at dusk, with Sue chasing fireflies, and all Jandy wanted in the world was to keep leaning against Sam, knowing that somehow if she put her faith in that mysterious connection they had, everything would be okay. All of it leading to the first night they'd made love.

She looked into his eyes as he began repeating his vows, but she was remembering the way she'd broken the speed limit driving Grandpa's pickup to the Revere place after she and Hud had their final conversation. She was sure Sam and Sue were already gone, were maybe even then at Yellowstone National Park. Sue would be an asset to Sam when he did research. As Jandy knew only too well, a dog helped initiate conversations. Before they knew it, strangers would share all kinds of private and potentially embarrassing information with Sam.

When she'd thrown gravel spinning into the driveway that day, Lark and the boys were sitting on the front porch. Whatever incoherent thing she'd said when she jumped out of the pickup had been enough for Lark to point her in the right direction. She ran through the trees with no thought that at any minute she could be attacked by a marauding band of guinea hens. She was ready to beg Sam's forgiveness for letting him leave her at the cabin that night, for not understanding her own feelings in time to keep from hurting his.

When she got her first look at his RV, she stared, dumbfounded, at the words she read on the panel next to the passenger door. She didn't know what shocked her more: that he'd remembered the name of her favorite lost childhood toy, or that he—or someone—had painted *Jandy's Star Traveler* on his RV.

She blinked, remembering what Madame Vorjean had told her: *You lost something when you were very young. Someone who loves you will return it to you, but the gift comes at a price.*

"I don't believe in fortune-tellers," she said out loud. "But I do believe in Sam."

Inside the RV, she could hear Paul McCartney and Wings singing "Helen Wheels." Sue barked twice, then stopped. Sam came around the back of the RV, stared at her for a few seconds, then met her halfway, as he had that day on the square. As he had on the first day they'd run toward each other and touched hands while petting the dog who'd brought them together.

After they kissed, she pointed to the name on the RV and said, "How did you know I'd go with you? Did you think you could make it happen just by wishing?"

"No," he said. "I thought *you* could. When other people called you a runaway bride, I knew they were wrong. The day I met you, first you ran to Sue. Then you ran to me. That's the way I'll always see you."

"Sometimes it's like you read my mind."

The road they'd started down on in Arizona on a hot day in late May, a road that had led them to the tiny town with the big heart, and from which she'd almost taken a bad detour, stretched ahead of them for a lifetime. She'd found her way to him in time to experience the sight of his eyes as he made love to her, the feel and scent of his skin against hers, and the sound of his laughter as they lay tangled in sheets, making plans for the future while Sue snored next to the bed.

"Jandy," Sam said quietly and brought her back to the present.

She blushed, realizing she'd missed her cue to repeat her vows.

"I'm sorry," she said.

"I'm not," Sam answered.

From behind her, she heard old Mr. Plochman say, "Can we please finish this while some of us are still alive?"

Jandy laughed, looked into Sam's eyes, and said, "I think the reason I never finish things is because I don't want them to be over."

"No worries," Sam said, and even though they hadn't finished their vows, exchanged their rings, or been pronounced husband and wife, he kissed her because their romance didn't follow the rules.

After the laughter died down, Reverend St. John said, "If you'll repeat after me, *I, January Day Halli*—"

"Call me Jandy."

More by Bestselling Author

Lori Foster

Available Wherever Books Are Sold!

Check out our website at **www.kensingtonbooks.com**

Put a Little Romance in Your Life with

Lisa Plumley